BUREAU FOR PARANORMAL RESEARCH AND DEFENSE

The Universal Machine

Created by Mike Mignola

CAPTAIN BENJAMIN DAIMIO

A United States Marine whose distinguished thirteen-year career ended in June of 2001 when he and the platoon he was leading were all killed during a mission. The details of his death remain classified. Exactly how it was that he came back to life is an outright mystery.

ABE SAPIEN

An amphibious man discovered in a long-forgotten subbasement beneath a Washington, D.C. hospital, sealed inside a primitive stasis chamber. All indications suggest a previous life, dating back to the Civil War, as scientist and occult investigator Langdon Everett Caul.

LIZ SHERMAN

A fire-starter since the age of eleven, when she accidentally burned her entire family to death. She has been a ward of the B.P.R.D. since then, learning to control her pyrokinetic abilities and cope with the trauma those abilities have wrought.

ROGER

A homunculus made from human blood and herbs. Discovered in Romania, Roger was first brought to life by Liz's pyrokinetic touch. Whether or not he is actually alive may be up for debate, even more so since his body was nearly destroyed in an explosion a few months ago.

JOHANN KRAUS

A medium whose physical form was destroyed while his ectoplasmic projection was out-of-body. That essence now resides in a containment suit. A psychic empath, Johann can create temporary forms for the dead to speak to the living.

DR. KATE CORRIGAN

A former professor at New York University, an authority on folklore and occult history. Dr. Corrigan has been a B.P.R.D. consultant for over ten years, now serving as special liaison to the enhanced-talents task force.

MIKE MIGNOLA'S

B.P.R.D.™

THE UNIVERSAL MACHINE

Story by
MIKE MIGNOLA and JOHN ARCUDI

Art by
GUY DAVIS

Colors by
DAVE STEWART

Letters by
CLEM ROBINS

Editor
SCOTT ALLIE

Assistant Editors
MATT DRYER and RACHEL EDIDIN

Collection Designer
AMY ARENDTS

Publisher
MIKE RICHARDSON

DARK HORSE BOOKS™

NEIL HANKERSON ✦ *executive vice president*

TOM WEDDLE ✦ *chief financial officer*

RANDY STRADLEY ✦ *vice president of publishing*

CHRIS WARNER ✦ *senior books editor, Dark Horse Books*

ROB SIMPSON ✦ *senior books editor, M Press/DH Press*

MICHAEL MARTENS ✦ *vice president of business development*

ANITA NELSON ✦ *vice president of marketing, sales, & licensing*

DAVID SCROGGY ✦ *vice president of product development*

DALE LaFOUNTAIN ✦ *vice president of information technology*

DARLENE VOGEL ✦ *director of purchasing*

KEN LIZZI ✦ *general counsel*

LIA RIBACCHI ✦ *art director*

Special thanks to Jason Hvam and John Nortz

www.hellboy.com

Published by Dark Horse Books
A division of Dark Horse Comics, Inc.
10956 SE Main Street
Milwaukie, OR 97222

First edition January 2007
ISBN 10: 1-59307-710-6
ISBN 13: 978-1-59307-710-5

1 3 5 7 9 10 8 6 4 2

Printed in China

B.P.R.D.: The Universal Machine.
January 2007. Published by Dark Horse Comics, Inc., 10956 SE Main Street, Milwaukie, Oregon 97222. B.P.R.D.: The Universal Machine copyright © 2007 Mike Mignola. Abe Sapien™, Liz Sherman™, Hellboy™, and all other prominently featured characters are trademarks of Mike Mignola. Dark Horse Comics® and the Dark Horse logo are trademarks of Dark Horse Comics, Inc., registered in various categories and countries. All rights reserved. No portion of this publication may be reproduced or transmitted, in any form or by any means, without the express written permission of Dark Horse Comics, Inc. Names, characters, places, and incidents featured in this publication either are the product of the author's imagination or are used fictitiously. Any resemblance to actual persons (living or dead), events, institutions, or locales, without satiric intent, is coincidental.

This book collects the *B.P.R.D.: The Universal Machine* comic-book series, issues 1-5, published by Dark Horse Comics.

CHAPTER ONE

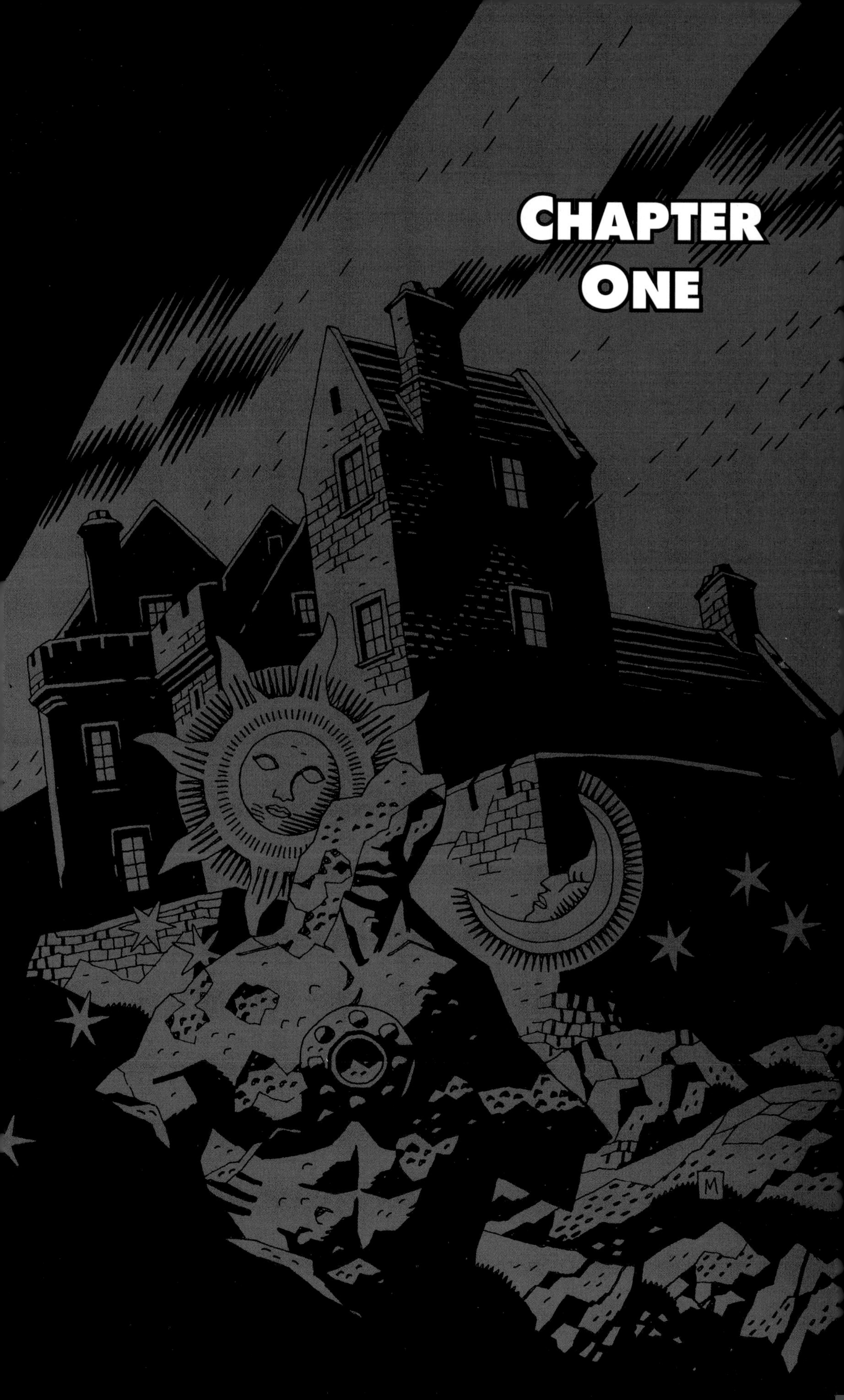

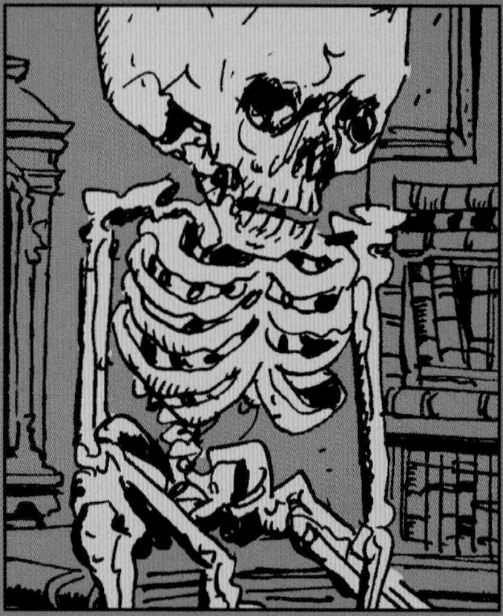

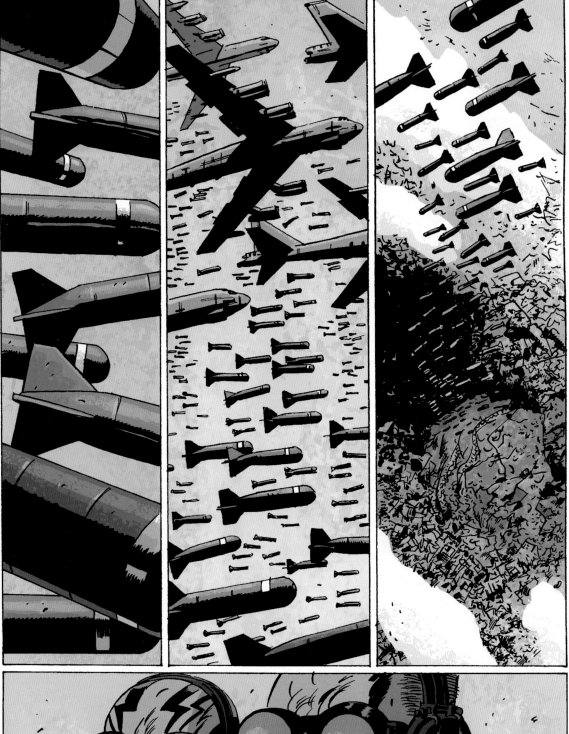

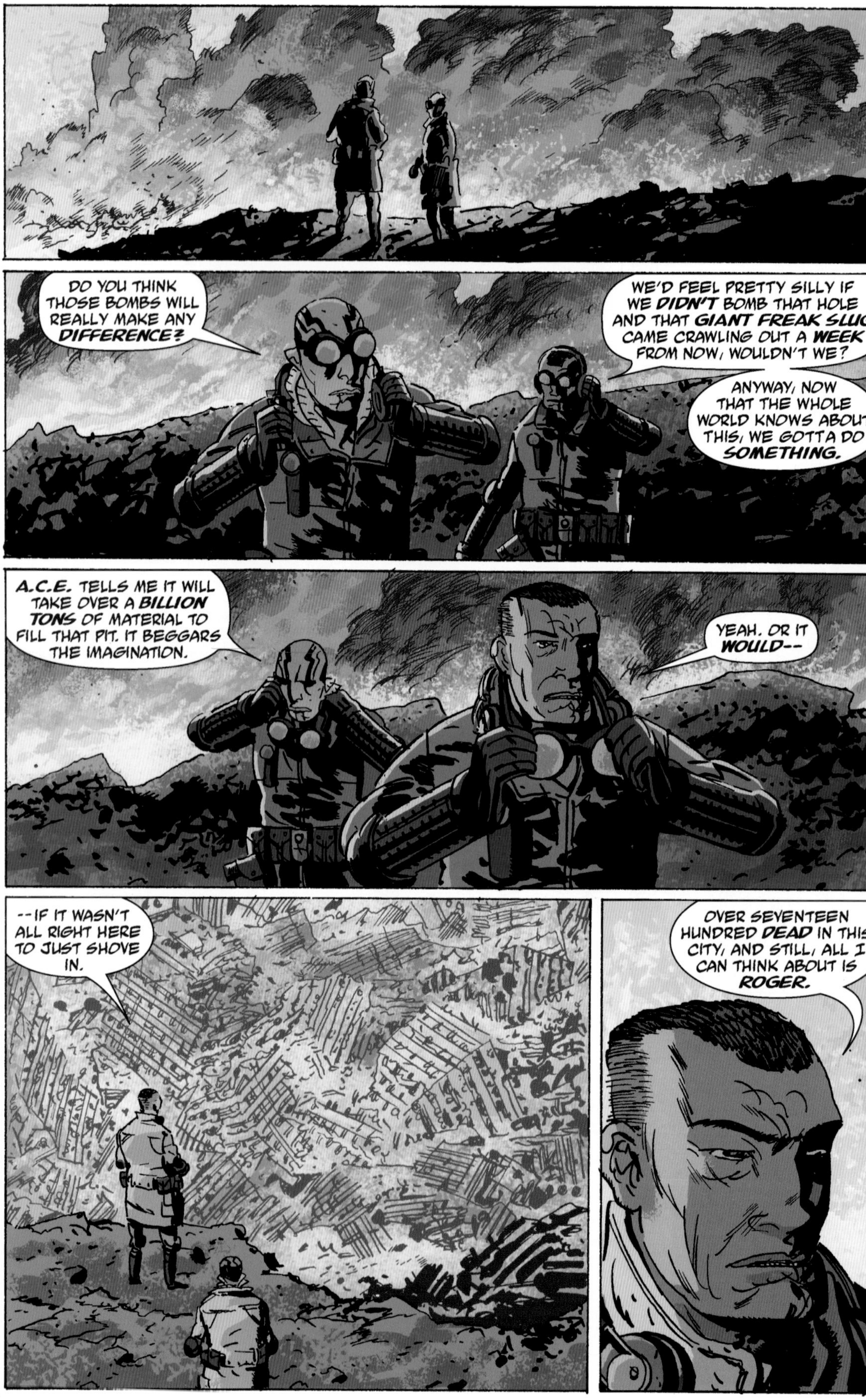
DO YOU THINK THOSE BOMBS WILL REALLY MAKE ANY DIFFERENCE?
WE'D FEEL PRETTY SILLY IF WE DIDN'T BOMB THAT HOLE AND THAT GIANT FREAK SLUG CAME CRAWLING OUT A WEEK FROM NOW, WOULDN'T WE?
ANYWAY, NOW THAT THE WHOLE WORLD KNOWS ABOUT THIS, WE GOTTA DO SOMETHING.
A.C.E. TELLS ME IT WILL TAKE OVER A BILLION TONS OF MATERIAL TO FILL THAT PIT. IT BEGGARS THE IMAGINATION.
YEAH. OR IT WOULD--
--IF IT WASN'T ALL RIGHT HERE TO JUST SHOVE IN.
OVER SEVENTEEN HUNDRED DEAD IN THIS CITY, AND STILL, ALL I CAN THINK ABOUT IS ROGER.

IT'S IMPOSSIBLE.

THAT'S WHAT EVERYBODY IN *RESEARCH* SAYS. THERE ARE NO PRECEDENTS FOR IT, NO GUIDELINES FOR REGROWING *HOMUNCULUS* TISSUE.

"AND ALL THOSE *BOOKS* WE FOUND WITH *ROGER* BEFORE HE WAS REVIVED? A LOT OF THEM SEEM TO BE IN *CODE*.

"ALTHOUGH *JOHANN* KEEPS TRYING, THINKING HE CAN FIND THE KEY AMONG THEM."

WELL, THAT'S OBVIOUSLY NOT HIS DISCIPLINE --

RRIIING

EXCUSE ME.

DR. CORRIGAN? THIS IS ANDREW *DEVON?* WE HAD A TEN-THIRTY APPOINTMENT--

OOOOH, RIGHT. *SORRY.*

DR. KATE CORRIGAN

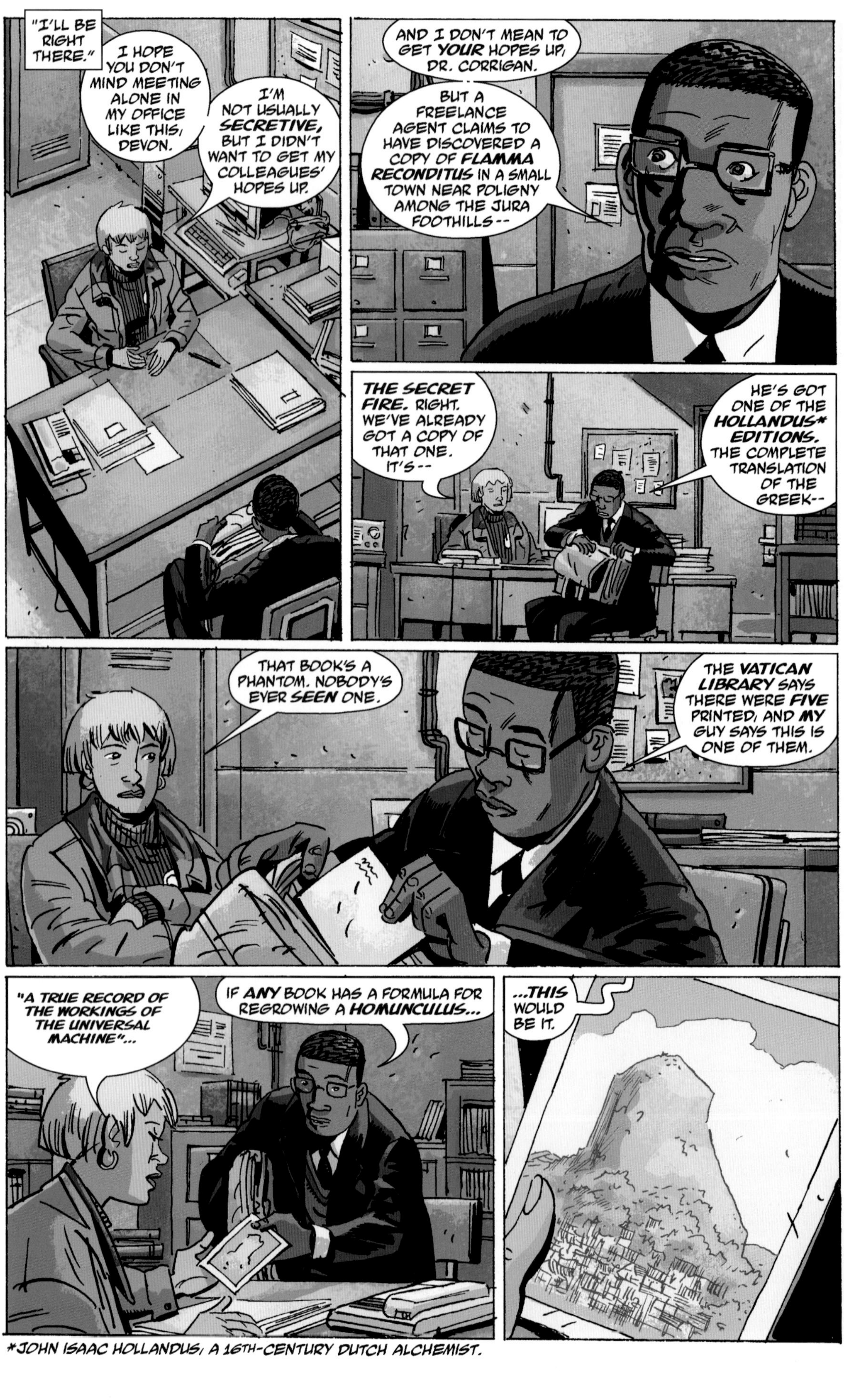
"I'LL BE RIGHT THERE."
I HOPE YOU DON'T MIND MEETING ALONE IN MY OFFICE LIKE THIS, DEVON.
I'M NOT USUALLY SECRETIVE, BUT I DIDN'T WANT TO GET MY COLLEAGUES' HOPES UP.
AND I DON'T MEAN TO GET YOUR HOPES UP, DR. CORRIGAN.
BUT A FREELANCE AGENT CLAIMS TO HAVE DISCOVERED A COPY OF FLAMMA RECONDITUS IN A SMALL TOWN NEAR POLIGNY AMONG THE JURA FOOTHILLS--
THE SECRET FIRE. RIGHT. WE'VE ALREADY GOT A COPY OF THAT ONE. IT'S--
HE'S GOT ONE OF THE HOLLANDUS* EDITIONS. THE COMPLETE TRANSLATION OF THE GREEK--
THAT BOOK'S A PHANTOM. NOBODY'S EVER SEEN ONE.
THE VATICAN LIBRARY SAYS THERE WERE FIVE PRINTED, AND MY GUY SAYS THIS IS ONE OF THEM.
"A TRUE RECORD OF THE WORKINGS OF THE UNIVERSAL MACHINE"...
IF ANY BOOK HAS A FORMULA FOR REGROWING A HOMUNCULUS...
...THIS WOULD BE IT.

*JOHN ISAAC HOLLANDUS, A 16TH-CENTURY DUTCH ALCHEMIST.

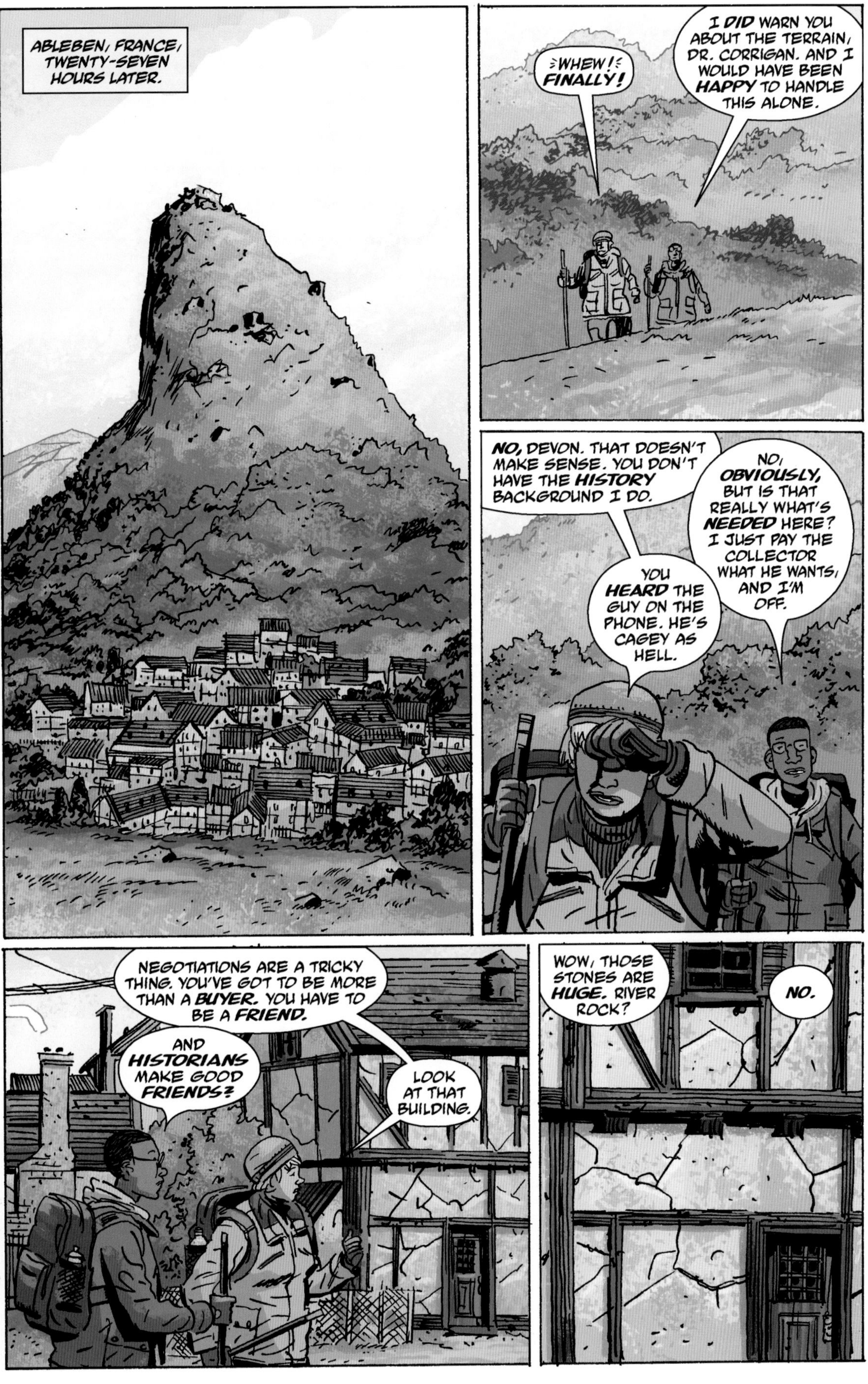
ABLEBEN, FRANCE, TWENTY-SEVEN HOURS LATER.
WHEW! FINALLY!
I DID WARN YOU ABOUT THE TERRAIN, DR. CORRIGAN. AND I WOULD HAVE BEEN HAPPY TO HANDLE THIS ALONE.
NO, DEVON. THAT DOESN'T MAKE SENSE. YOU DON'T HAVE THE HISTORY BACKGROUND I DO.
NO, OBVIOUSLY, BUT IS THAT REALLY WHAT'S NEEDED HERE? I JUST PAY THE COLLECTOR WHAT HE WANTS, AND I'M OFF.
YOU HEARD THE GUY ON THE PHONE. HE'S CAGEY AS HELL.
NEGOTIATIONS ARE A TRICKY THING. YOU'VE GOT TO BE MORE THAN A BUYER. YOU HAVE TO BE A FRIEND.
AND HISTORIANS MAKE GOOD FRIENDS?
LOOK AT THAT BUILDING.
WOW, THOSE STONES ARE HUGE. RIVER ROCK?
NO.

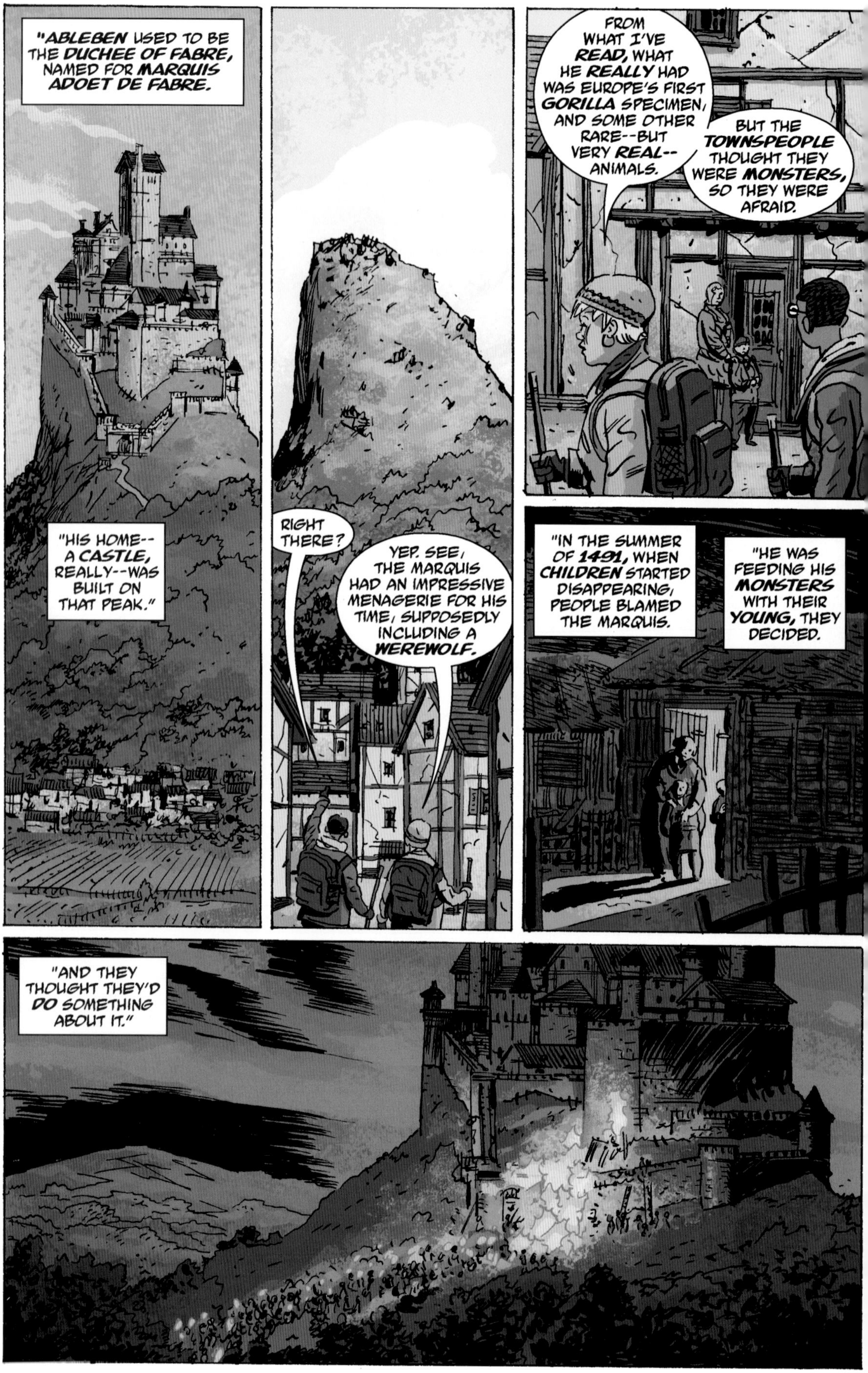

"ABLEBEN USED TO BE THE DUCHEE OF FABRE, NAMED FOR MARQUIS ADOET DE FABRE.
"HIS HOME--A CASTLE, REALLY--WAS BUILT ON THAT PEAK."
RIGHT THERE?
YEP. SEE, THE MARQUIS HAD AN IMPRESSIVE MENAGERIE FOR HIS TIME, SUPPOSEDLY INCLUDING A WEREWOLF.
FROM WHAT I'VE READ, WHAT HE REALLY HAD WAS EUROPE'S FIRST GORILLA SPECIMEN, AND SOME OTHER RARE--BUT VERY REAL--ANIMALS.
BUT THE TOWNSPEOPLE THOUGHT THEY WERE MONSTERS, SO THEY WERE AFRAID.
"IN THE SUMMER OF 1491, WHEN CHILDREN STARTED DISAPPEARING, PEOPLE BLAMED THE MARQUIS.
"HE WAS FEEDING HIS MONSTERS WITH THEIR YOUNG, THEY DECIDED.
"AND THEY THOUGHT THEY'D DO SOMETHING ABOUT IT."

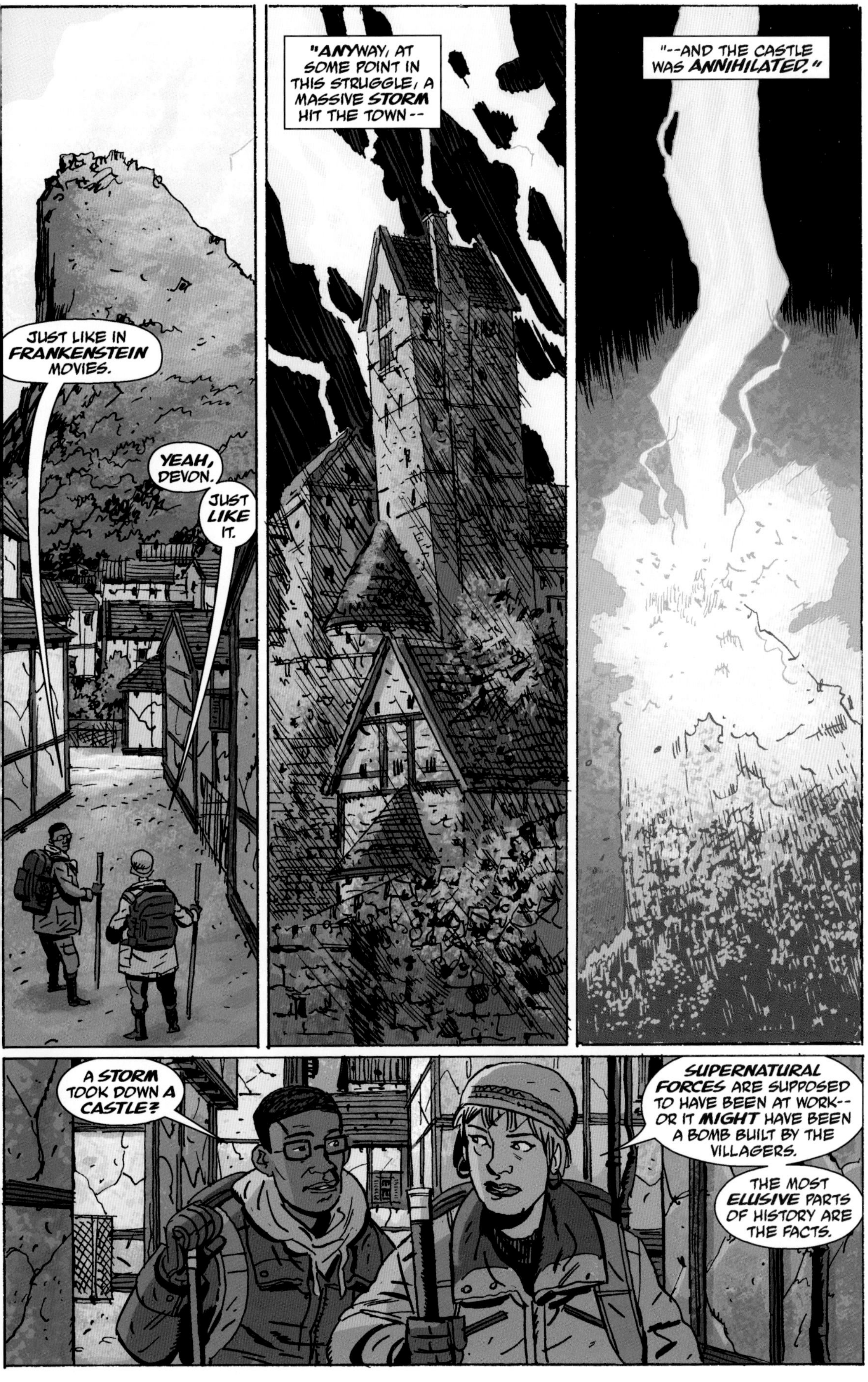
JUST LIKE IN FRANKENSTEIN MOVIES.
YEAH, DEVON.
JUST LIKE IT.
"ANYWAY, AT SOME POINT IN THIS STRUGGLE, A MASSIVE STORM HIT THE TOWN--
"--AND THE CASTLE WAS ANNIHILATED."
A STORM TOOK DOWN A CASTLE?
SUPERNATURAL FORCES ARE SUPPOSED TO HAVE BEEN AT WORK--OR IT MIGHT HAVE BEEN A BOMB BUILT BY THE VILLAGERS.
THE MOST ELUSIVE PARTS OF HISTORY ARE THE FACTS.

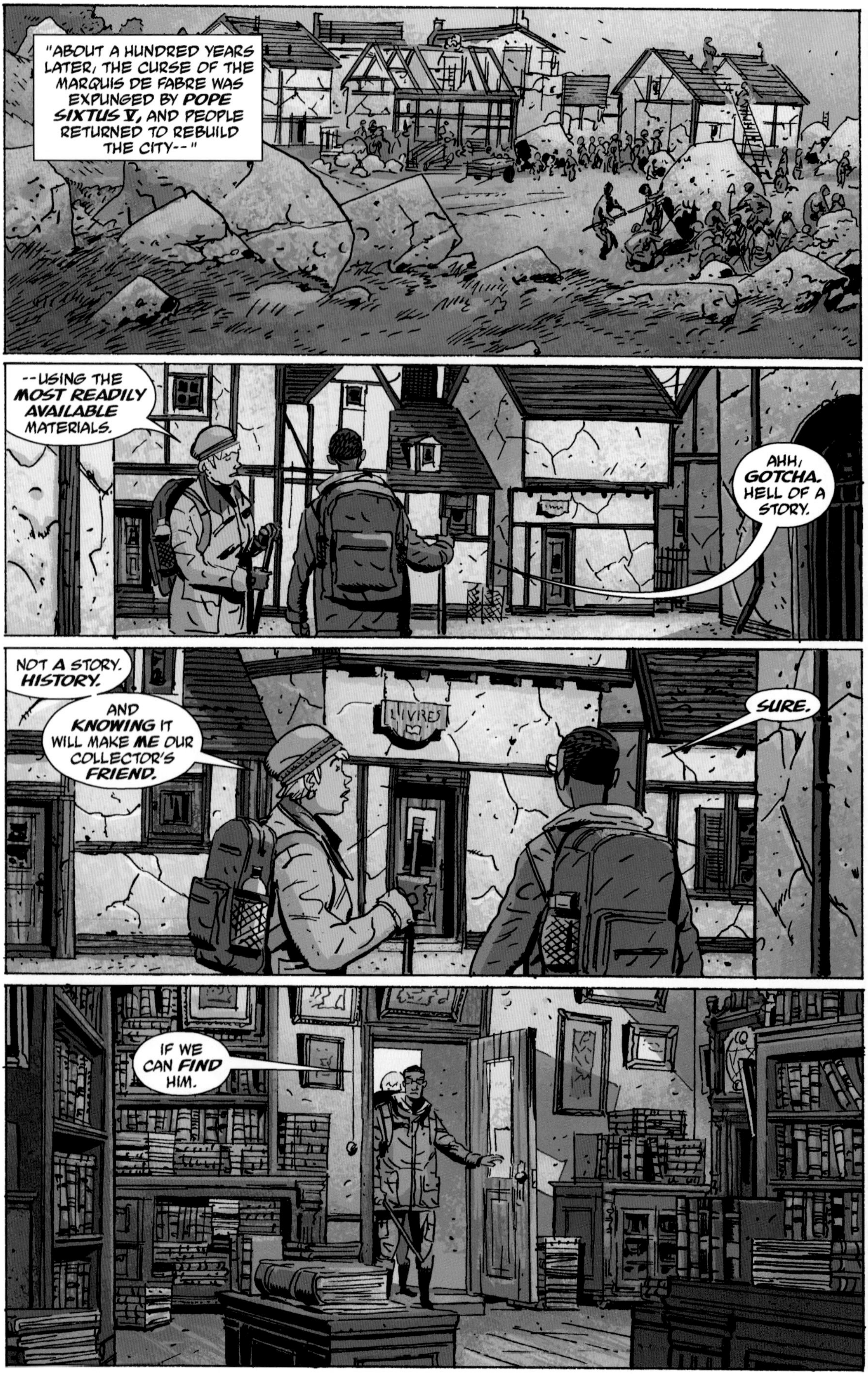
"ABOUT A HUNDRED YEARS LATER, THE CURSE OF THE MARQUIS DE FABRE WAS EXPUNGED BY POPE SIXTUS V, AND PEOPLE RETURNED TO REBUILD THE CITY--"
--USING THE MOST READILY AVAILABLE MATERIALS.
AHH, GOTCHA. HELL OF A STORY.
NOT A STORY. HISTORY.
AND KNOWING IT WILL MAKE ME OUR COLLECTOR'S FRIEND.
SURE.
LIVRES
IF WE CAN FIND HIM.

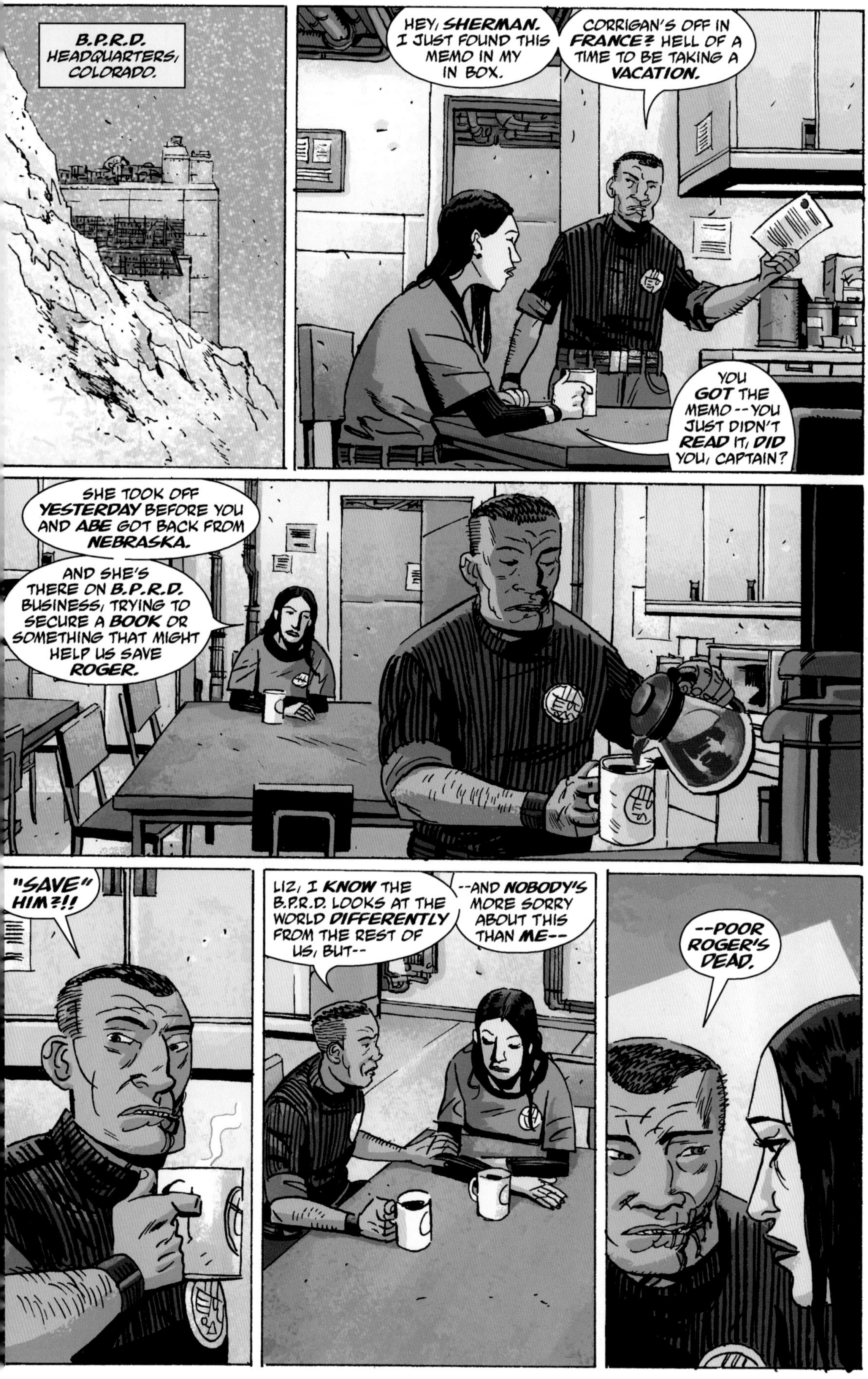
B.P.R.D. HEADQUARTERS, COLORADO.
HEY, SHERMAN. I JUST FOUND THIS MEMO IN MY IN BOX.
CORRIGAN'S OFF IN FRANCE? HELL OF A TIME TO BE TAKING A VACATION.
YOU GOT THE MEMO--YOU JUST DIDN'T READ IT, DID YOU, CAPTAIN?
SHE TOOK OFF YESTERDAY BEFORE YOU AND ABE GOT BACK FROM NEBRASKA.
AND SHE'S THERE ON B.P.R.D. BUSINESS, TRYING TO SECURE A BOOK OR SOMETHING THAT MIGHT HELP US SAVE ROGER.
"SAVE" HIM?!!
LIZ, I KNOW THE B.P.R.D. LOOKS AT THE WORLD DIFFERENTLY FROM THE REST OF US, BUT--
--AND NOBODY'S MORE SORRY ABOUT THIS THAN ME--
--POOR ROGER'S DEAD.

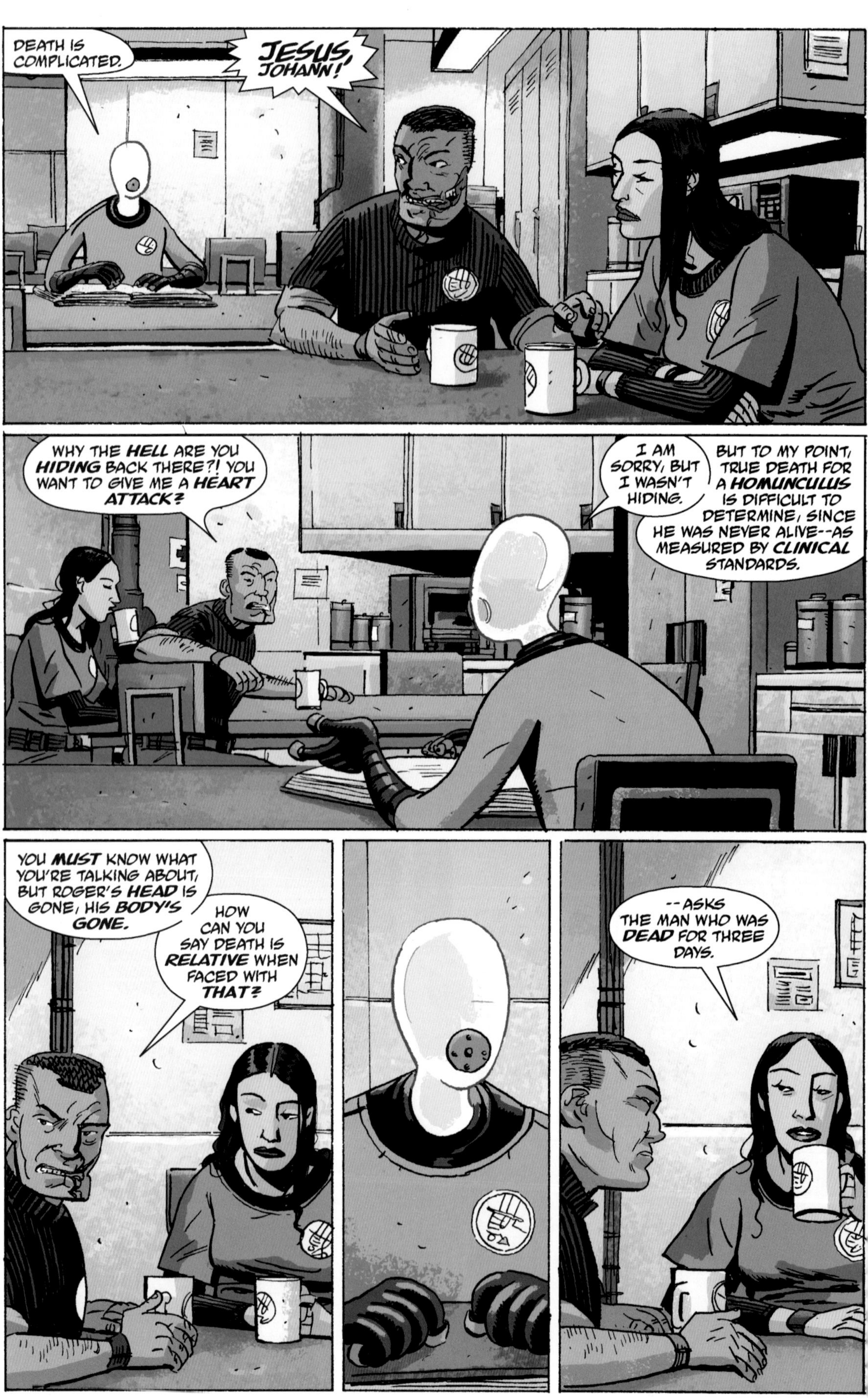
DEATH IS COMPLICATED.
JESUS, JOHANN!
WHY THE HELL ARE YOU HIDING BACK THERE?! YOU WANT TO GIVE ME A HEART ATTACK?
I AM SORRY, BUT I WASN'T HIDING.
BUT TO MY POINT, TRUE DEATH FOR A HOMUNCULUS IS DIFFICULT TO DETERMINE, SINCE HE WAS NEVER ALIVE--AS MEASURED BY CLINICAL STANDARDS.
YOU MUST KNOW WHAT YOU'RE TALKING ABOUT, BUT ROGER'S HEAD IS GONE, HIS BODY'S GONE.
HOW CAN YOU SAY DEATH IS RELATIVE WHEN FACED WITH THAT?
--ASKS THE MAN WHO WAS DEAD FOR THREE DAYS.

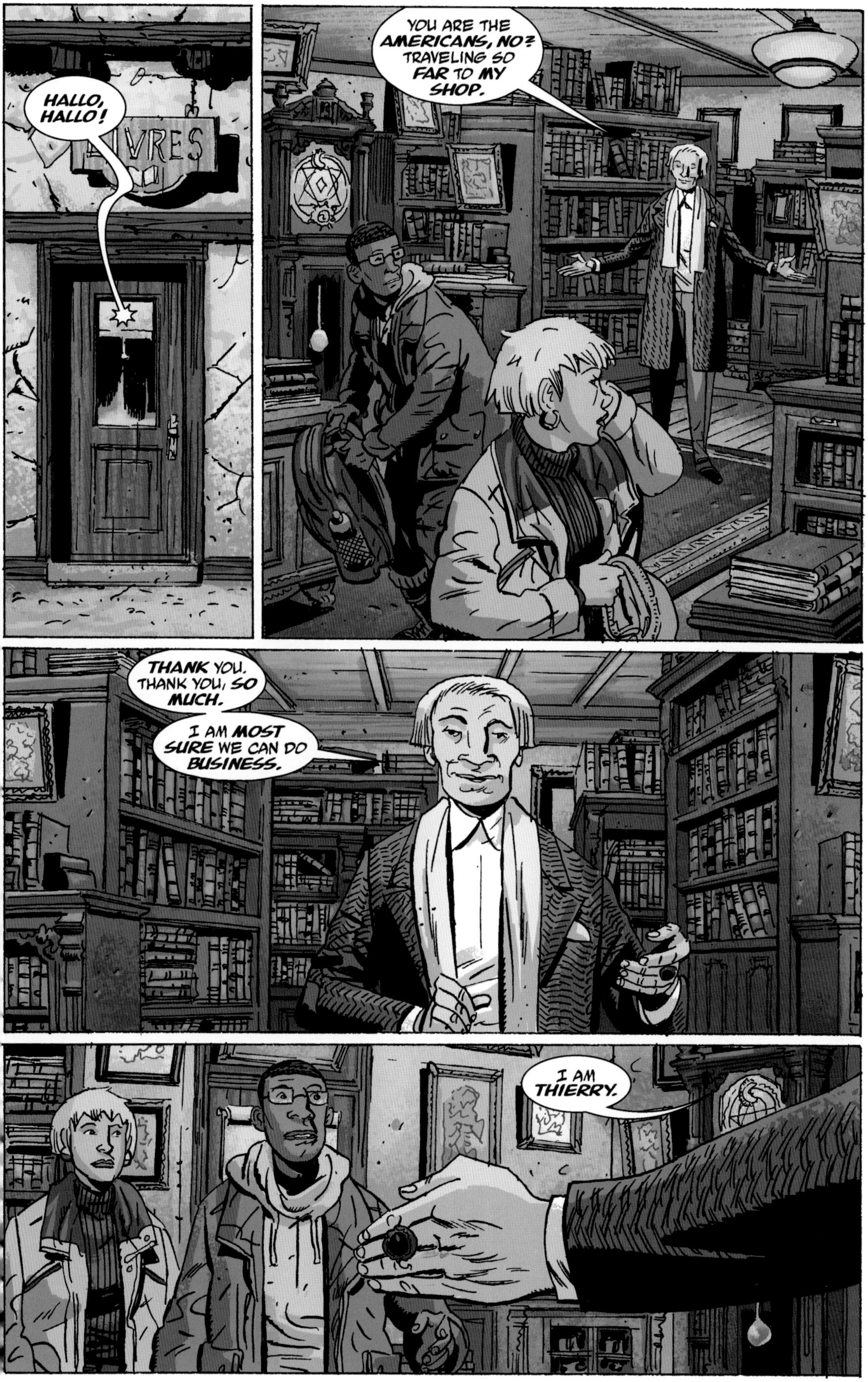
LIVRES
HALLO, HALLO!
YOU ARE THE AMERICANS, NO? TRAVELING SO FAR TO MY SHOP.
THANK YOU. THANK YOU, SO MUCH.
I AM MOST SURE WE CAN DO BUSINESS.
I AM THIERRY.

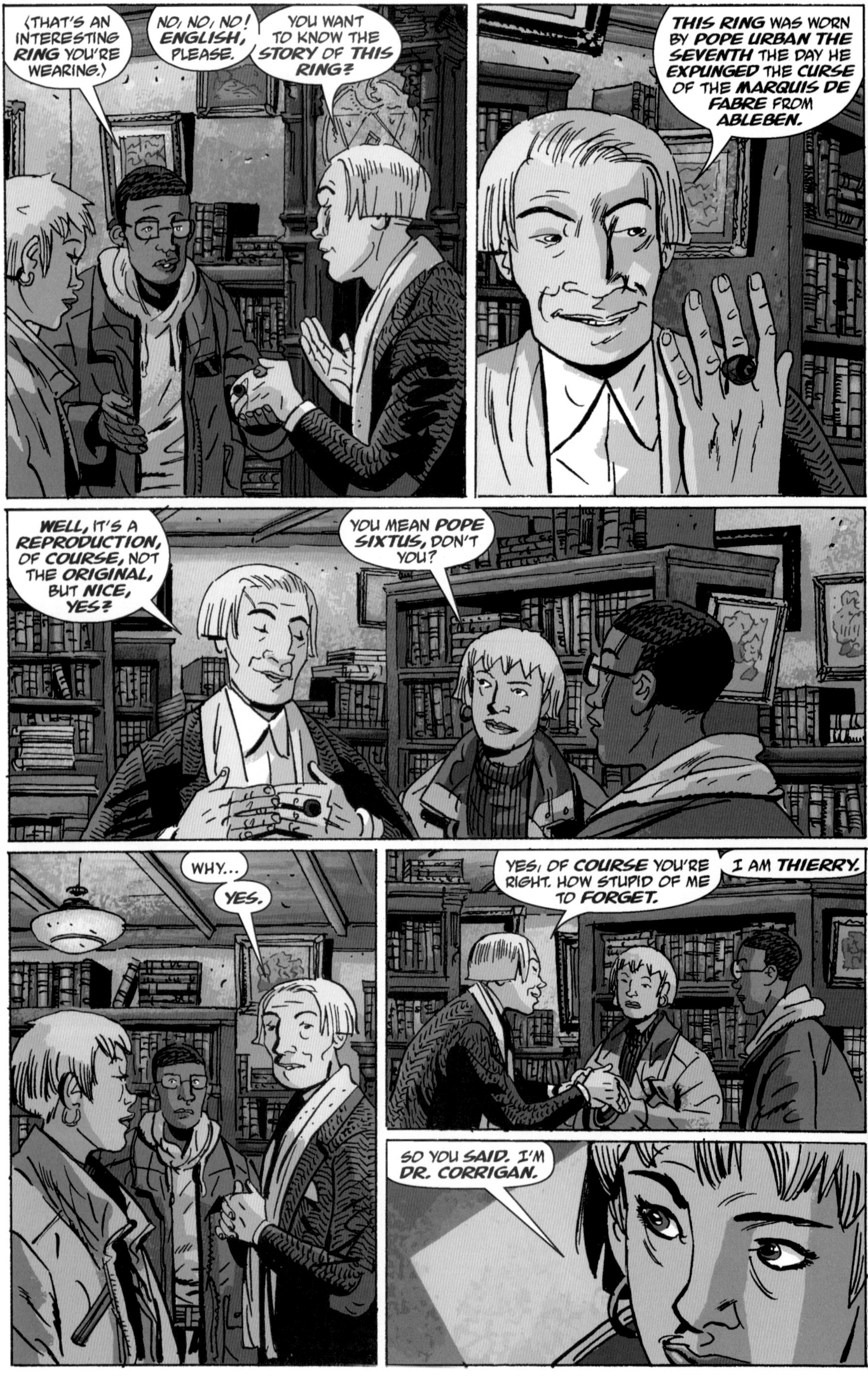

‹THAT'S AN INTERESTING RING YOU'RE WEARING.›
NO, NO, NO! ENGLISH, PLEASE.
YOU WANT TO KNOW THE STORY OF THIS RING?
THIS RING WAS WORN BY POPE URBAN THE SEVENTH THE DAY HE EXPUNGED THE CURSE OF THE MARQUIS DE FABRE FROM ABLEBEN.
WELL, IT'S A REPRODUCTION, OF COURSE, NOT THE ORIGINAL, BUT NICE, YES?
YOU MEAN POPE SIXTUS, DON'T YOU?
WHY...
YES.
YES, OF COURSE YOU'RE RIGHT. HOW STUPID OF ME TO FORGET.
I AM THIERRY.
SO YOU SAID. I'M DR. CORRIGAN.

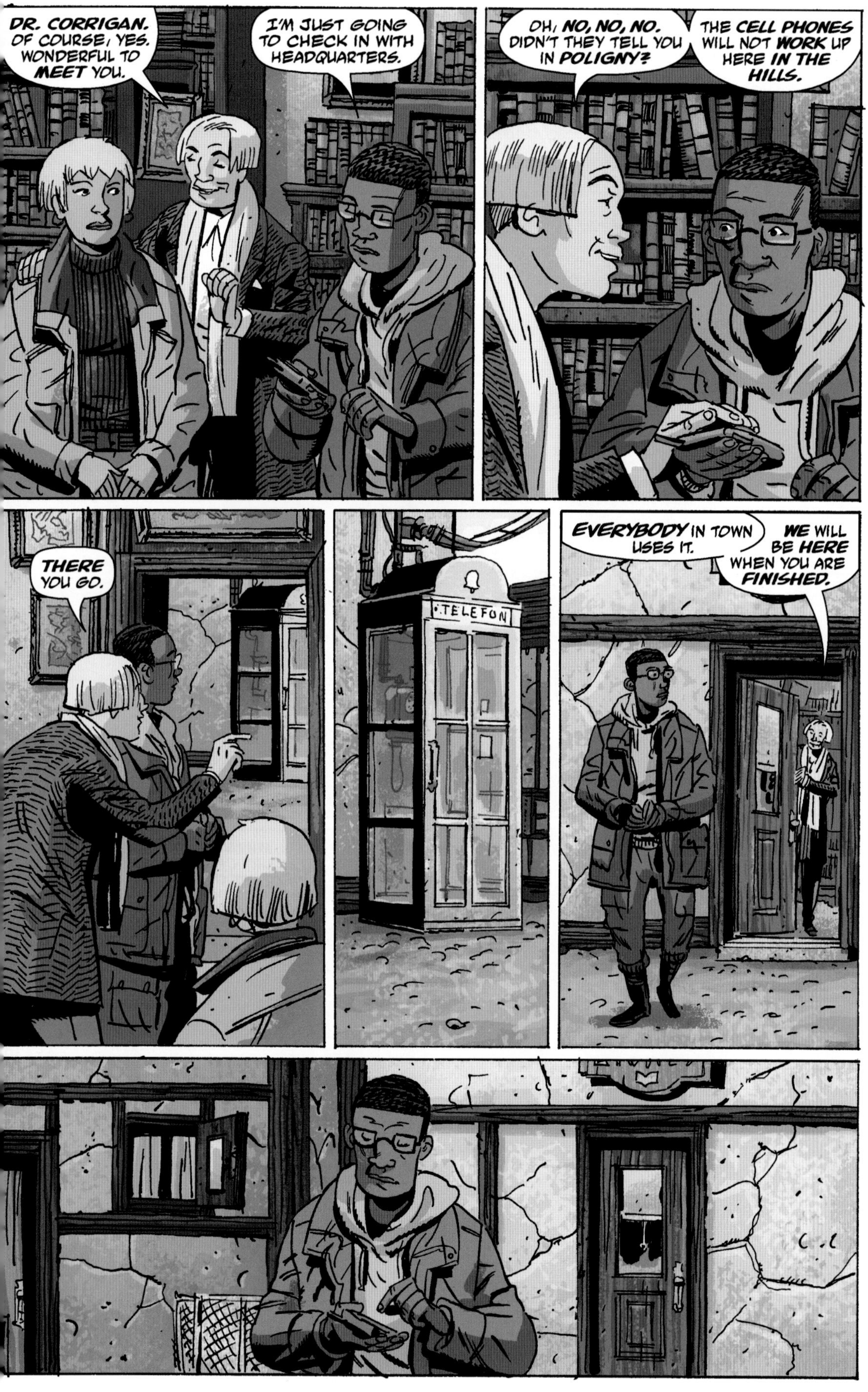
DR. CORRIGAN. OF COURSE, YES. WONDERFUL TO MEET YOU.
I'M JUST GOING TO CHECK IN WITH HEADQUARTERS.
OH, NO, NO, NO. DIDN'T THEY TELL YOU IN POLIGNY?
THE CELL PHONES WILL NOT WORK UP HERE IN THE HILLS.
THERE YOU GO.
TELEFON
EVERYBODY IN TOWN USES IT.
WE WILL BE HERE WHEN YOU ARE FINISHED.

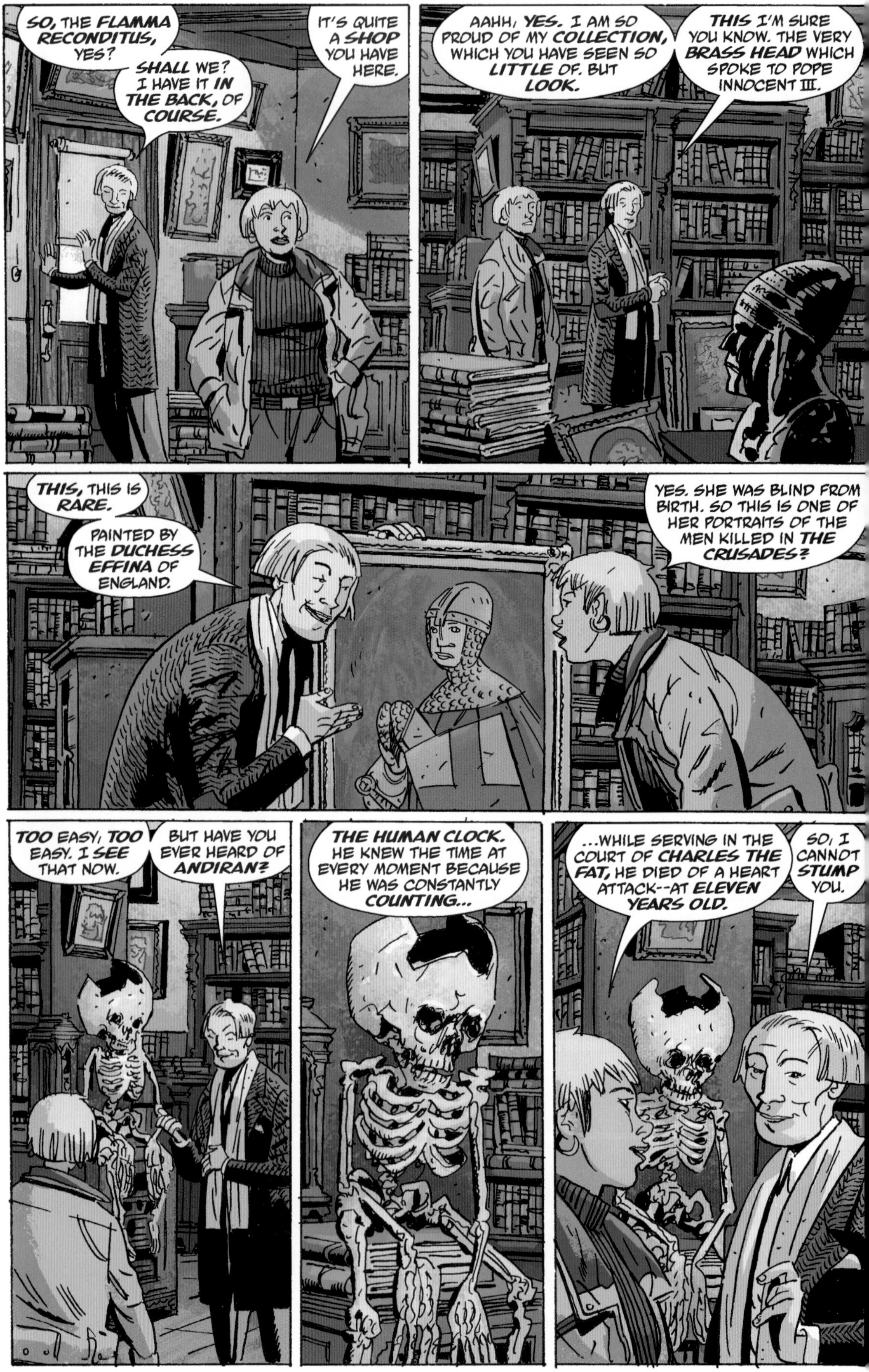
SO, THE FLAMMA RECONDITUS, YES?
SHALL WE? I HAVE IT IN THE BACK, OF COURSE.
IT'S QUITE A SHOP YOU HAVE HERE.
AAHH, YES. I AM SO PROUD OF MY COLLECTION, WHICH YOU HAVE SEEN SO LITTLE OF. BUT LOOK.
THIS I'M SURE YOU KNOW. THE VERY BRASS HEAD WHICH SPOKE TO POPE INNOCENT III.
THIS, THIS IS RARE.
PAINTED BY THE DUCHESS EFFINA OF ENGLAND.
YES. SHE WAS BLIND FROM BIRTH. SO THIS IS ONE OF HER PORTRAITS OF THE MEN KILLED IN THE CRUSADES?
TOO EASY, TOO EASY. I SEE THAT NOW.
BUT HAVE YOU EVER HEARD OF ANDIRAN?
THE HUMAN CLOCK. HE KNEW THE TIME AT EVERY MOMENT BECAUSE HE WAS CONSTANTLY COUNTING...
...WHILE SERVING IN THE COURT OF CHARLES THE FAT, HE DIED OF A HEART ATTACK--AT ELEVEN YEARS OLD.
SO, I CANNOT STUMP YOU.

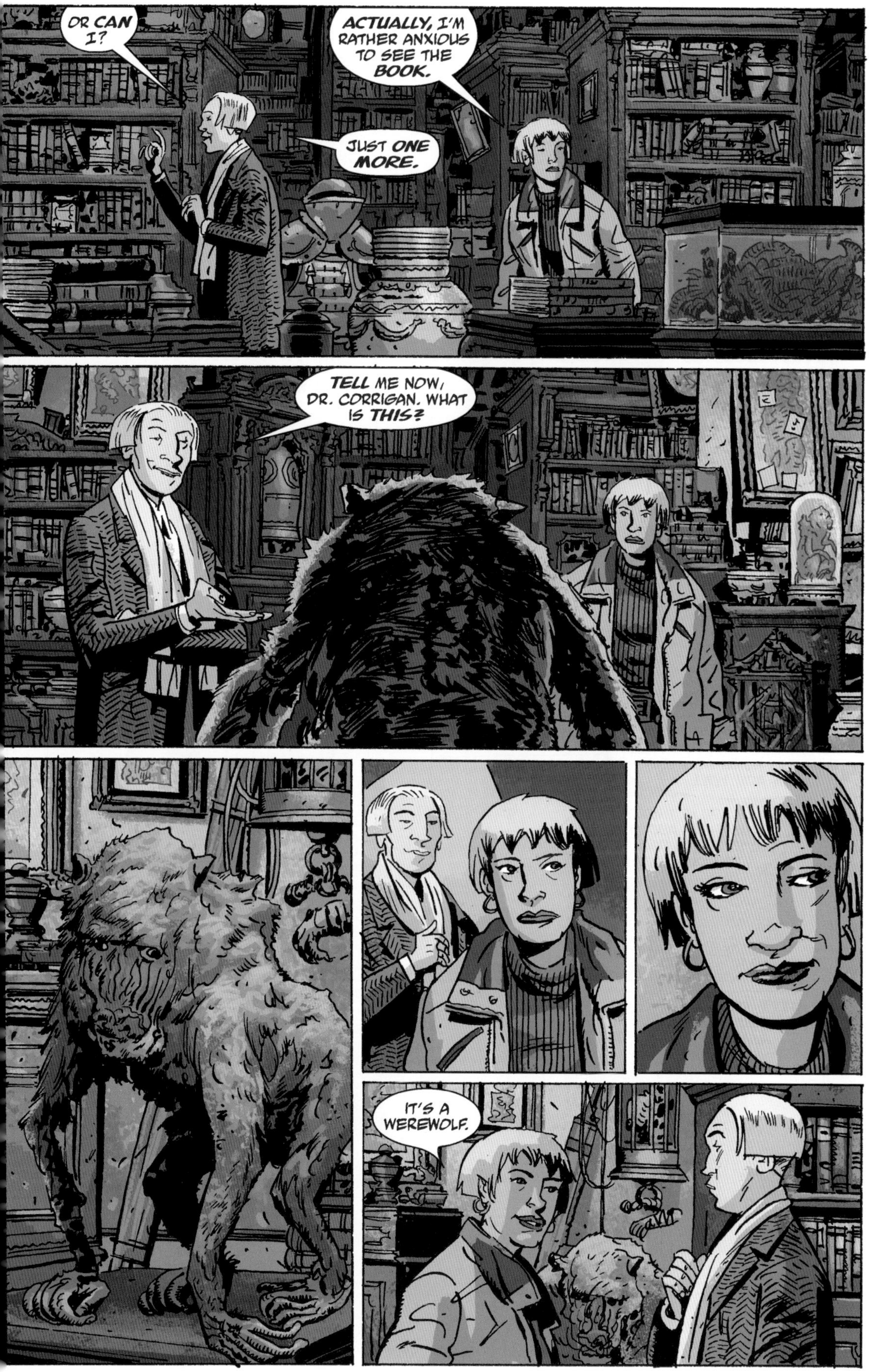
OR CAN I?
ACTUALLY, I'M RATHER ANXIOUS TO SEE THE BOOK.
JUST ONE MORE.
TELL ME NOW, DR. CORRIGAN. WHAT IS THIS?
IT'S A WEREWOLF.

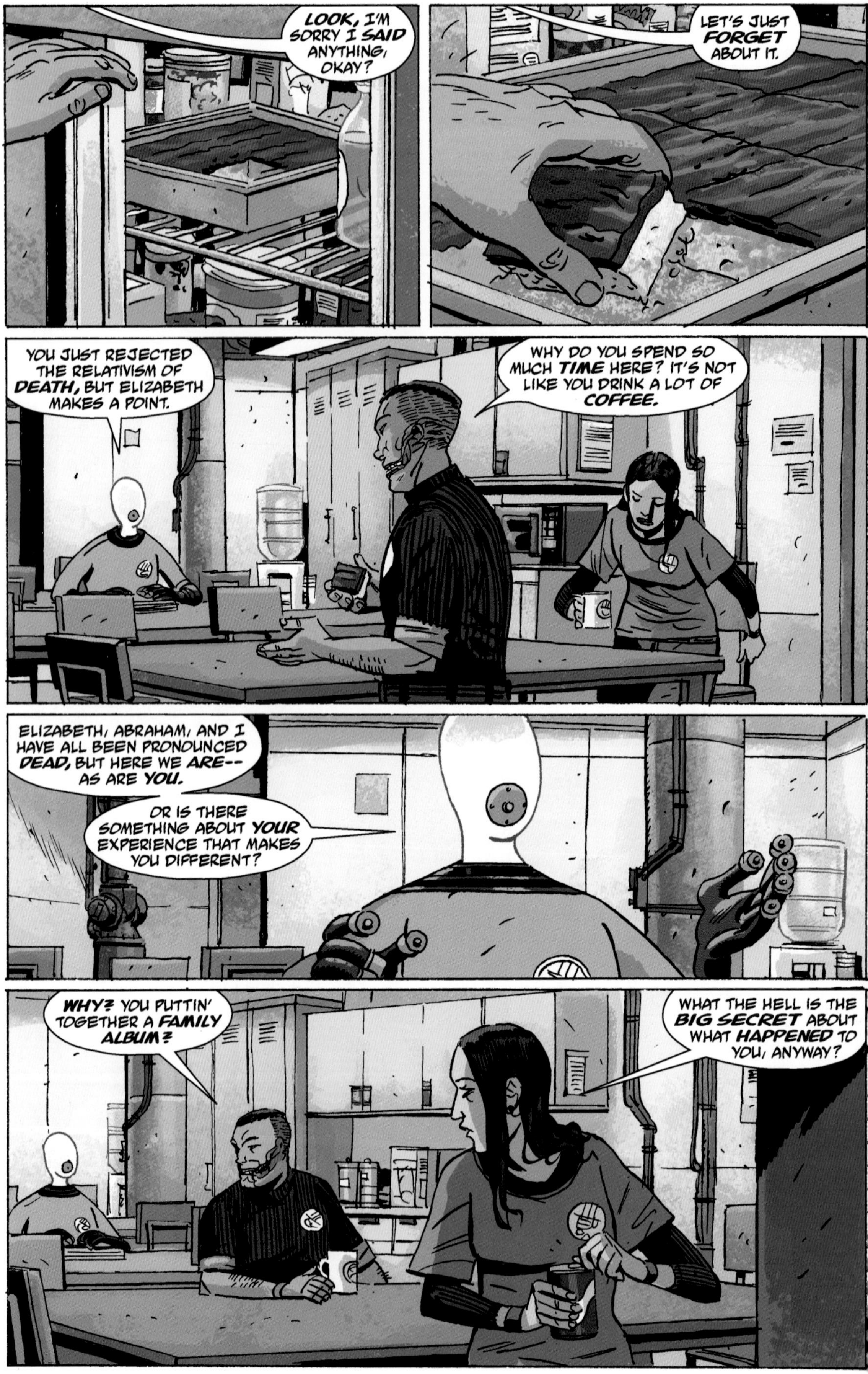
LOOK, I'M SORRY I SAID ANYTHING, OKAY?
LET'S JUST FORGET ABOUT IT.
YOU JUST REJECTED THE RELATIVISM OF DEATH, BUT ELIZABETH MAKES A POINT.
WHY DO YOU SPEND SO MUCH TIME HERE? IT'S NOT LIKE YOU DRINK A LOT OF COFFEE.
ELIZABETH, ABRAHAM, AND I HAVE ALL BEEN PRONOUNCED DEAD, BUT HERE WE ARE-- AS ARE YOU.
OR IS THERE SOMETHING ABOUT YOUR EXPERIENCE THAT MAKES YOU DIFFERENT?
WHY? YOU PUTTIN' TOGETHER A FAMILY ALBUM?
WHAT THE HELL IS THE BIG SECRET ABOUT WHAT HAPPENED TO YOU, ANYWAY?

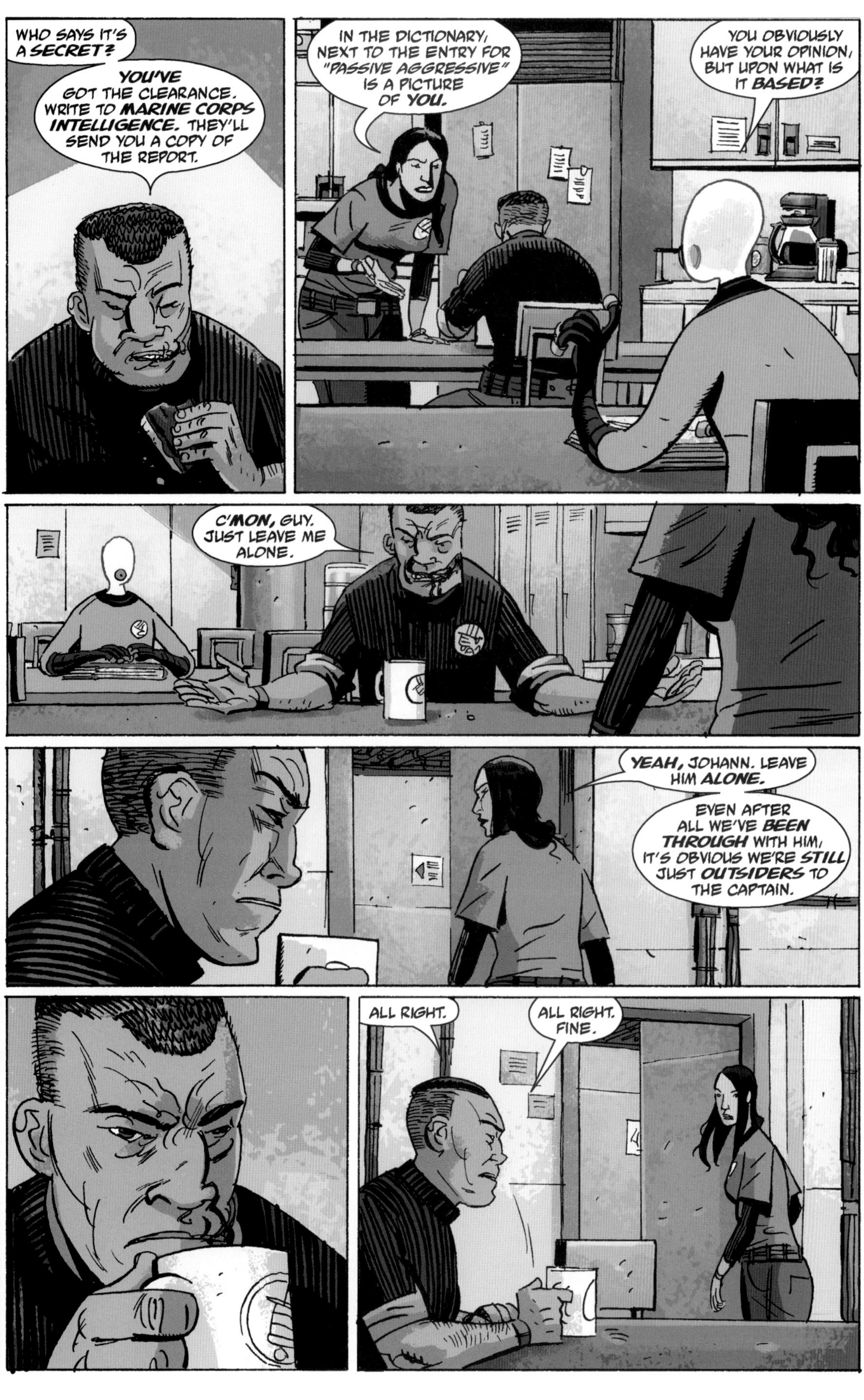

WHO SAYS IT'S A SECRET?
YOU'VE GOT THE CLEARANCE. WRITE TO MARINE CORPS INTELLIGENCE. THEY'LL SEND YOU A COPY OF THE REPORT.
IN THE DICTIONARY, NEXT TO THE ENTRY FOR "PASSIVE AGGRESSIVE" IS A PICTURE OF YOU.
YOU OBVIOUSLY HAVE YOUR OPINION, BUT UPON WHAT IS IT BASED?
C'MON, GUY. JUST LEAVE ME ALONE.
YEAH, JOHANN. LEAVE HIM ALONE.
EVEN AFTER ALL WE'VE BEEN THROUGH WITH HIM, IT'S OBVIOUS WE'RE STILL JUST OUTSIDERS TO THE CAPTAIN.
ALL RIGHT.
ALL RIGHT. FINE.

YES, A "WEREWOLF" FROM THE MENAGERIE OF THE *MARQUIS ADOET DE FABRE.*

I *CONCEDE* YOUR *EXCEPTIONAL* KNOWLEDGE IN THE FIELD, *DR. CORRIGAN.*

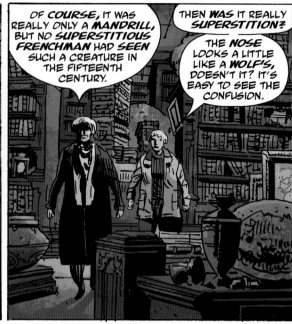

OF *COURSE*, IT WAS REALLY ONLY A *MANDRILL*, BUT NO *SUPERSTITIOUS FRENCHMAN* HAD SEEN SUCH A CREATURE IN THE FIFTEENTH CENTURY.

THEN *WAS* IT REALLY *SUPERSTITION?*

THE *NOSE* LOOKS A LITTLE LIKE A *WOLF'S*, DOESN'T IT? IT'S EASY TO SEE THE CONFUSION.

IGNORANCE DOESN'T EQUAL *SUPERSTITION.* THEY SIMPLY WERE GRAPPLING WITH A STRANGE WORLD, USING THE BEST MEANS *AVAILABLE* TO THEM AT THE MOMENT TO UNDERSTAND IT.

EVERY TIME NEW *DATA* EMERGES THAT OVERTURNS *ALL* CONVENTIONAL WISDOM, I THINK THAT WE'RE NOT SO VERY *DIFFERENT.*

WORDS *EXPRESSIVE* OF A *TRULY* ENLIGHTENED *MIND*, IF ANYONE WANTS *MY* OPINION.

AH, BUT WE HAVE A *BOOK* TO FIND.

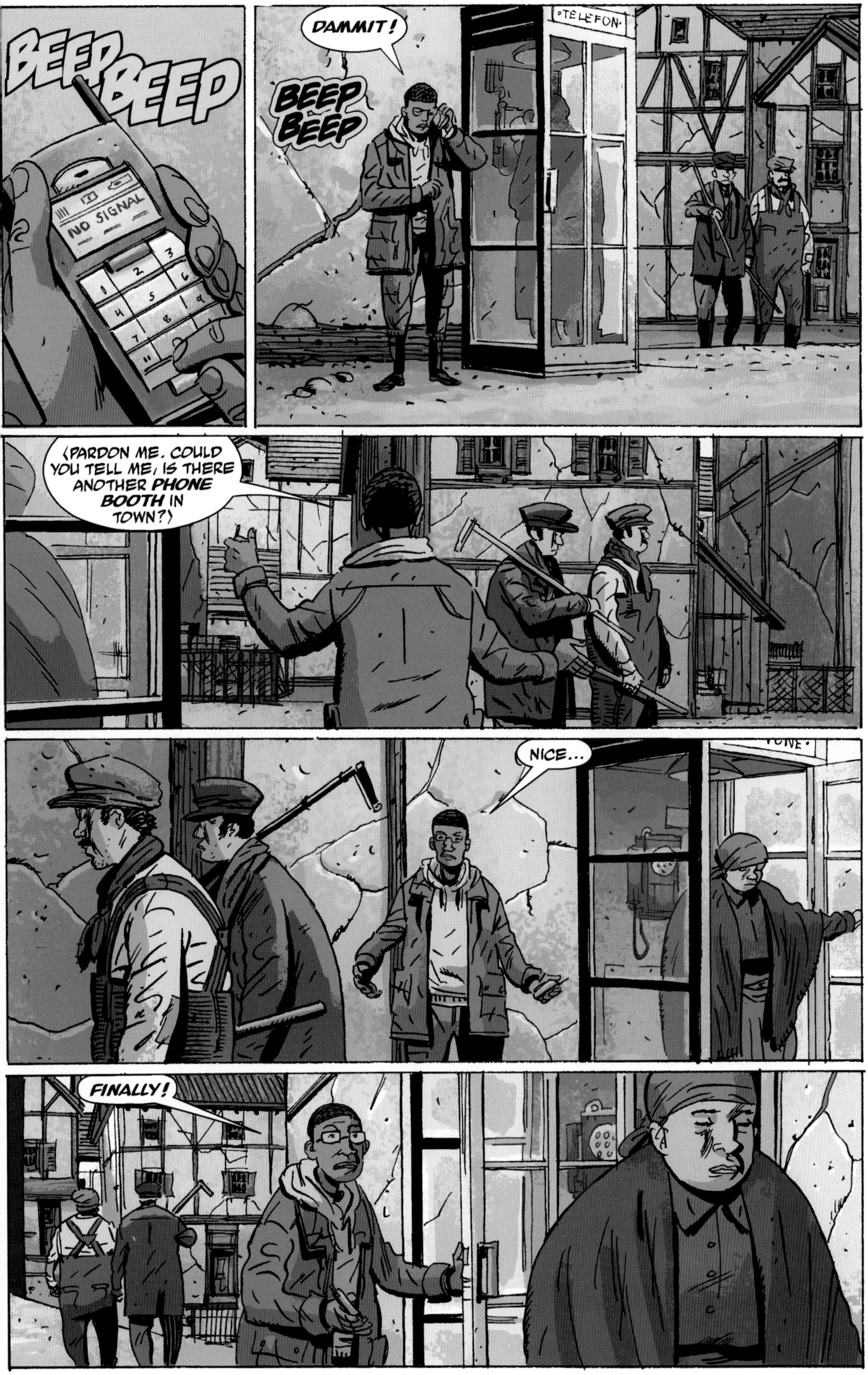
BEEP BEEP
NO SIGNAL
DAMMIT!
BEEP BEEP
TELEFON
⟨PARDON ME. COULD YOU TELL ME, IS THERE ANOTHER PHONE BOOTH IN TOWN?⟩
NICE...
FINALLY!

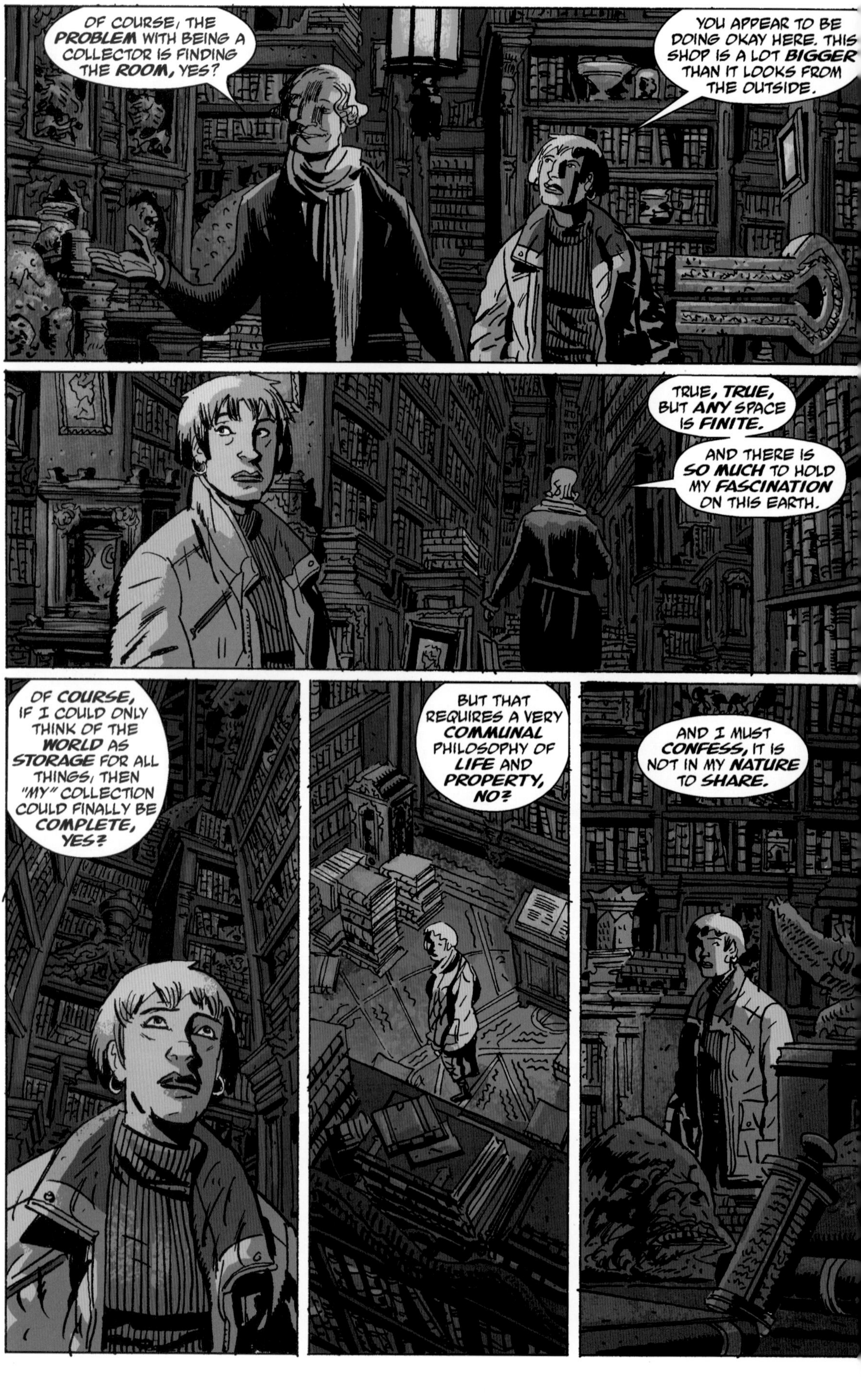
OF COURSE, THE PROBLEM WITH BEING A COLLECTOR IS FINDING THE ROOM, YES?
YOU APPEAR TO BE DOING OKAY HERE. THIS SHOP IS A LOT BIGGER THAN IT LOOKS FROM THE OUTSIDE.
TRUE, TRUE, BUT ANY SPACE IS FINITE.
AND THERE IS SO MUCH TO HOLD MY FASCINATION ON THIS EARTH.
OF COURSE, IF I COULD ONLY THINK OF THE WORLD AS STORAGE FOR ALL THINGS, THEN "MY" COLLECTION COULD FINALLY BE COMPLETE, YES?
BUT THAT REQUIRES A VERY COMMUNAL PHILOSOPHY OF LIFE AND PROPERTY, NO?
AND I MUST CONFESS, IT IS NOT IN MY NATURE TO SHARE.

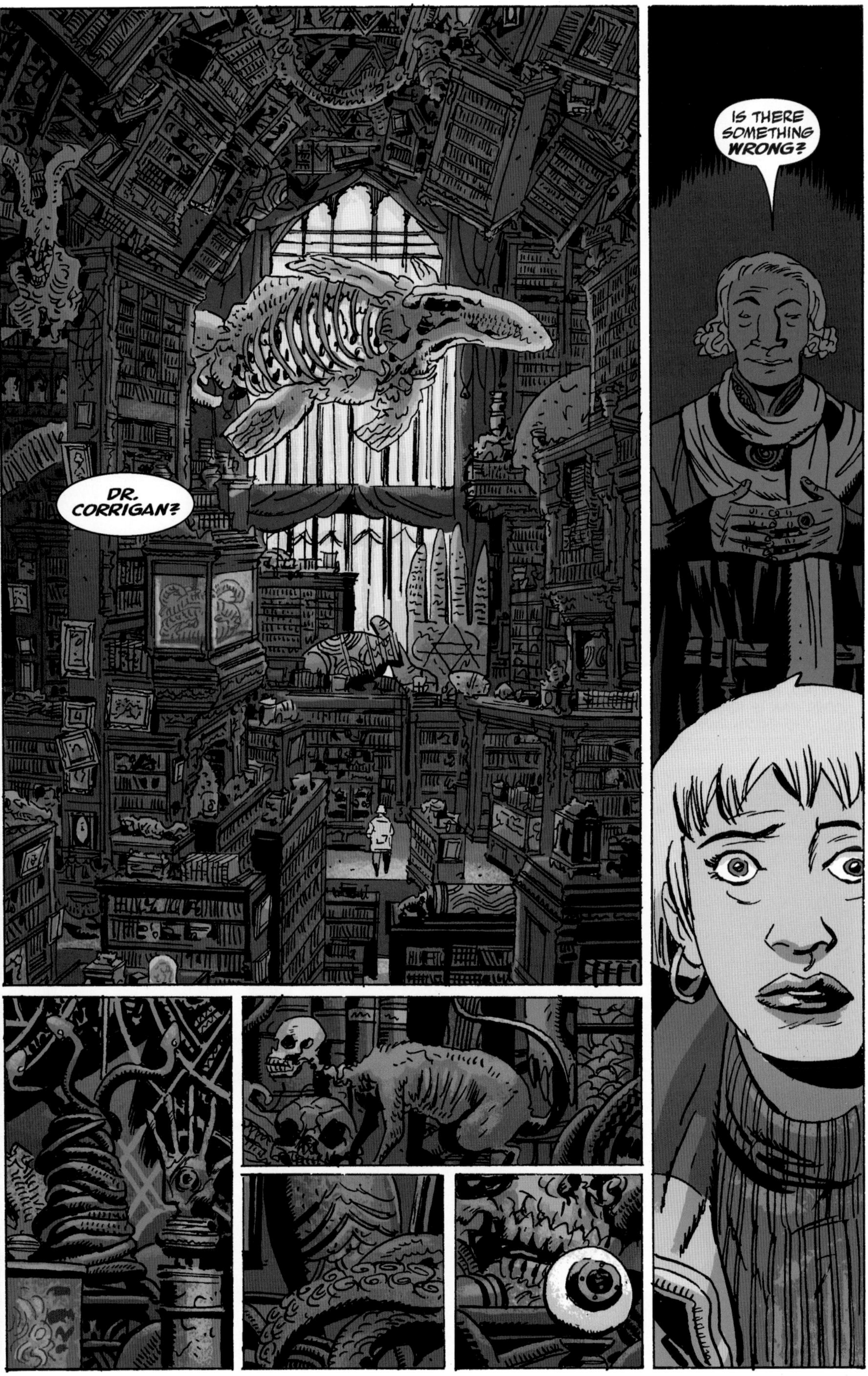
DR. CORRIGAN?
IS THERE SOMETHING WRONG?

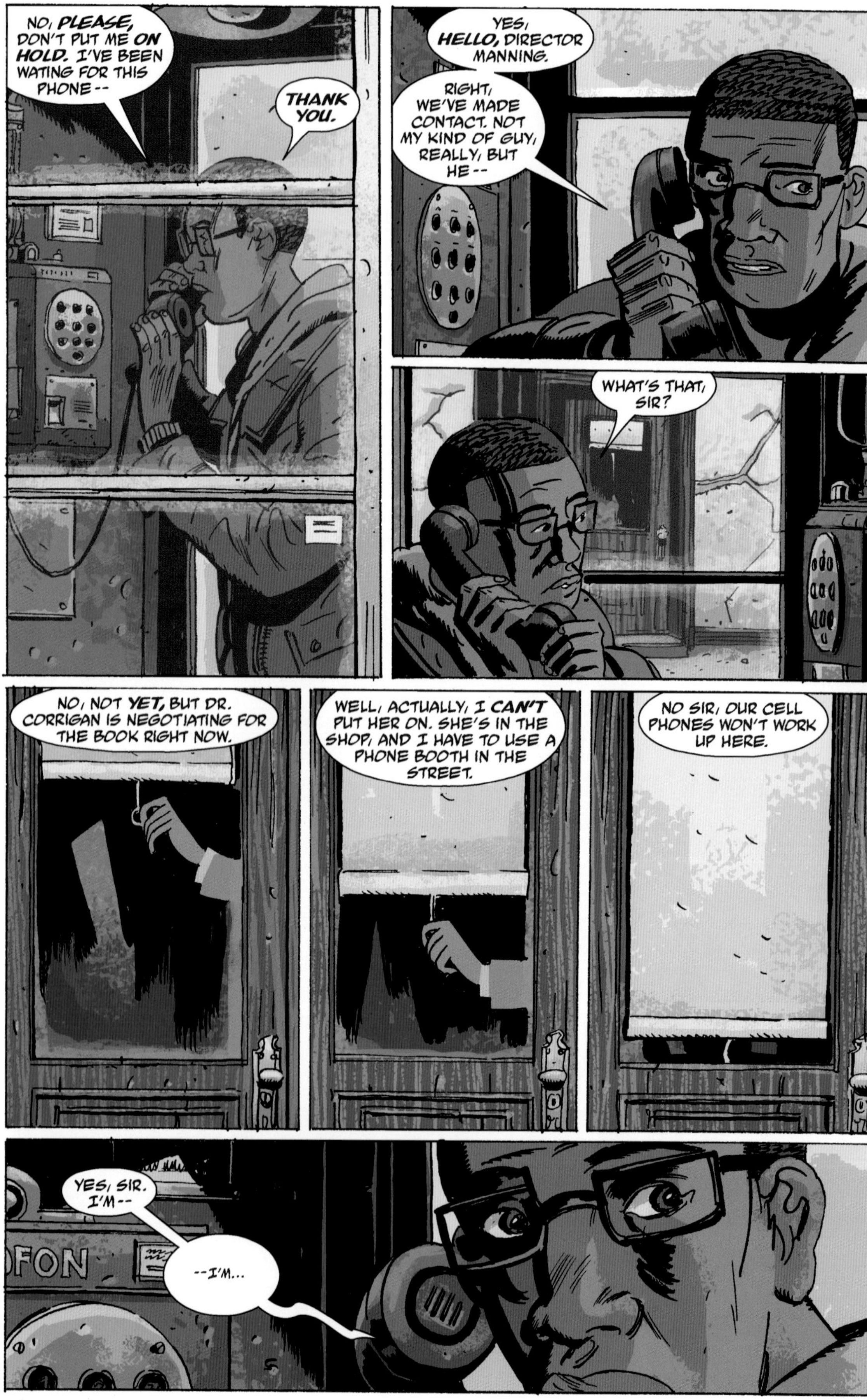
NO, PLEASE, DON'T PUT ME ON HOLD. I'VE BEEN WATING FOR THIS PHONE --
THANK YOU.
YES, HELLO, DIRECTOR MANNING.
RIGHT, WE'VE MADE CONTACT. NOT MY KIND OF GUY, REALLY, BUT HE --
WHAT'S THAT, SIR?
NO, NOT YET, BUT DR. CORRIGAN IS NEGOTIATING FOR THE BOOK RIGHT NOW.
WELL, ACTUALLY, I CAN'T PUT HER ON. SHE'S IN THE SHOP, AND I HAVE TO USE A PHONE BOOTH IN THE STREET.
NO SIR, OUR CELL PHONES WON'T WORK UP HERE.
YES, SIR. I'M --
--I'M...
FON

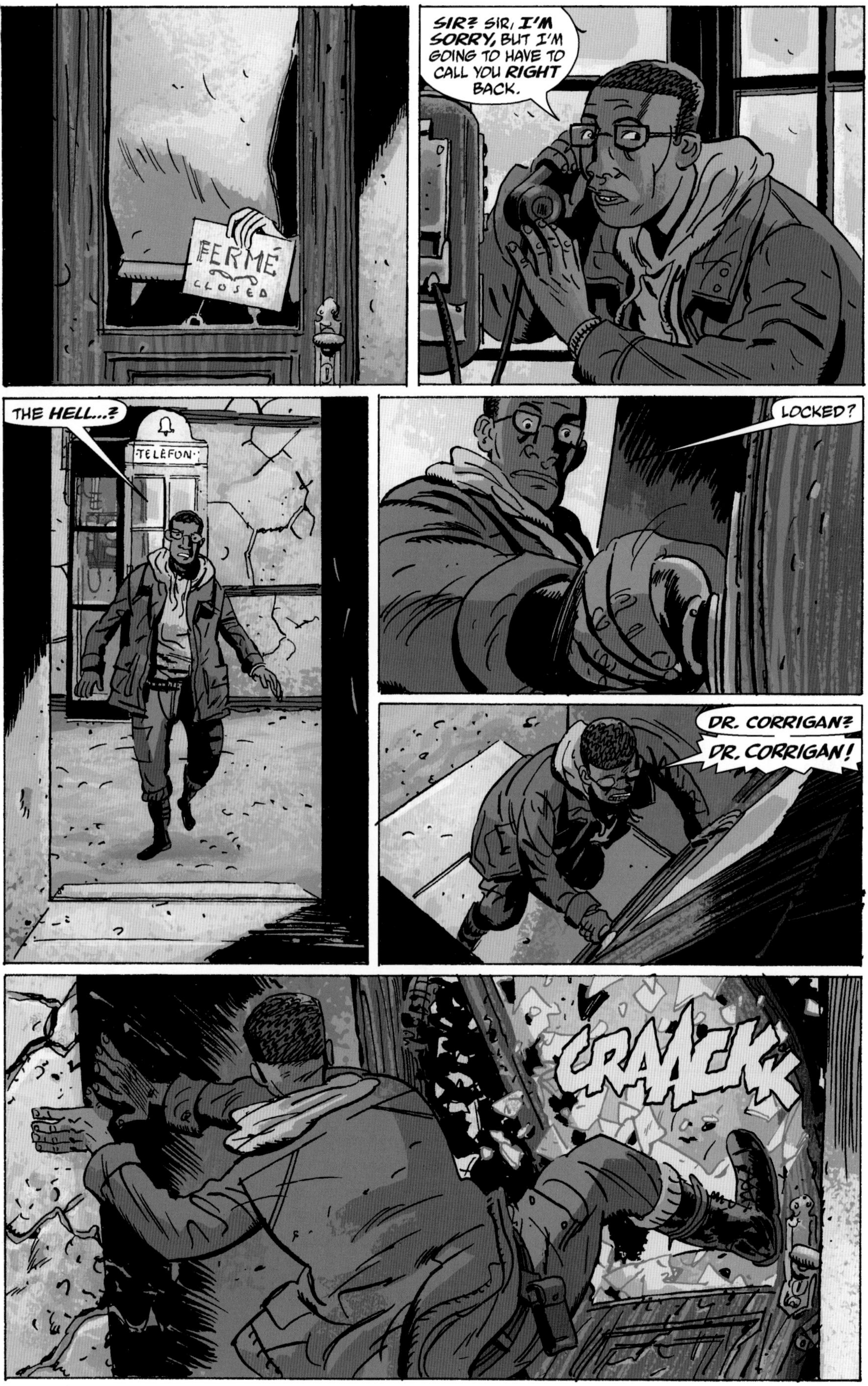
FERMÉ
CLOSED
SIR? SIR, I'M SORRY, BUT I'M GOING TO HAVE TO CALL YOU RIGHT BACK.
THE HELL...?
TELEFON
LOCKED?
DR. CORRIGAN?
DR. CORRIGAN!
CRAACK

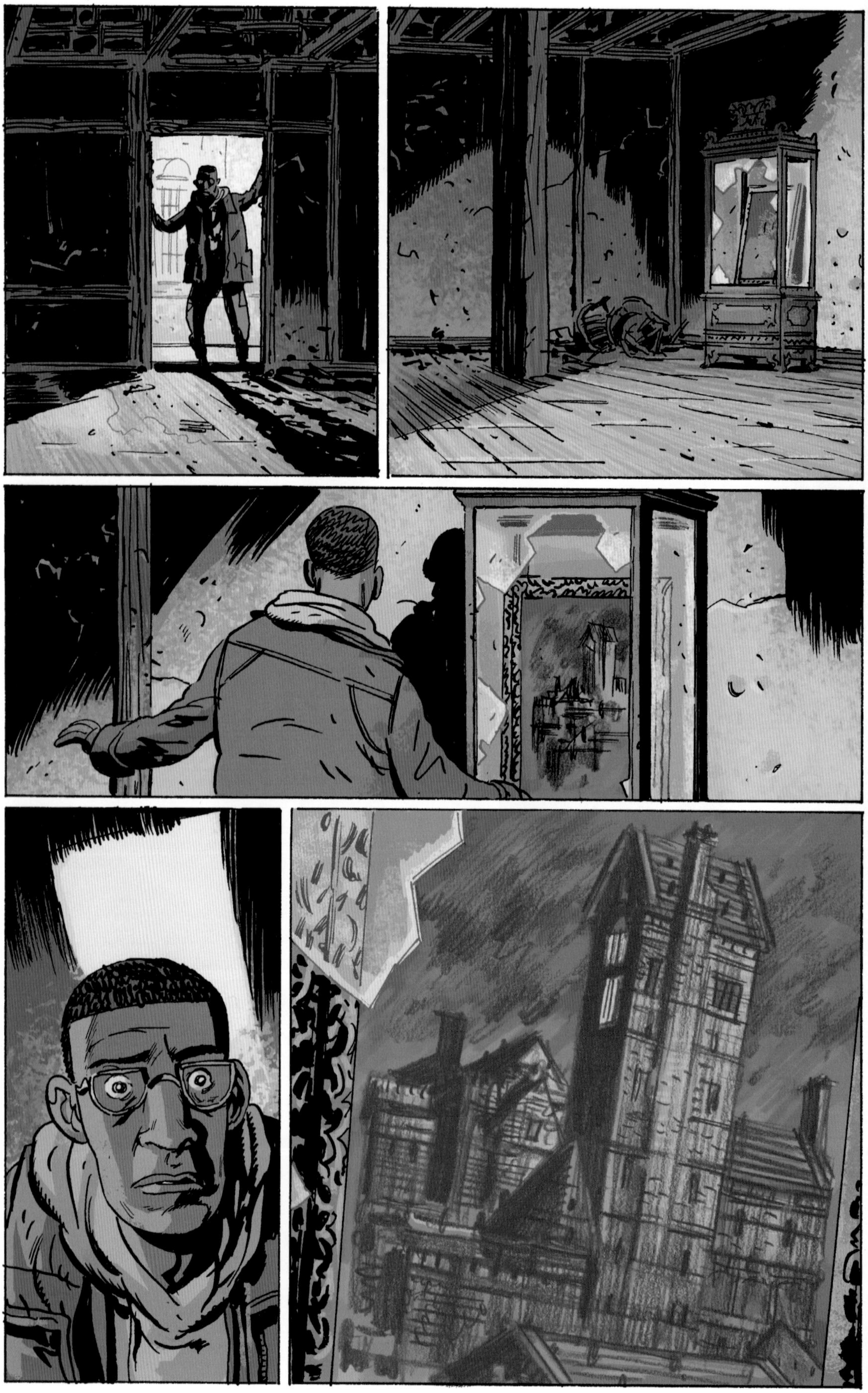

CHAPTER TWO

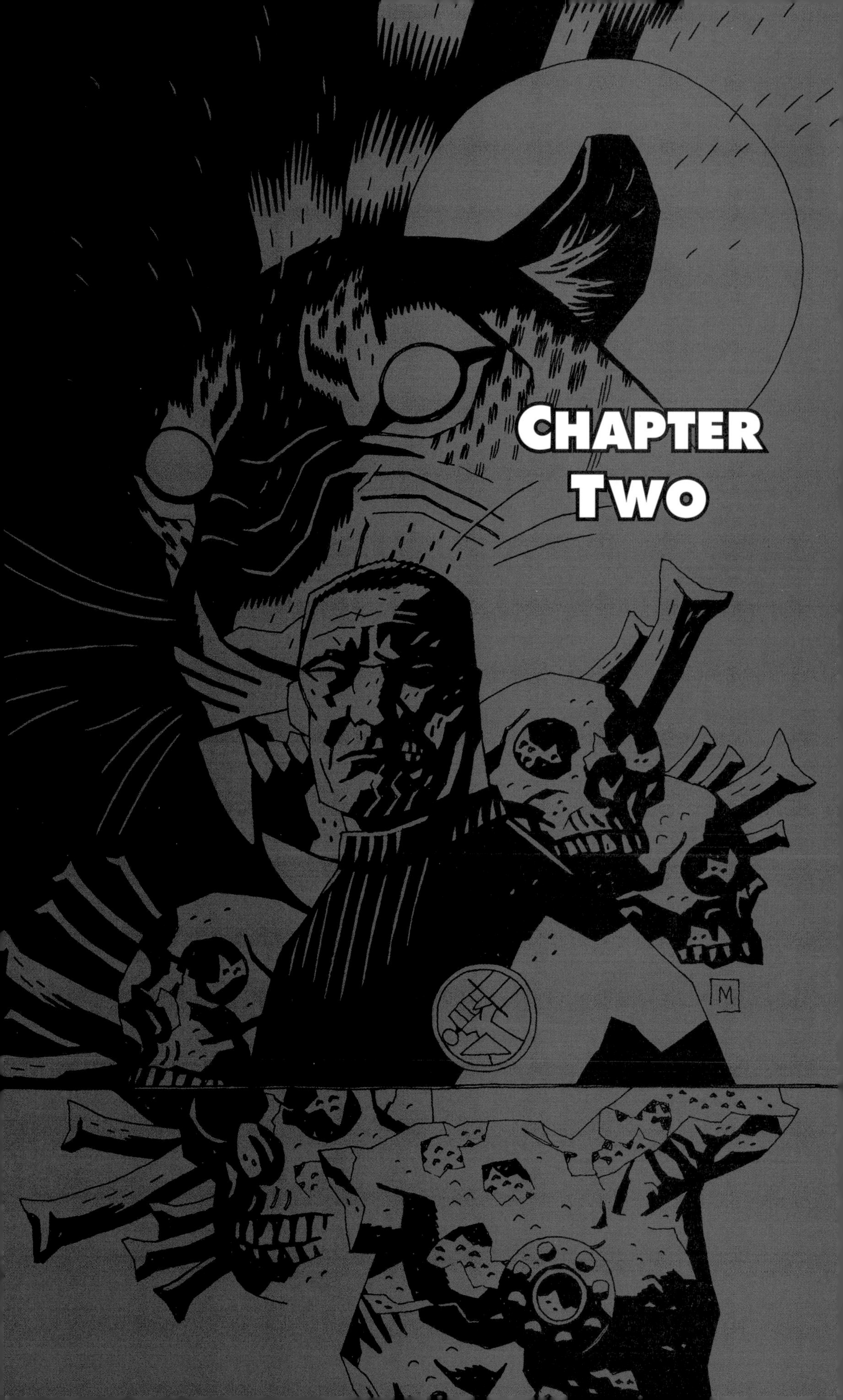

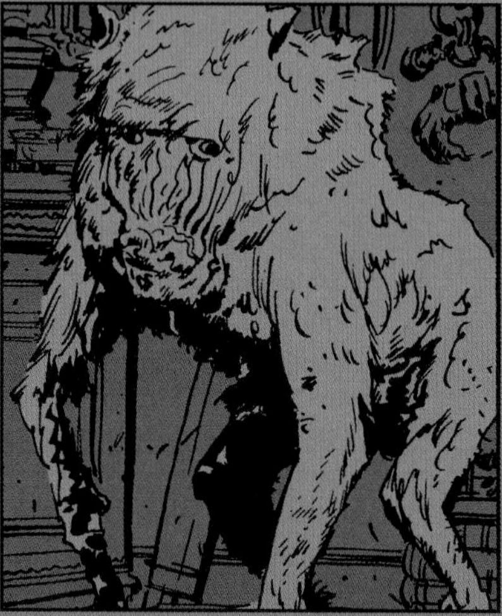

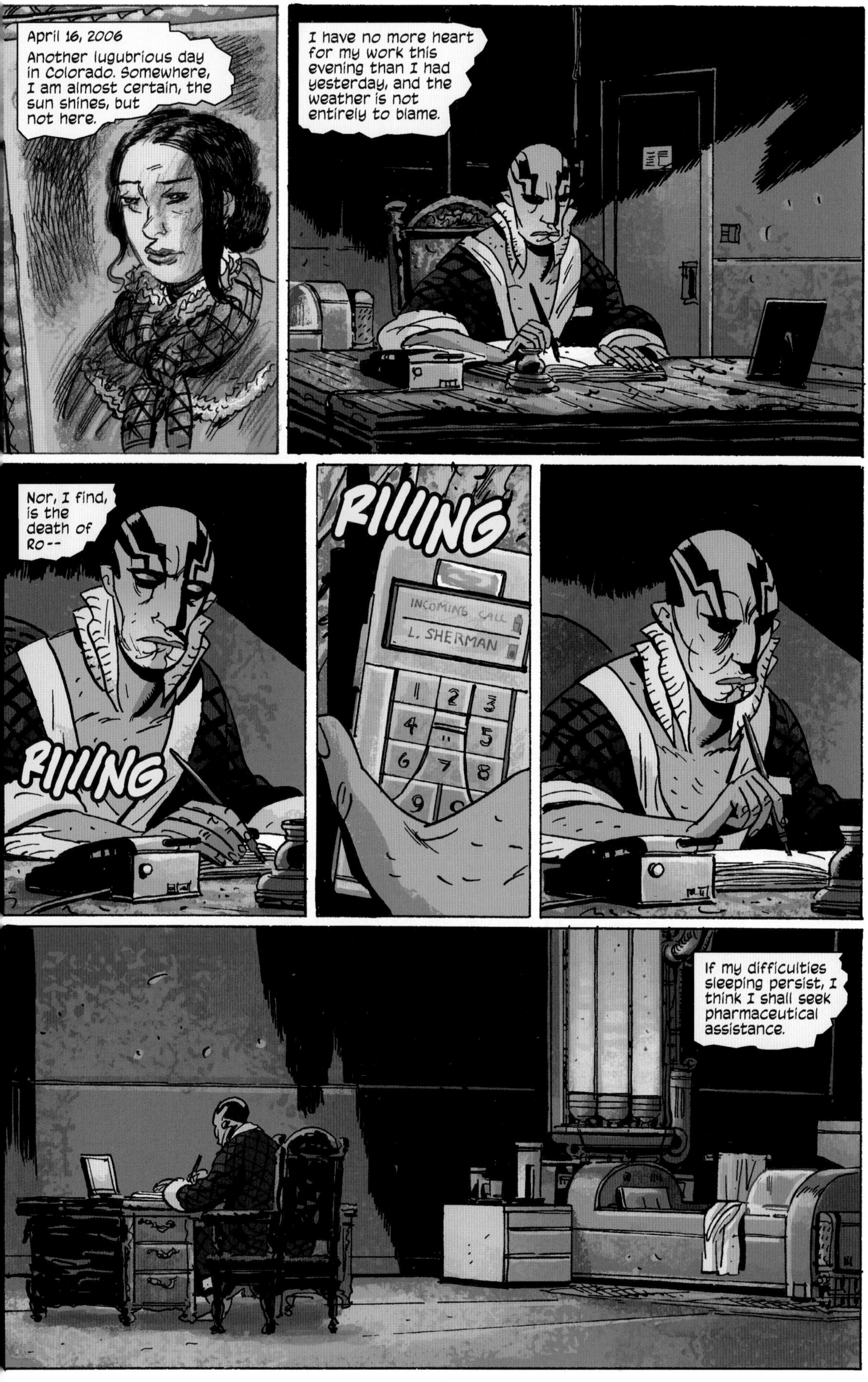
April 16, 2006
Another lugubrious day in Colorado. Somewhere, I am almost certain, the sun shines, but not here.
I have no more heart for my work this evening than I had yesterday, and the weather is not entirely to blame.
Nor, I find, is the death of Ro--
RIIIING
RIIIING
INCOMING CALL
L. SHERMAN
If my difficulties sleeping persist, I think I shall seek pharmaceutical assistance.

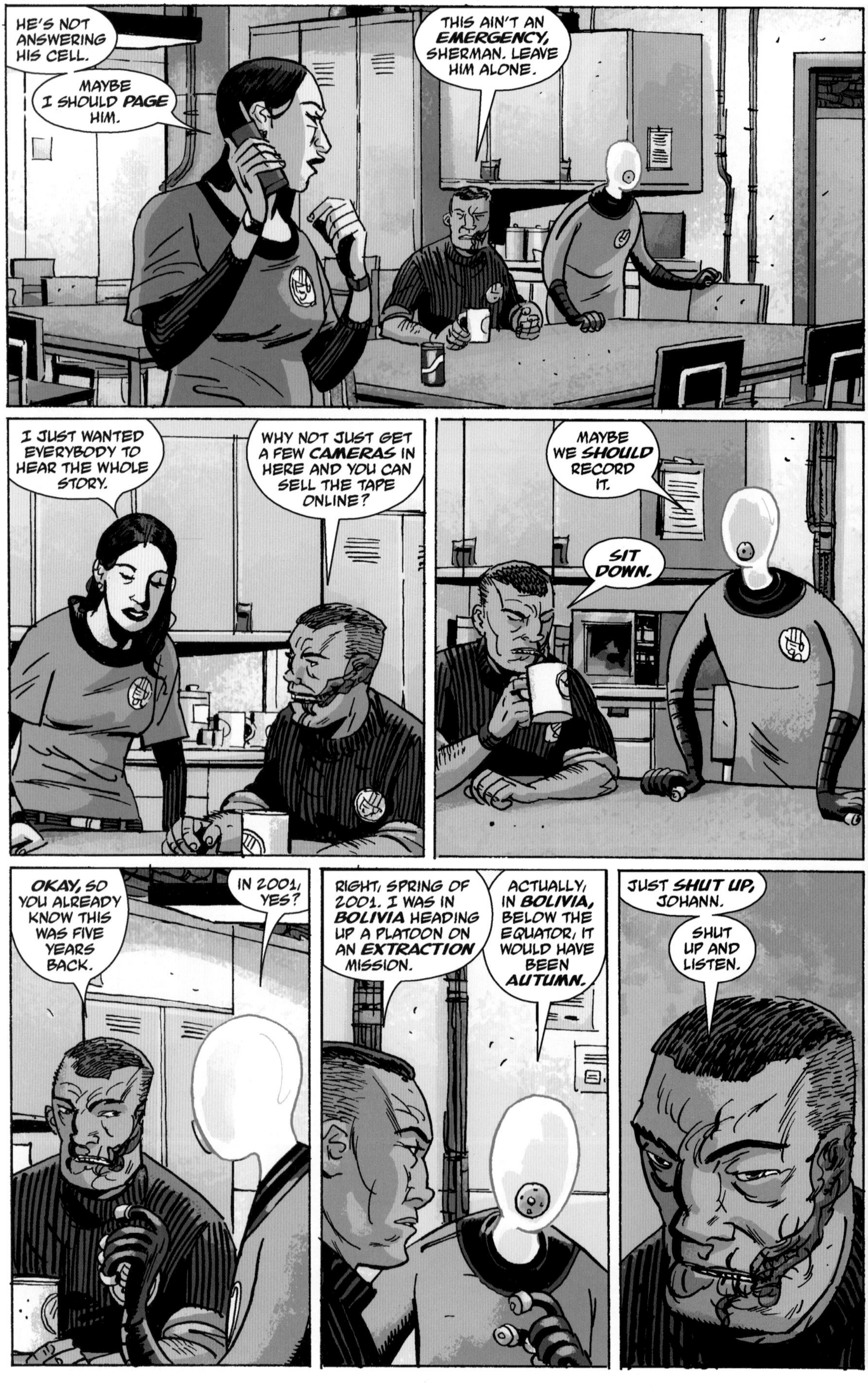
HE'S NOT ANSWERING HIS CELL.
MAYBE I SHOULD PAGE HIM.
THIS AIN'T AN EMERGENCY, SHERMAN. LEAVE HIM ALONE.
I JUST WANTED EVERYBODY TO HEAR THE WHOLE STORY.
WHY NOT JUST GET A FEW CAMERAS IN HERE AND YOU CAN SELL THE TAPE ONLINE?
MAYBE WE SHOULD RECORD IT.
SIT DOWN.
OKAY, SO YOU ALREADY KNOW THIS WAS FIVE YEARS BACK.
IN 2001, YES?
RIGHT, SPRING OF 2001. I WAS IN BOLIVIA HEADING UP A PLATOON ON AN EXTRACTION MISSION.
ACTUALLY, IN BOLIVIA, BELOW THE EQUATOR, IT WOULD HAVE BEEN AUTUMN.
JUST SHUT UP, JOHANN.
SHUT UP AND LISTEN.

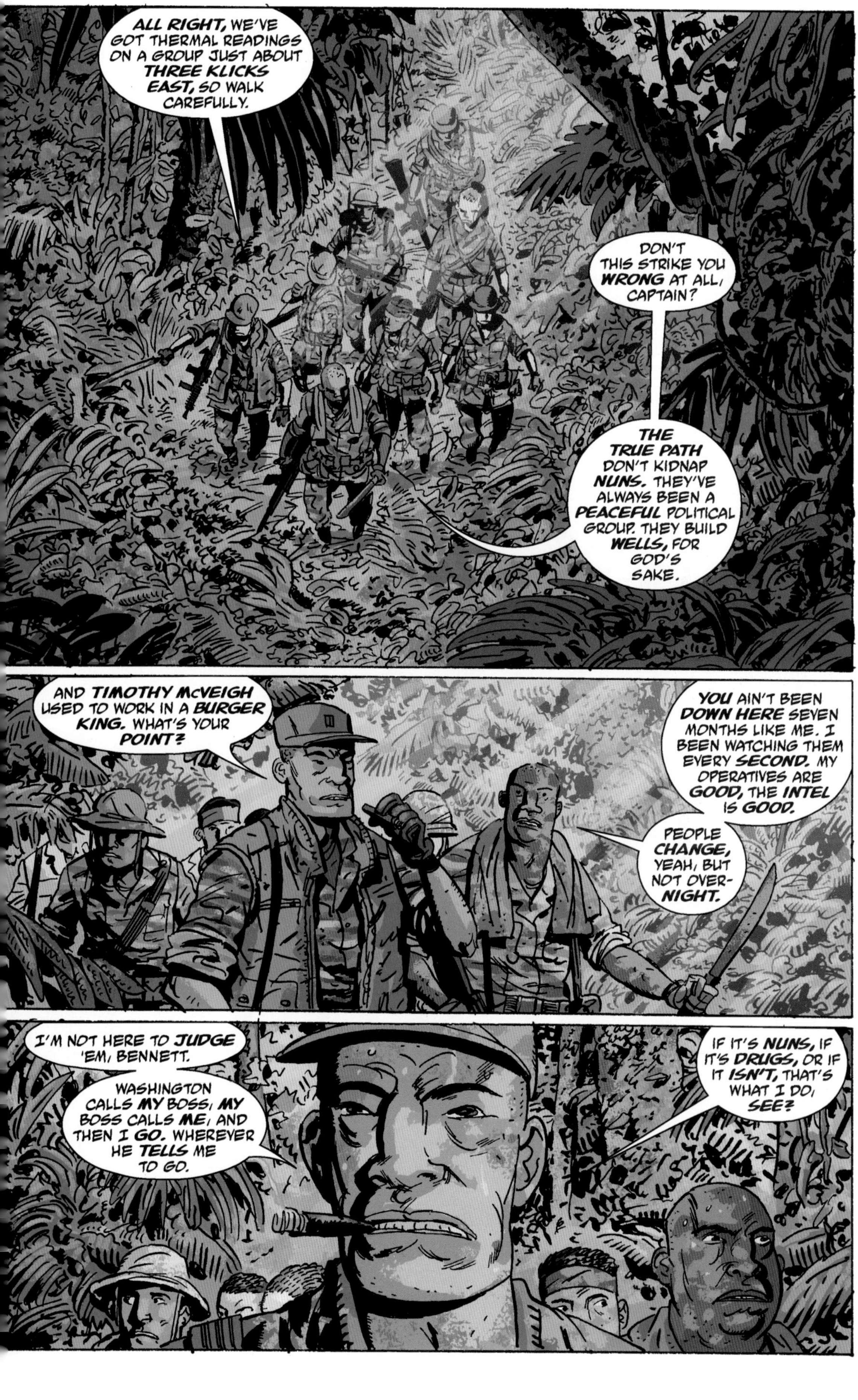
ALL RIGHT, WE'VE GOT THERMAL READINGS ON A GROUP JUST ABOUT THREE KLICKS EAST, SO WALK CAREFULLY.
DON'T THIS STRIKE YOU WRONG AT ALL, CAPTAIN?
THE TRUE PATH DON'T KIDNAP NUNS. THEY'VE ALWAYS BEEN A PEACEFUL POLITICAL GROUP. THEY BUILD WELLS, FOR GOD'S SAKE.
AND TIMOTHY McVEIGH USED TO WORK IN A BURGER KING. WHAT'S YOUR POINT?
YOU AIN'T BEEN DOWN HERE SEVEN MONTHS LIKE ME. I BEEN WATCHING THEM EVERY SECOND. MY OPERATIVES ARE GOOD, THE INTEL IS GOOD.
PEOPLE CHANGE, YEAH, BUT NOT OVER-NIGHT.
I'M NOT HERE TO JUDGE 'EM, BENNETT.
WASHINGTON CALLS MY BOSS, MY BOSS CALLS ME, AND THEN I GO. WHEREVER HE TELLS ME TO GO.
IF IT'S NUNS, IF IT'S DRUGS, OR IF IT ISN'T, THAT'S WHAT I DO, SEE?

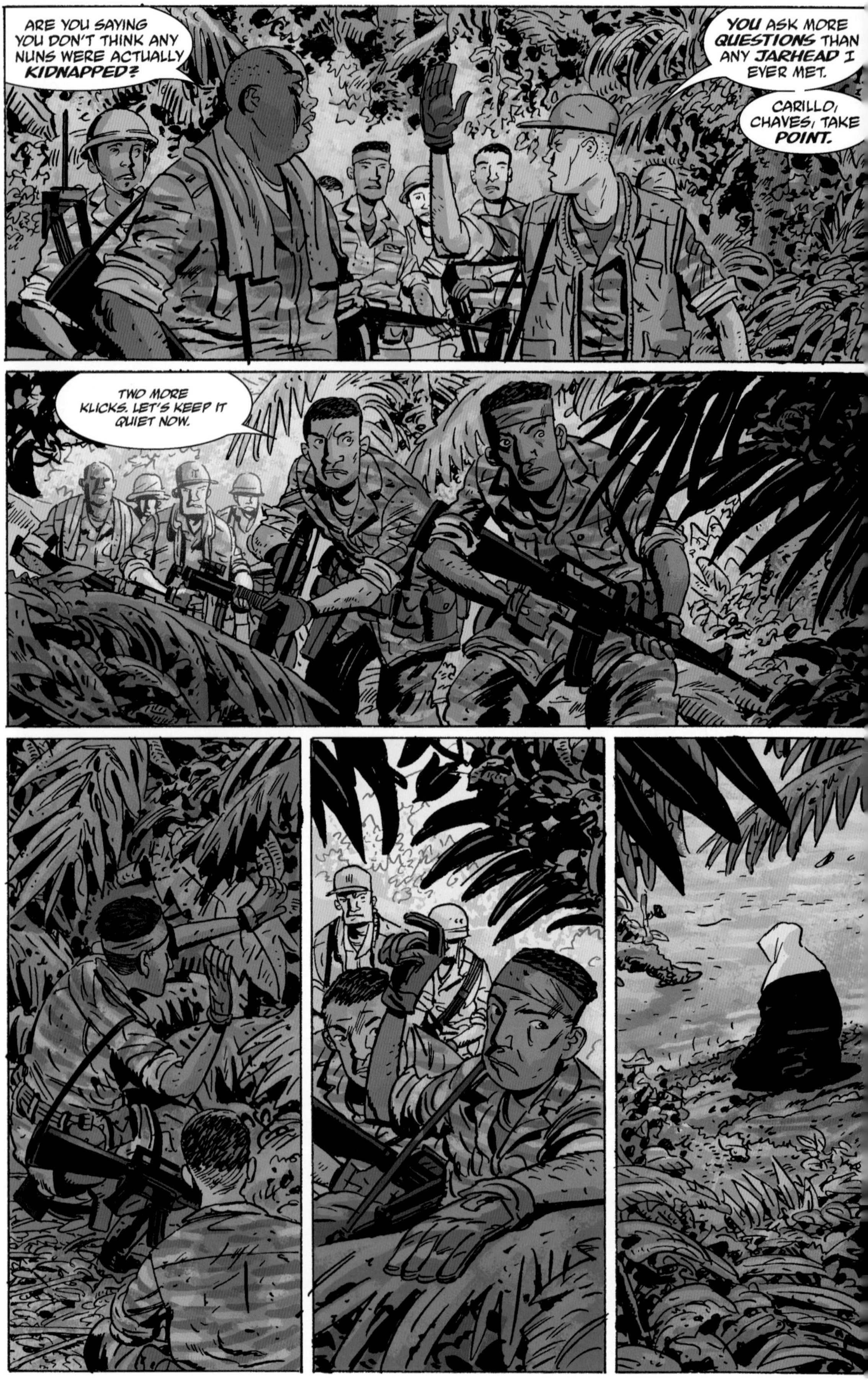

ARE YOU SAYING YOU DON'T THINK ANY NUNS WERE ACTUALLY KIDNAPPED?
YOU ASK MORE QUESTIONS THAN ANY JARHEAD I EVER MET.
CARILLO, CHAVES, TAKE POINT.
TWO MORE KLICKS. LET'S KEEP IT QUIET NOW.

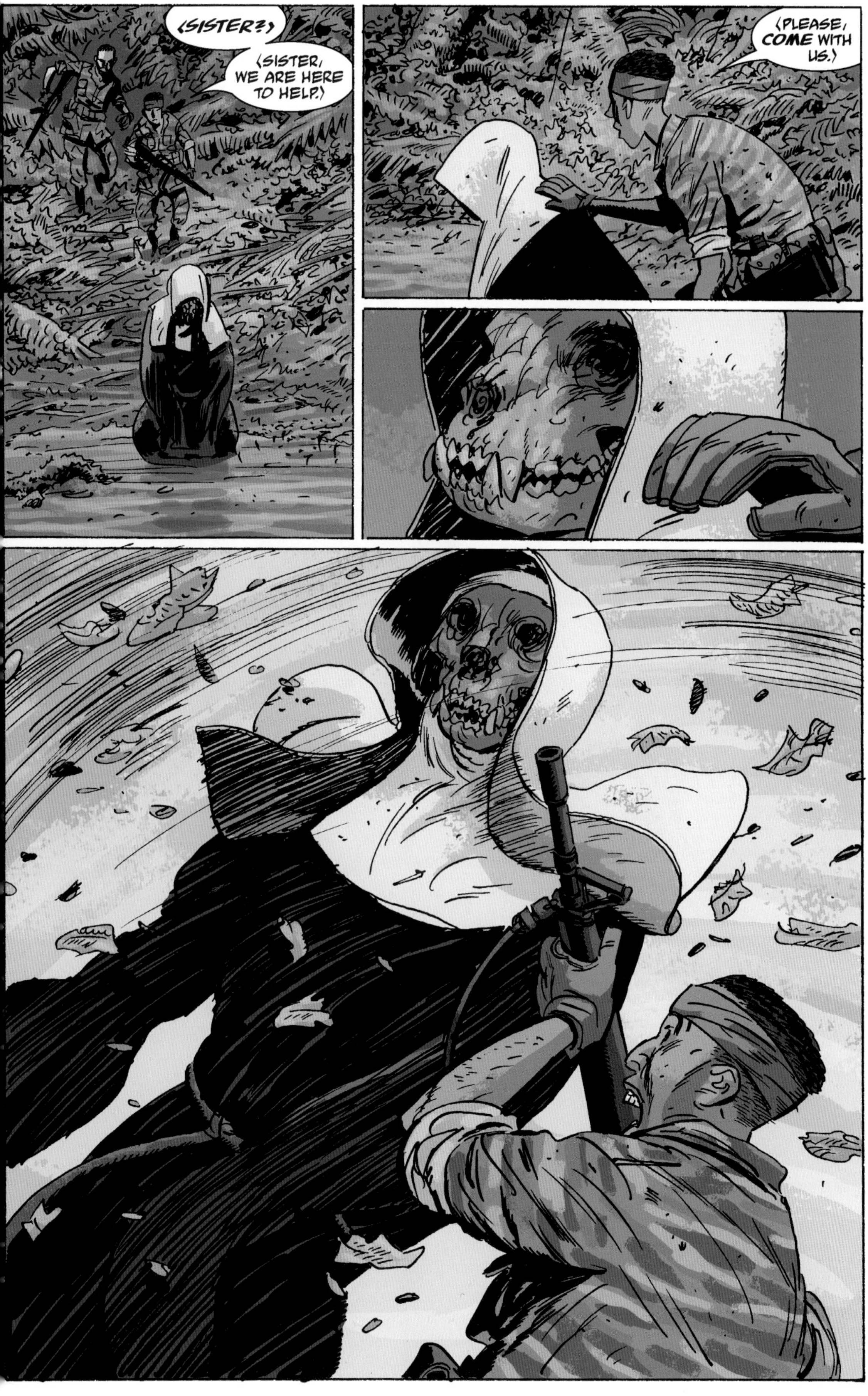
‹SISTER?›
‹SISTER, WE ARE HERE TO HELP.›
‹PLEASE, COME WITH US.›

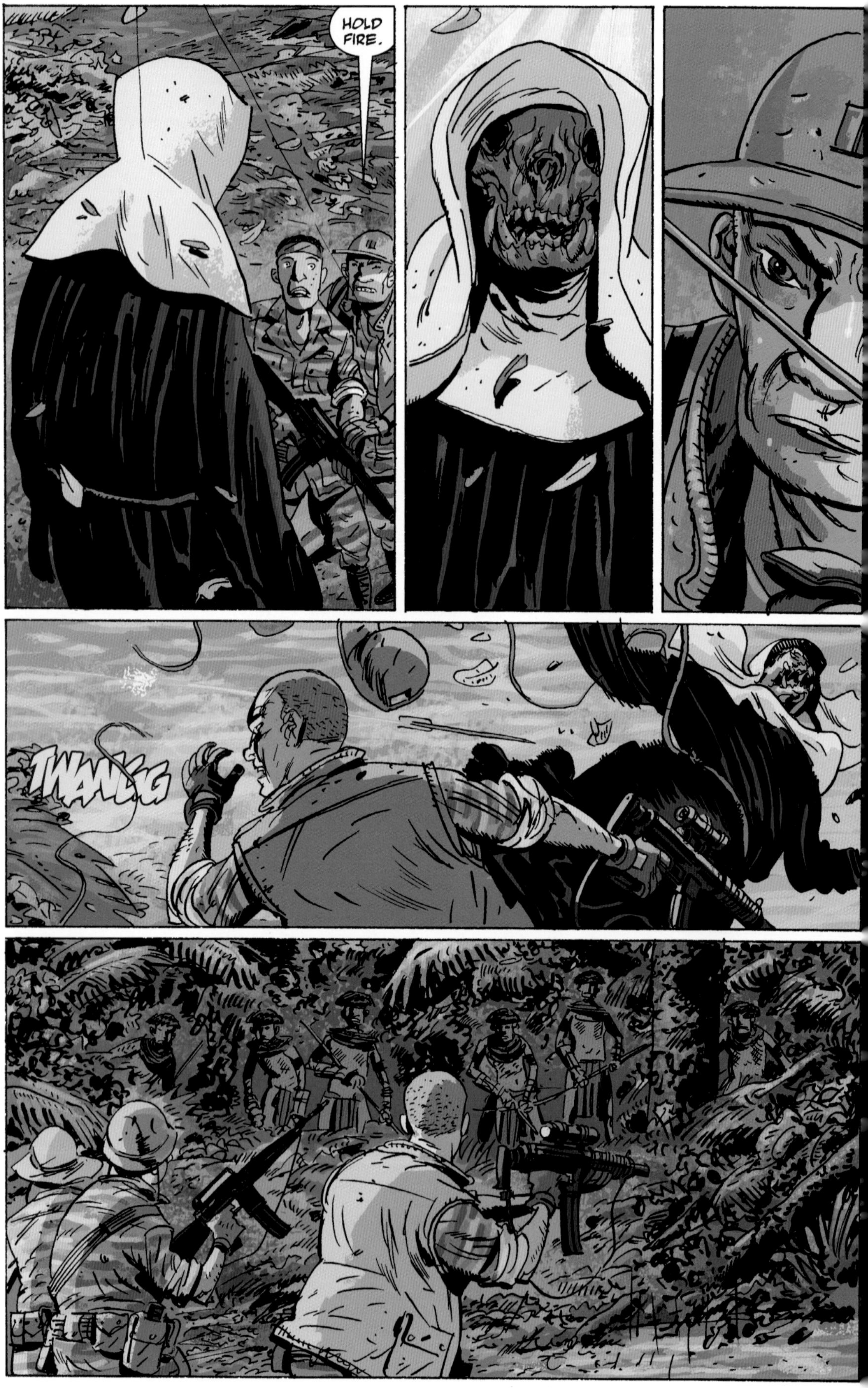
HOLD FIRE.
TWANG

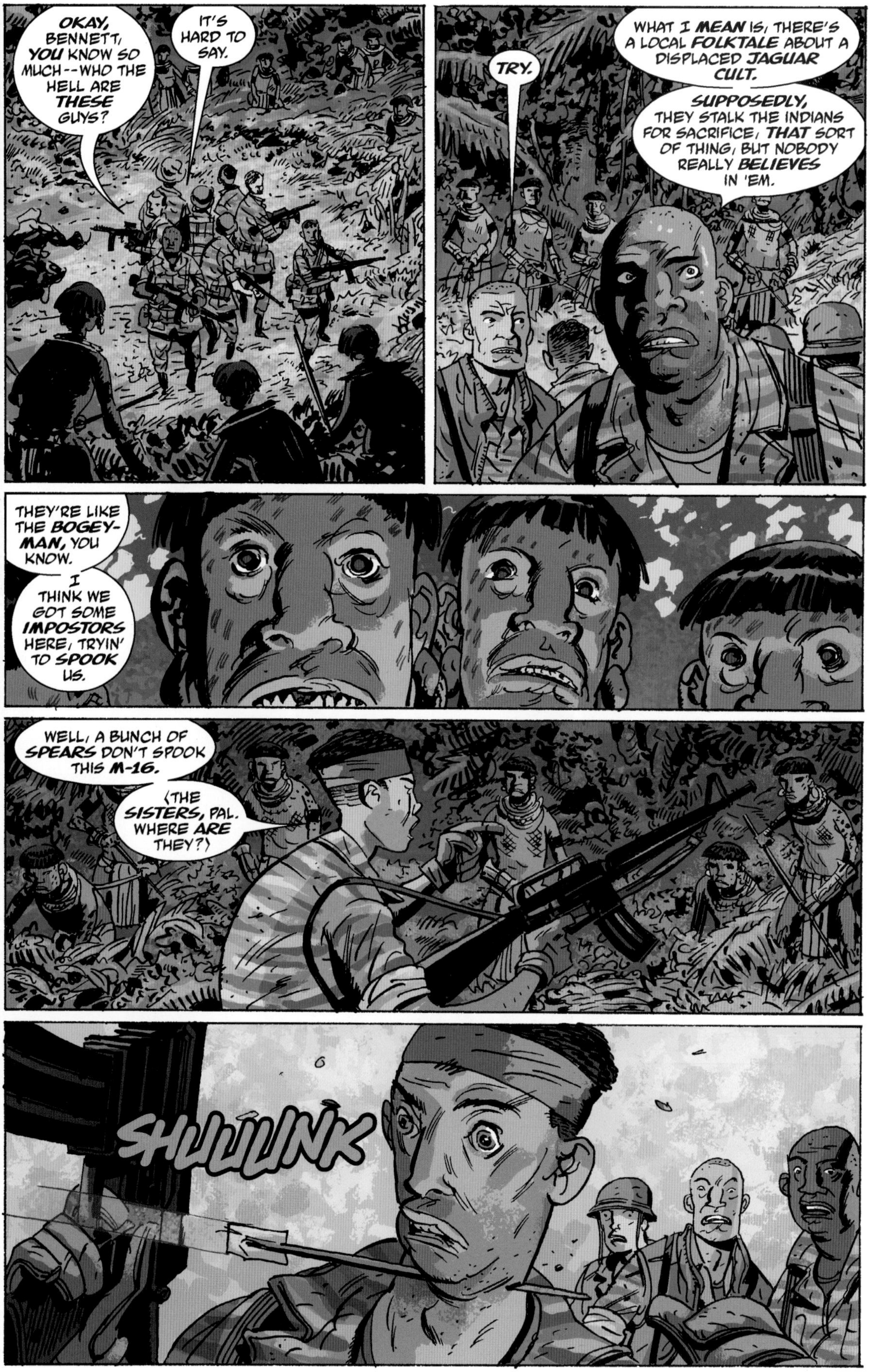

OKAY, BENNETT, YOU KNOW SO MUCH--WHO THE HELL ARE THESE GUYS?
IT'S HARD TO SAY.
TRY.
WHAT I MEAN IS, THERE'S A LOCAL FOLKTALE ABOUT A DISPLACED JAGUAR CULT.
SUPPOSEDLY, THEY STALK THE INDIANS FOR SACRIFICE, THAT SORT OF THING, BUT NOBODY REALLY BELIEVES IN 'EM.
THEY'RE LIKE THE BOGEY-MAN, YOU KNOW.
I THINK WE GOT SOME IMPOSTORS HERE, TRYIN' TO SPOOK US.
WELL, A BUNCH OF SPEARS DON'T SPOOK THIS M-16.
⟨THE SISTERS, PAL. WHERE ARE THEY?⟩
SHULUNK

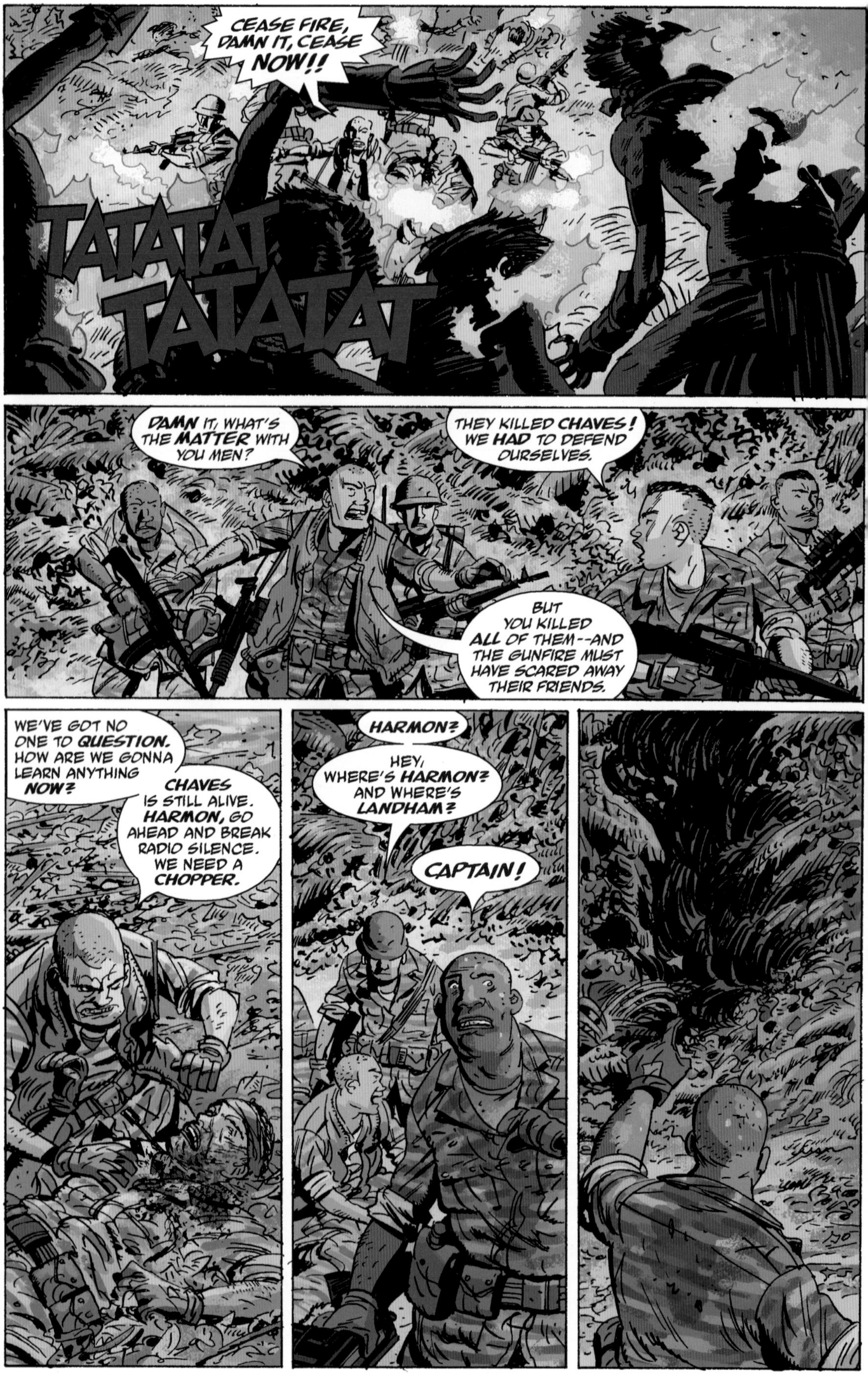
CEASE FIRE, DAMN IT, CEASE NOW!!
TATATAT TATATAT
DAMN IT, WHAT'S THE MATTER WITH YOU MEN?
THEY KILLED CHAVES! WE HAD TO DEFEND OURSELVES.
BUT YOU KILLED ALL OF THEM--AND THE GUNFIRE MUST HAVE SCARED AWAY THEIR FRIENDS.
WE'VE GOT NO ONE TO QUESTION. HOW ARE WE GONNA LEARN ANYTHING NOW?
CHAVES IS STILL ALIVE. HARMON, GO AHEAD AND BREAK RADIO SILENCE. WE NEED A CHOPPER.
HARMON?
HEY, WHERE'S HARMON? AND WHERE'S LANDHAM?
CAPTAIN!

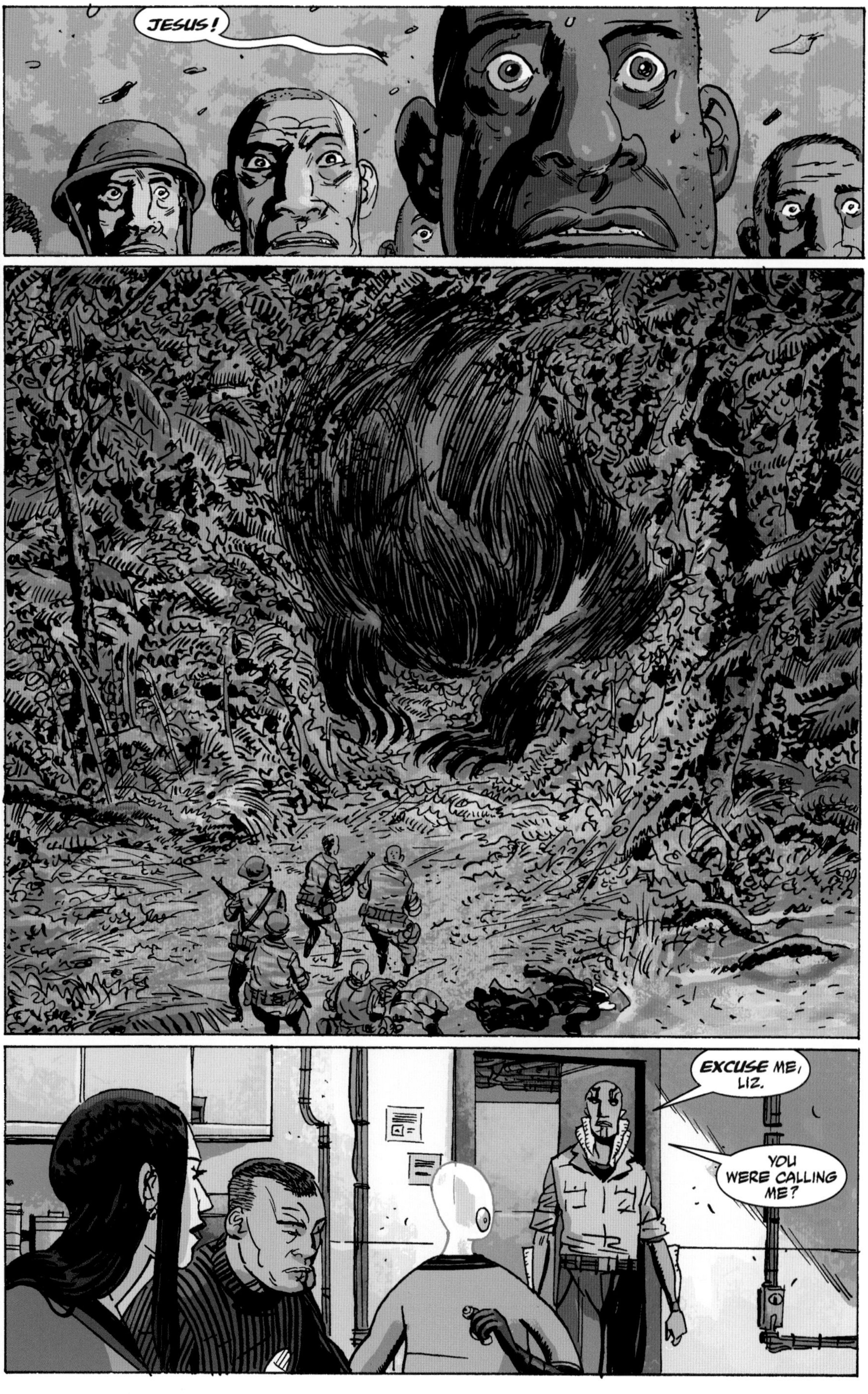
JESUS!
EXCUSE ME, LIZ.
YOU WERE CALLING ME?

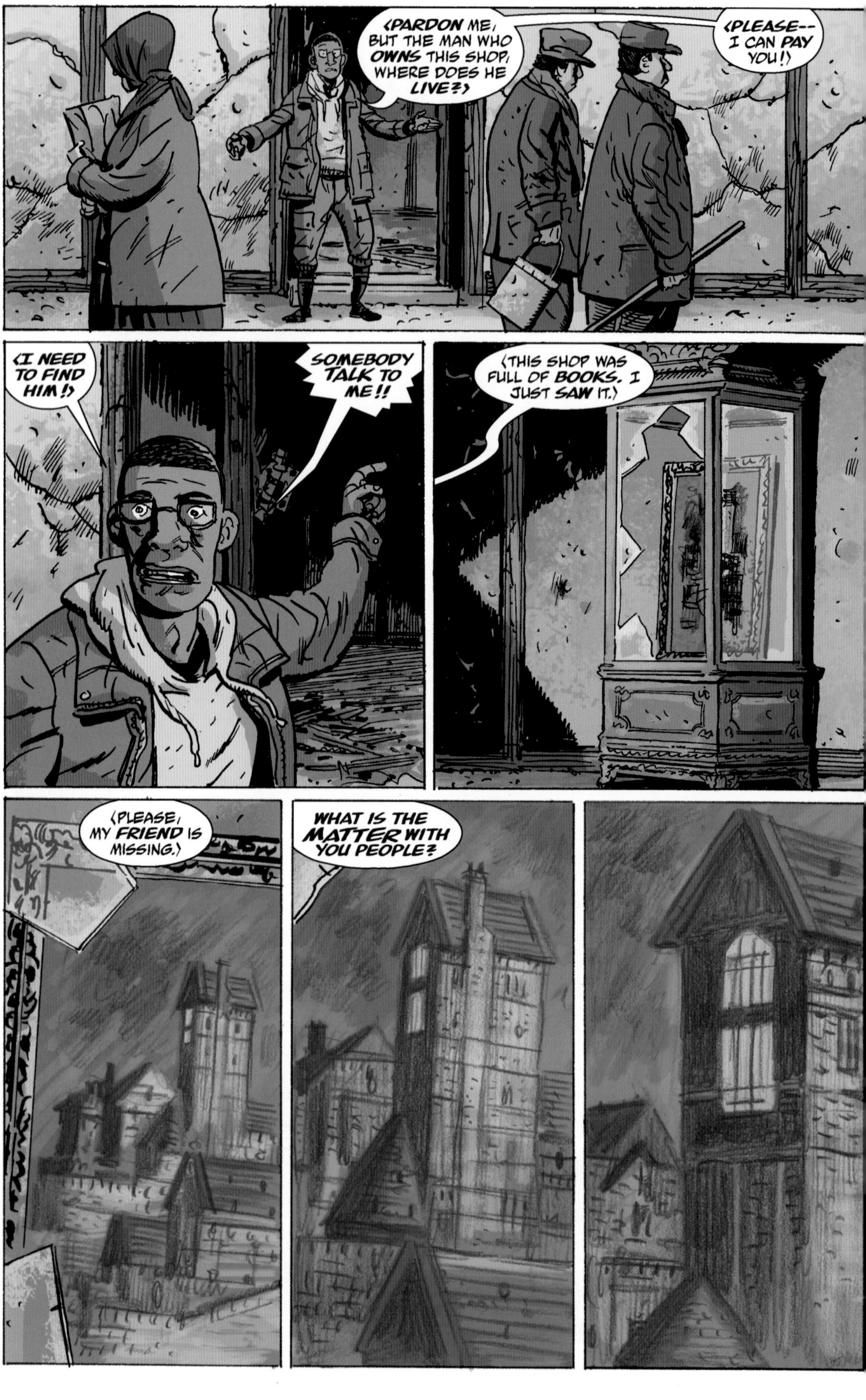

‹PARDON ME, BUT THE MAN WHO OWNS THIS SHOP, WHERE DOES HE LIVE?›
‹PLEASE-- I CAN PAY YOU!›
‹I NEED TO FIND HIM!›
SOMEBODY TALK TO ME!!
‹THIS SHOP WAS FULL OF BOOKS. I JUST SAW IT.›
‹PLEASE, MY FRIEND IS MISSING.›
WHAT IS THE MATTER WITH YOU PEOPLE?

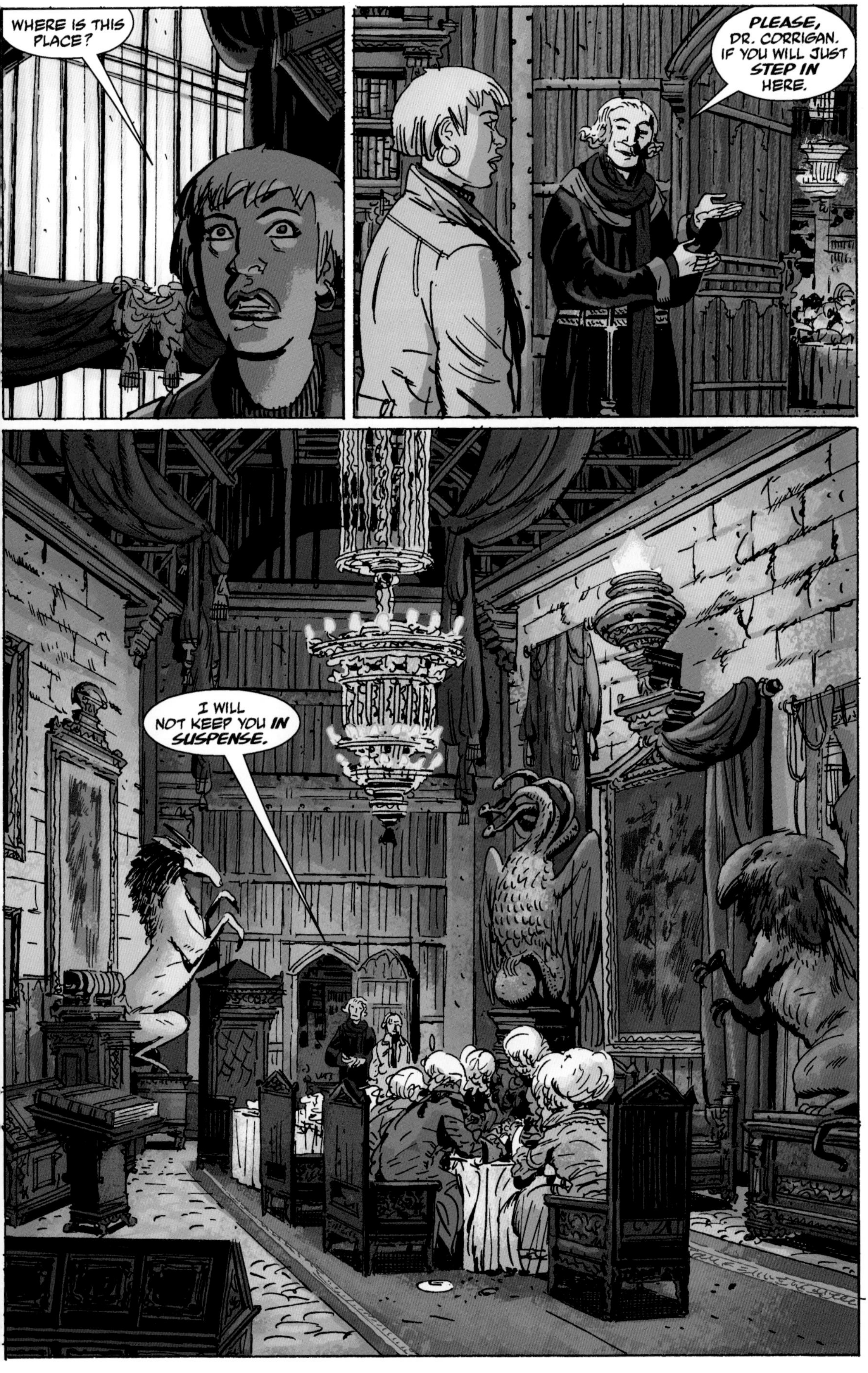
WHERE IS THIS PLACE?
PLEASE, DR. CORRIGAN. IF YOU WILL JUST STEP IN HERE.
I WILL NOT KEEP YOU IN SUSPENSE.

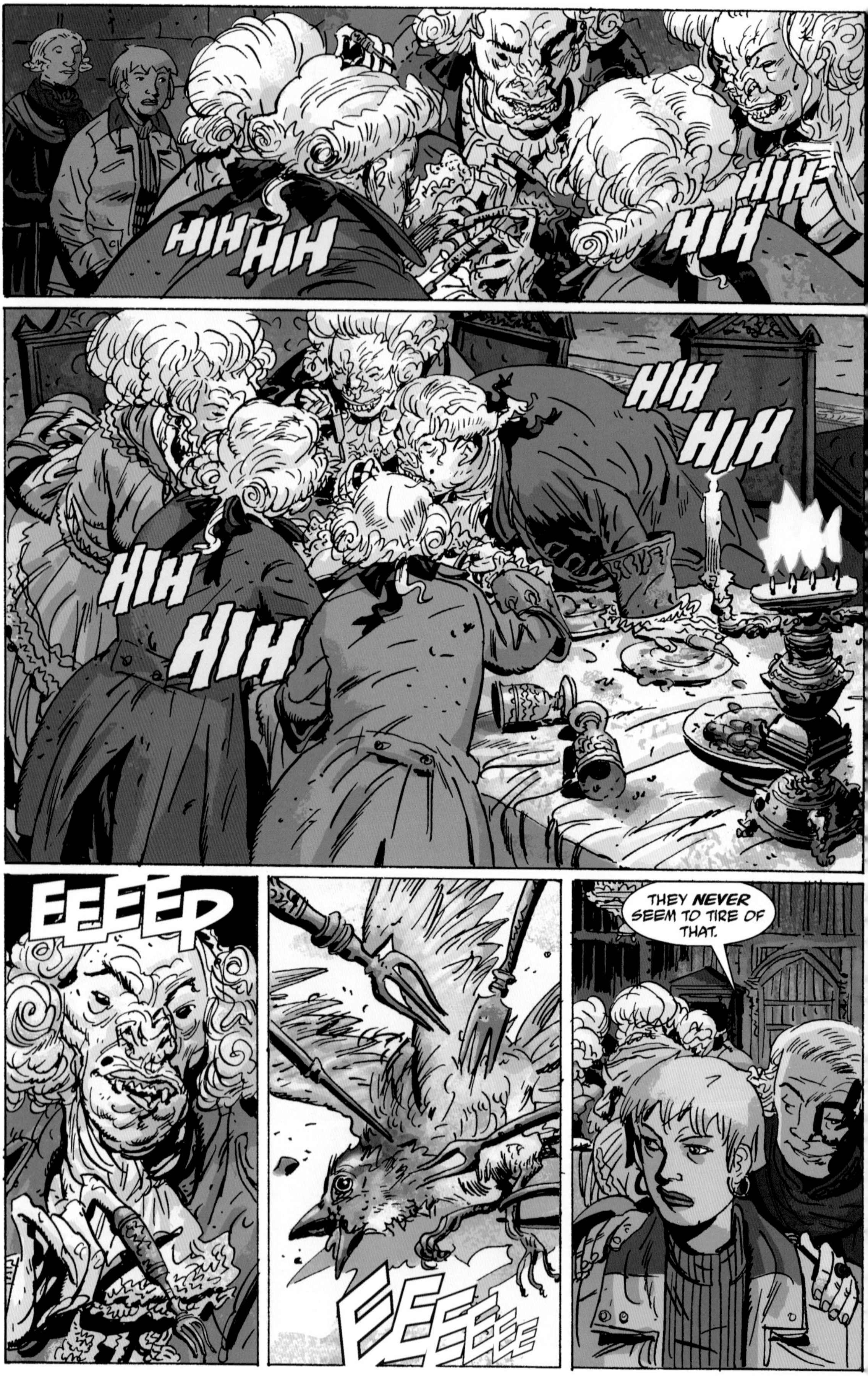

HIH HIH
HIH HIH
HIH HIH
HIH HIH
EEEEP
EEEEEEEE
THEY NEVER SEEM TO TIRE OF THAT.

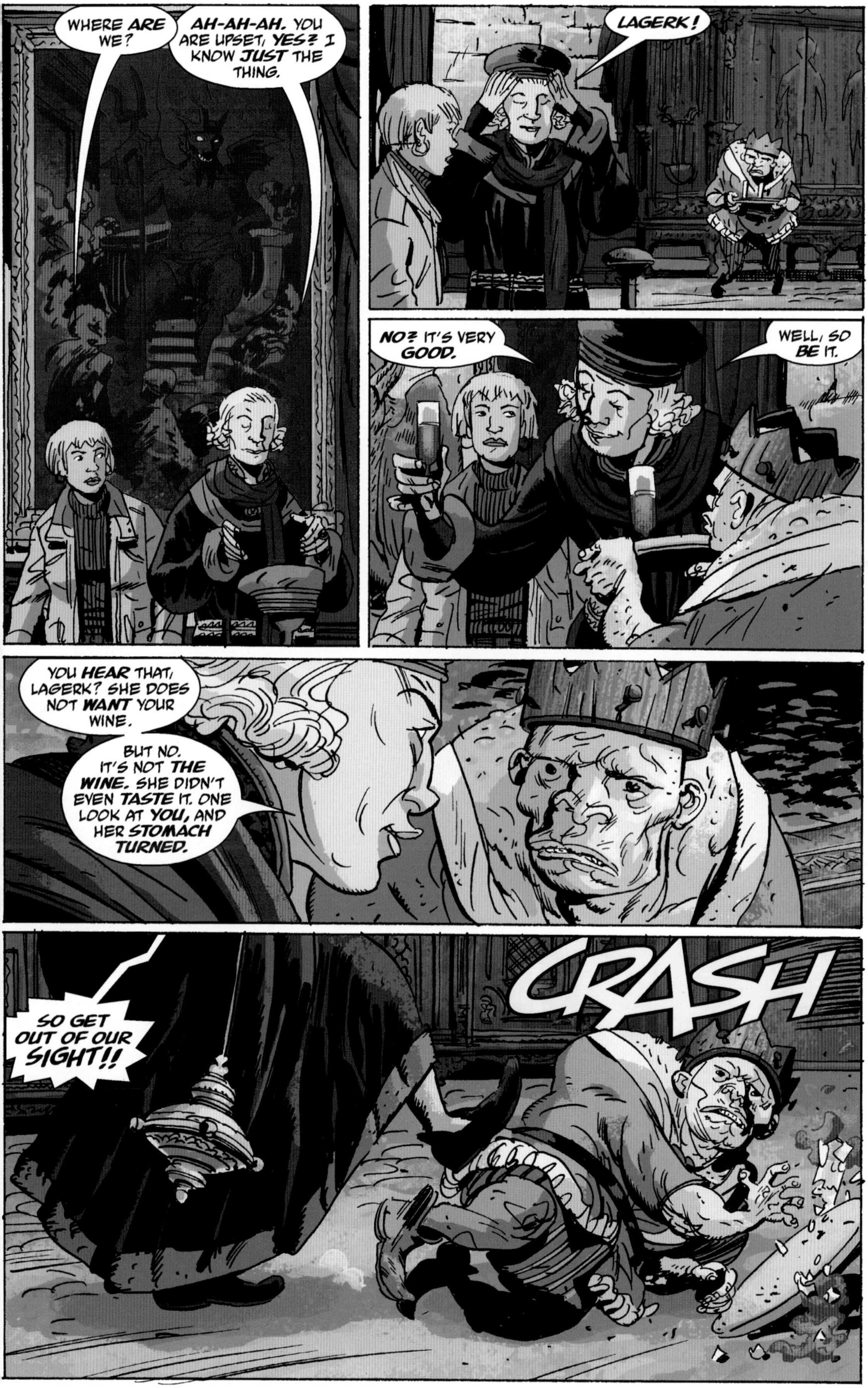
WHERE ARE WE?
AH-AH-AH. YOU ARE UPSET, YES? I KNOW JUST THE THING.
LAGERK!
NO? IT'S VERY GOOD.
WELL, SO BE IT.
YOU HEAR THAT, LAGERK? SHE DOES NOT WANT YOUR WINE.
BUT NO. IT'S NOT THE WINE. SHE DIDN'T EVEN TASTE IT. ONE LOOK AT YOU, AND HER STOMACH TURNED.
SO GET OUT OF OUR SIGHT!!
CRASH

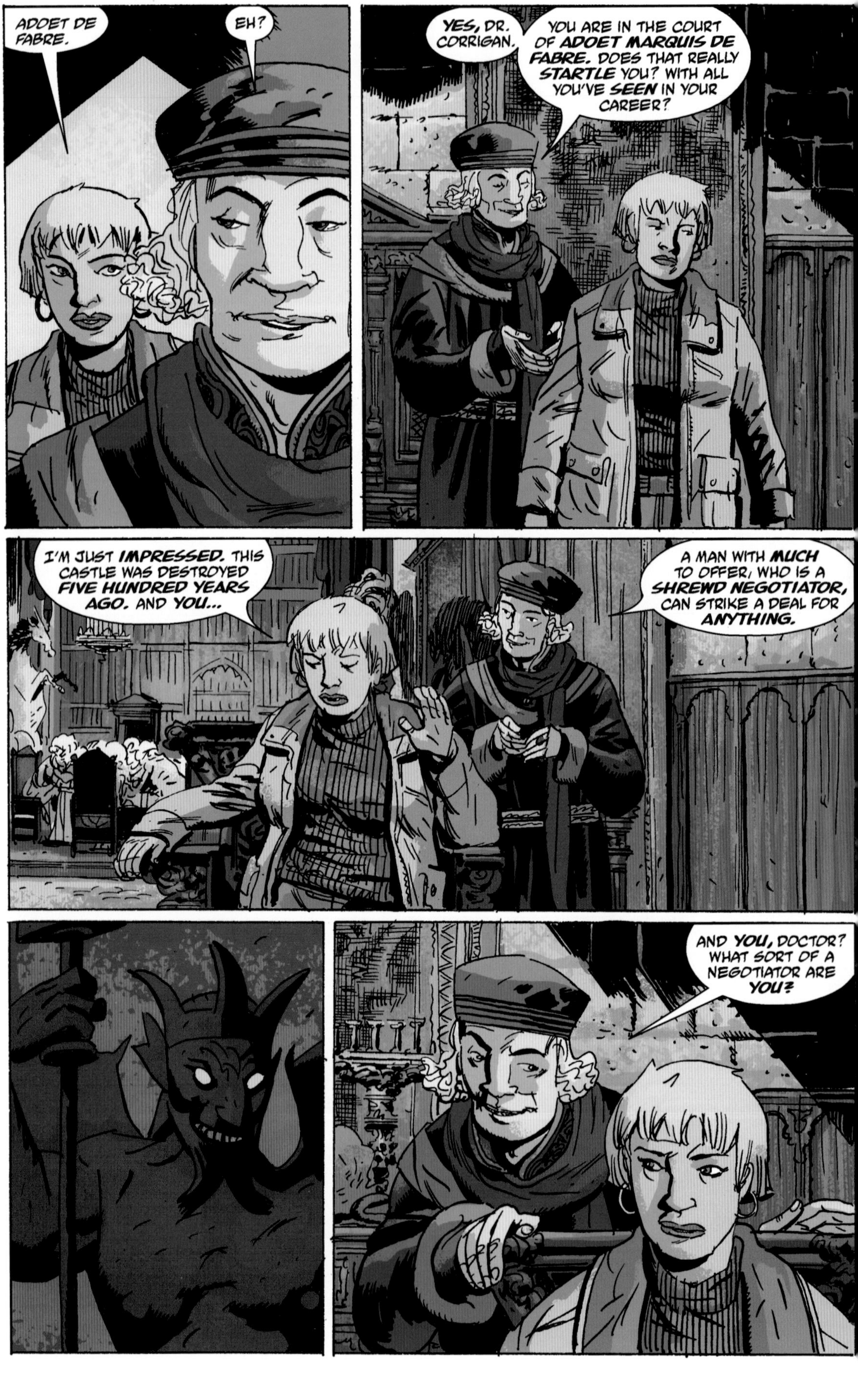
ADOET DE FABRE.
EH?
YES, DR. CORRIGAN.
YOU ARE IN THE COURT OF ADOET MARQUIS DE FABRE. DOES THAT REALLY STARTLE YOU? WITH ALL YOU'VE SEEN IN YOUR CAREER?
I'M JUST IMPRESSED. THIS CASTLE WAS DESTROYED FIVE HUNDRED YEARS AGO. AND YOU...
A MAN WITH MUCH TO OFFER, WHO IS A SHREWD NEGOTIATOR, CAN STRIKE A DEAL FOR ANYTHING.
AND YOU, DOCTOR? WHAT SORT OF A NEGOTIATOR ARE YOU?

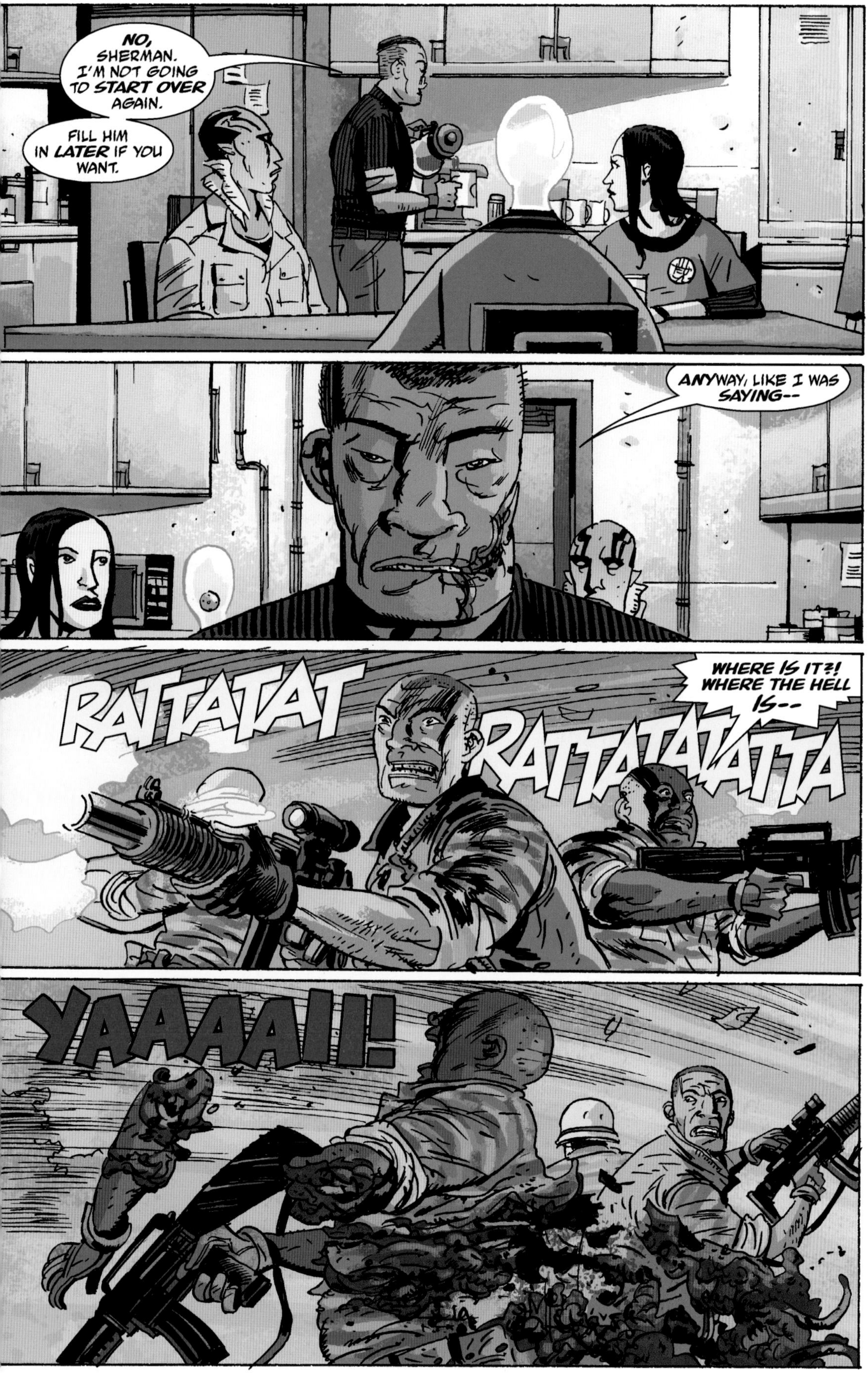
NO, SHERMAN. I'M NOT GOING TO START OVER AGAIN.
FILL HIM IN LATER IF YOU WANT.
ANYWAY, LIKE I WAS SAYING--
RATTATAT
WHERE IS IT?! WHERE THE HELL IS--
RATTATATATTA
YAAAAII!

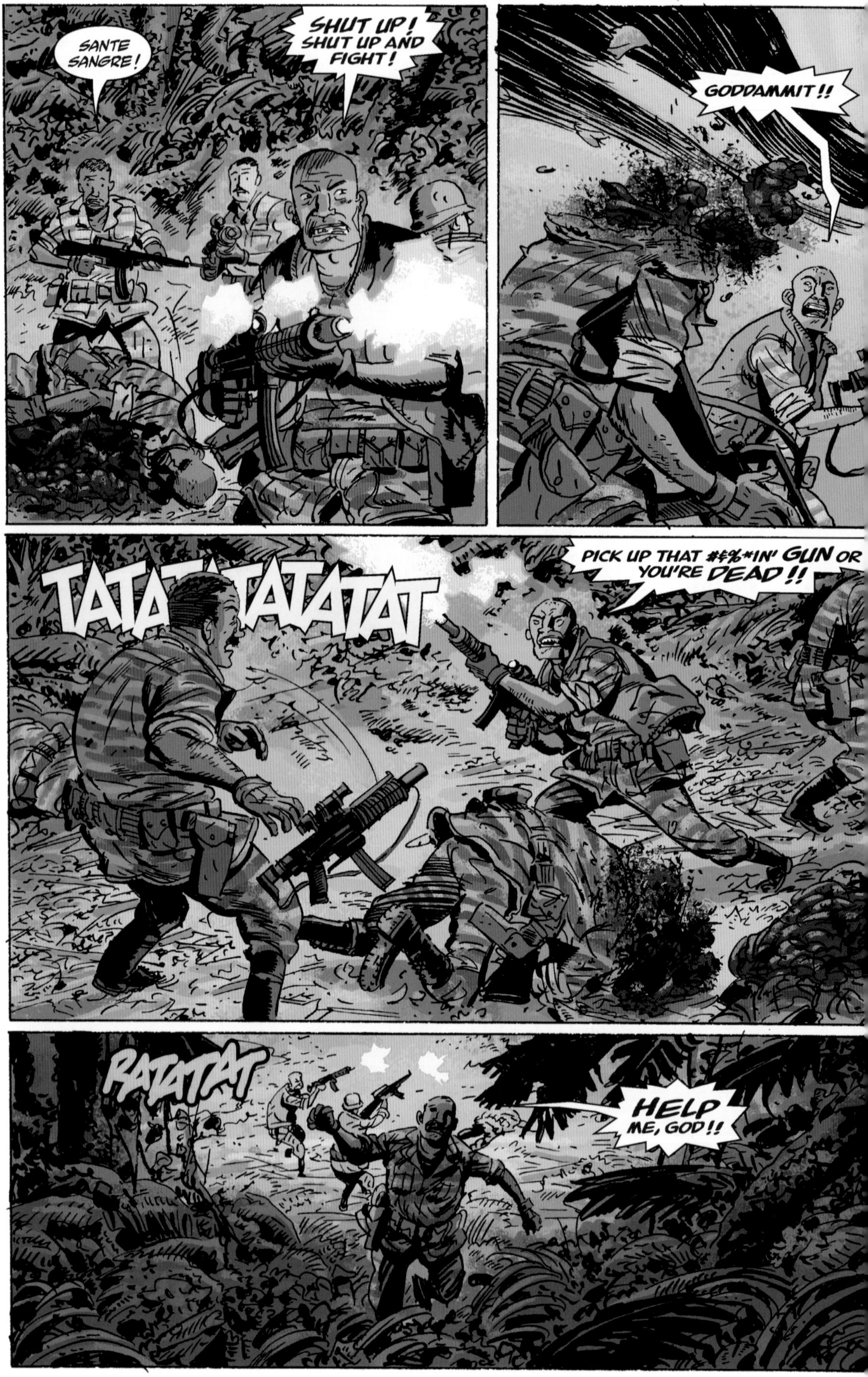
SANTE SANGRE!
SHUT UP! SHUT UP AND FIGHT!
GODDAMMIT!!
TATATATATATAT
PICK UP THAT #$%*IN' GUN OR YOU'RE DEAD!!
RATATAT
HELP ME, GOD!!

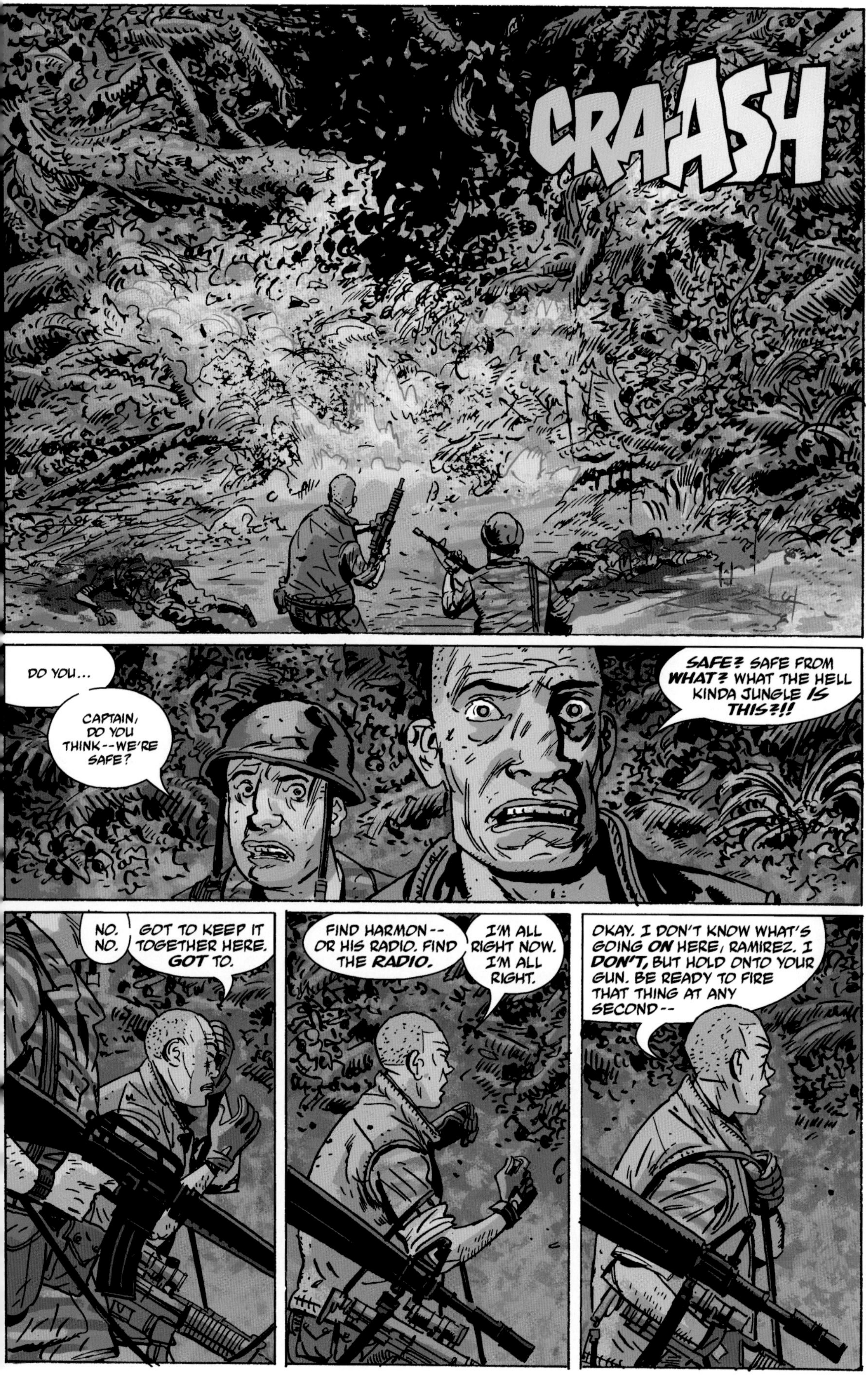
CRA-ASH
DO YOU...
CAPTAIN, DO YOU THINK--WE'RE SAFE?
SAFE? SAFE FROM WHAT? WHAT THE HELL KINDA JUNGLE IS THIS?!!
NO. NO.
GOT TO KEEP IT TOGETHER HERE. GOT TO.
FIND HARMON-- OR HIS RADIO. FIND THE RADIO.
I'M ALL RIGHT NOW. I'M ALL RIGHT.
OKAY. I DON'T KNOW WHAT'S GOING ON HERE, RAMIREZ. I DON'T, BUT HOLD ONTO YOUR GUN. BE READY TO FIRE THAT THING AT ANY SECOND--

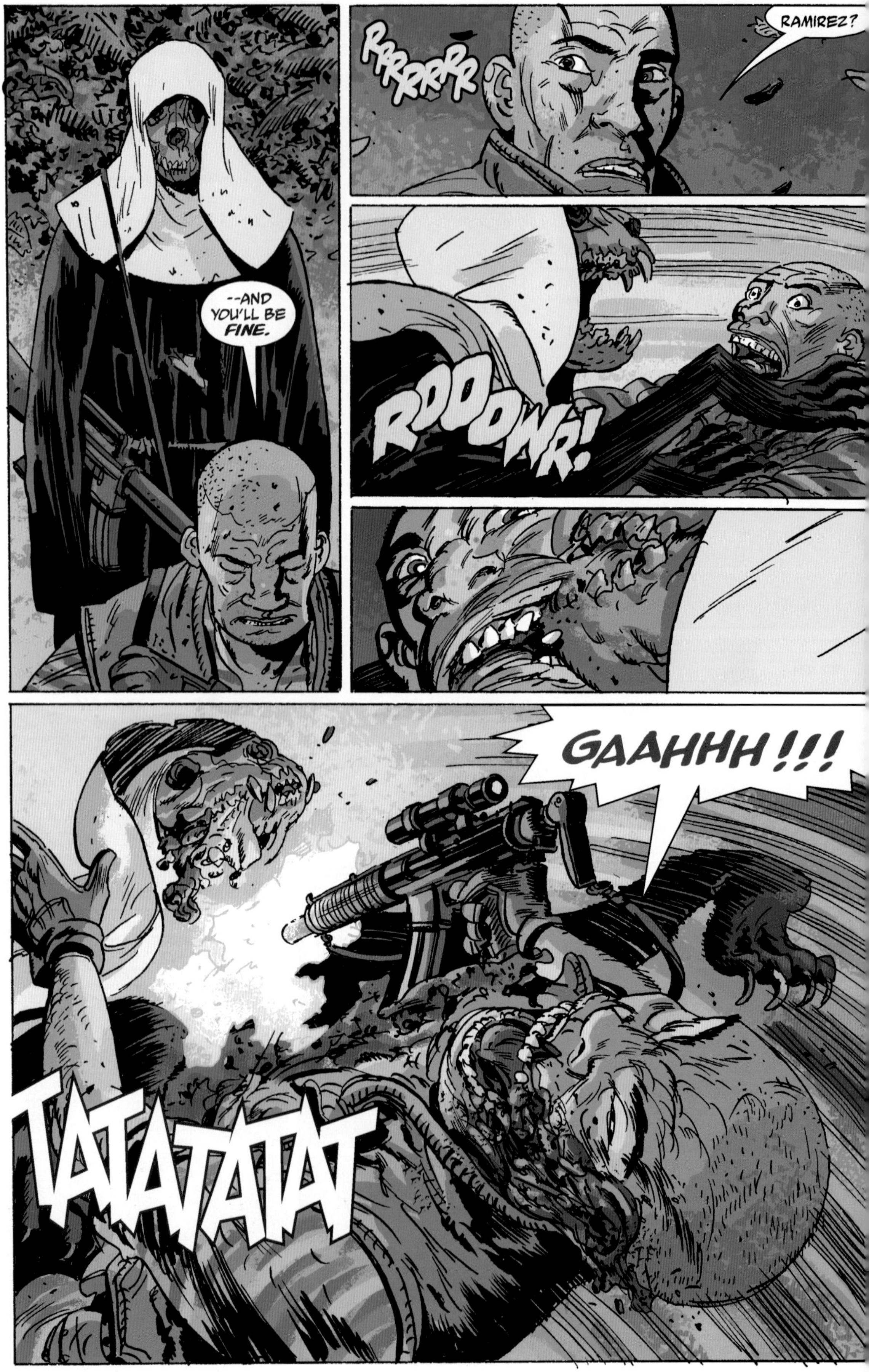
--AND YOU'LL BE FINE.
RRRRRRR
RAMIREZ?
ROOOWR!
GAAHHH!!!
TATATATAT

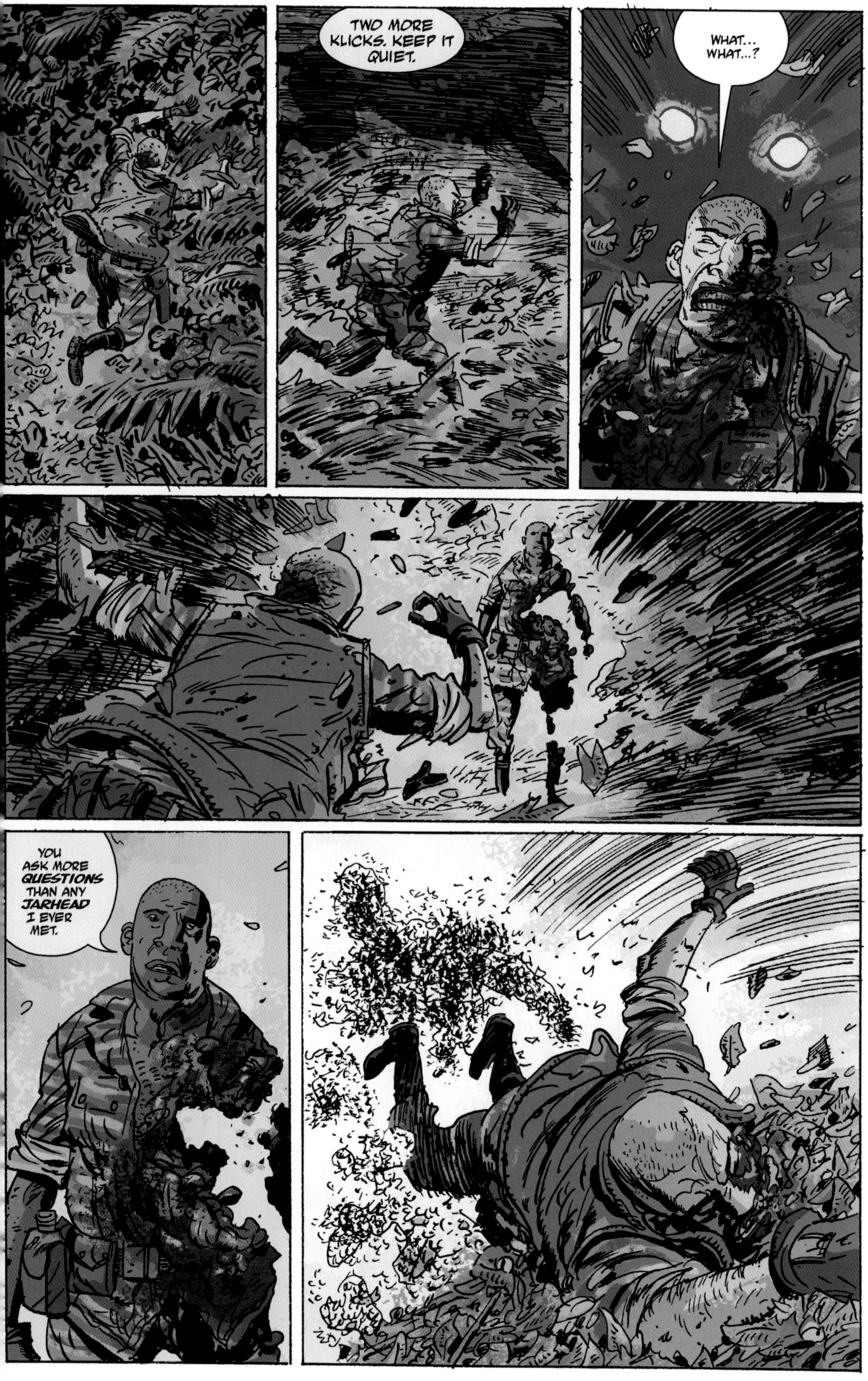
TWO MORE KLICKS. KEEP IT QUIET.
WHAT... WHAT...?
YOU ASK MORE QUESTIONS THAN ANY JARHEAD I EVER MET.

I SAY AGAIN, ROMEO FOXTROT KILO, THIS IS ECHO COMPANY. WE HAVE FULL MISSION ABORT.

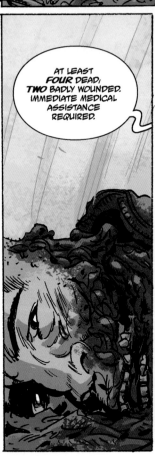

AT LEAST *FOUR* DEAD, *TWO* BADLY WOUNDED. IMMEDIATE MEDICAL ASSISTANCE REQUIRED.

HOLD ONTO YOUR GUN AND YOU'LL BE *FINE*.

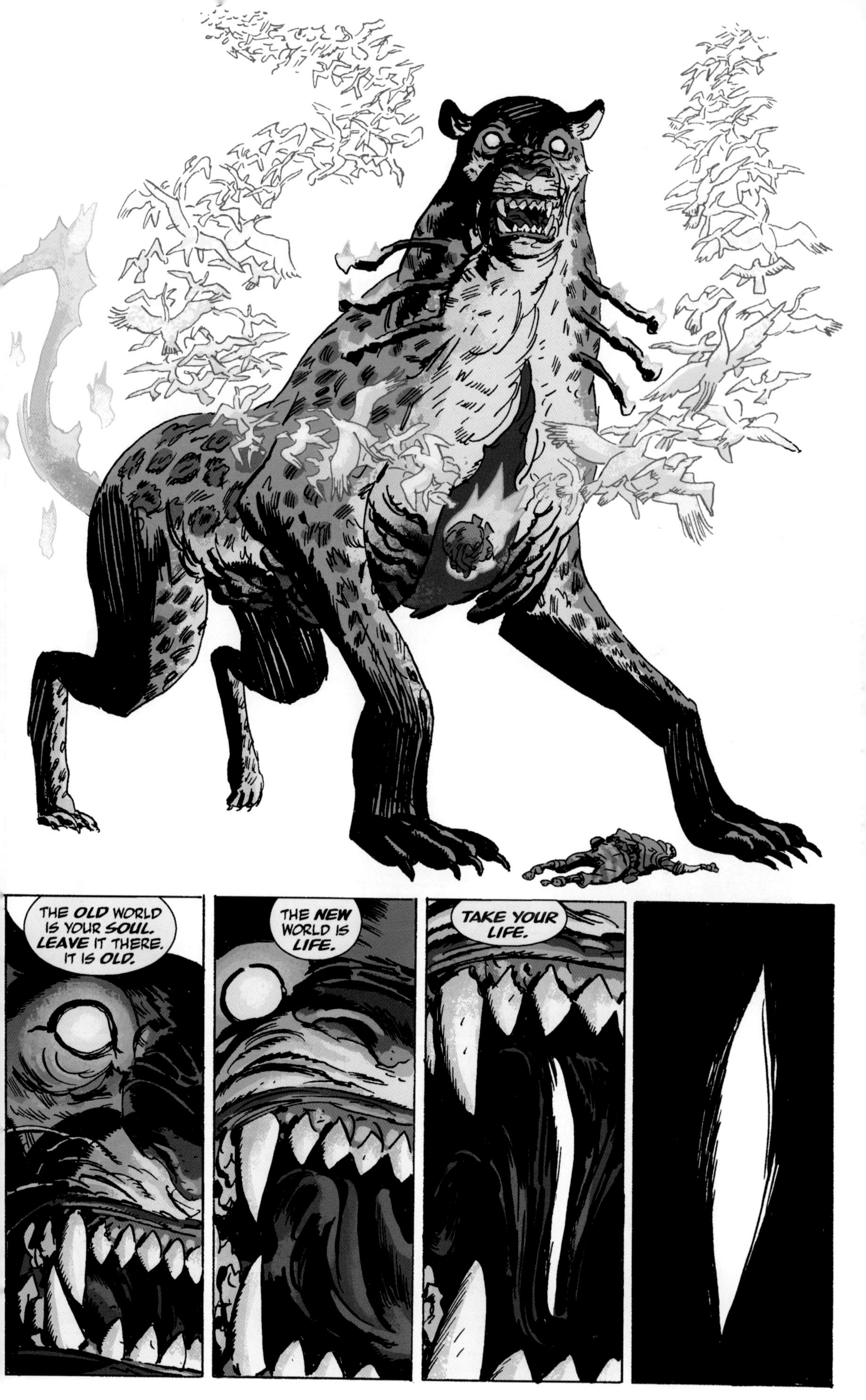
THE OLD WORLD IS YOUR SOUL. LEAVE IT THERE. IT IS OLD.
THE NEW WORLD IS LIFE.
TAKE YOUR LIFE.

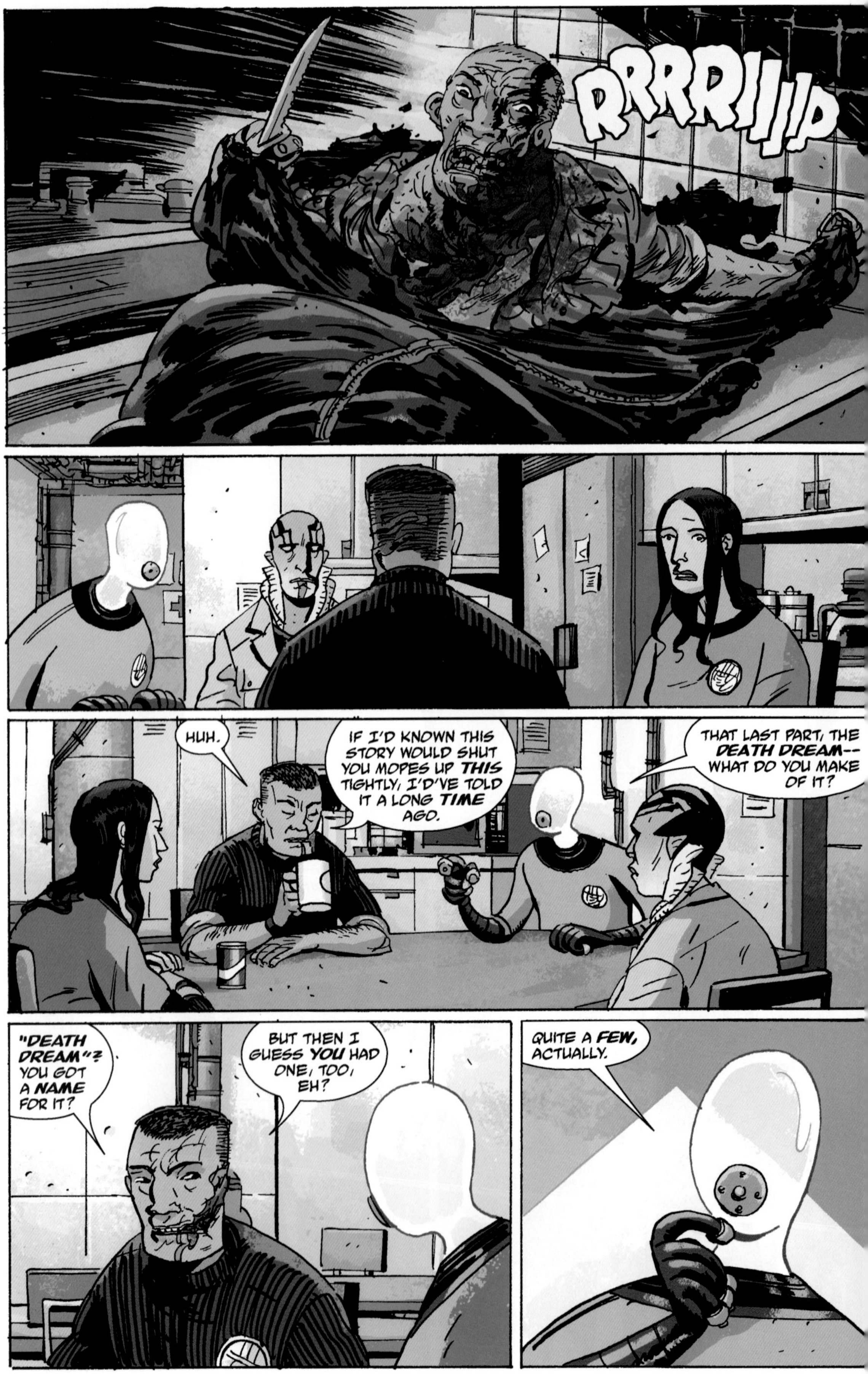
RRRRIIIIP
HUH.
IF I'D KNOWN THIS STORY WOULD SHUT YOU MOPES UP THIS TIGHTLY, I'D'VE TOLD IT A LONG TIME AGO.
THAT LAST PART, THE DEATH DREAM-- WHAT DO YOU MAKE OF IT?
"DEATH DREAM"? YOU GOT A NAME FOR IT?
BUT THEN I GUESS YOU HAD ONE, TOO, EH?
QUITE A FEW, ACTUALLY.

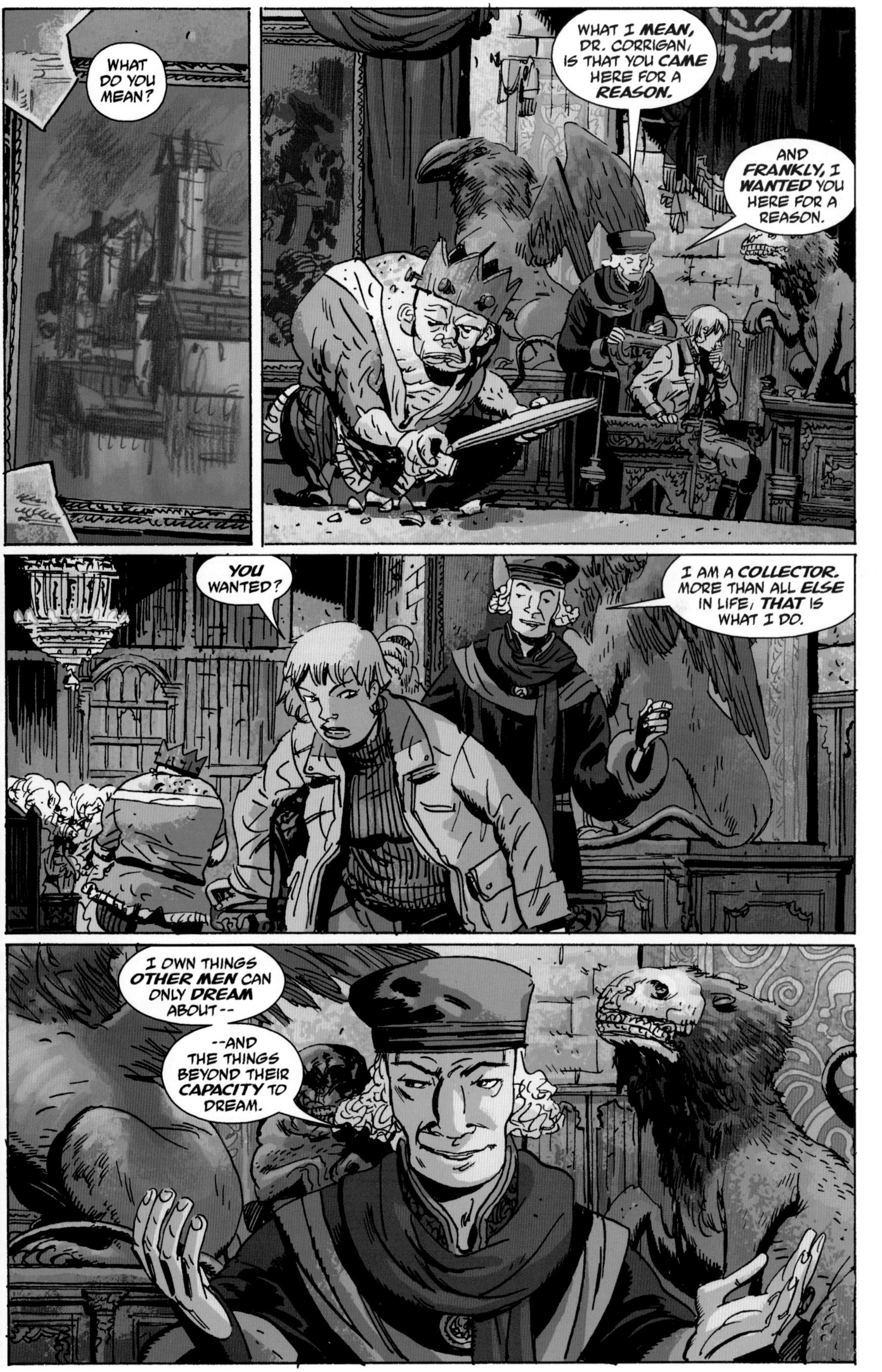
WHAT DO YOU MEAN?
WHAT I MEAN, DR. CORRIGAN, IS THAT YOU CAME HERE FOR A REASON.
AND FRANKLY, I WANTED YOU HERE FOR A REASON.
YOU WANTED?
I AM A COLLECTOR. MORE THAN ALL ELSE IN LIFE, THAT IS WHAT I DO.
I OWN THINGS OTHER MEN CAN ONLY DREAM ABOUT--
--AND THE THINGS BEYOND THEIR CAPACITY TO DREAM.

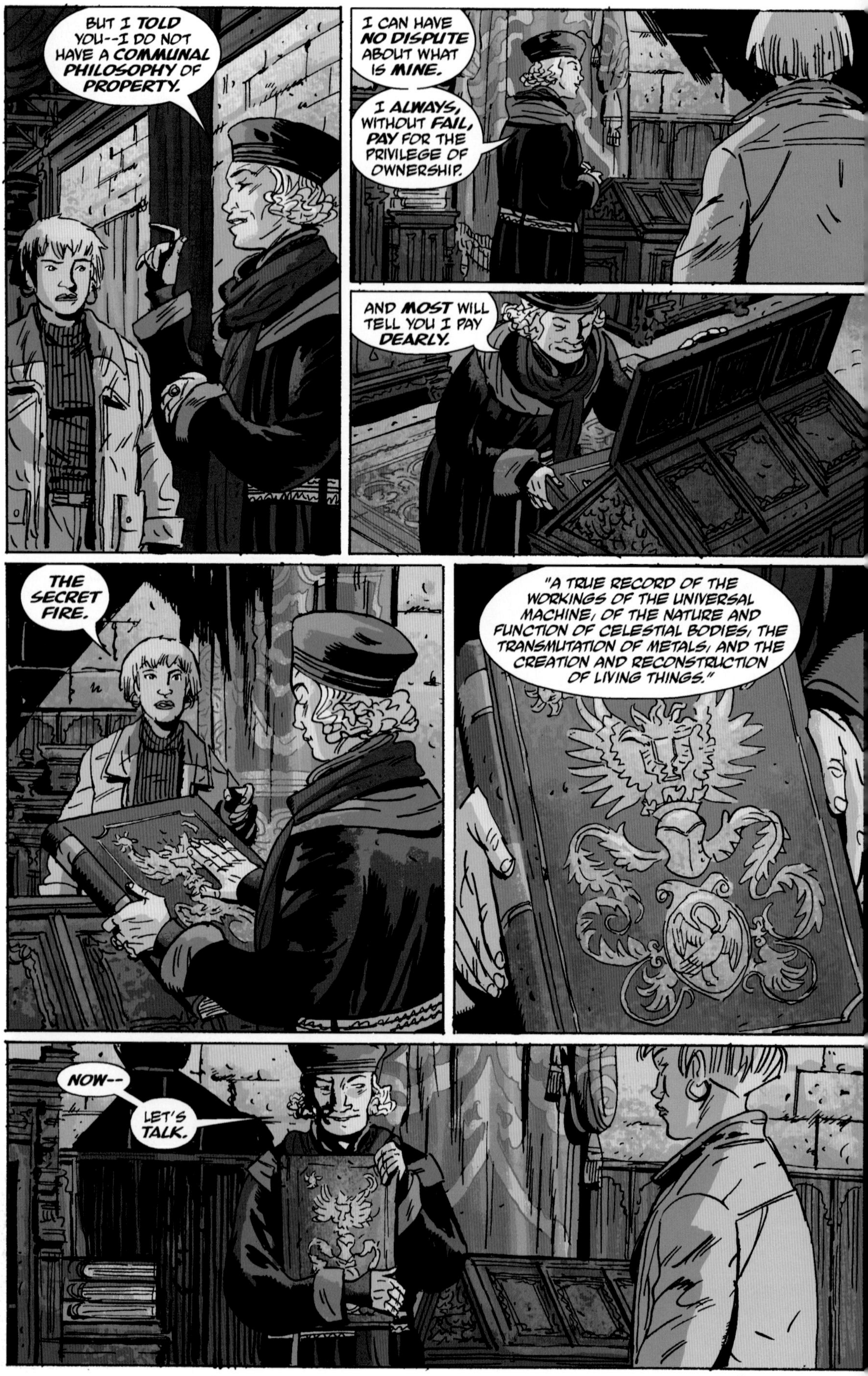
BUT I TOLD YOU--I DO NOT HAVE A COMMUNAL PHILOSOPHY OF PROPERTY.
I CAN HAVE NO DISPUTE ABOUT WHAT IS MINE.
I ALWAYS, WITHOUT FAIL, PAY FOR THE PRIVILEGE OF OWNERSHIP.
AND MOST WILL TELL YOU I PAY DEARLY.
THE SECRET FIRE.
"A TRUE RECORD OF THE WORKINGS OF THE UNIVERSAL MACHINE, OF THE NATURE AND FUNCTION OF CELESTIAL BODIES, THE TRANSMUTATION OF METALS, AND THE CREATION AND RECONSTRUCTION OF LIVING THINGS."
NOW--
LET'S TALK.

CHAPTER THREE

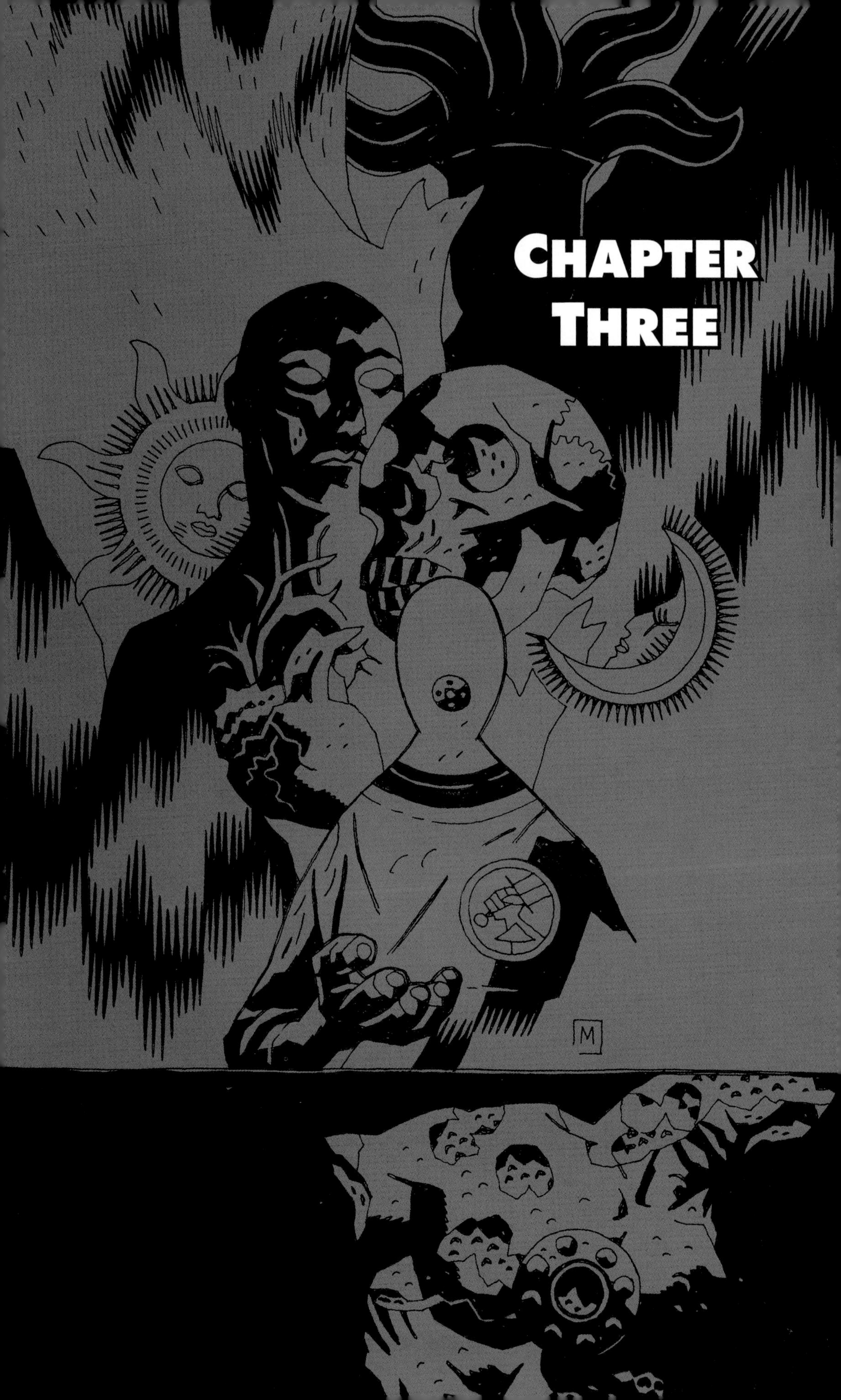

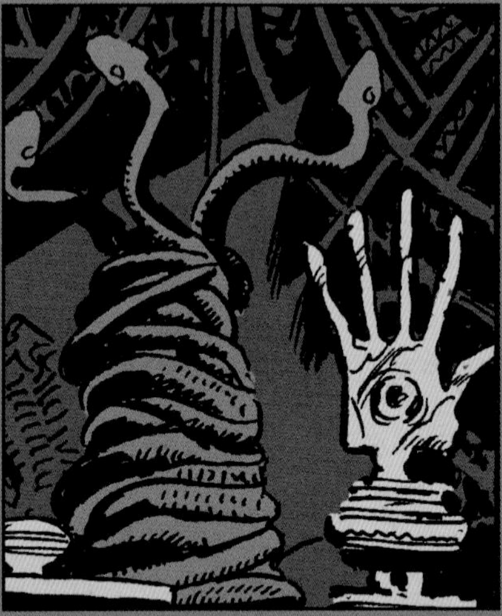

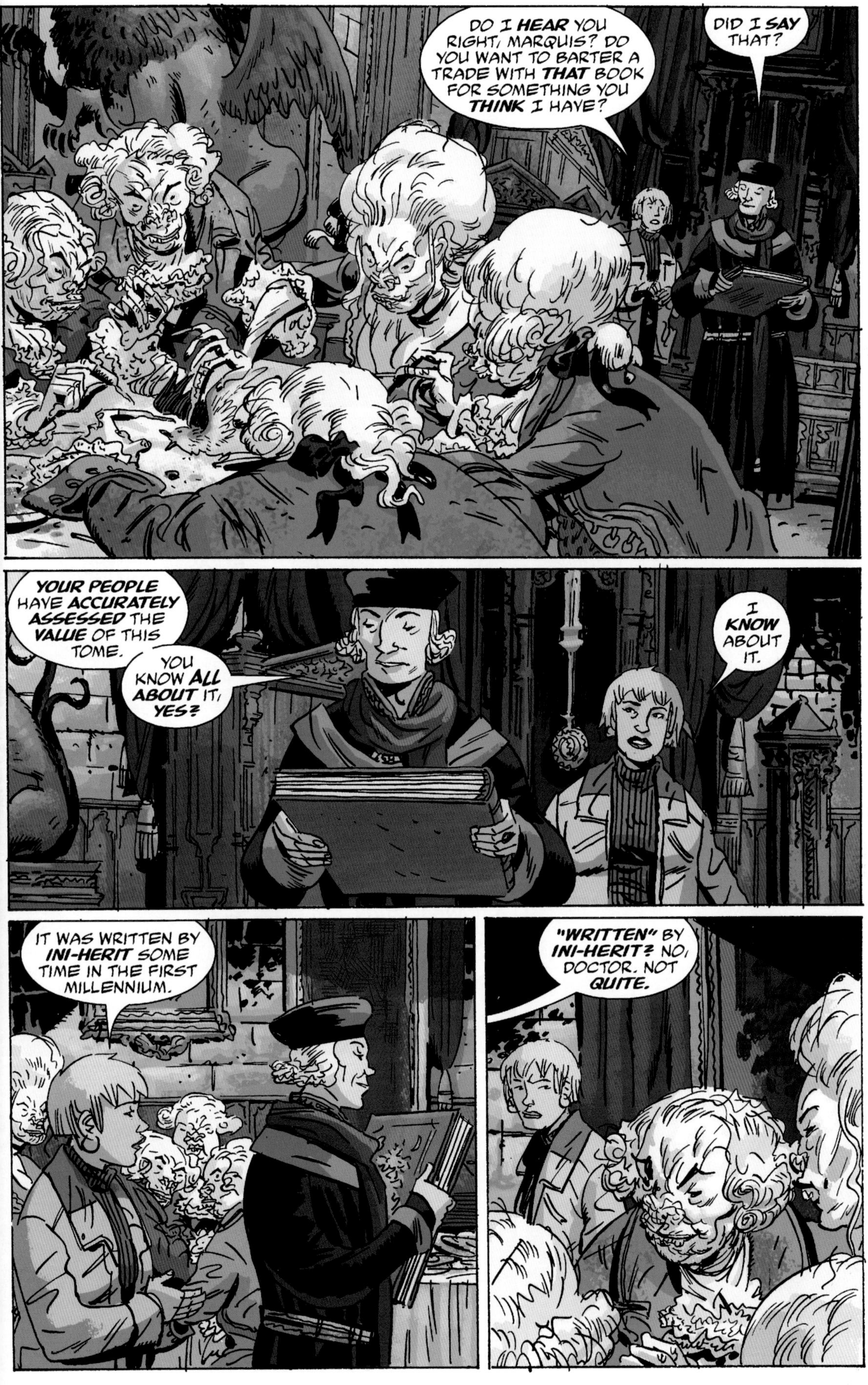
DO I HEAR YOU RIGHT, MARQUIS? DO YOU WANT TO BARTER A TRADE WITH THAT BOOK FOR SOMETHING YOU THINK I HAVE?
DID I SAY THAT?
YOUR PEOPLE HAVE ACCURATELY ASSESSED THE VALUE OF THIS TOME.
YOU KNOW ALL ABOUT IT, YES?
I KNOW ABOUT IT.
IT WAS WRITTEN BY INI-HERIT SOME TIME IN THE FIRST MILLENNIUM.
"WRITTEN" BY INI-HERIT? NO, DOCTOR. NOT QUITE.

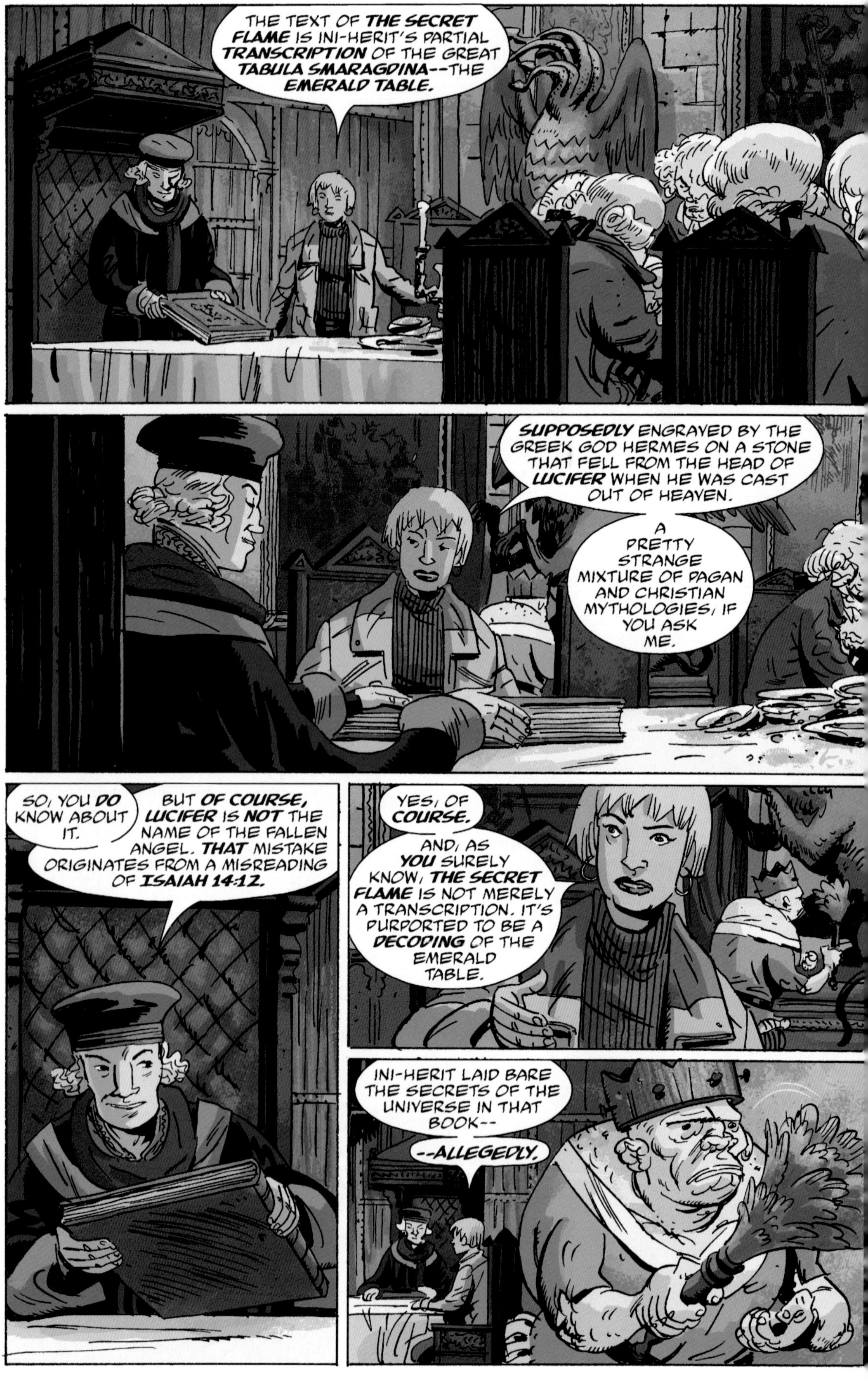
THE TEXT OF THE SECRET FLAME IS INI-HERIT'S PARTIAL TRANSCRIPTION OF THE GREAT TABULA SMARAGDINA--THE EMERALD TABLE.
SUPPOSEDLY ENGRAVED BY THE GREEK GOD HERMES ON A STONE THAT FELL FROM THE HEAD OF LUCIFER WHEN HE WAS CAST OUT OF HEAVEN.
A PRETTY STRANGE MIXTURE OF PAGAN AND CHRISTIAN MYTHOLOGIES, IF YOU ASK ME.
SO, YOU DO KNOW ABOUT IT.
BUT OF COURSE, LUCIFER IS NOT THE NAME OF THE FALLEN ANGEL. THAT MISTAKE ORIGINATES FROM A MISREADING OF ISAIAH 14:12.
YES, OF COURSE.
AND, AS YOU SURELY KNOW, THE SECRET FLAME IS NOT MERELY A TRANSCRIPTION. IT'S PURPORTED TO BE A DECODING OF THE EMERALD TABLE.
INI-HERIT LAID BARE THE SECRETS OF THE UNIVERSE IN THAT BOOK--
--ALLEGEDLY.

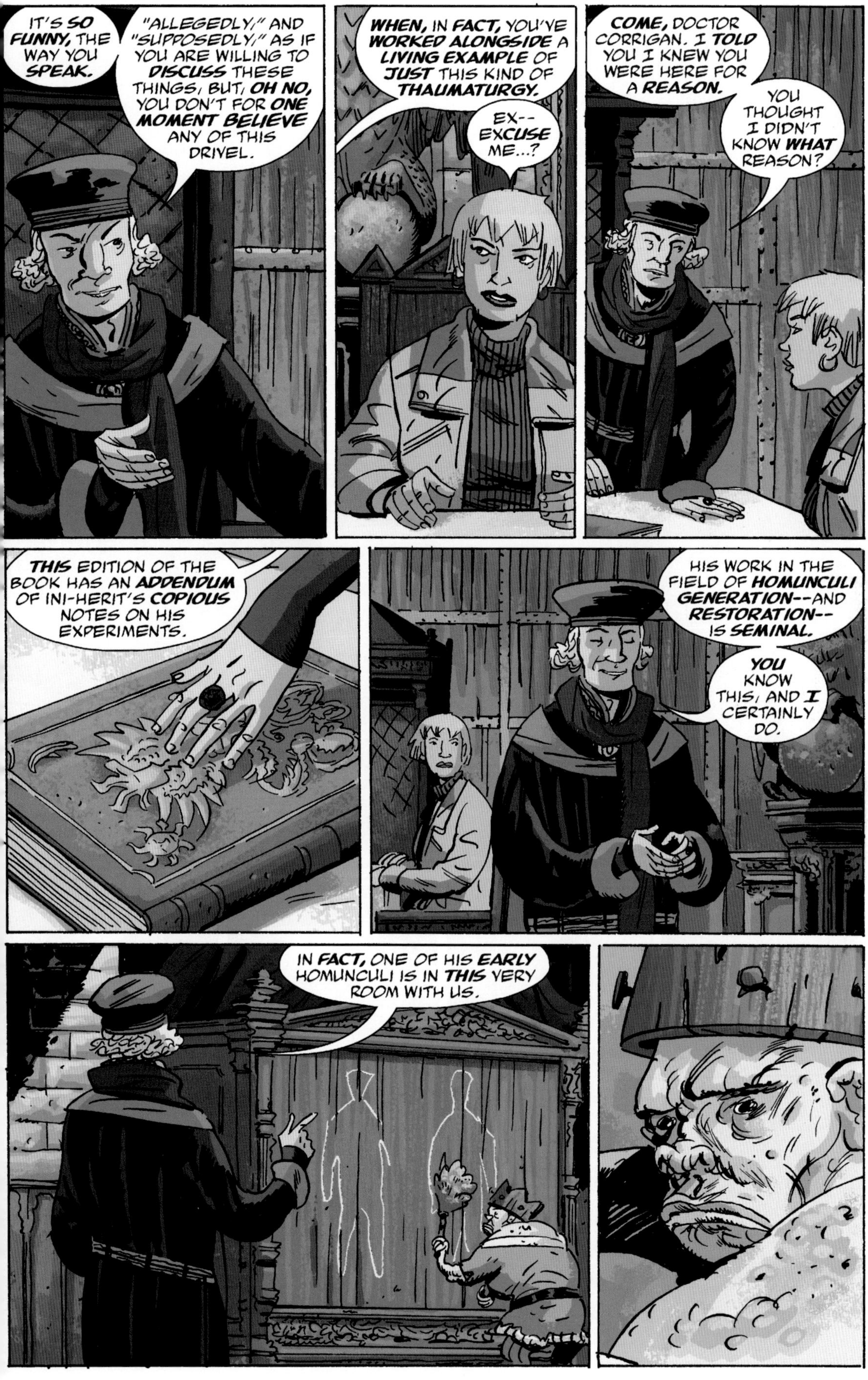

IT'S SO FUNNY, THE WAY YOU SPEAK.
"ALLEGEDLY," AND "SUPPOSEDLY," AS IF YOU ARE WILLING TO DISCUSS THESE THINGS, BUT, OH NO, YOU DON'T FOR ONE MOMENT BELIEVE ANY OF THIS DRIVEL.
WHEN, IN FACT, YOU'VE WORKED ALONGSIDE A LIVING EXAMPLE OF JUST THIS KIND OF THAUMATURGY.
EX-- EXCUSE ME...?
COME, DOCTOR CORRIGAN. I TOLD YOU I KNEW YOU WERE HERE FOR A REASON.
YOU THOUGHT I DIDN'T KNOW WHAT REASON?
THIS EDITION OF THE BOOK HAS AN ADDENDUM OF INI-HERIT'S COPIOUS NOTES ON HIS EXPERIMENTS.
HIS WORK IN THE FIELD OF HOMUNCULI GENERATION--AND RESTORATION-- IS SEMINAL.
YOU KNOW THIS, AND I CERTAINLY DO.
IN FACT, ONE OF HIS EARLY HOMUNCULI IS IN THIS VERY ROOM WITH US.

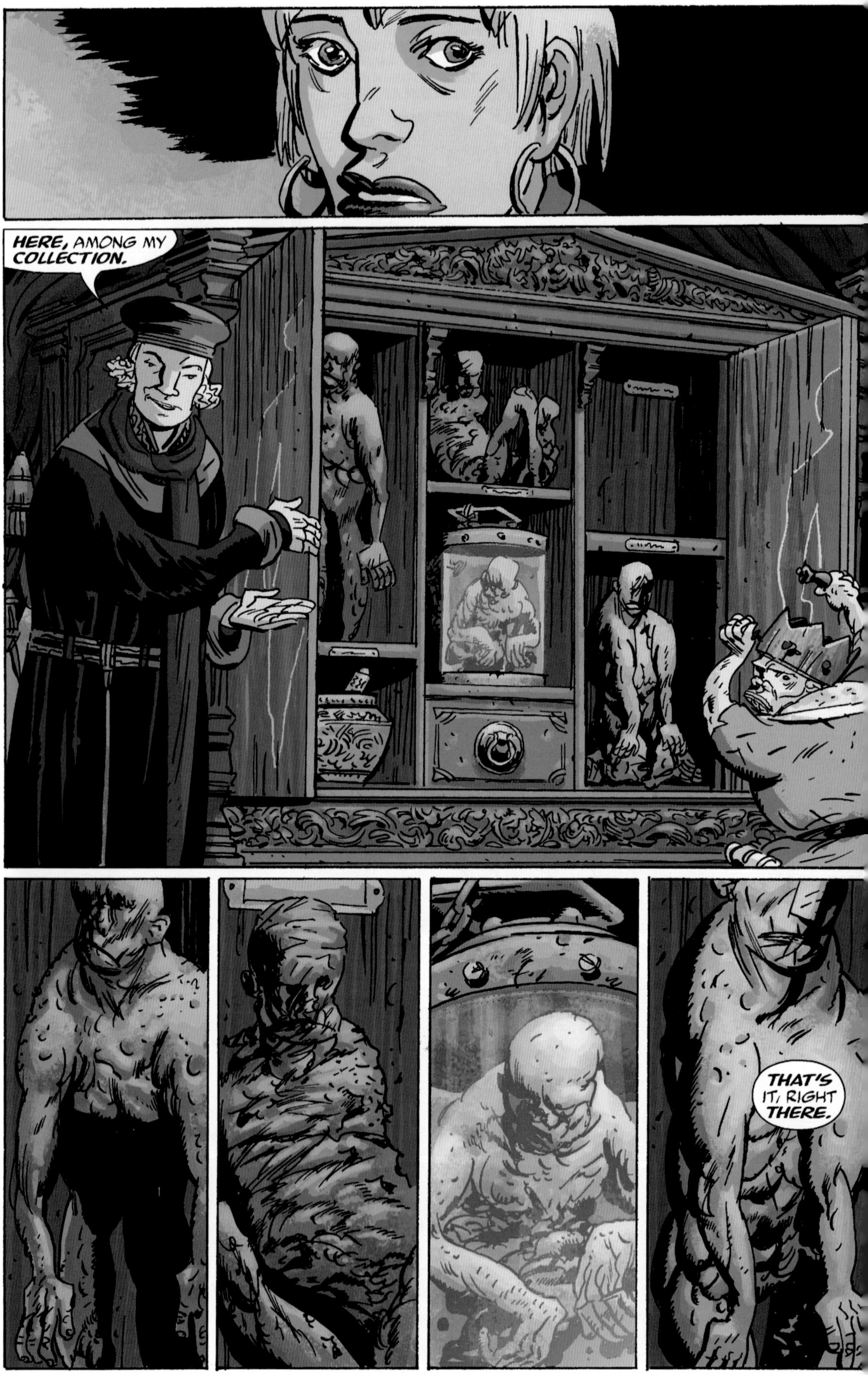
HERE, AMONG MY COLLECTION.
THAT'S IT, RIGHT THERE.

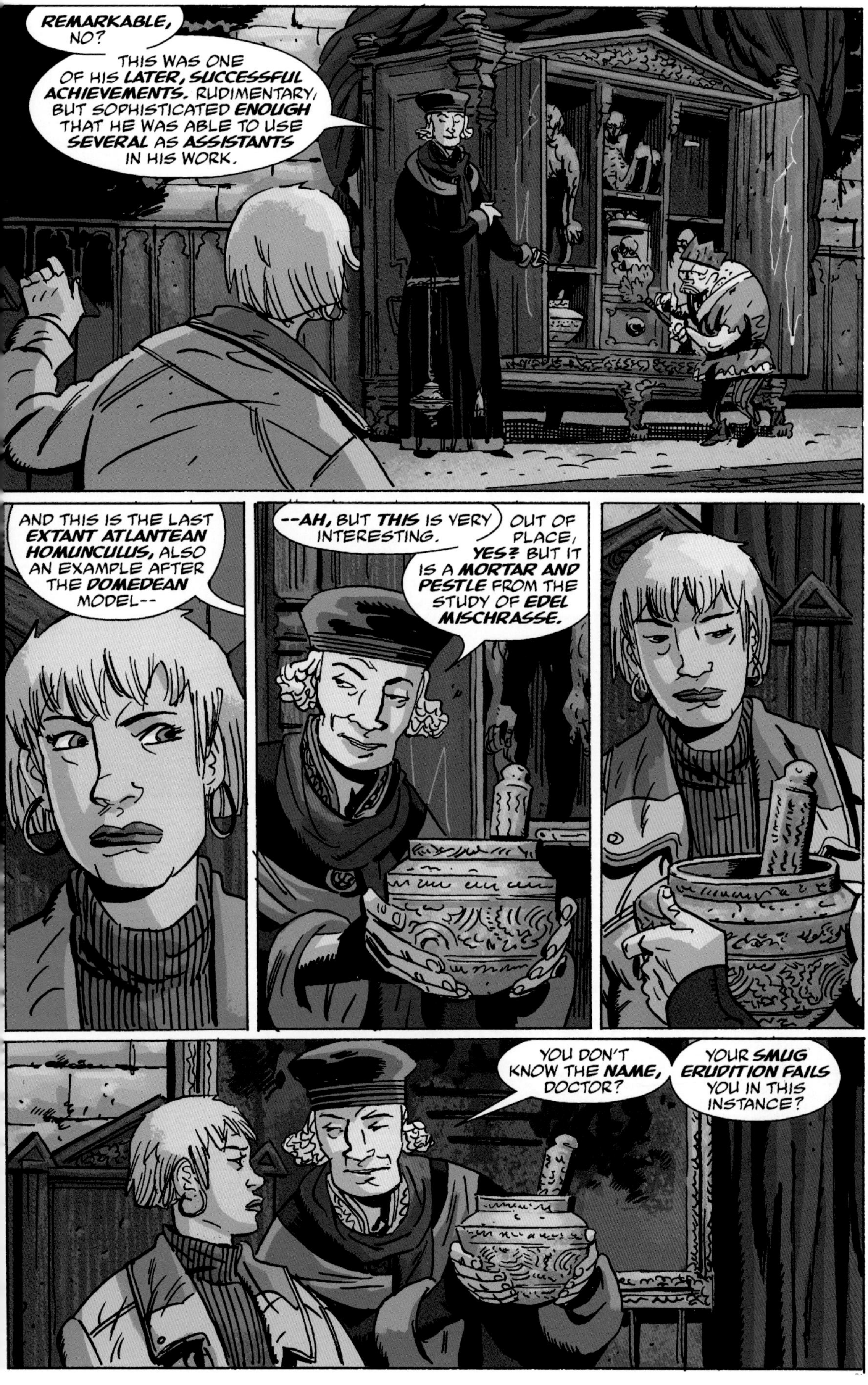

REMARKABLE, NO?
THIS WAS ONE OF HIS LATER, SUCCESSFUL ACHIEVEMENTS. RUDIMENTARY, BUT SOPHISTICATED ENOUGH THAT HE WAS ABLE TO USE SEVERAL AS ASSISTANTS IN HIS WORK.
AND THIS IS THE LAST EXTANT ATLANTEAN HOMUNCULUS, ALSO AN EXAMPLE AFTER THE DOMEDEAN MODEL--
--AH, BUT THIS IS VERY INTERESTING.
OUT OF PLACE, YES? BUT IT IS A MORTAR AND PESTLE FROM THE STUDY OF EDEL MISCHRASSE.
YOU DON'T KNOW THE NAME, DOCTOR?
YOUR SMUG ERUDITION FAILS YOU IN THIS INSTANCE?

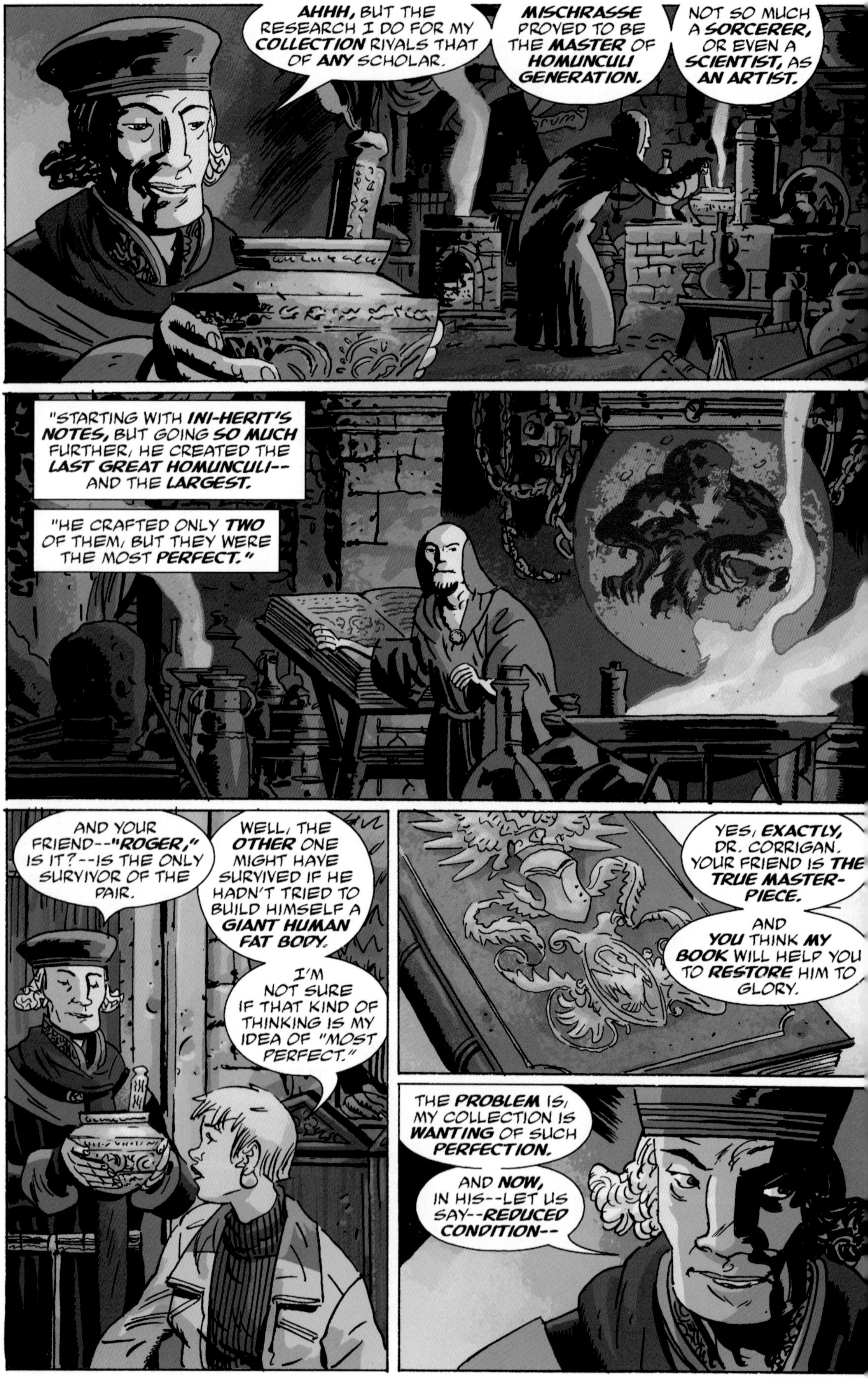
AHHH, BUT THE RESEARCH I DO FOR MY COLLECTION RIVALS THAT OF ANY SCHOLAR.
MISCHRASSE PROVED TO BE THE MASTER OF HOMUNCULI GENERATION.
NOT SO MUCH A SORCERER, OR EVEN A SCIENTIST, AS AN ARTIST.
"STARTING WITH INI-HERIT'S NOTES, BUT GOING SO MUCH FURTHER, HE CREATED THE LAST GREAT HOMUNCULI-- AND THE LARGEST.
"HE CRAFTED ONLY TWO OF THEM, BUT THEY WERE THE MOST PERFECT."
AND YOUR FRIEND--"ROGER," IS IT?--IS THE ONLY SURVIVOR OF THE PAIR.
WELL, THE OTHER ONE MIGHT HAVE SURVIVED IF HE HADN'T TRIED TO BUILD HIMSELF A GIANT HUMAN FAT BODY.
I'M NOT SURE IF THAT KIND OF THINKING IS MY IDEA OF "MOST PERFECT."
YES, EXACTLY, DR. CORRIGAN. YOUR FRIEND IS THE TRUE MASTER-PIECE.
AND YOU THINK MY BOOK WILL HELP YOU TO RESTORE HIM TO GLORY.
THE PROBLEM IS, MY COLLECTION IS WANTING OF SUCH PERFECTION.
AND NOW, IN HIS--LET US SAY--REDUCED CONDITION--

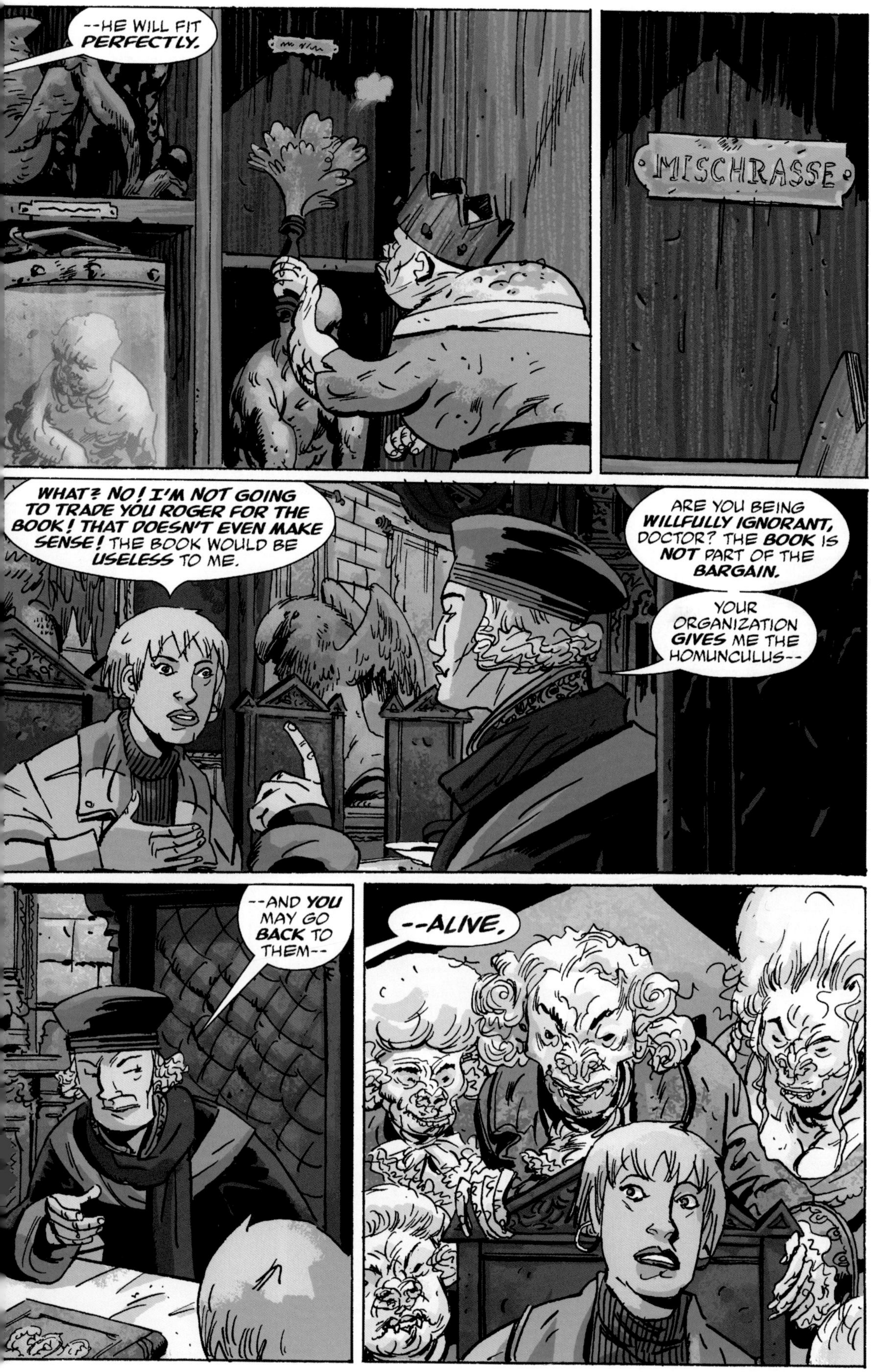
--HE WILL FIT PERFECTLY.
MISCHRASSE
WHAT? NO! I'M NOT GOING TO TRADE YOU ROGER FOR THE BOOK! THAT DOESN'T EVEN MAKE SENSE! THE BOOK WOULD BE USELESS TO ME.
ARE YOU BEING WILLFULLY IGNORANT, DOCTOR? THE BOOK IS NOT PART OF THE BARGAIN.
YOUR ORGANIZATION GIVES ME THE HOMUNCULUS--
--AND YOU MAY GO BACK TO THEM--
--ALIVE.

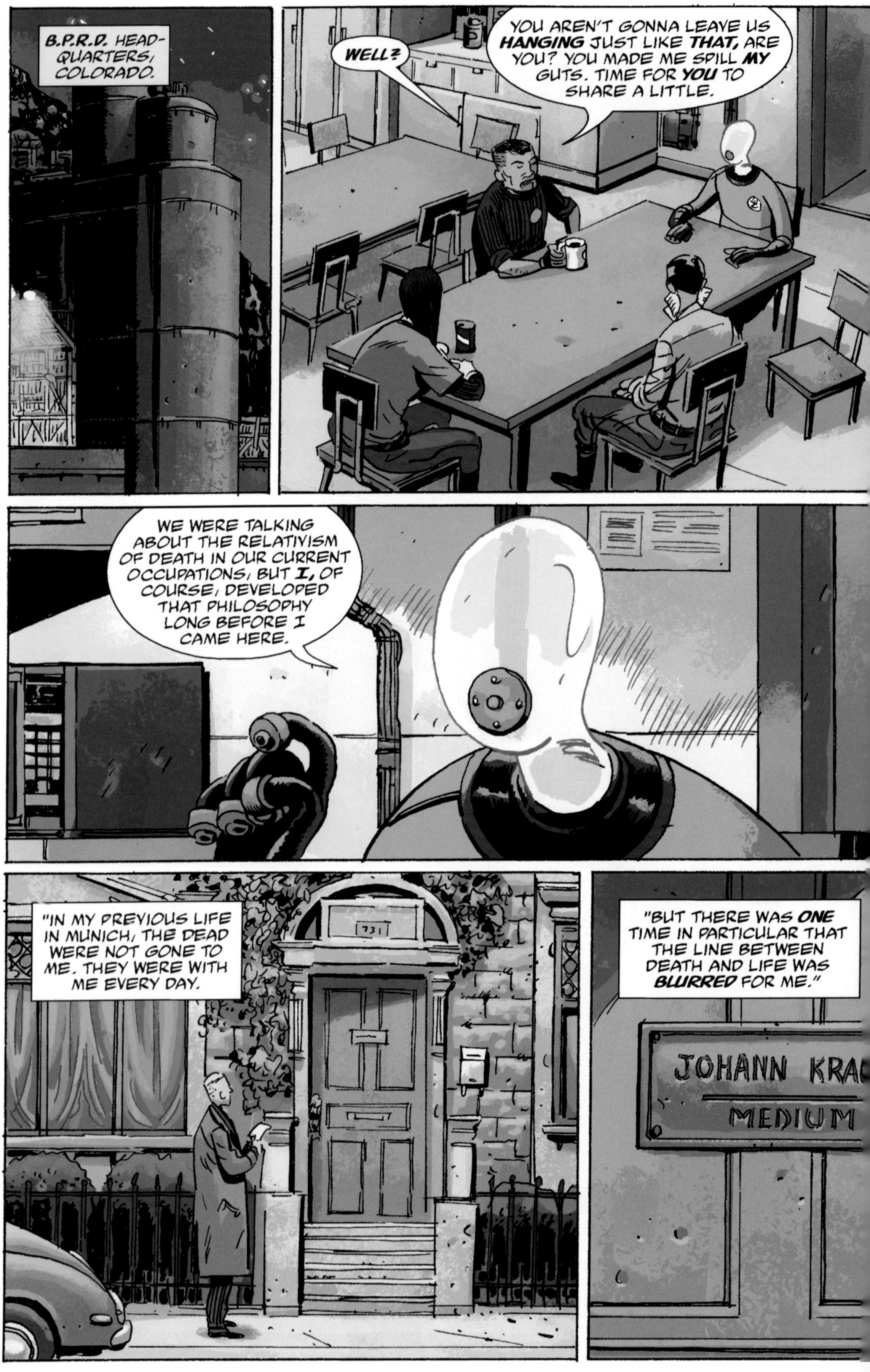
B.P.R.D. HEADQUARTERS, COLORADO.
WELL?
YOU AREN'T GONNA LEAVE US HANGING JUST LIKE THAT, ARE YOU? YOU MADE ME SPILL MY GUTS. TIME FOR YOU TO SHARE A LITTLE.
WE WERE TALKING ABOUT THE RELATIVISM OF DEATH IN OUR CURRENT OCCUPATIONS, BUT I, OF COURSE, DEVELOPED THAT PHILOSOPHY LONG BEFORE I CAME HERE.
"IN MY PREVIOUS LIFE IN MUNICH, THE DEAD WERE NOT GONE TO ME. THEY WERE WITH ME EVERY DAY.
731
"BUT THERE WAS ONE TIME IN PARTICULAR THAT THE LINE BETWEEN DEATH AND LIFE WAS BLURRED FOR ME."
JOHANN KRA
MEDIUM

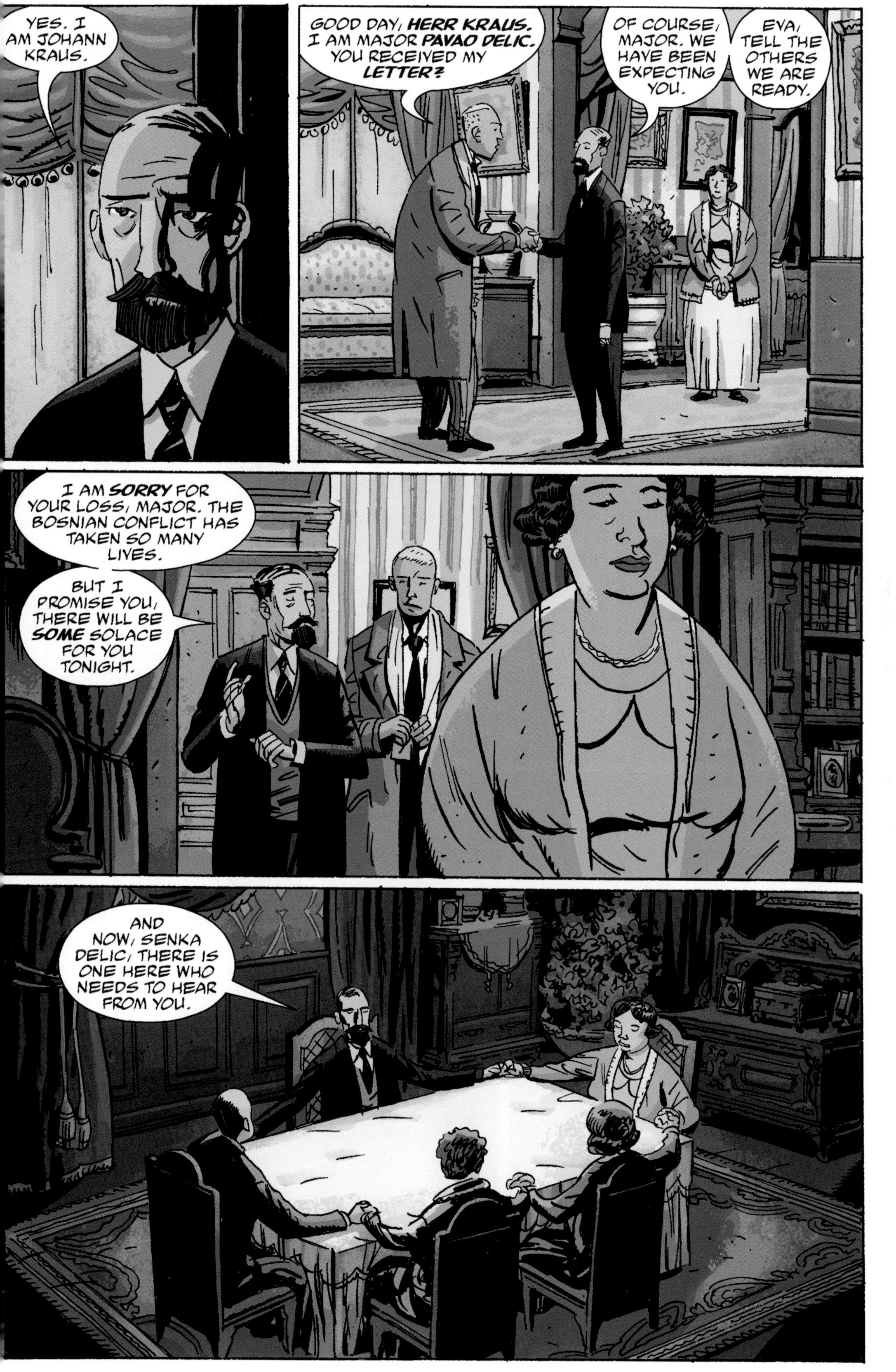
YES. I AM JOHANN KRAUS.
GOOD DAY, HERR KRAUS. I AM MAJOR PAVAO DELIC. YOU RECEIVED MY LETTER?
OF COURSE, MAJOR. WE HAVE BEEN EXPECTING YOU.
EVA, TELL THE OTHERS WE ARE READY.
I AM SORRY FOR YOUR LOSS, MAJOR. THE BOSNIAN CONFLICT HAS TAKEN SO MANY LIVES.
BUT I PROMISE YOU, THERE WILL BE SOME SOLACE FOR YOU TONIGHT.
AND NOW, SENKA DELIC, THERE IS ONE HERE WHO NEEDS TO HEAR FROM YOU.

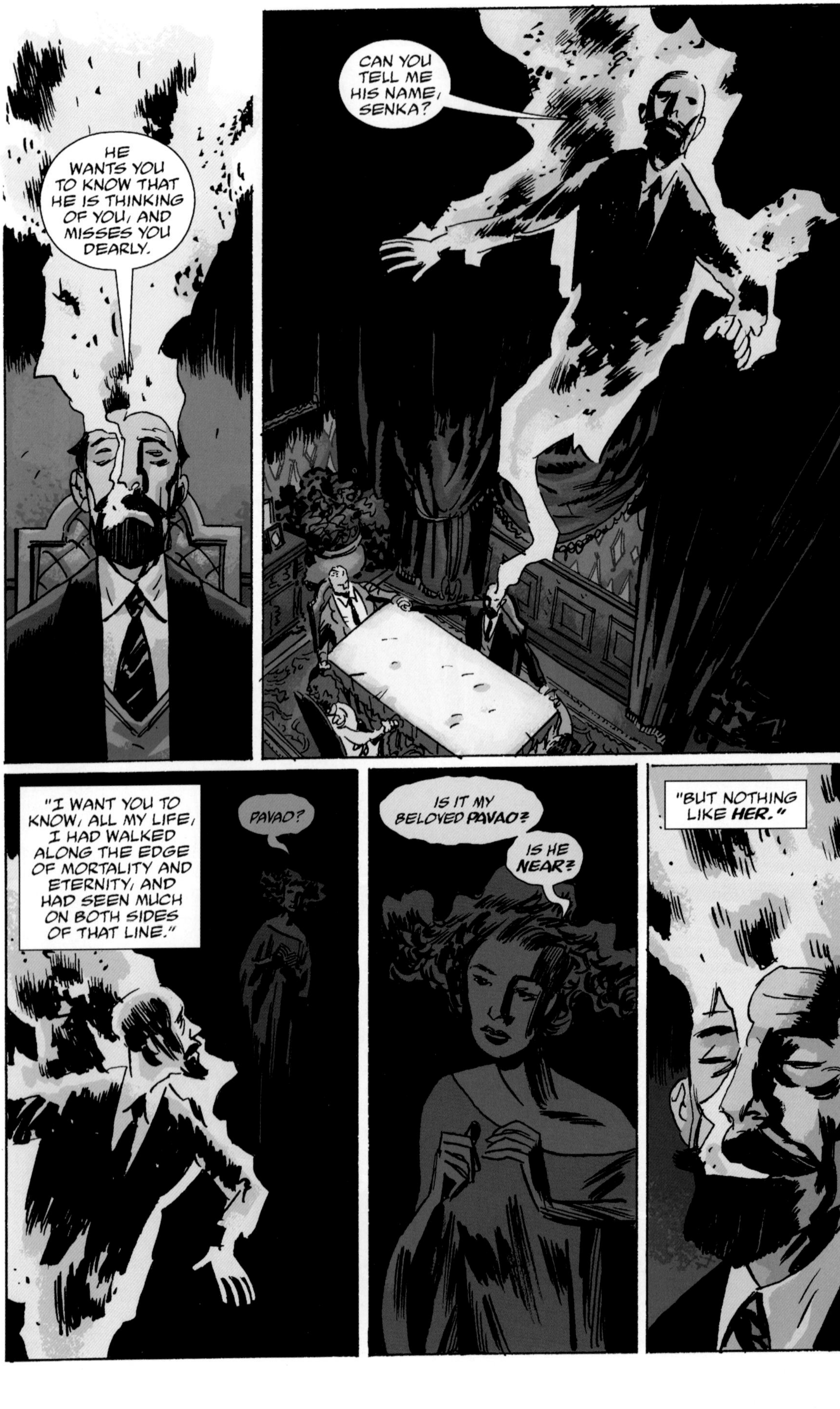
HE WANTS YOU TO KNOW THAT HE IS THINKING OF YOU, AND MISSES YOU DEARLY.
CAN YOU TELL ME HIS NAME, SENKA?
"I WANT YOU TO KNOW, ALL MY LIFE, I HAD WALKED ALONG THE EDGE OF MORTALITY AND ETERNITY, AND HAD SEEN MUCH ON BOTH SIDES OF THAT LINE."
PAVAO?
IS IT MY BELOVED PAVAO?
IS HE NEAR?
"BUT NOTHING LIKE HER."

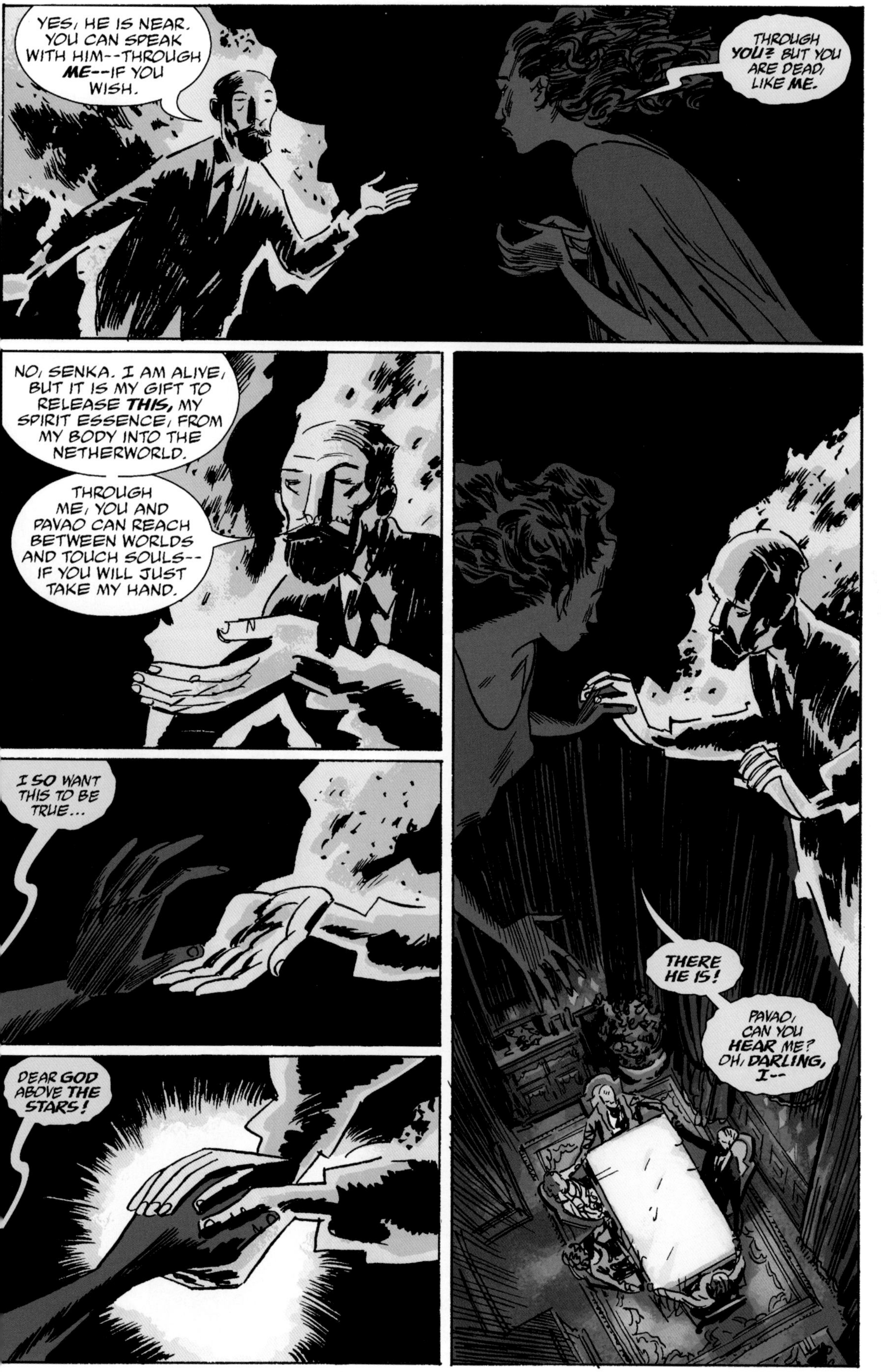

YES, HE IS NEAR. YOU CAN SPEAK WITH HIM--THROUGH ME--IF YOU WISH.
THROUGH YOU? BUT YOU ARE DEAD, LIKE ME.
NO, SENKA. I AM ALIVE, BUT IT IS MY GIFT TO RELEASE THIS, MY SPIRIT ESSENCE, FROM MY BODY INTO THE NETHERWORLD.
THROUGH ME, YOU AND PAVAO CAN REACH BETWEEN WORLDS AND TOUCH SOULS-- IF YOU WILL JUST TAKE MY HAND.
I SO WANT THIS TO BE TRUE...
DEAR GOD ABOVE THE STARS!
THERE HE IS!
PAVAO, CAN YOU HEAR ME? OH, DARLING, I--

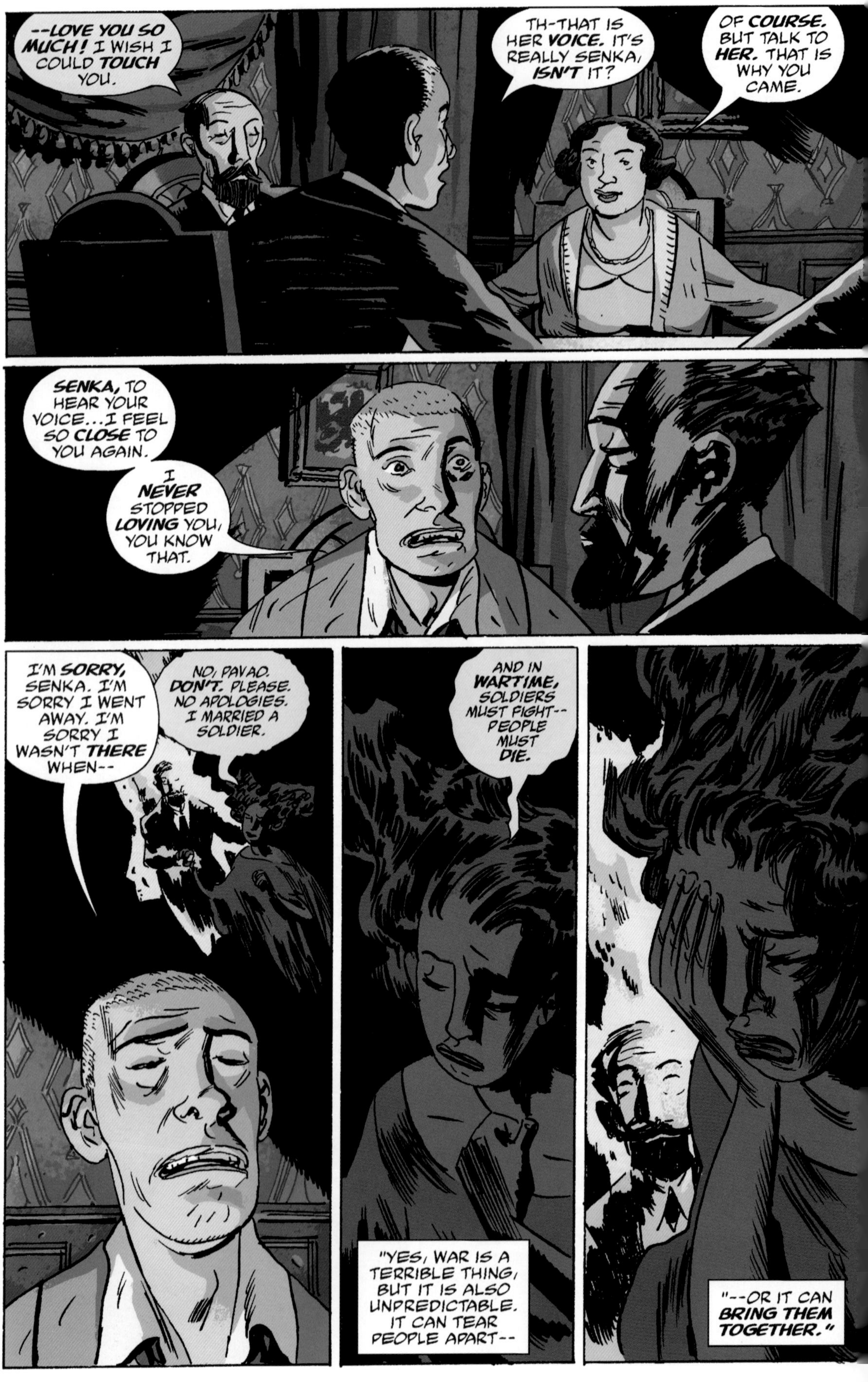
--LOVE YOU SO MUCH! I WISH I COULD TOUCH YOU.
TH-THAT IS HER VOICE. IT'S REALLY SENKA, ISN'T IT?
OF COURSE. BUT TALK TO HER. THAT IS WHY YOU CAME.
SENKA, TO HEAR YOUR VOICE... I FEEL SO CLOSE TO YOU AGAIN.
I NEVER STOPPED LOVING YOU, YOU KNOW THAT.
I'M SORRY, SENKA. I'M SORRY I WENT AWAY. I'M SORRY I WASN'T THERE WHEN--
NO, PAVAO. DON'T. PLEASE. NO APOLOGIES. I MARRIED A SOLDIER.
AND IN WARTIME, SOLDIERS MUST FIGHT-- PEOPLE MUST DIE.
"YES, WAR IS A TERRIBLE THING, BUT IT IS ALSO UNPREDICTABLE. IT CAN TEAR PEOPLE APART--
"--OR IT CAN BRING THEM TOGETHER."

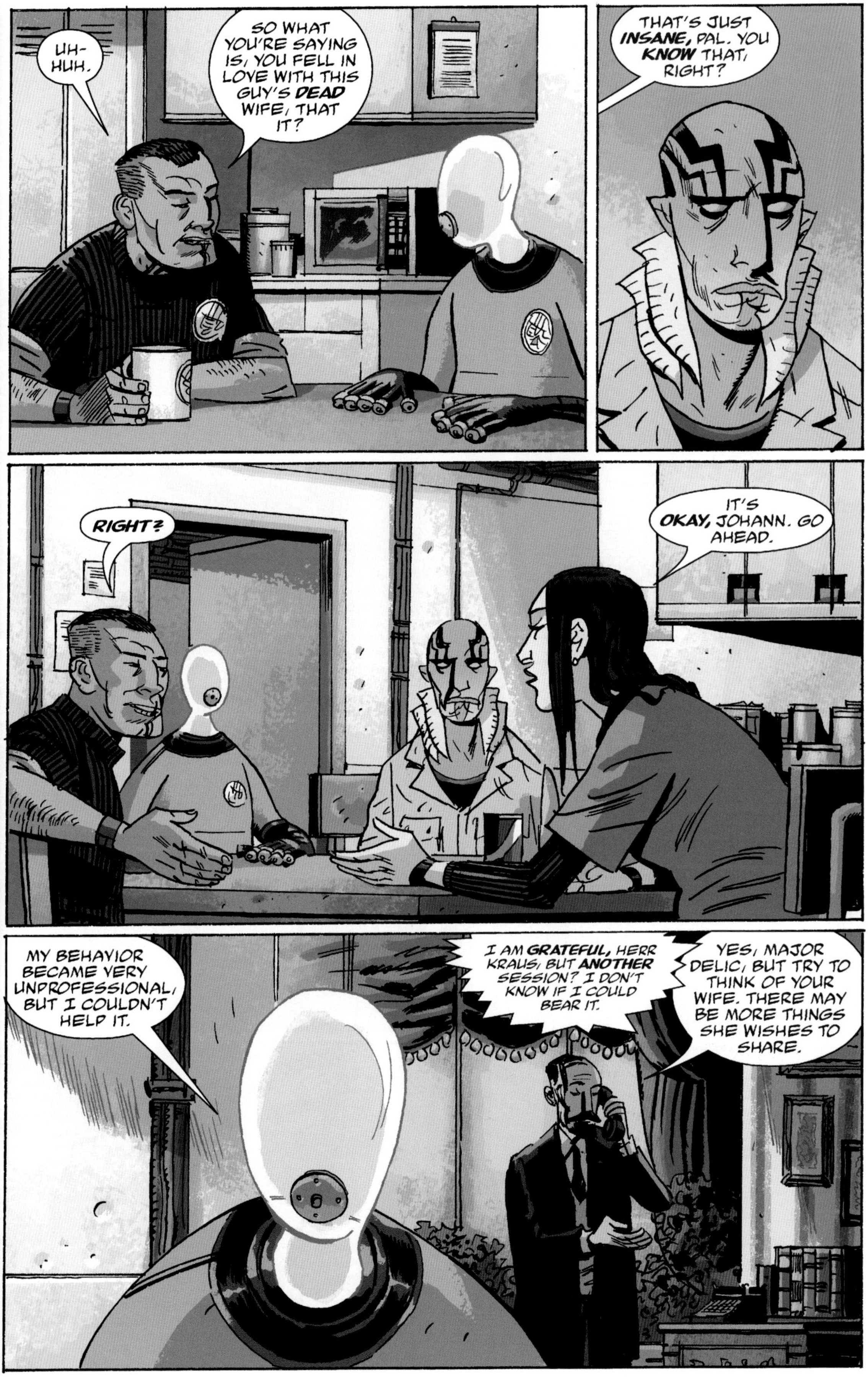
UH-HUH.
SO WHAT YOU'RE SAYING IS, YOU FELL IN LOVE WITH THIS GUY'S **DEAD** WIFE, THAT IT?
THAT'S JUST **INSANE,** PAL. YOU **KNOW** THAT, RIGHT?
RIGHT?
IT'S **OKAY,** JOHANN. GO AHEAD.
MY BEHAVIOR BECAME VERY UNPROFESSIONAL, BUT I COULDN'T HELP IT.
I AM **GRATEFUL,** HERR KRAUS, BUT **ANOTHER** SESSION? I DON'T KNOW IF I COULD BEAR IT.
YES, MAJOR DELIC, BUT TRY TO THINK OF YOUR WIFE. THERE MAY BE MORE THINGS SHE WISHES TO SHARE.

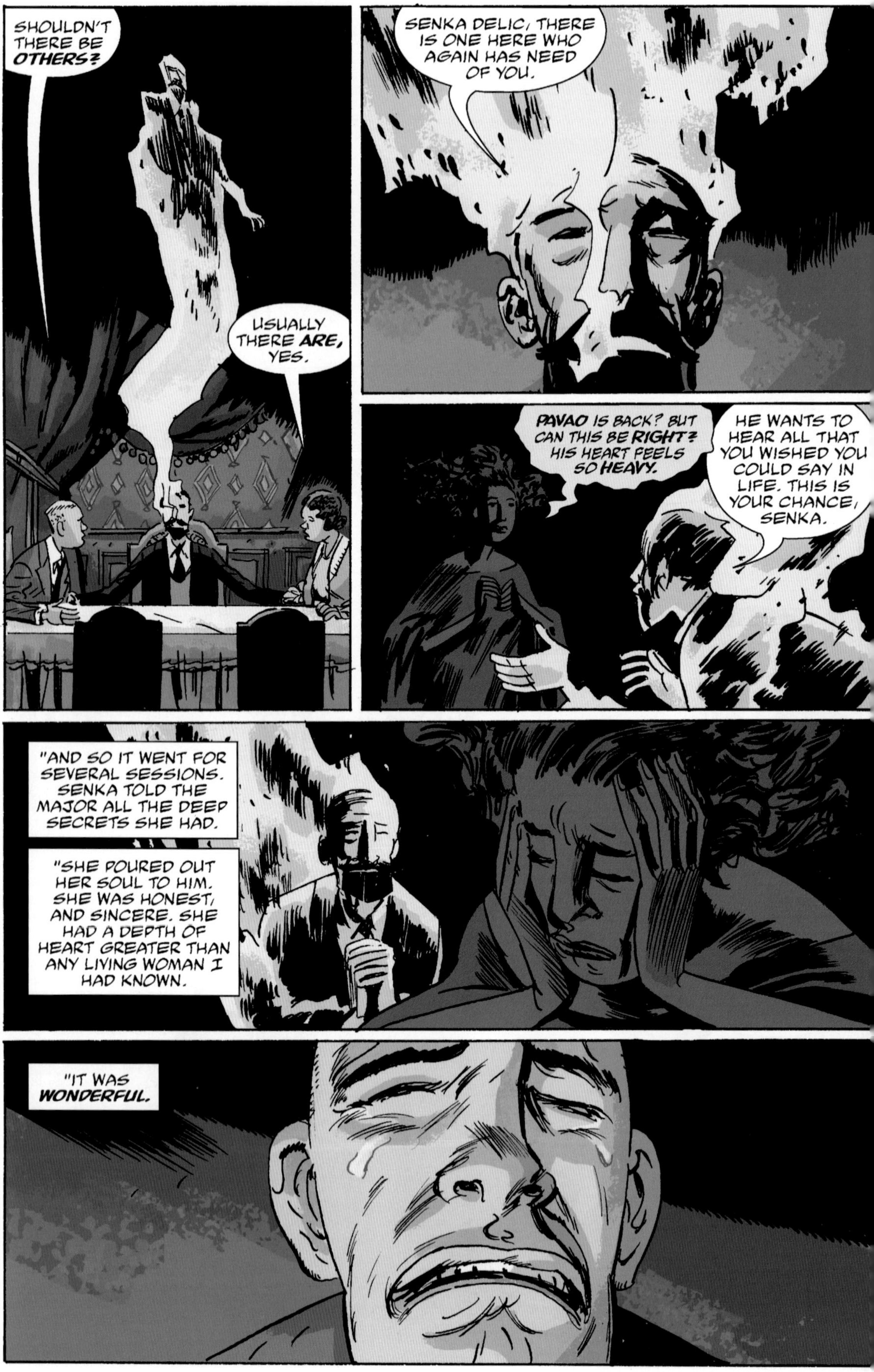

SHOULDN'T THERE BE OTHERS?
USUALLY THERE ARE, YES.
SENKA DELIC, THERE IS ONE HERE WHO AGAIN HAS NEED OF YOU.
PAVAO IS BACK? BUT CAN THIS BE RIGHT? HIS HEART FEELS SO HEAVY.
HE WANTS TO HEAR ALL THAT YOU WISHED YOU COULD SAY IN LIFE. THIS IS YOUR CHANCE, SENKA.
"AND SO IT WENT FOR SEVERAL SESSIONS. SENKA TOLD THE MAJOR ALL THE DEEP SECRETS SHE HAD.
"SHE POURED OUT HER SOUL TO HIM. SHE WAS HONEST, AND SINCERE. SHE HAD A DEPTH OF HEART GREATER THAN ANY LIVING WOMAN I HAD KNOWN.
"IT WAS WONDERFUL.

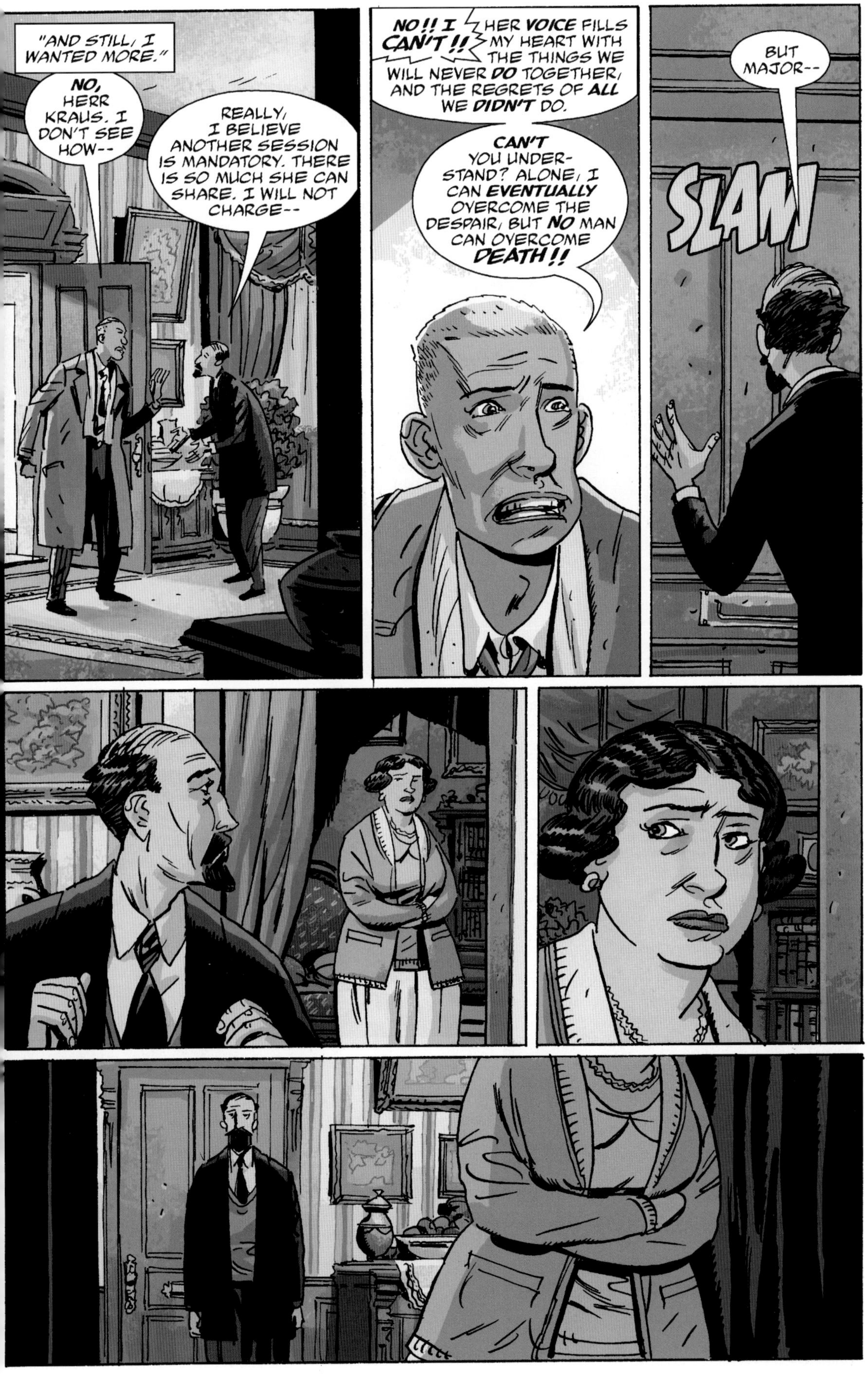
"AND STILL, I WANTED MORE."
NO, HERR KRAUS. I DON'T SEE HOW--
REALLY, I BELIEVE ANOTHER SESSION IS MANDATORY. THERE IS SO MUCH SHE CAN SHARE. I WILL NOT CHARGE--
NO!! I CAN'T!!
HER VOICE FILLS MY HEART WITH THE THINGS WE WILL NEVER DO TOGETHER, AND THE REGRETS OF ALL WE DIDN'T DO.
CAN'T YOU UNDERSTAND? ALONE, I CAN EVENTUALLY OVERCOME THE DESPAIR, BUT NO MAN CAN OVERCOME DEATH!!
BUT MAJOR--
SLAM

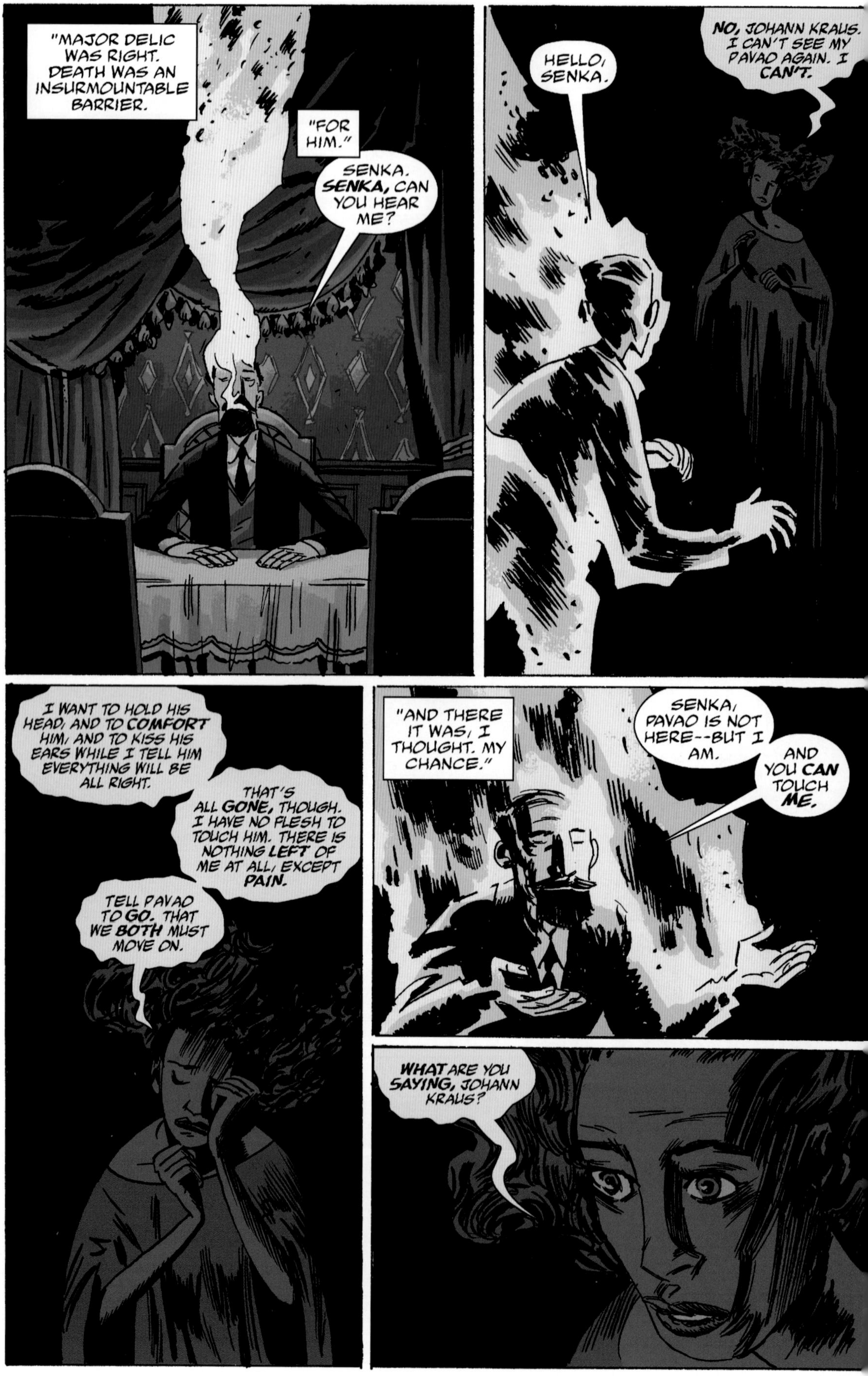
"MAJOR DELIC WAS RIGHT. DEATH WAS AN INSURMOUNTABLE BARRIER.
"FOR HIM."
SENKA. SENKA, CAN YOU HEAR ME?
HELLO, SENKA.
NO, JOHANN KRAUS. I CAN'T SEE MY PAVAO AGAIN. I CAN'T.
I WANT TO HOLD HIS HEAD, AND TO COMFORT HIM, AND TO KISS HIS EARS WHILE I TELL HIM EVERYTHING WILL BE ALL RIGHT.
THAT'S ALL GONE, THOUGH. I HAVE NO FLESH TO TOUCH HIM. THERE IS NOTHING LEFT OF ME AT ALL, EXCEPT PAIN.
TELL PAVAO TO GO. THAT WE BOTH MUST MOVE ON.
"AND THERE IT WAS, I THOUGHT. MY CHANCE."
SENKA, PAVAO IS NOT HERE--BUT I AM.
AND YOU CAN TOUCH ME.
WHAT ARE YOU SAYING, JOHANN KRAUS?

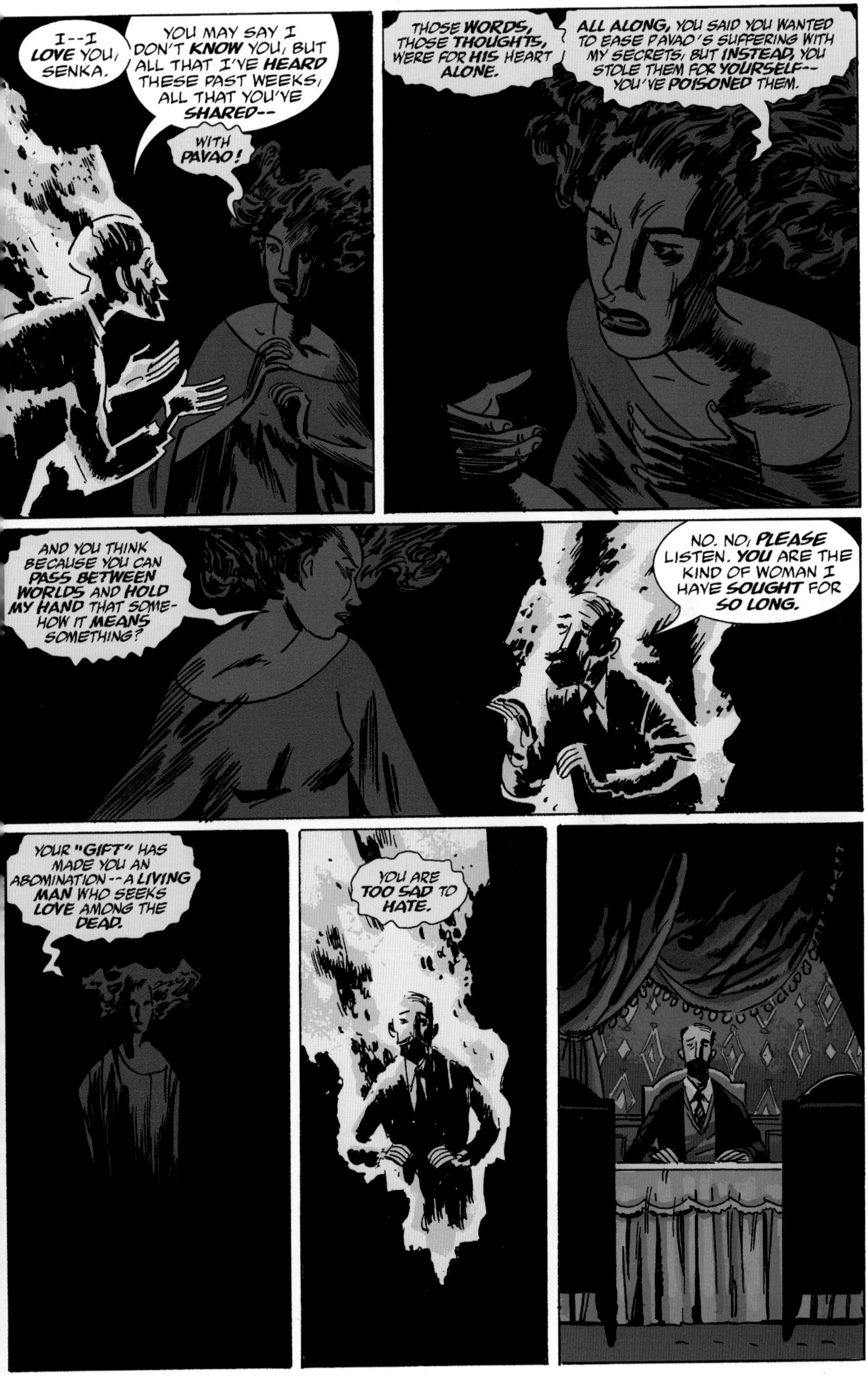
I--I LOVE YOU, SENKA.
YOU MAY SAY I DON'T KNOW YOU, BUT ALL THAT I'VE HEARD THESE PAST WEEKS, ALL THAT YOU'VE SHARED--
WITH PAVAO!
THOSE WORDS, THOSE THOUGHTS, WERE FOR HIS HEART ALONE.
ALL ALONG, YOU SAID YOU WANTED TO EASE PAVAO'S SUFFERING WITH MY SECRETS, BUT INSTEAD, YOU STOLE THEM FOR YOURSELF--YOU'VE POISONED THEM.
AND YOU THINK BECAUSE YOU CAN PASS BETWEEN WORLDS AND HOLD MY HAND THAT SOMEHOW IT MEANS SOMETHING?
NO. NO, PLEASE LISTEN. YOU ARE THE KIND OF WOMAN I HAVE SOUGHT FOR SO LONG.
YOUR "GIFT" HAS MADE YOU AN ABOMINATION--A LIVING MAN WHO SEEKS LOVE AMONG THE DEAD.
YOU ARE TOO SAD TO HATE.

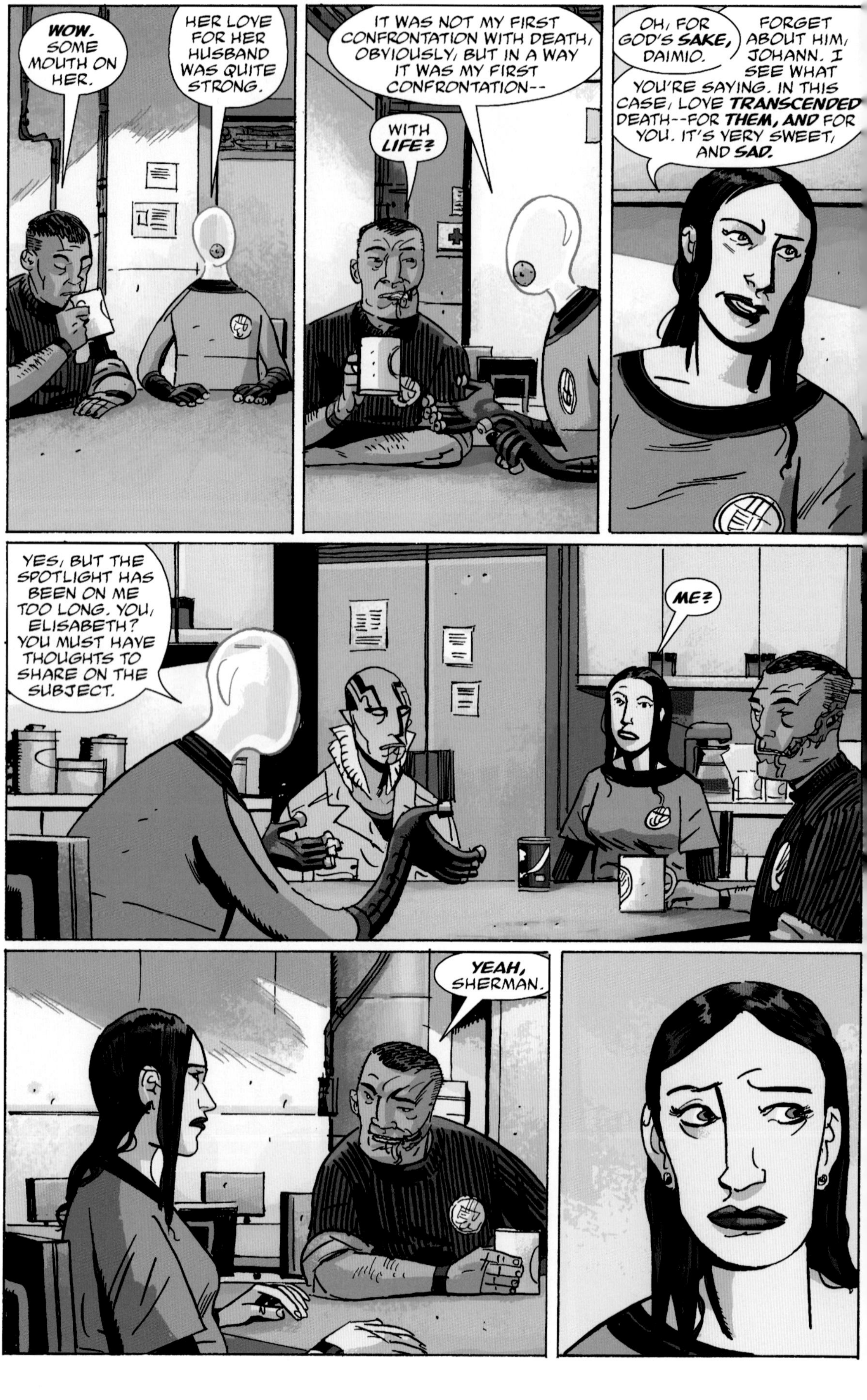

WOW. SOME MOUTH ON HER.
HER LOVE FOR HER HUSBAND WAS QUITE STRONG.
IT WAS NOT MY FIRST CONFRONTATION WITH DEATH, OBVIOUSLY, BUT IN A WAY IT WAS MY FIRST CONFRONTATION--
WITH LIFE?
OH, FOR GOD'S SAKE, DAIMIO.
FORGET ABOUT HIM, JOHANN. I SEE WHAT YOU'RE SAYING. IN THIS CASE, LOVE TRANSCENDED DEATH--FOR THEM, AND FOR YOU. IT'S VERY SWEET, AND SAD.
YES, BUT THE SPOTLIGHT HAS BEEN ON ME TOO LONG. YOU, ELISABETH? YOU MUST HAVE THOUGHTS TO SHARE ON THE SUBJECT.
ME?
YEAH, SHERMAN.

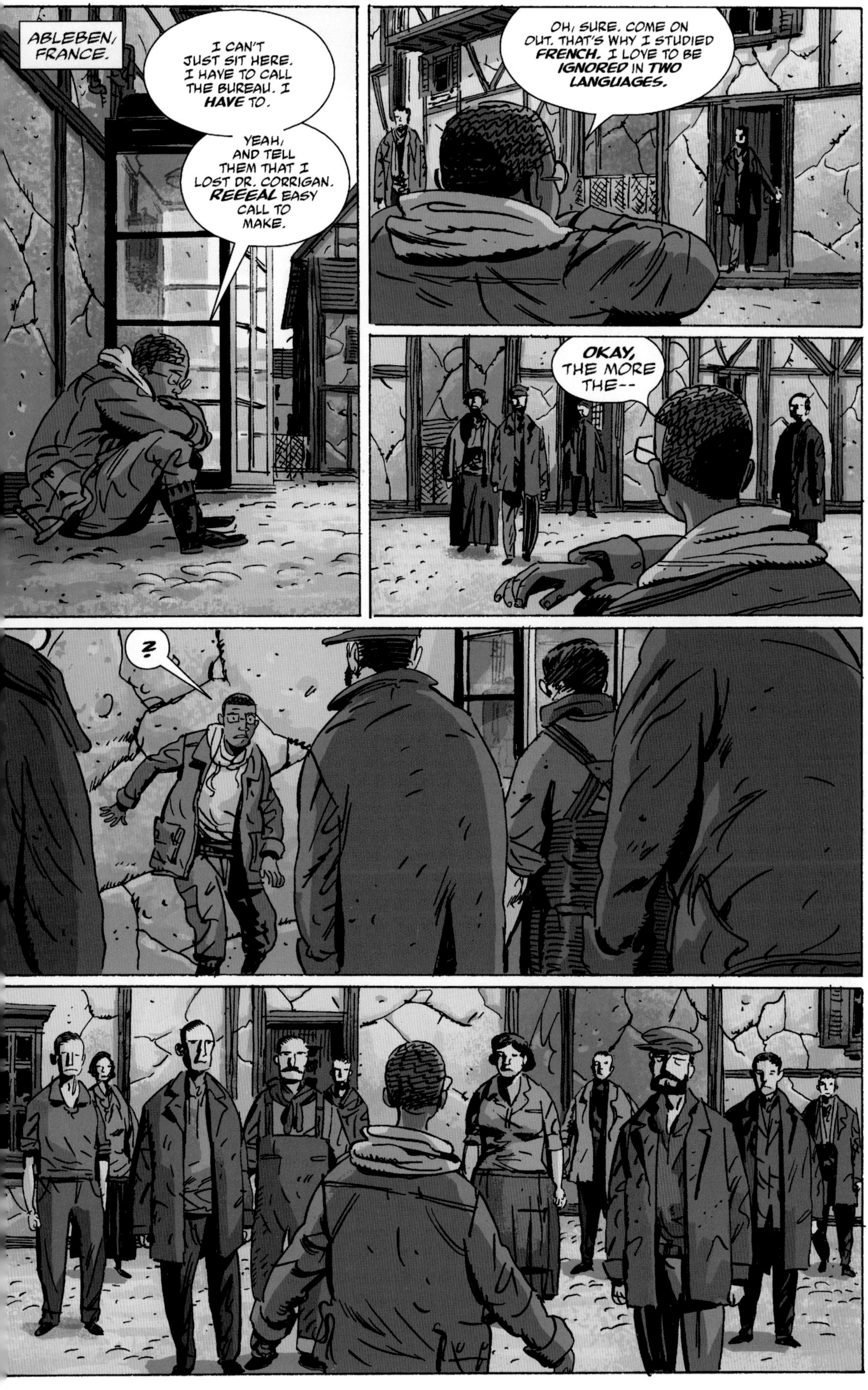
ABLEBEN, FRANCE.
I CAN'T JUST SIT HERE. I HAVE TO CALL THE BUREAU. I HAVE TO.
YEAH, AND TELL THEM THAT I LOST DR. CORRIGAN. REEEAL EASY CALL TO MAKE.
OH, SURE. COME ON OUT. THAT'S WHY I STUDIED FRENCH. I LOVE TO BE IGNORED IN TWO LANGUAGES.
OKAY, THE MORE THE--
?

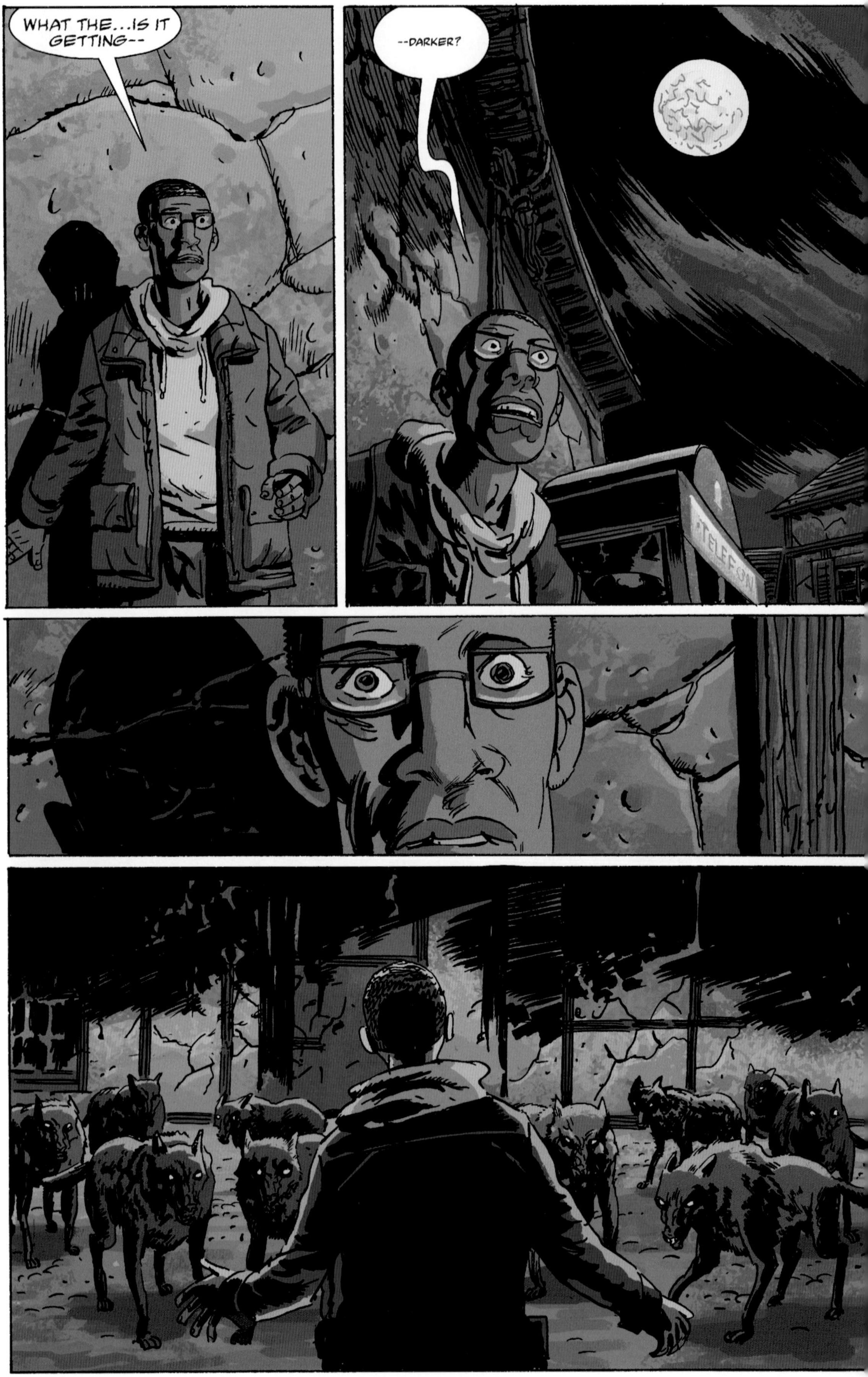
WHAT THE...IS IT GETTING--
--DARKER?
TELEFON

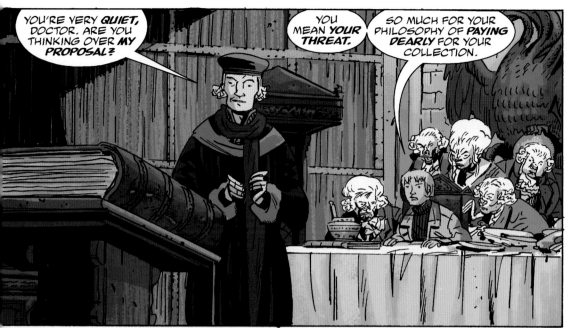

YOU'RE VERY *QUIET*, DOCTOR. ARE YOU THINKING OVER *MY PROPOSAL?*

YOU MEAN *YOUR THREAT.*

SO MUCH FOR YOUR PHILOSOPHY OF *PAYING DEARLY* FOR YOUR COLLECTION.

BELIEVE ME, DOCTOR, IT WILL COST ME *VERY DEARLY* TO WREST YOUR LIFE FROM *THESE* PARASITES.

THE FACT IS, IF THEY COULD SPEAK ENGLISH... WELL, I DON'T KNOW THAT YOU WOULD STILL BE *ALIVE.*

ALL RIGHT. I'M NOT *AGREEING* TO ANYTHING, BUT I JUST HAVE ONE QUESTION.

ASK IT SITTING *DOWN.*

PLEASE.

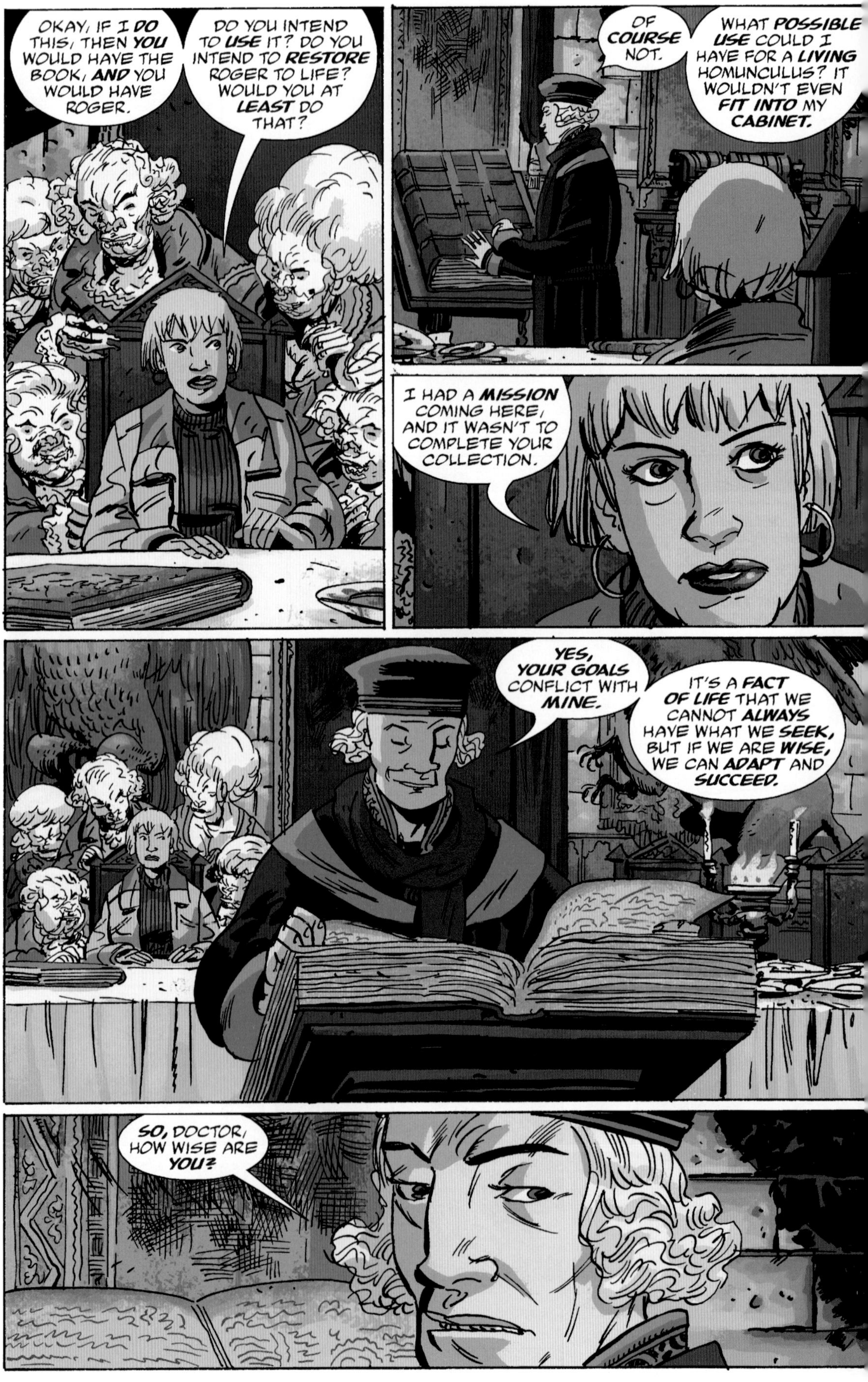

OKAY, IF I DO THIS, THEN YOU WOULD HAVE THE BOOK, AND YOU WOULD HAVE ROGER.
DO YOU INTEND TO USE IT? DO YOU INTEND TO RESTORE ROGER TO LIFE? WOULD YOU AT LEAST DO THAT?
OF COURSE NOT.
WHAT POSSIBLE USE COULD I HAVE FOR A LIVING HOMUNCULUS? IT WOULDN'T EVEN FIT INTO MY CABINET.
I HAD A MISSION COMING HERE, AND IT WASN'T TO COMPLETE YOUR COLLECTION.
YES, YOUR GOALS CONFLICT WITH MINE.
IT'S A FACT OF LIFE THAT WE CANNOT ALWAYS HAVE WHAT WE SEEK, BUT IF WE ARE WISE, WE CAN ADAPT AND SUCCEED.
SO, DOCTOR, HOW WISE ARE YOU?

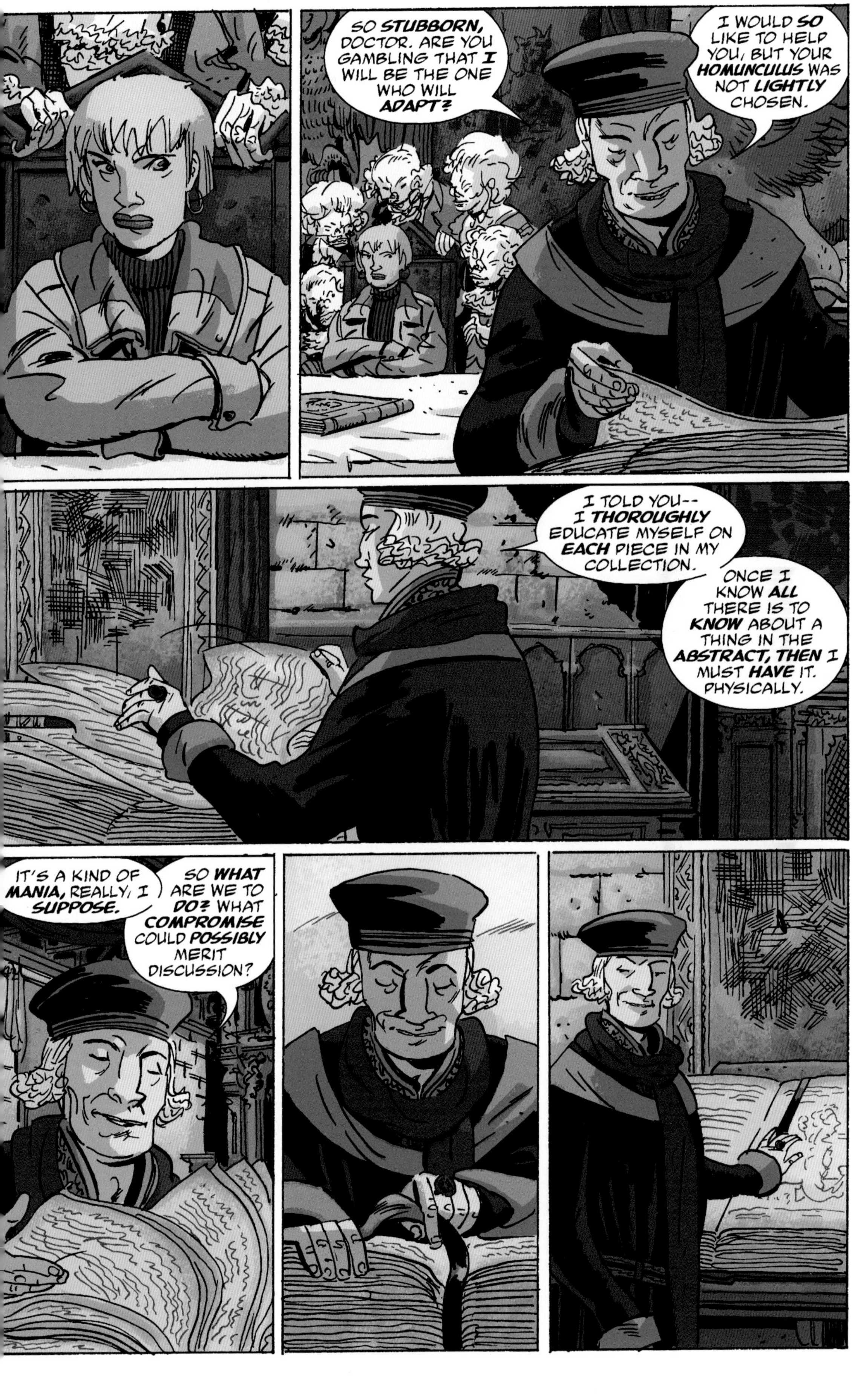

SO **STUBBORN,** DOCTOR. ARE YOU GAMBLING THAT **I** WILL BE THE ONE WHO WILL **ADAPT?**
I WOULD **SO** LIKE TO HELP YOU, BUT YOUR **HOMUNCULUS** WAS NOT **LIGHTLY** CHOSEN.
I TOLD YOU-- I **THOROUGHLY** EDUCATE MYSELF ON **EACH** PIECE IN MY COLLECTION.
ONCE I KNOW **ALL** THERE IS TO **KNOW** ABOUT A THING IN THE **ABSTRACT, THEN** I MUST **HAVE** IT. PHYSICALLY.
IT'S A KIND OF **MANIA,** REALLY, I **SUPPOSE.**
SO **WHAT** ARE WE TO **DO?** WHAT **COMPROMISE** COULD **POSSIBLY** MERIT DISCUSSION?

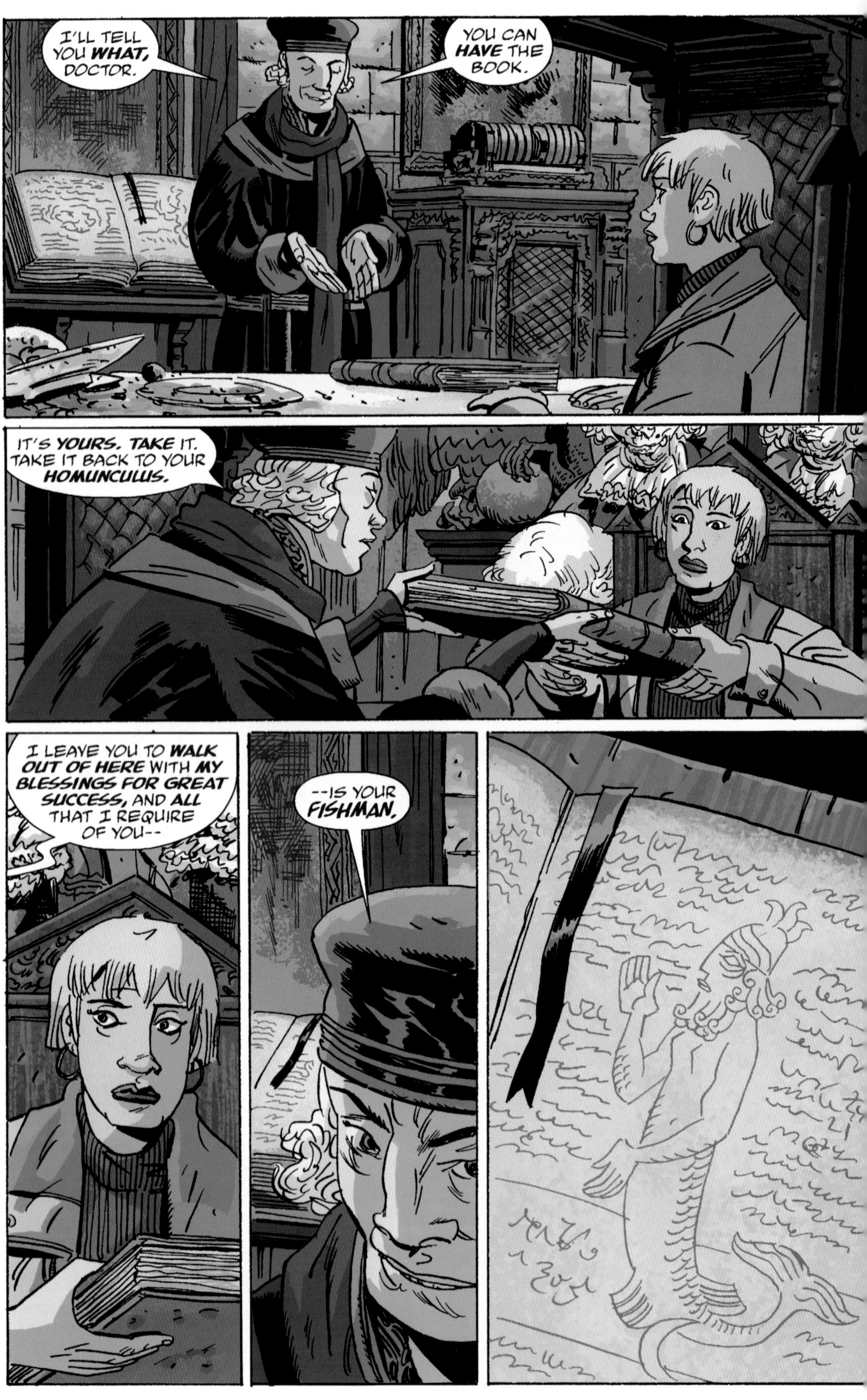
I'LL TELL YOU WHAT, DOCTOR.
YOU CAN HAVE THE BOOK.
IT'S YOURS. TAKE IT. TAKE IT BACK TO YOUR HOMUNCULUS.
I LEAVE YOU TO WALK OUT OF HERE WITH MY BLESSINGS FOR GREAT SUCCESS, AND ALL THAT I REQUIRE OF YOU--
--IS YOUR FISHMAN.

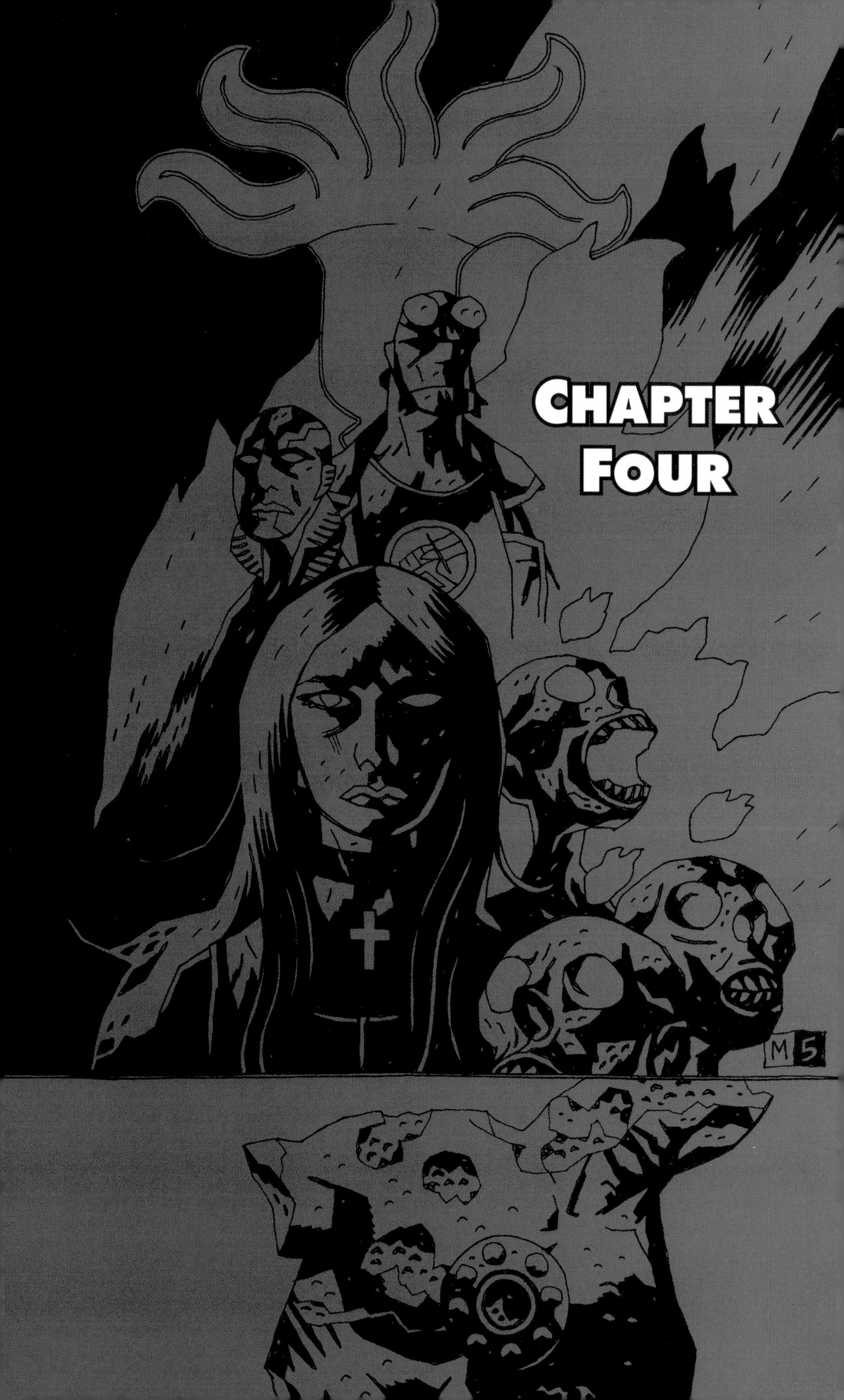
CHAPTER FOUR
M5

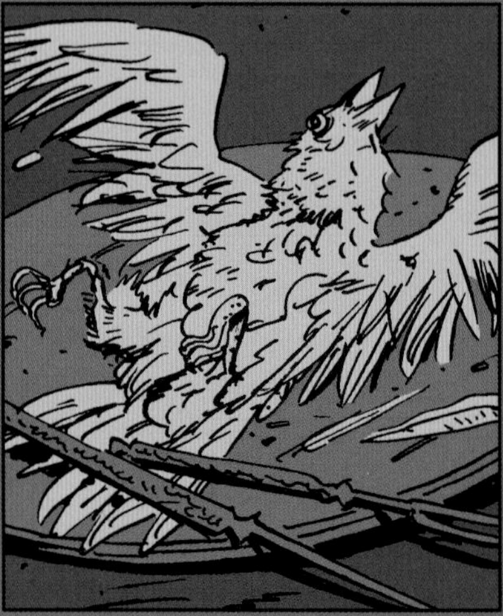

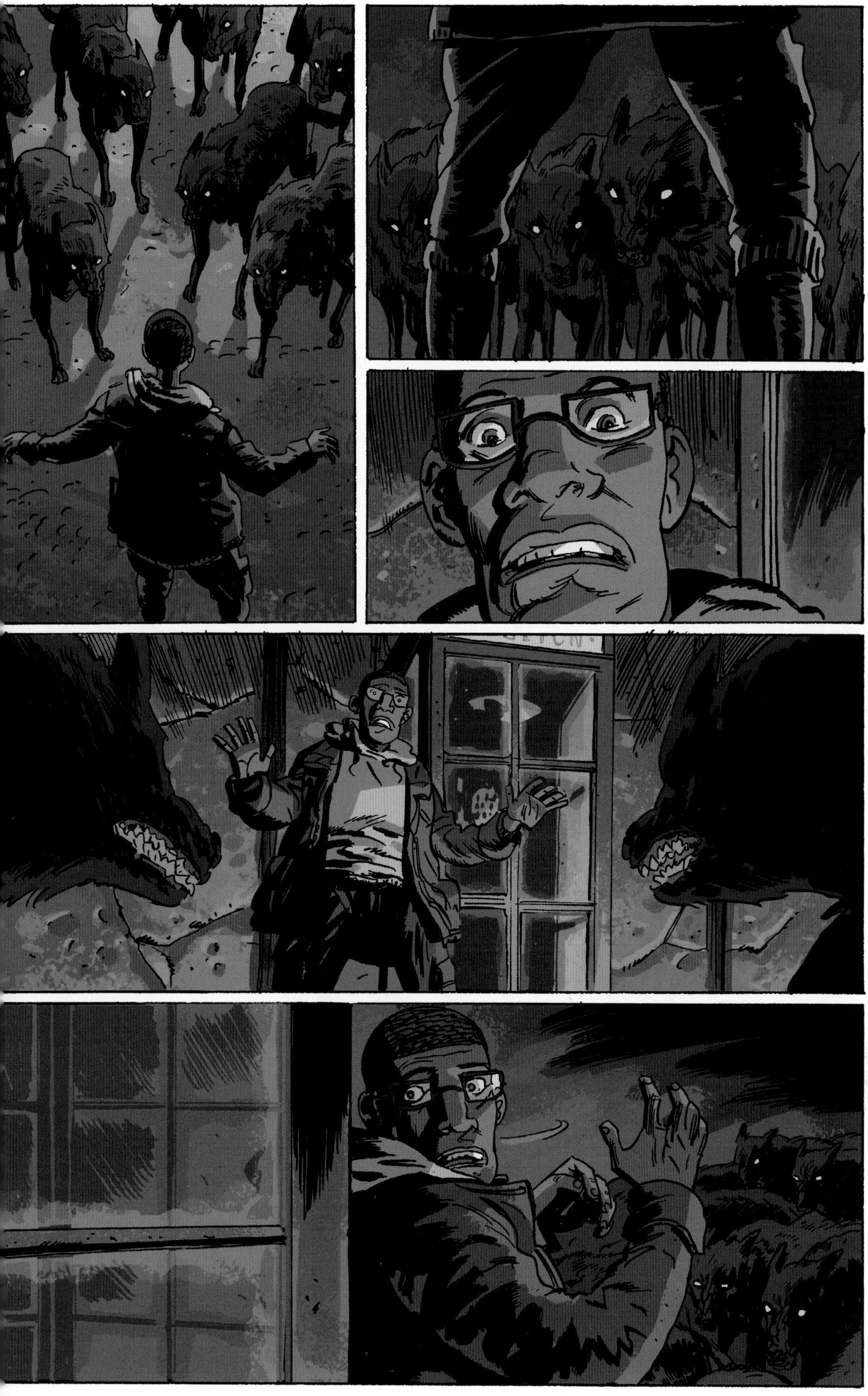

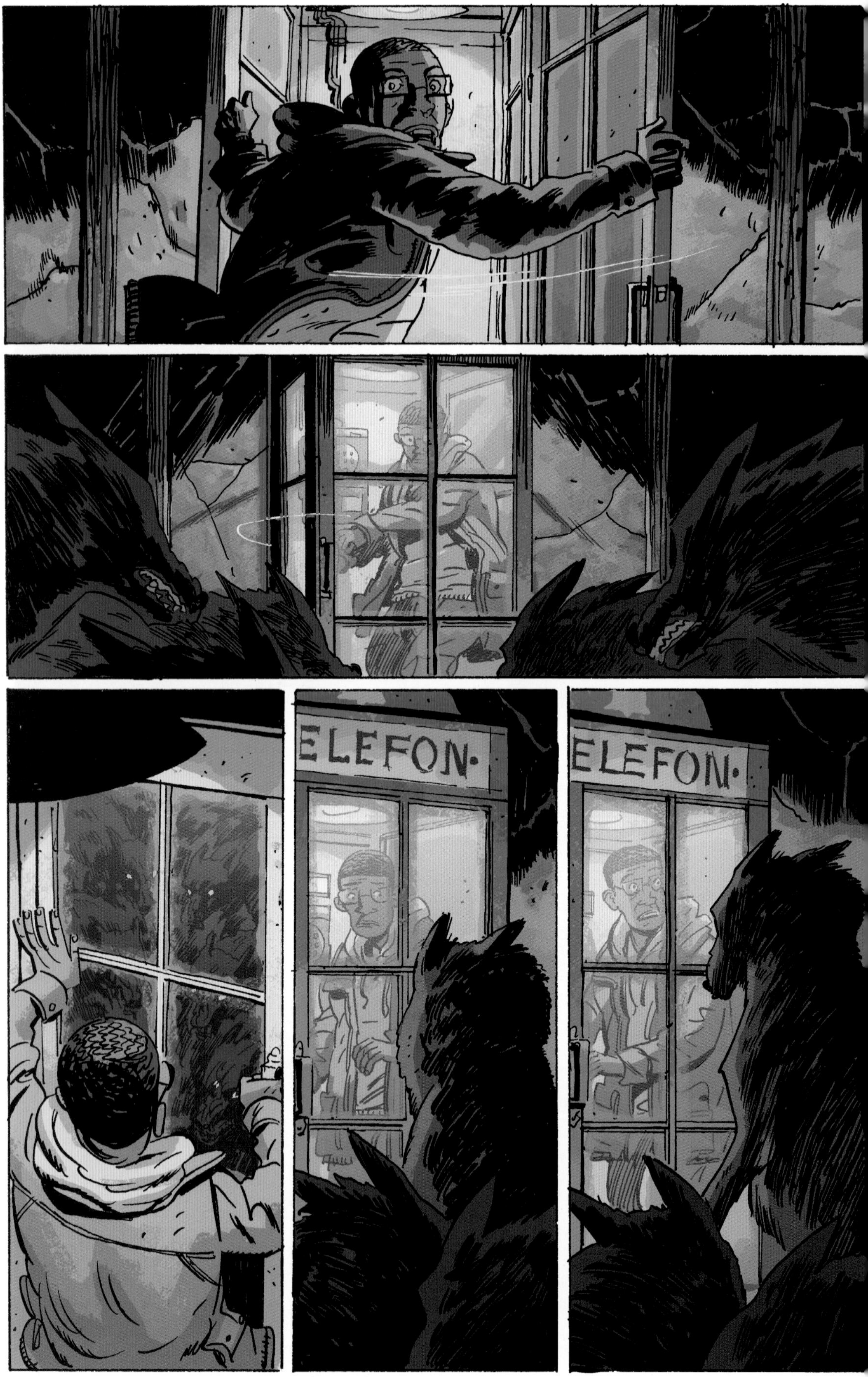
ELEFON•
ELEFON•

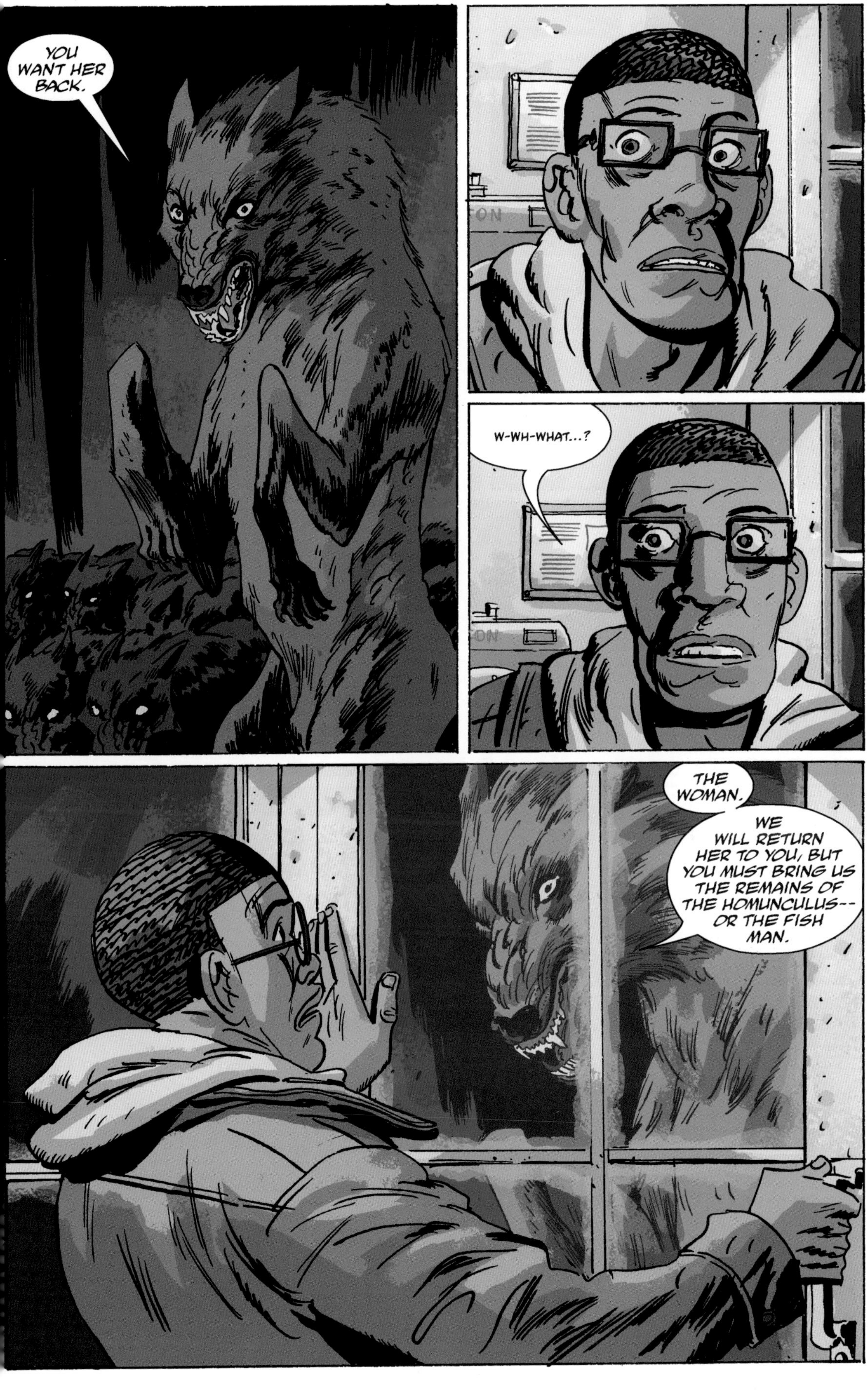
YOU WANT HER BACK.
W-WH-WHAT...?
THE WOMAN.
WE WILL RETURN HER TO YOU, BUT YOU MUST BRING US THE REMAINS OF THE HOMUNCULUS--OR THE FISH MAN.

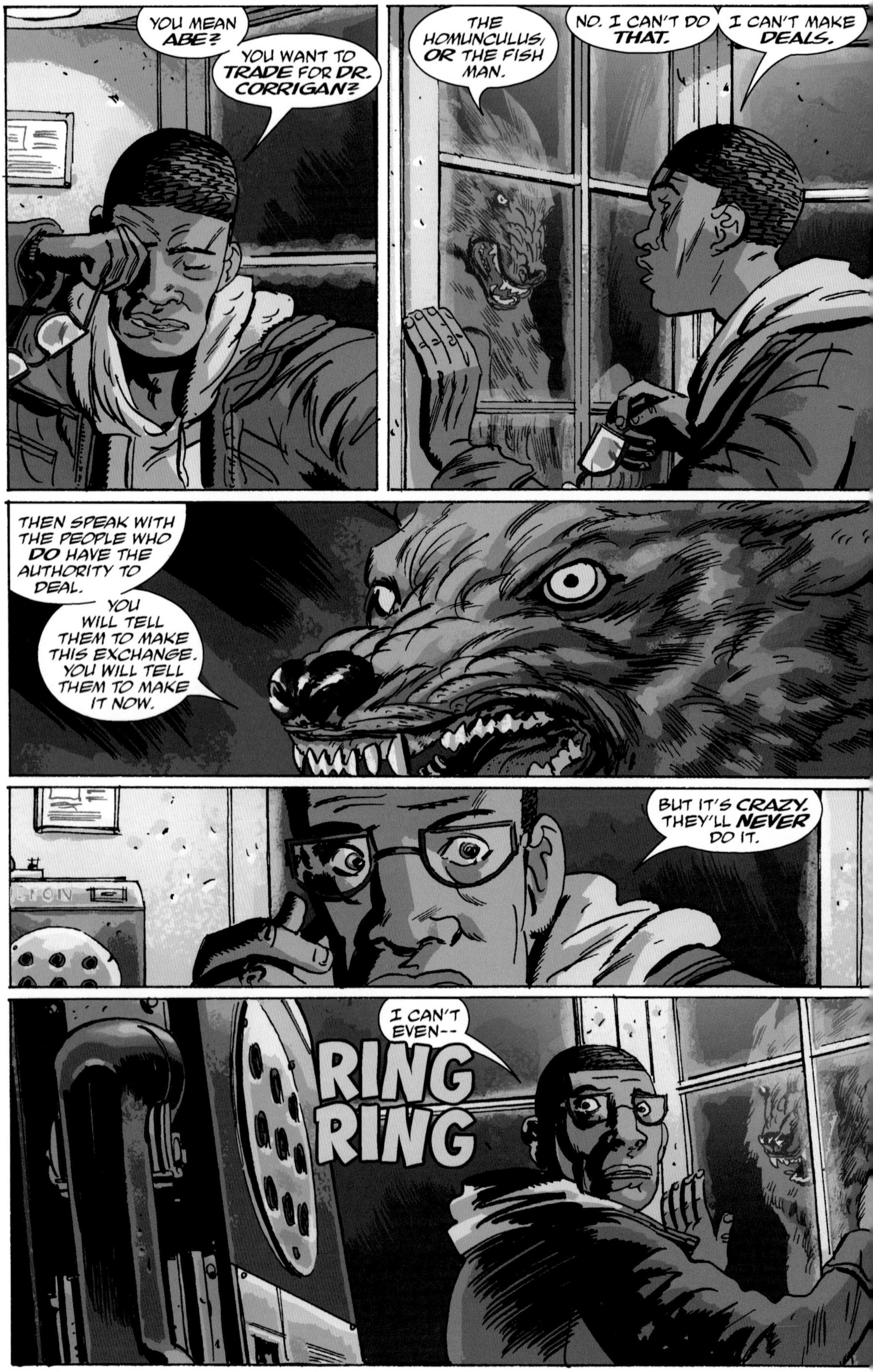

YOU MEAN ABE?
YOU WANT TO TRADE FOR DR. CORRIGAN?
THE HOMUNCULUS, OR THE FISH MAN.
NO. I CAN'T DO THAT.
I CAN'T MAKE DEALS.
THEN SPEAK WITH THE PEOPLE WHO DO HAVE THE AUTHORITY TO DEAL.
YOU WILL TELL THEM TO MAKE THIS EXCHANGE. YOU WILL TELL THEM TO MAKE IT NOW.
BUT IT'S CRAZY. THEY'LL NEVER DO IT.
I CAN'T EVEN--
RING RING

ALL RIGHT. YOU WANT A *STORY?*

HOW ABOUT THIS...

I'M *SORRY,* LIZ. TIME FOR *BED.*

THIS IS *SILLY,* JENNY. IT'S NOT EVEN *EIGHT O'CLOCK.* I'M TOO *OLD* TO GO TO BED THIS EARLY.

AND, *JEEZ,* DON'T MOM AND DAD KNOW I'M TOO OLD FOR A *BABYSITTER?*

LET'S NOT GO THROUGH *THAT* AGAIN, LIZ. *YOU* KNOW WHY I'M HERE.

SLEEP TIGHT, SWEETIE.

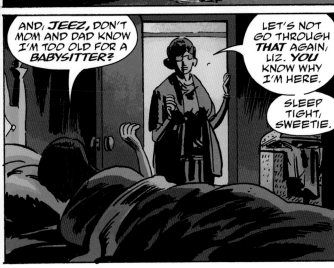

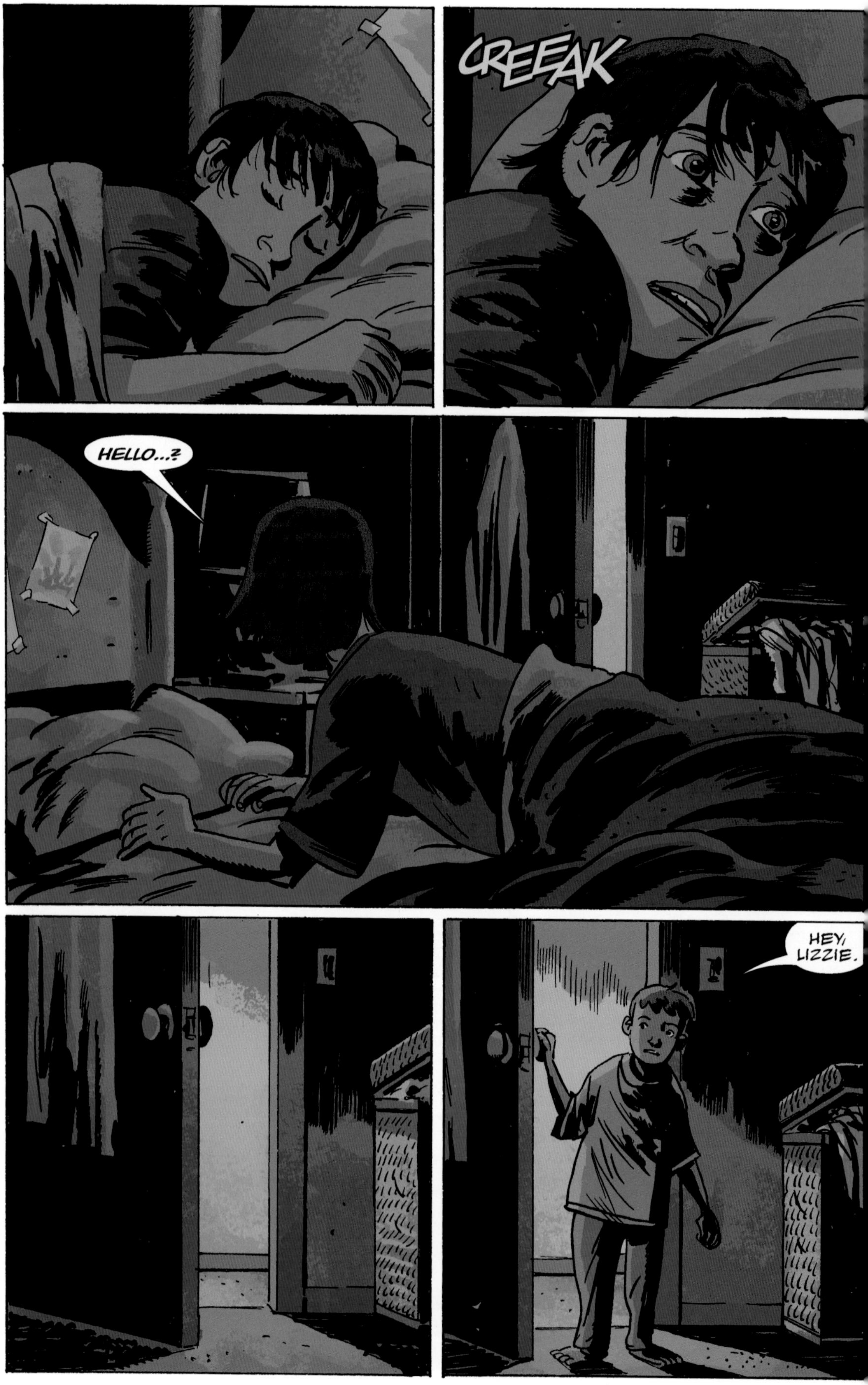
CREEAK
HELLO...?
HEY, LIZZIE.

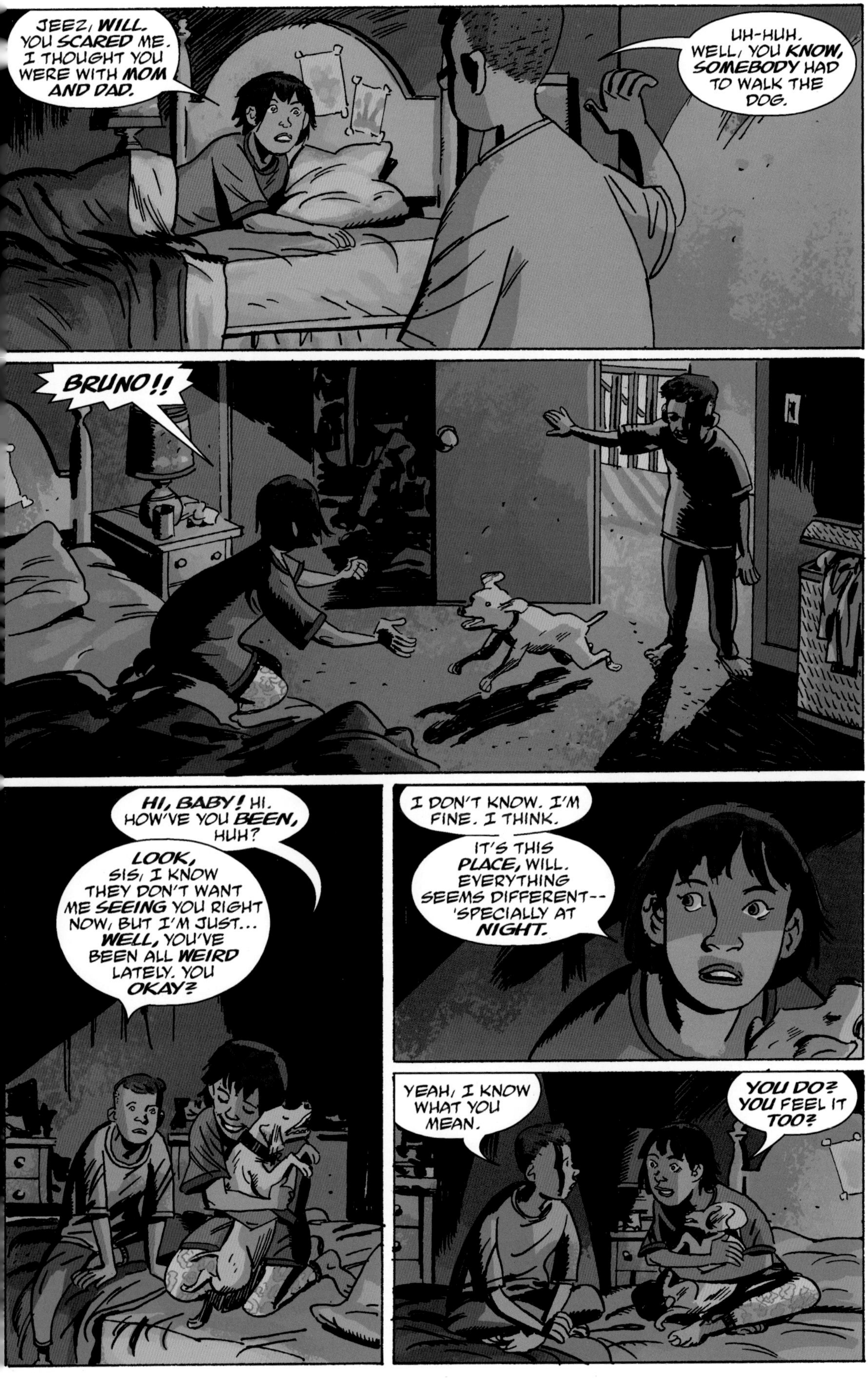

JEEZ, WILL. YOU SCARED ME. I THOUGHT YOU WERE WITH MOM AND DAD.
UH-HUH. WELL, YOU KNOW, SOMEBODY HAD TO WALK THE DOG.
BRUNO!!
HI, BABY! HI. HOW'VE YOU BEEN, HUH?
LOOK, SIS, I KNOW THEY DON'T WANT ME SEEING YOU RIGHT NOW, BUT I'M JUST... WELL, YOU'VE BEEN ALL WEIRD LATELY. YOU OKAY?
I DON'T KNOW. I'M FINE. I THINK.
IT'S THIS PLACE, WILL. EVERYTHING SEEMS DIFFERENT-- 'SPECIALLY AT NIGHT.
YEAH, I KNOW WHAT YOU MEAN.
YOU DO? YOU FEEL IT TOO?

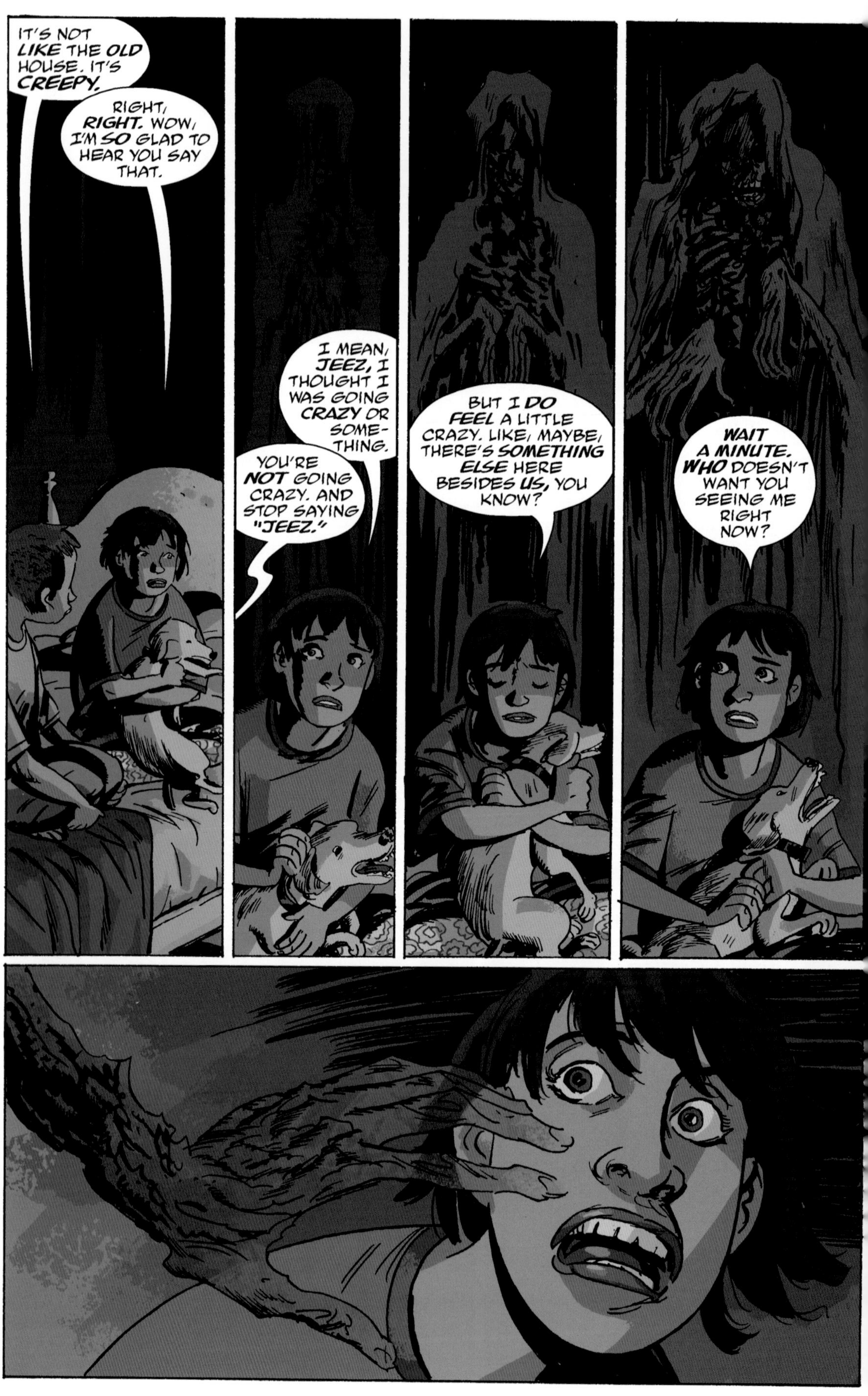
IT'S NOT LIKE THE OLD HOUSE. IT'S CREEPY.
RIGHT, RIGHT. WOW, I'M SO GLAD TO HEAR YOU SAY THAT.
I MEAN, JEEZ, I THOUGHT I WAS GOING CRAZY OR SOME-THING.
YOU'RE NOT GOING CRAZY. AND STOP SAYING "JEEZ."
BUT I DO FEEL A LITTLE CRAZY. LIKE, MAYBE, THERE'S SOMETHING ELSE HERE BESIDES US, YOU KNOW?
WAIT A MINUTE. WHO DOESN'T WANT YOU SEEING ME RIGHT NOW?

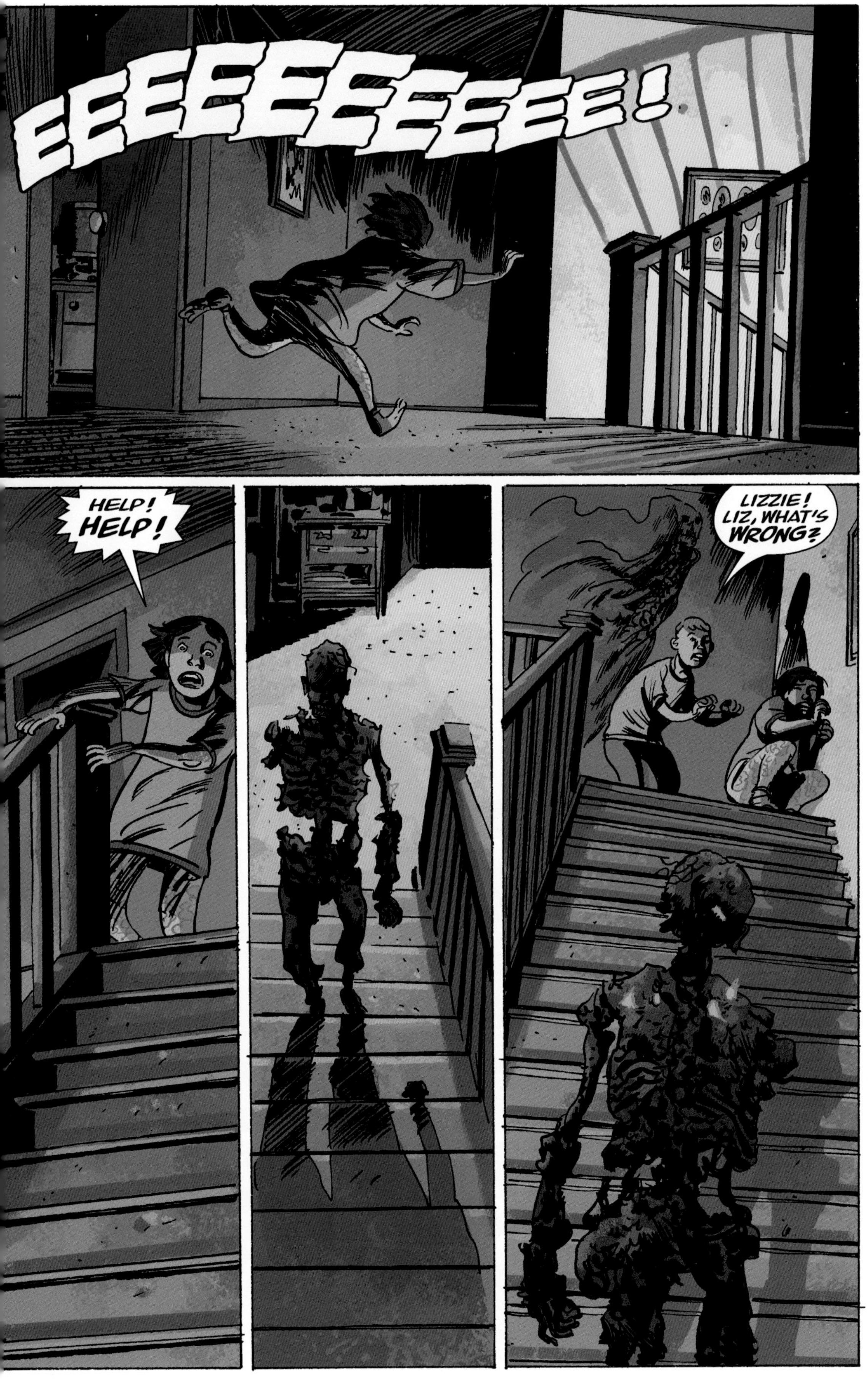
EEEEEEEEEEEEEE!
HELP! HELP!
LIZZIE! LIZ, WHAT'S WRONG?

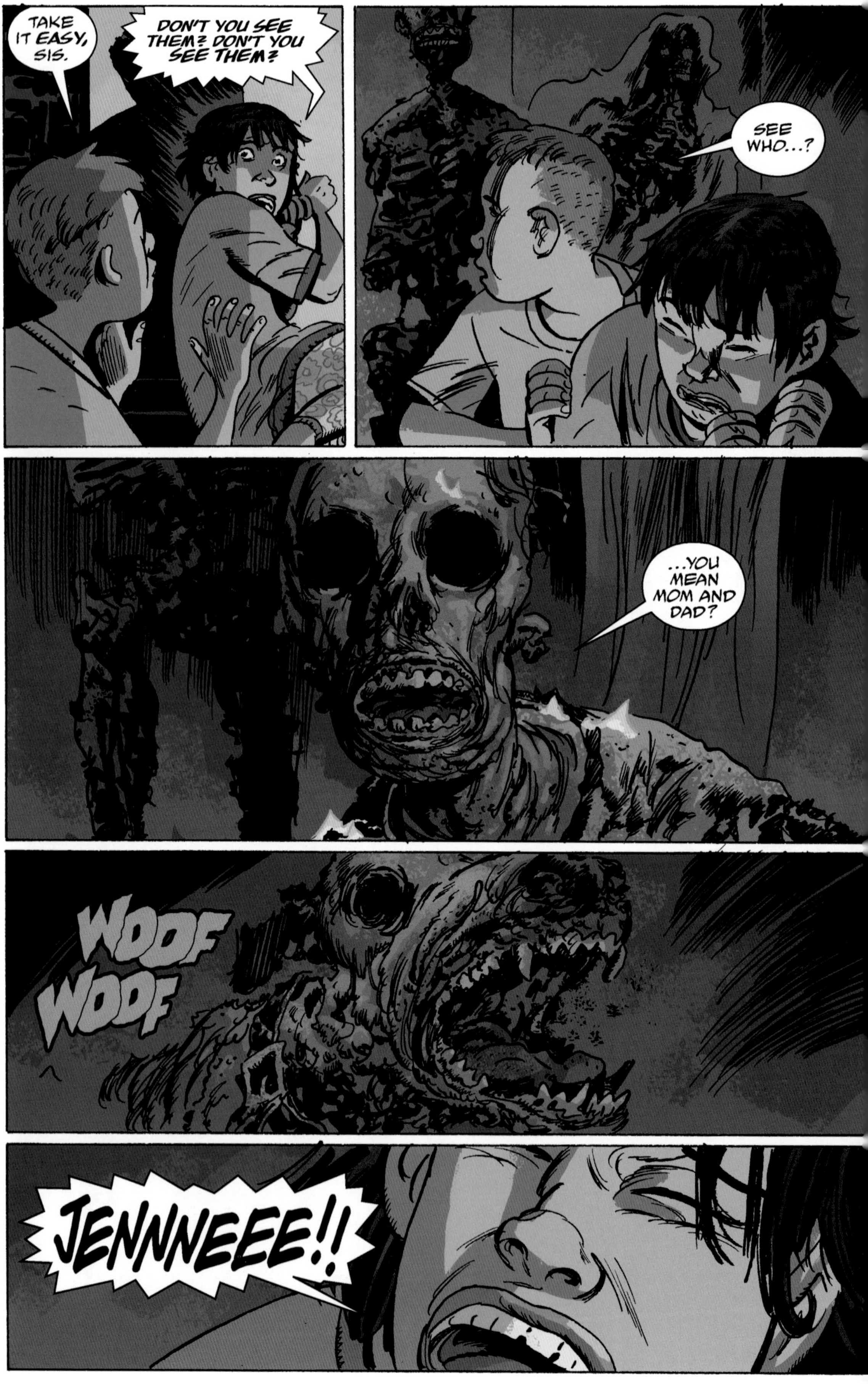
TAKE IT EASY, SIS.
DON'T YOU SEE THEM? DON'T YOU SEE THEM?
SEE WHO...?
...YOU MEAN MOM AND DAD?
WOOF WOOF
JENNEEE!!

IT'S OKAY, LIZZIE. IT'S OKAY.

I'M *HERE,* SWEETIE.

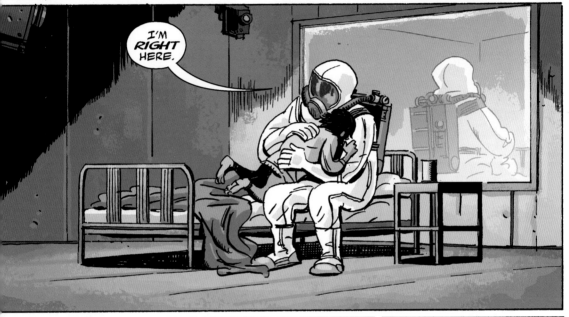

I'M *RIGHT* HERE.

WHAT? THAT DOESN'T COUNT. THAT WAS A *DREAM!*

I THINK IT WAS *MORE* THAN A *DREAM.*

MORE LIKELY A VISITATION-- THE SPIRITS OF YOUR FAMILY REACHING OUT TO HELP YOU MOVE ON.

THAT'S WHAT *I* THINK.

WHEN I CAME TO THE *B.P.R.D.,* I COULDN'T REMEMBER ANYTHING, AND NOBODY *TOLD* ME.

IT WASN'T UNTIL *THAT* DAY THAT I WAS ABLE TO ACCEPT THAT MY PARENTS, AND MY BROTHER, WERE REALLY DEAD.

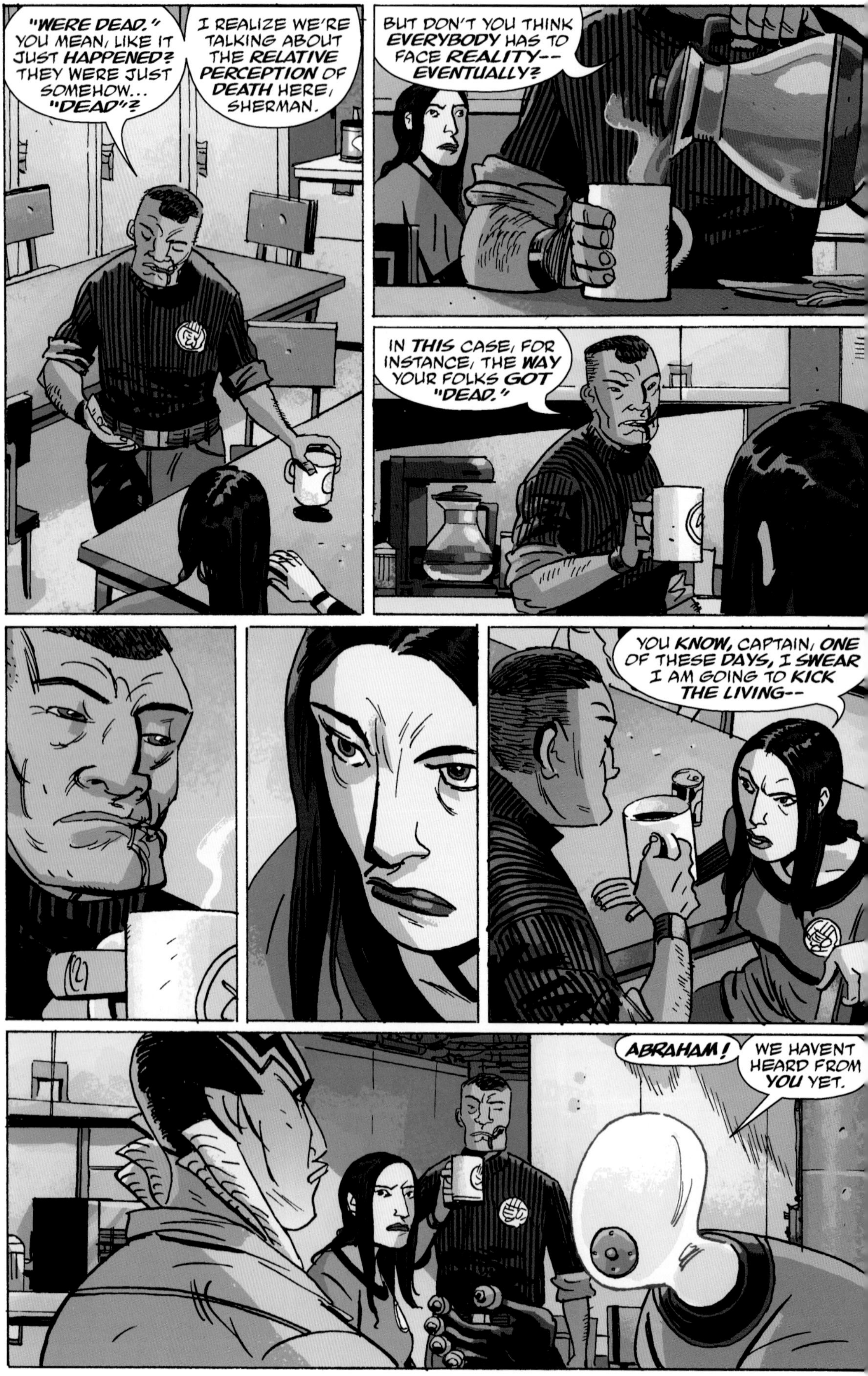
"WERE DEAD." YOU MEAN, LIKE IT JUST HAPPENED? THEY WERE JUST SOMEHOW... "DEAD"?
I REALIZE WE'RE TALKING ABOUT THE RELATIVE PERCEPTION OF DEATH HERE, SHERMAN.
BUT DON'T YOU THINK EVERYBODY HAS TO FACE REALITY-- EVENTUALLY?
IN THIS CASE, FOR INSTANCE, THE WAY YOUR FOLKS GOT "DEAD."
YOU KNOW, CAPTAIN, ONE OF THESE DAYS, I SWEAR I AM GOING TO KICK THE LIVING--
ABRAHAM!
WE HAVENT HEARD FROM YOU YET.

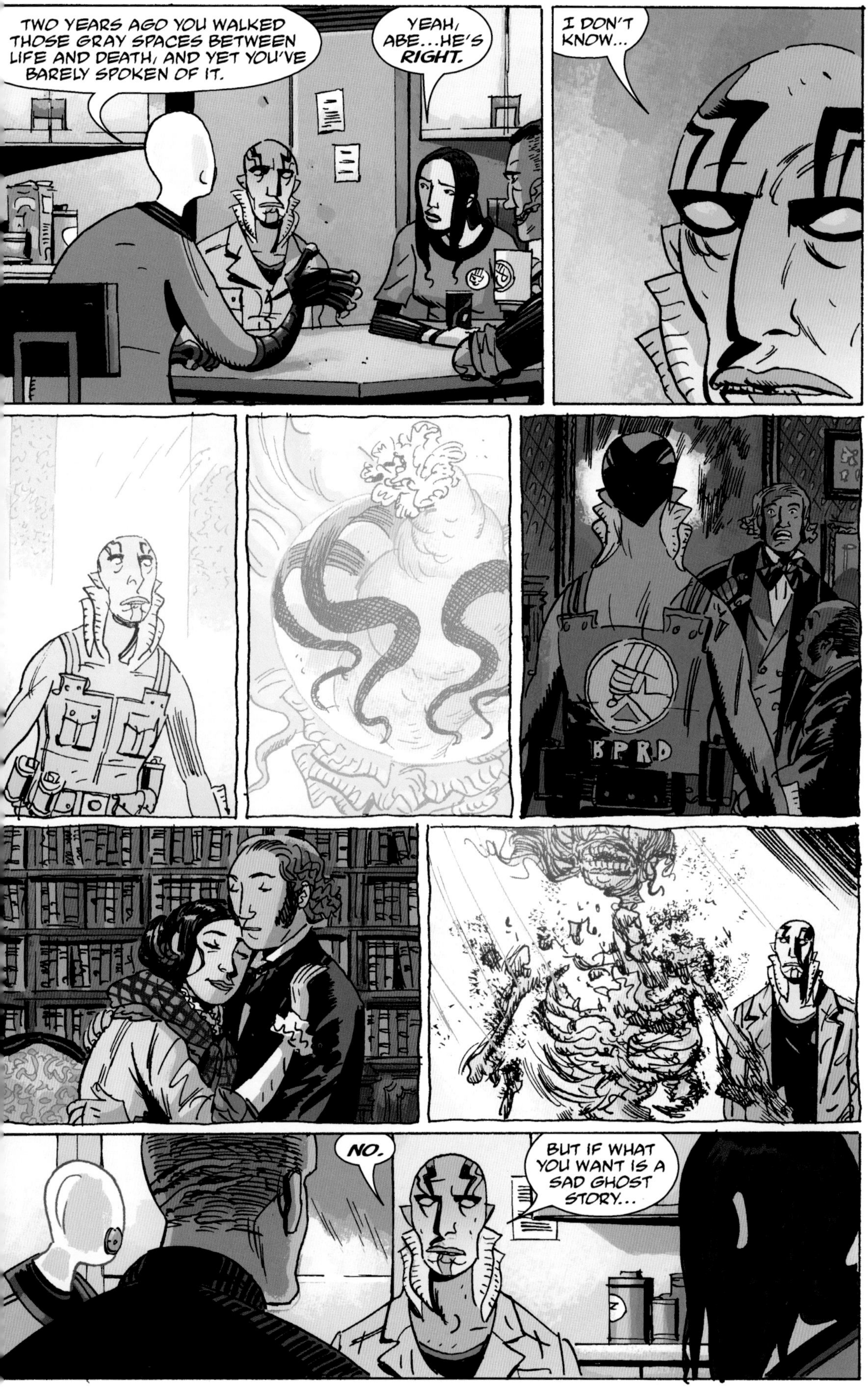
TWO YEARS AGO YOU WALKED THOSE GRAY SPACES BETWEEN LIFE AND DEATH, AND YET YOU'VE BARELY SPOKEN OF IT.
YEAH, ABE...HE'S *RIGHT.*
I DON'T KNOW...
BPRD
NO.
BUT IF WHAT YOU WANT IS A SAD GHOST STORY...

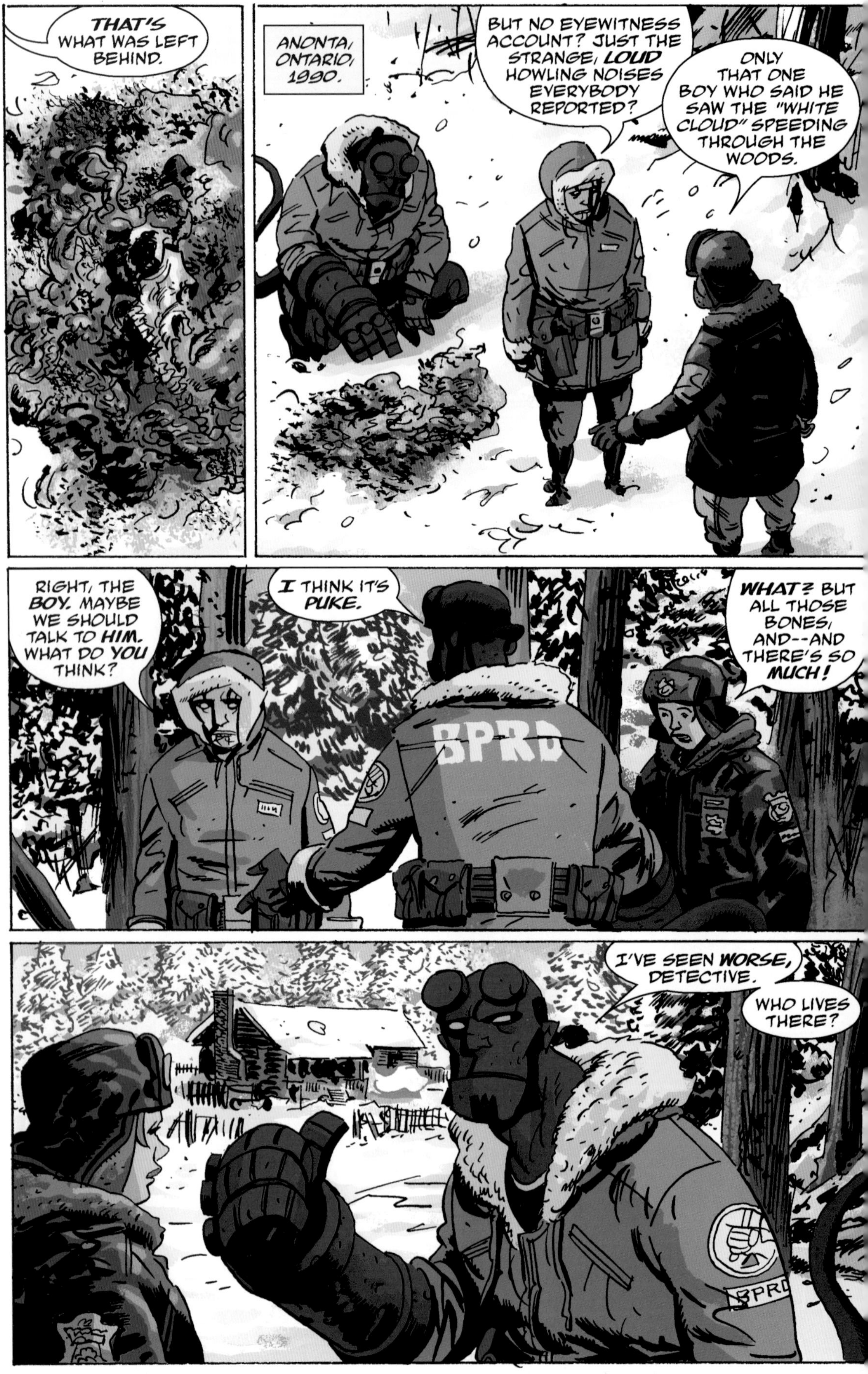
THAT'S WHAT WAS LEFT BEHIND.
ANONTA, ONTARIO, 1990.
BUT NO EYEWITNESS ACCOUNT? JUST THE STRANGE, LOUD HOWLING NOISES EVERYBODY REPORTED?
ONLY THAT ONE BOY WHO SAID HE SAW THE "WHITE CLOUD" SPEEDING THROUGH THE WOODS.
RIGHT, THE BOY. MAYBE WE SHOULD TALK TO HIM. WHAT DO YOU THINK?
I THINK IT'S PUKE.
WHAT? BUT ALL THOSE BONES, AND--AND THERE'S SO MUCH!
BPRD
I'VE SEEN WORSE, DETECTIVE.
WHO LIVES THERE?
BPRD

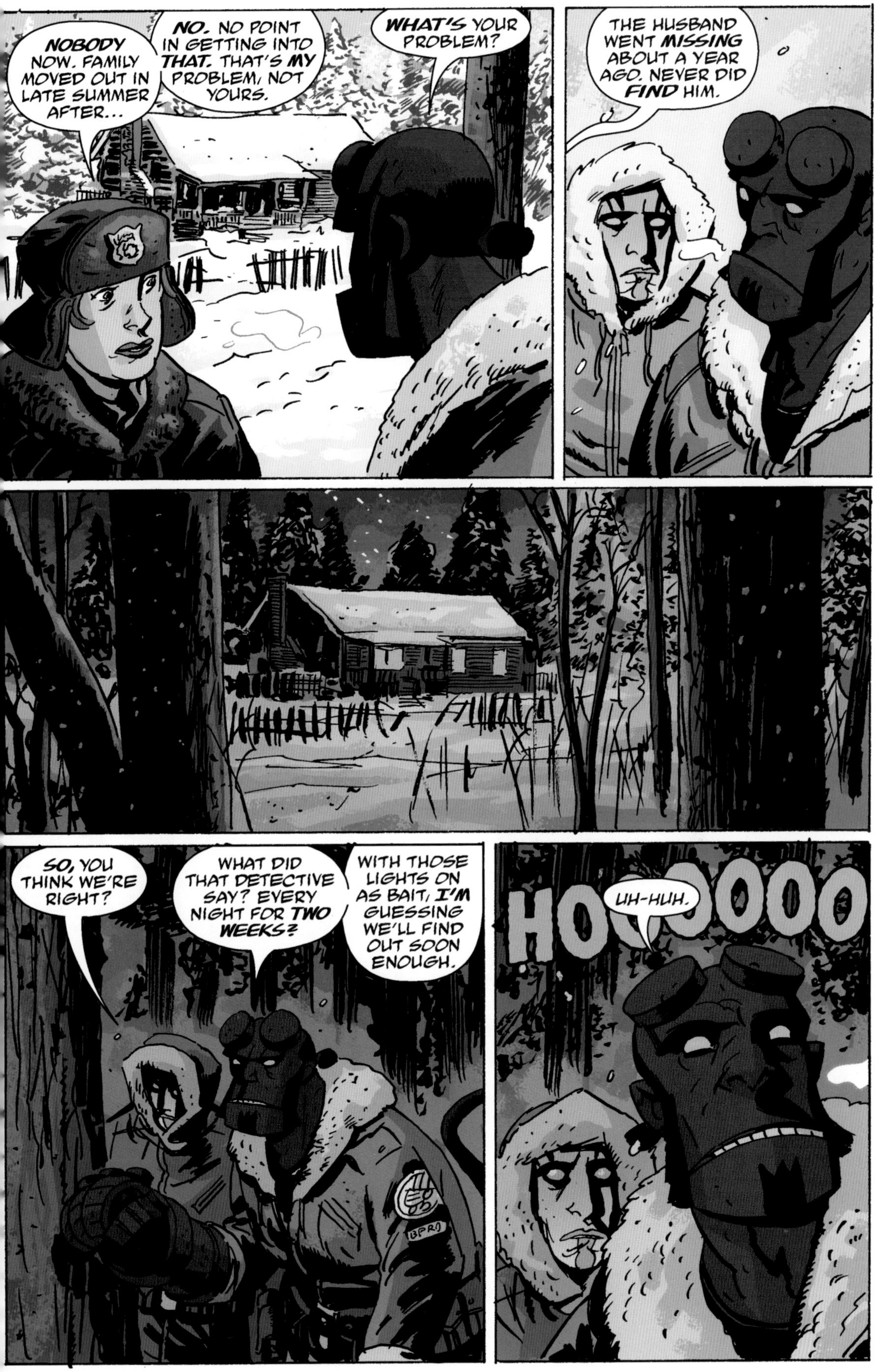
NOBODY NOW. FAMILY MOVED OUT IN LATE SUMMER AFTER...
NO. NO POINT IN GETTING INTO THAT. THAT'S MY PROBLEM, NOT YOURS.
WHAT'S YOUR PROBLEM?
THE HUSBAND WENT MISSING ABOUT A YEAR AGO. NEVER DID FIND HIM.
SO, YOU THINK WE'RE RIGHT?
WHAT DID THAT DETECTIVE SAY? EVERY NIGHT FOR TWO WEEKS?
WITH THOSE LIGHTS ON AS BAIT, I'M GUESSING WE'LL FIND OUT SOON ENOUGH.
HOOOOOO
UH-HUH.

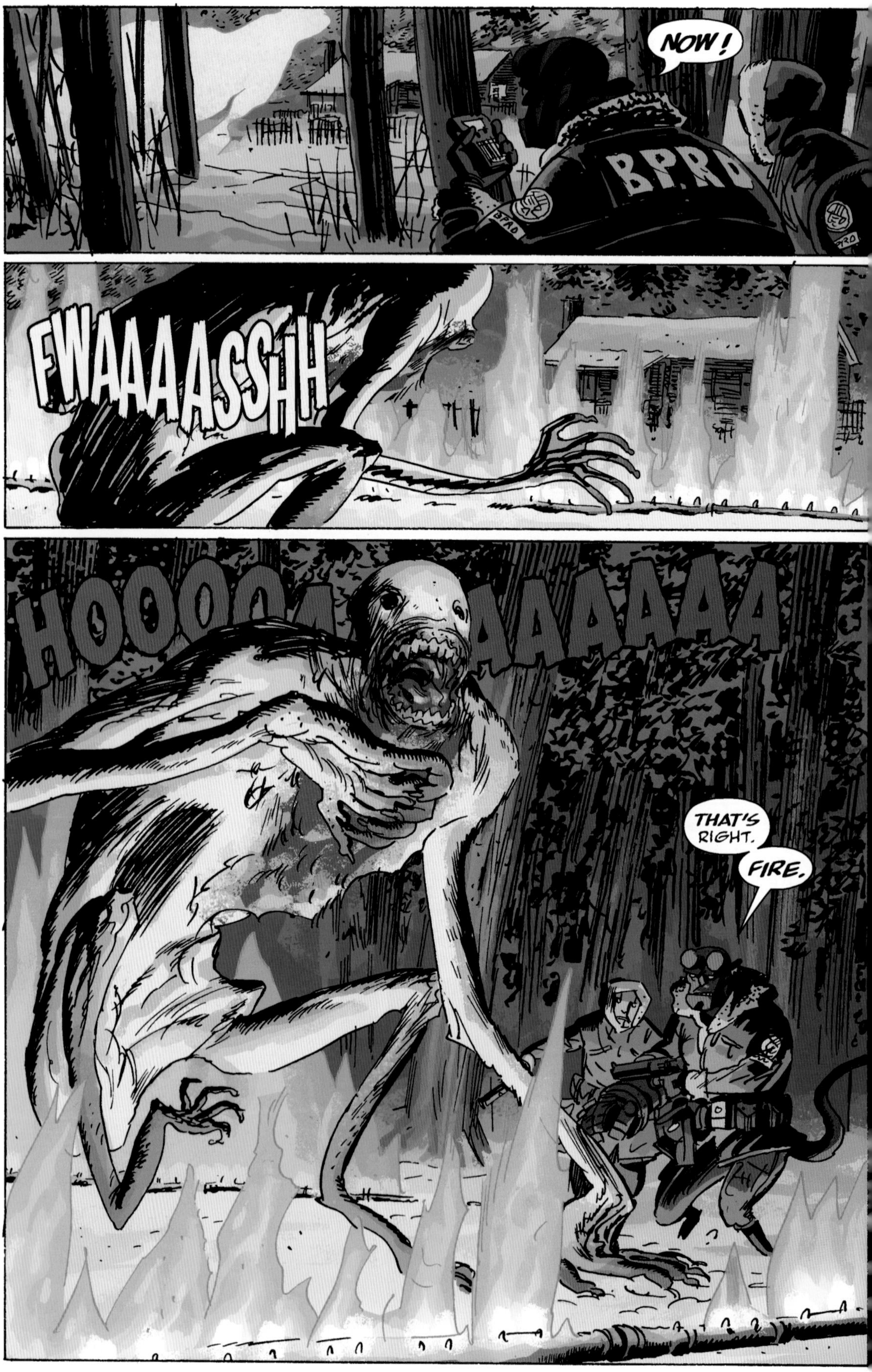
NOW!
B.P.R.D.
FWAAAASSHH
HOOOOAAAAAAA
THAT'S RIGHT.
FIRE.

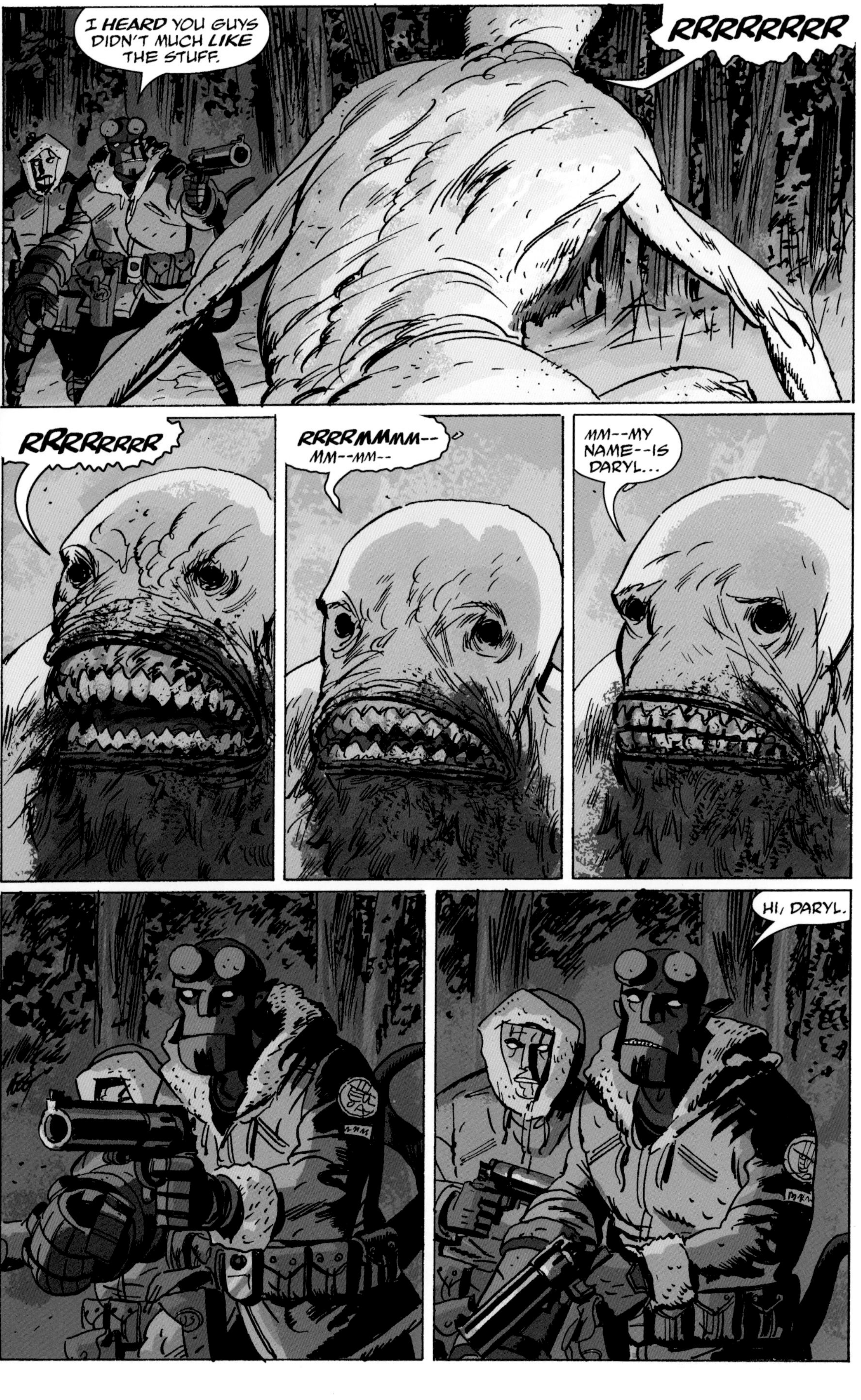

I HEARD YOU GUYS DIDN'T MUCH LIKE THE STUFF.
RRRRRRRR
RRRRRRRR
RRRRMMMM-- MM--MM--
MM--MY NAME--IS DARYL...
HI, DARYL.

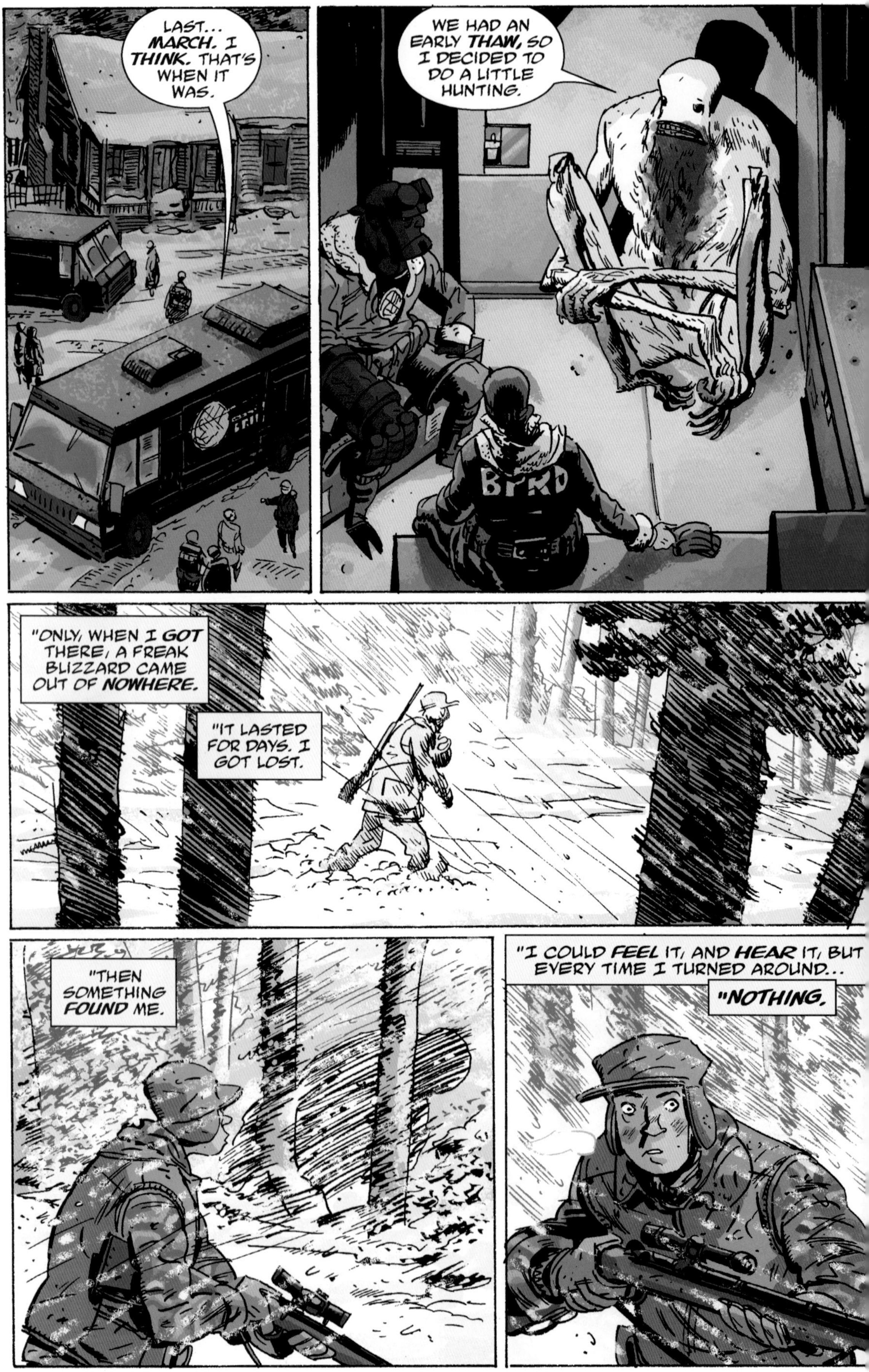
LAST... MARCH. I THINK. THAT'S WHEN IT WAS.
WE HAD AN EARLY THAW, SO I DECIDED TO DO A LITTLE HUNTING.
BPRD
"ONLY, WHEN I GOT THERE, A FREAK BLIZZARD CAME OUT OF NOWHERE.
"IT LASTED FOR DAYS. I GOT LOST.
"THEN SOMETHING FOUND ME.
"I COULD FEEL IT, AND HEAR IT, BUT EVERY TIME I TURNED AROUND...
"NOTHING.

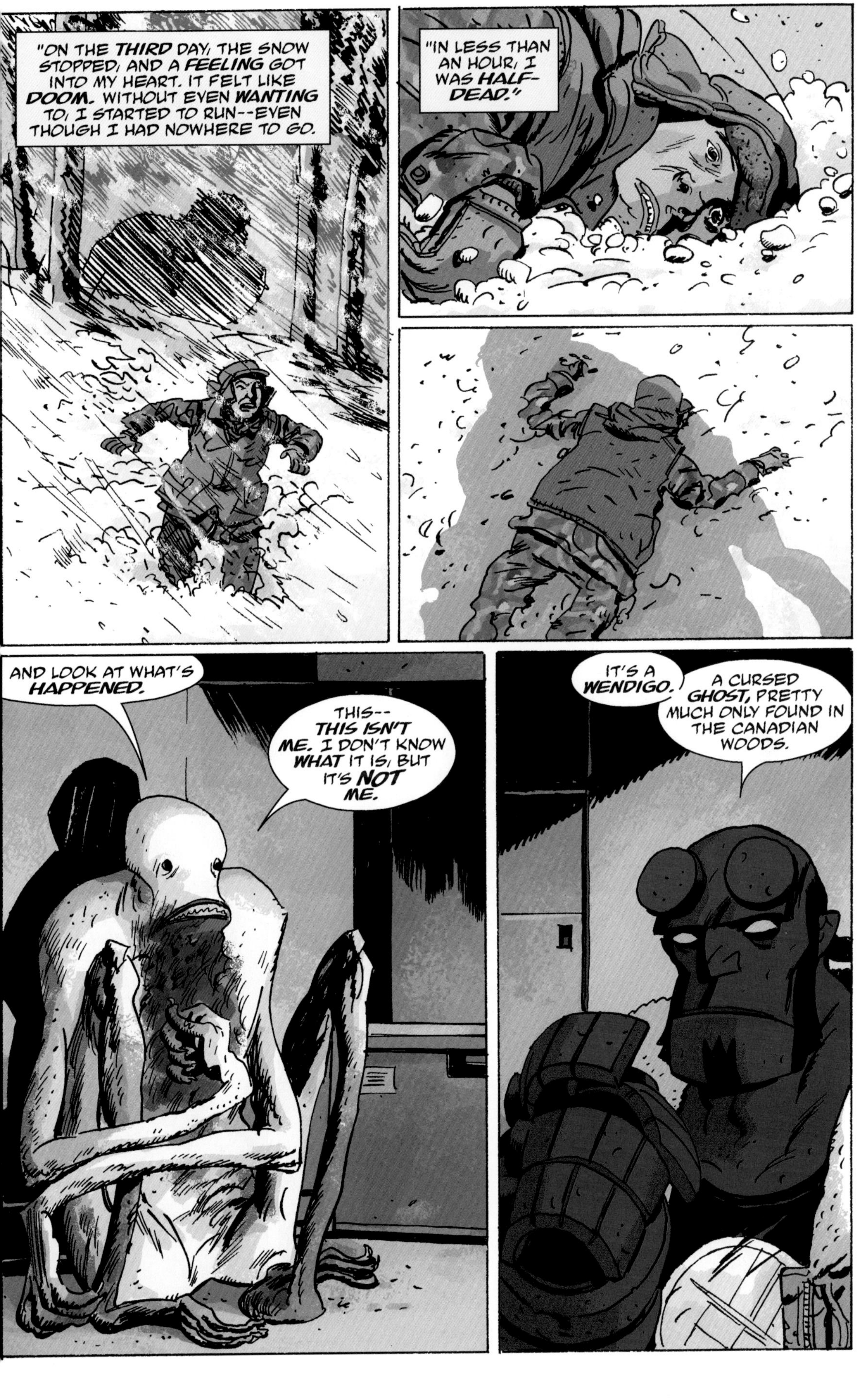
"ON THE THIRD DAY, THE SNOW STOPPED, AND A FEELING GOT INTO MY HEART. IT FELT LIKE DOOM. WITHOUT EVEN WANTING TO, I STARTED TO RUN--EVEN THOUGH I HAD NOWHERE TO GO.
"IN LESS THAN AN HOUR, I WAS HALF-DEAD."
AND LOOK AT WHAT'S HAPPENED.
THIS-- THIS ISN'T ME. I DON'T KNOW WHAT IT IS, BUT IT'S NOT ME.
IT'S A WENDIGO.
A CURSED GHOST, PRETTY MUCH ONLY FOUND IN THE CANADIAN WOODS.

THEY WANDER AROUND LOOKING FOR SOMEBODY, SOME *SOUL*, TO TAKE THEIR PLACE. THEY NEED TO STICK SOMEBODY *ELSE* WITH THE CURSE SO THEY CAN...

...REST IN PEACE.

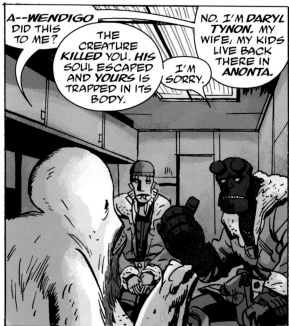

A--*WENDIGO* DID THIS TO ME?

THE CREATURE *KILLED* YOU. *HIS* SOUL ESCAPED AND *YOURS* IS TRAPPED IN ITS BODY.

NO. I'M *DARYL TYNON*. MY WIFE, MY KIDS LIVE BACK THERE IN *ANONTA*.

I'M SORRY.

ACTUALLY, THEY MOVED *OUT* OF THAT HOUSE LAST SUMMER.

WITH-OUT ME...?

THAT'S FOR THE *BEST*, DON'T YOU THINK?

Y-YOU SAID CURSED. WHY *ME*? I NEVER HURT ANYBODY IN MY LIFE.

I DON'T KNOW. BAD *LUCK*? THEY USUALLY TARGET *MURDERERS*.

SOME MYTHS LINK THEM TO CANNIBALISM, BUT--

I'M NO CANNIBAL! I'D REMEMBER THAT! I--

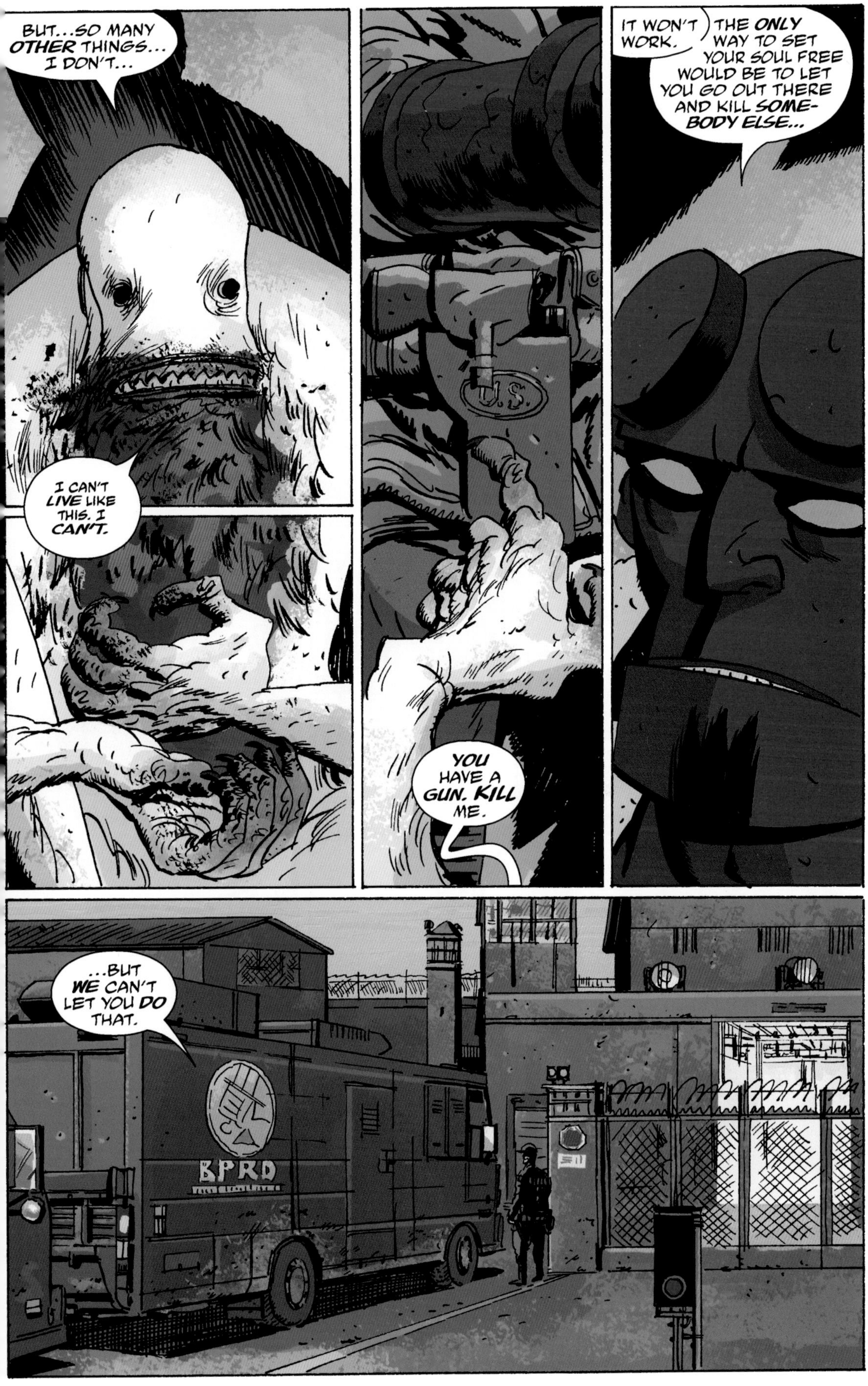

BUT...SO MANY OTHER THINGS... I DON'T...
I CAN'T LIVE LIKE THIS. I CAN'T.
YOU HAVE A GUN. KILL ME.
IT WON'T WORK.
THE ONLY WAY TO SET YOUR SOUL FREE WOULD BE TO LET YOU GO OUT THERE AND KILL SOME-BODY ELSE...
...BUT WE CAN'T LET YOU DO THAT.
BPRD
U.S.

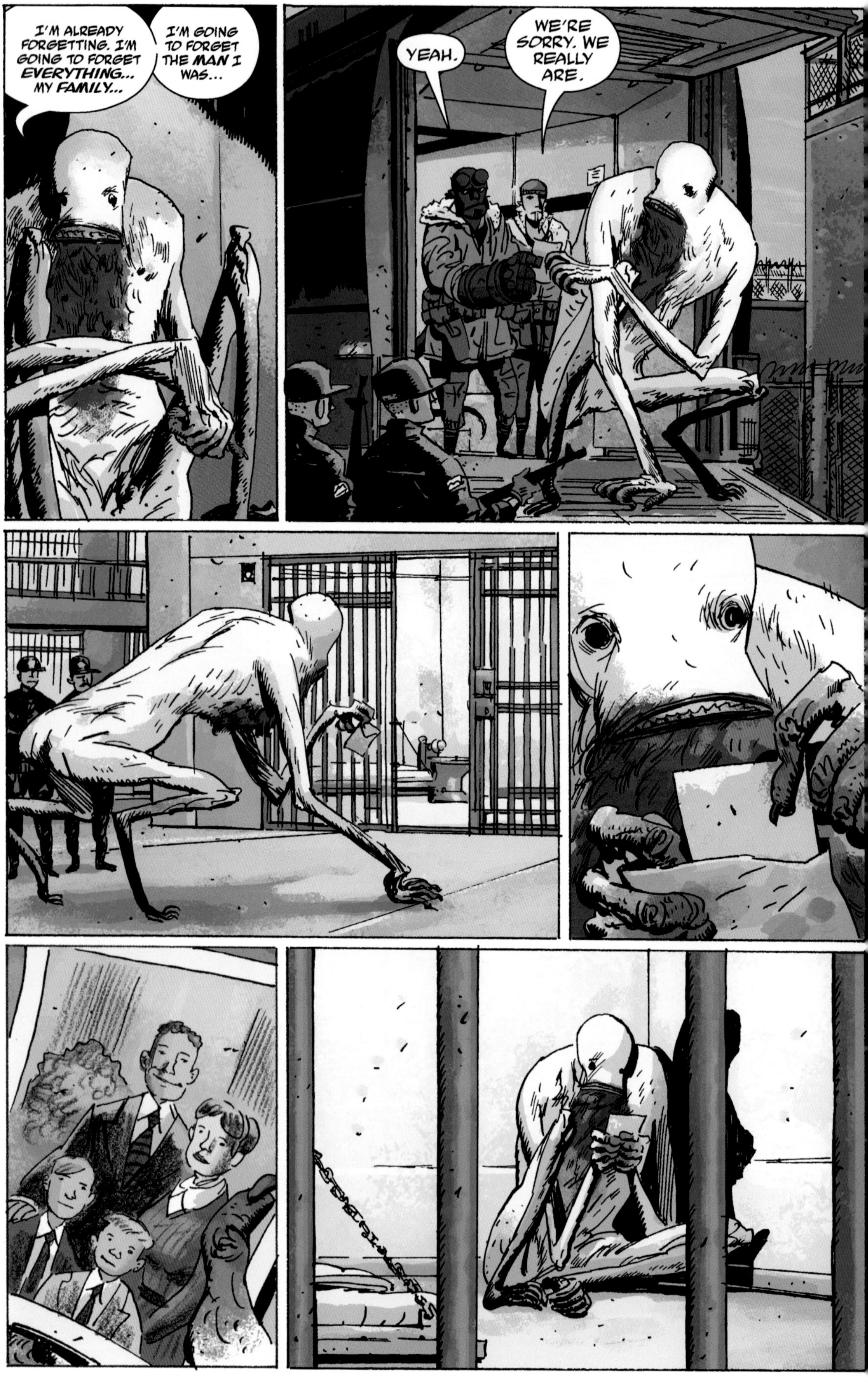
I'M ALREADY FORGETTING. I'M GOING TO FORGET EVERYTHING... MY FAMILY...
I'M GOING TO FORGET THE MAN I WAS...
YEAH.
WE'RE SORRY. WE REALLY ARE.

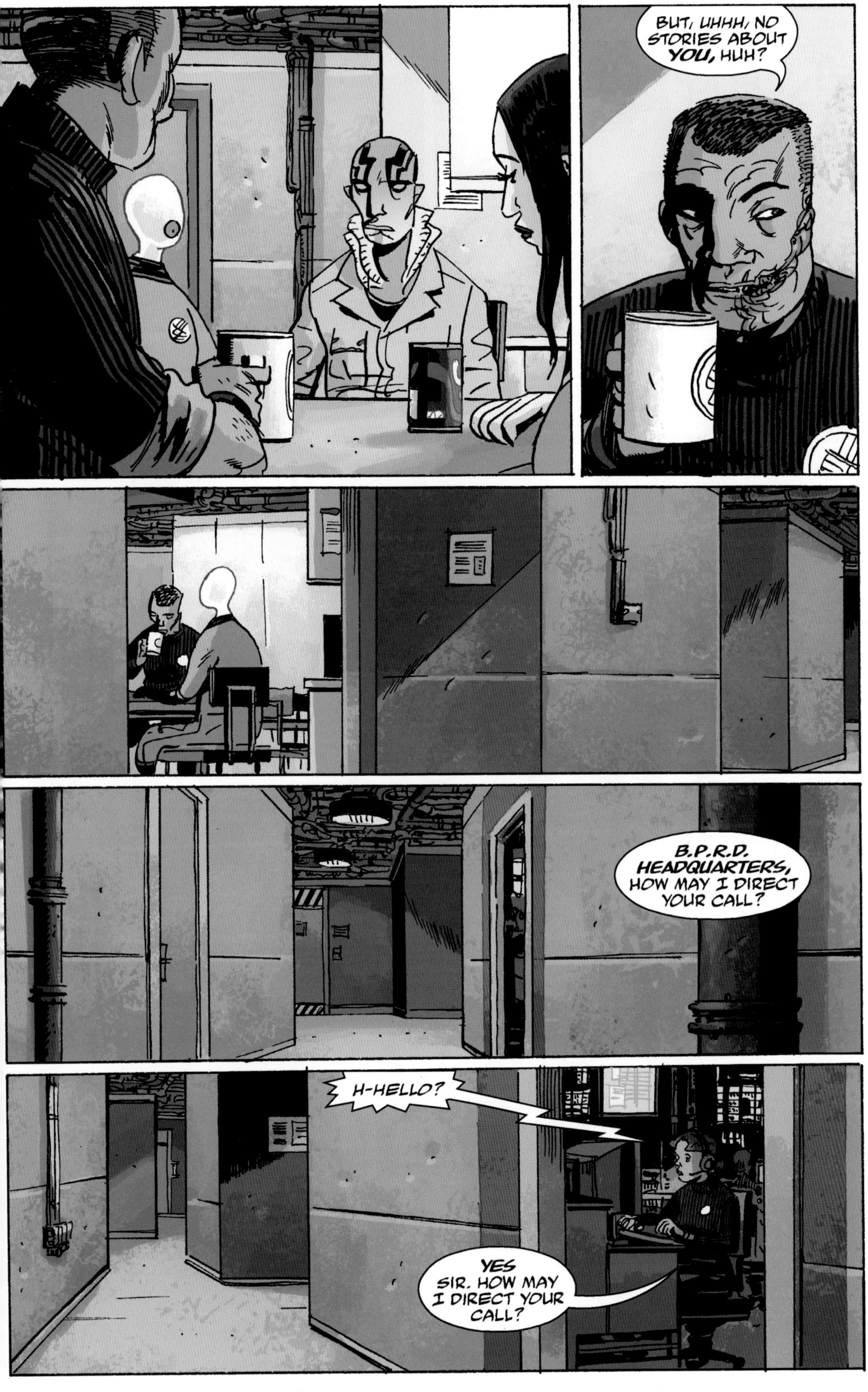
BUT, UHHH, NO STORIES ABOUT YOU, HUH?
B.P.R.D. HEADQUARTERS, HOW MAY I DIRECT YOUR CALL?
H-HELLO?
YES SIR. HOW MAY I DIRECT YOUR CALL?

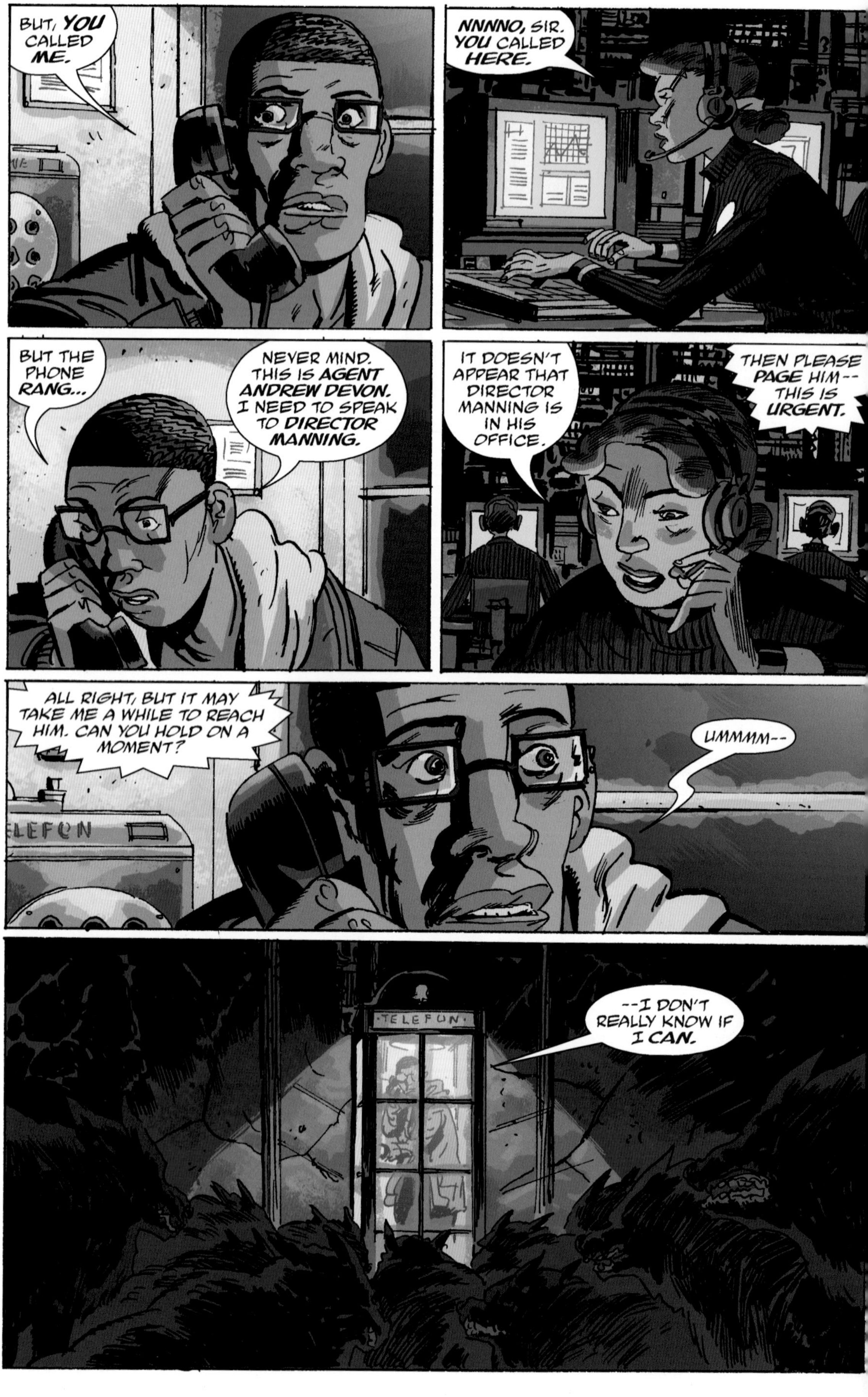

BUT, YOU CALLED ME.
NNNNO, SIR. YOU CALLED HERE.
BUT THE PHONE RANG...
NEVER MIND. THIS IS AGENT ANDREW DEVON. I NEED TO SPEAK TO DIRECTOR MANNING.
IT DOESN'T APPEAR THAT DIRECTOR MANNING IS IN HIS OFFICE.
THEN PLEASE PAGE HIM-- THIS IS URGENT.
ALL RIGHT, BUT IT MAY TAKE ME A WHILE TO REACH HIM. CAN YOU HOLD ON A MOMENT?
UMMMM--
TELEFON
--I DON'T REALLY KNOW IF I CAN.
TELEFON

CHAPTER FIVE

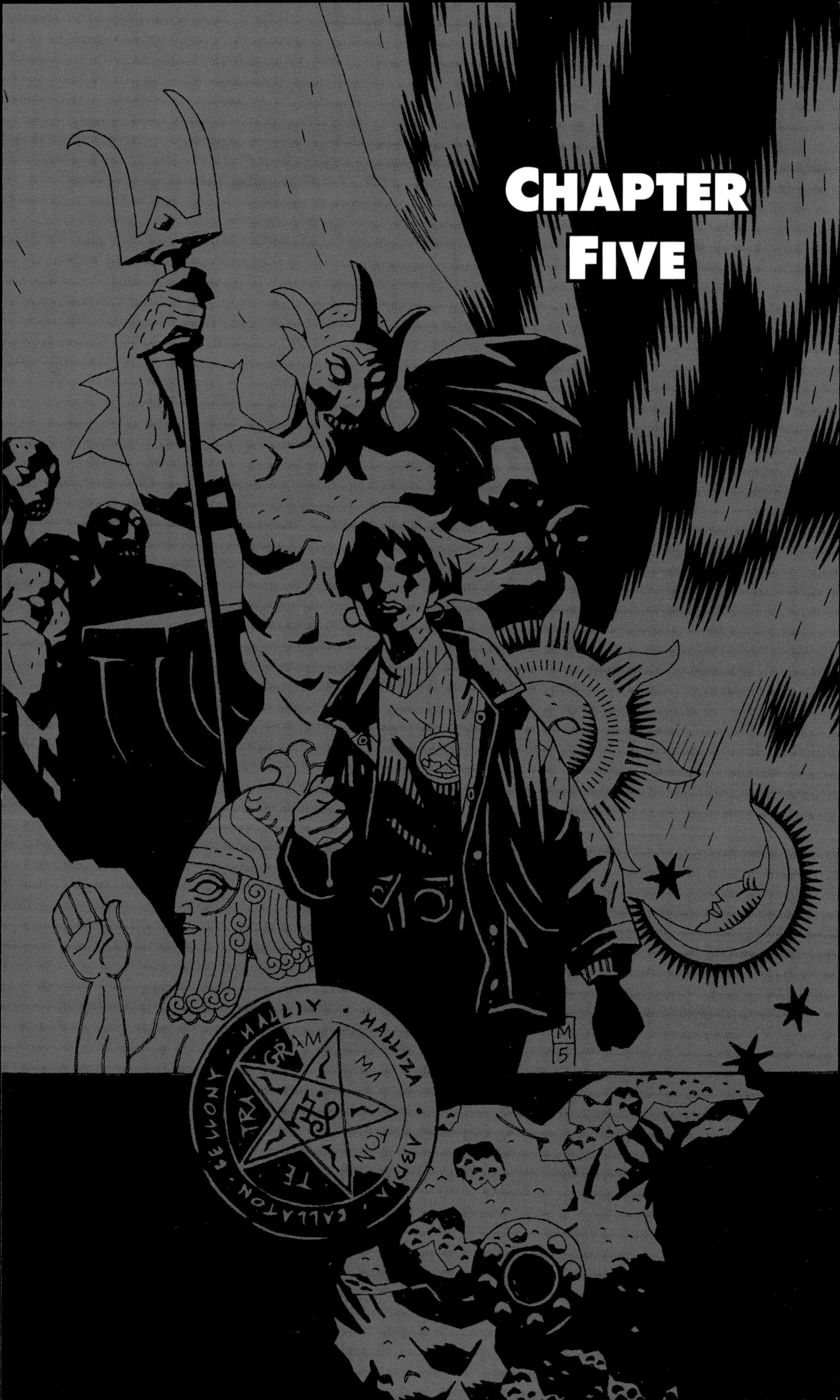

MALLIY · HALLIZA · ABDIA · GALLATON · BELLONY
TE TRA GRAM MA TON

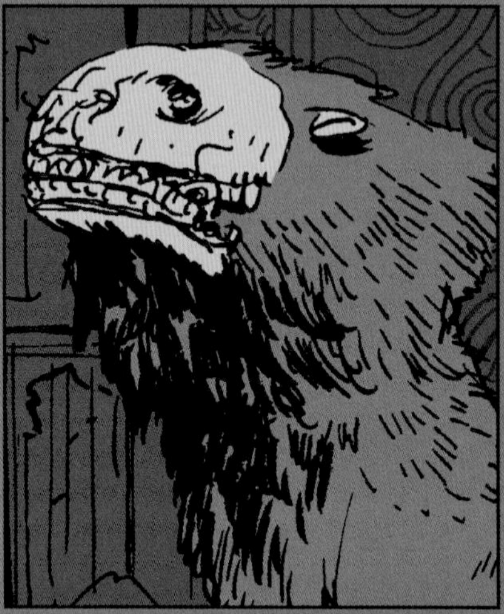

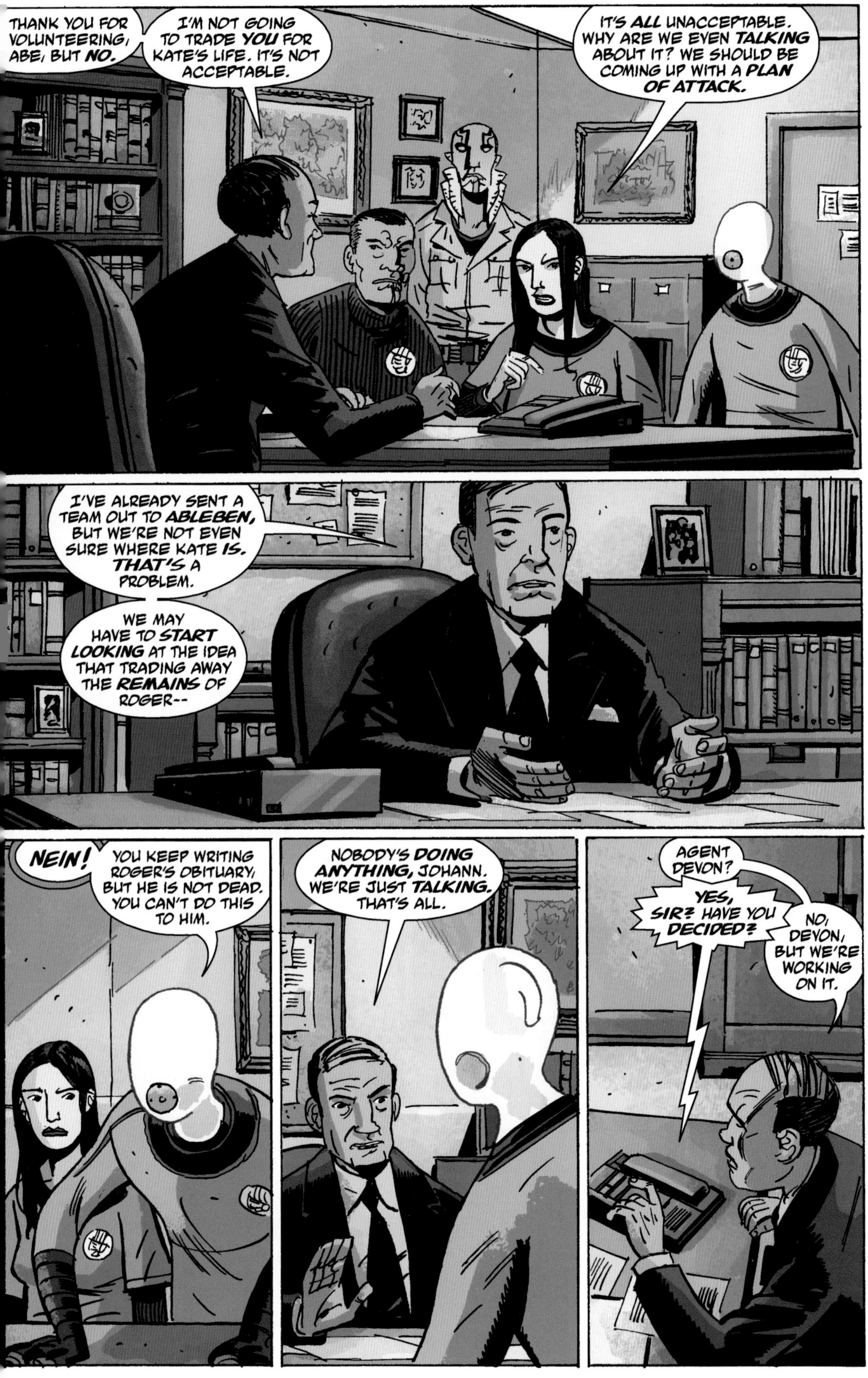
THANK YOU FOR VOLUNTEERING, ABE, BUT NO.
I'M NOT GOING TO TRADE YOU FOR KATE'S LIFE. IT'S NOT ACCEPTABLE.
IT'S ALL UNACCEPTABLE. WHY ARE WE EVEN TALKING ABOUT IT? WE SHOULD BE COMING UP WITH A PLAN OF ATTACK.
I'VE ALREADY SENT A TEAM OUT TO ABLEBEN, BUT WE'RE NOT EVEN SURE WHERE KATE IS. THAT'S A PROBLEM.
WE MAY HAVE TO START LOOKING AT THE IDEA THAT TRADING AWAY THE REMAINS OF ROGER--
NEIN!
YOU KEEP WRITING ROGER'S OBITUARY, BUT HE IS NOT DEAD. YOU CAN'T DO THIS TO HIM.
NOBODY'S DOING ANYTHING, JOHANN. WE'RE JUST TALKING. THAT'S ALL.
AGENT DEVON?
YES, SIR? HAVE YOU DECIDED?
NO, DEVON, BUT WE'RE WORKING ON IT.

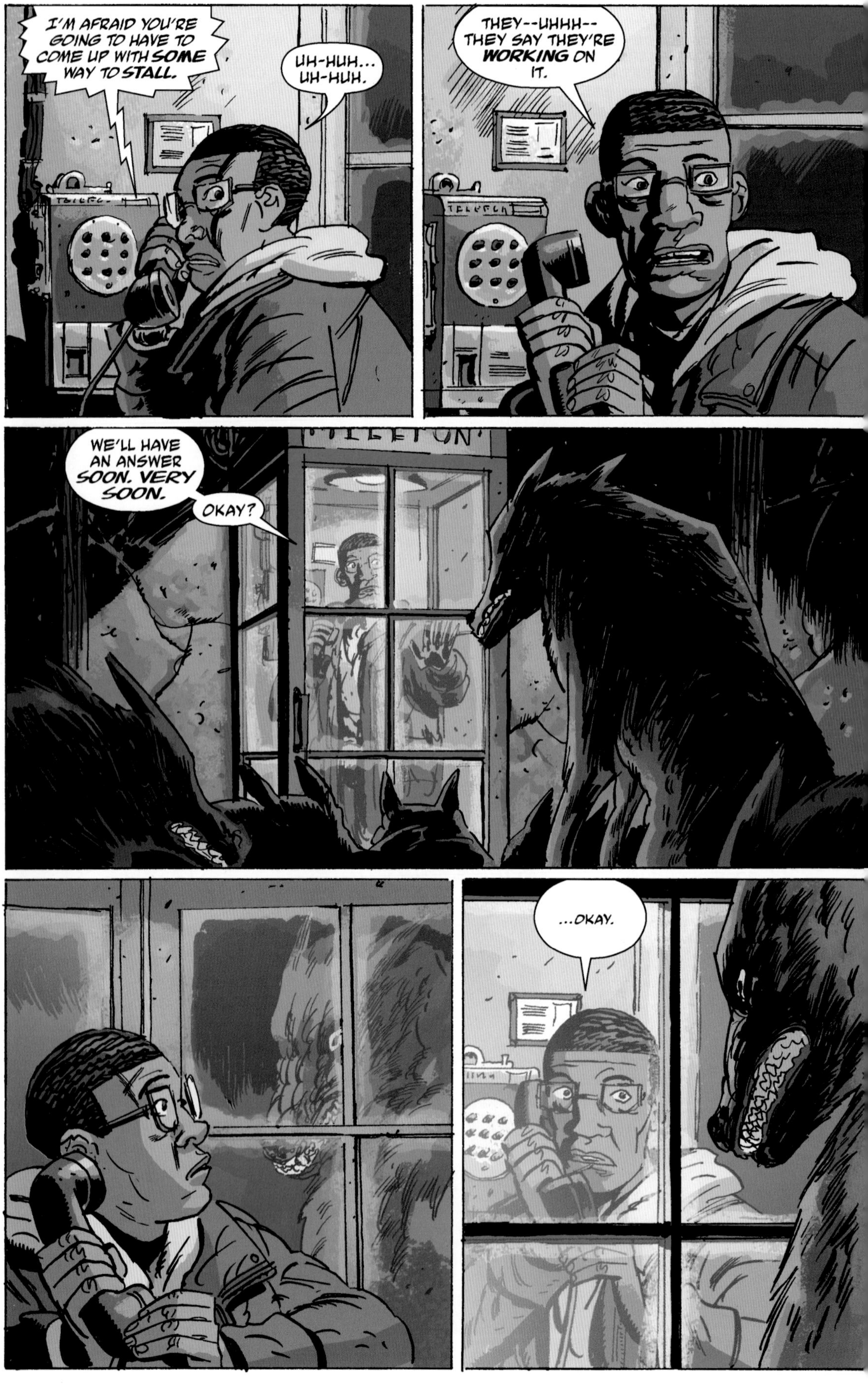
I'M AFRAID YOU'RE GOING TO HAVE TO COME UP WITH SOME WAY TO STALL.
UH-HUH... UH-HUH.
THEY--UHHH-- THEY SAY THEY'RE WORKING ON IT.
WE'LL HAVE AN ANSWER SOON. VERY SOON.
OKAY?
...OKAY.

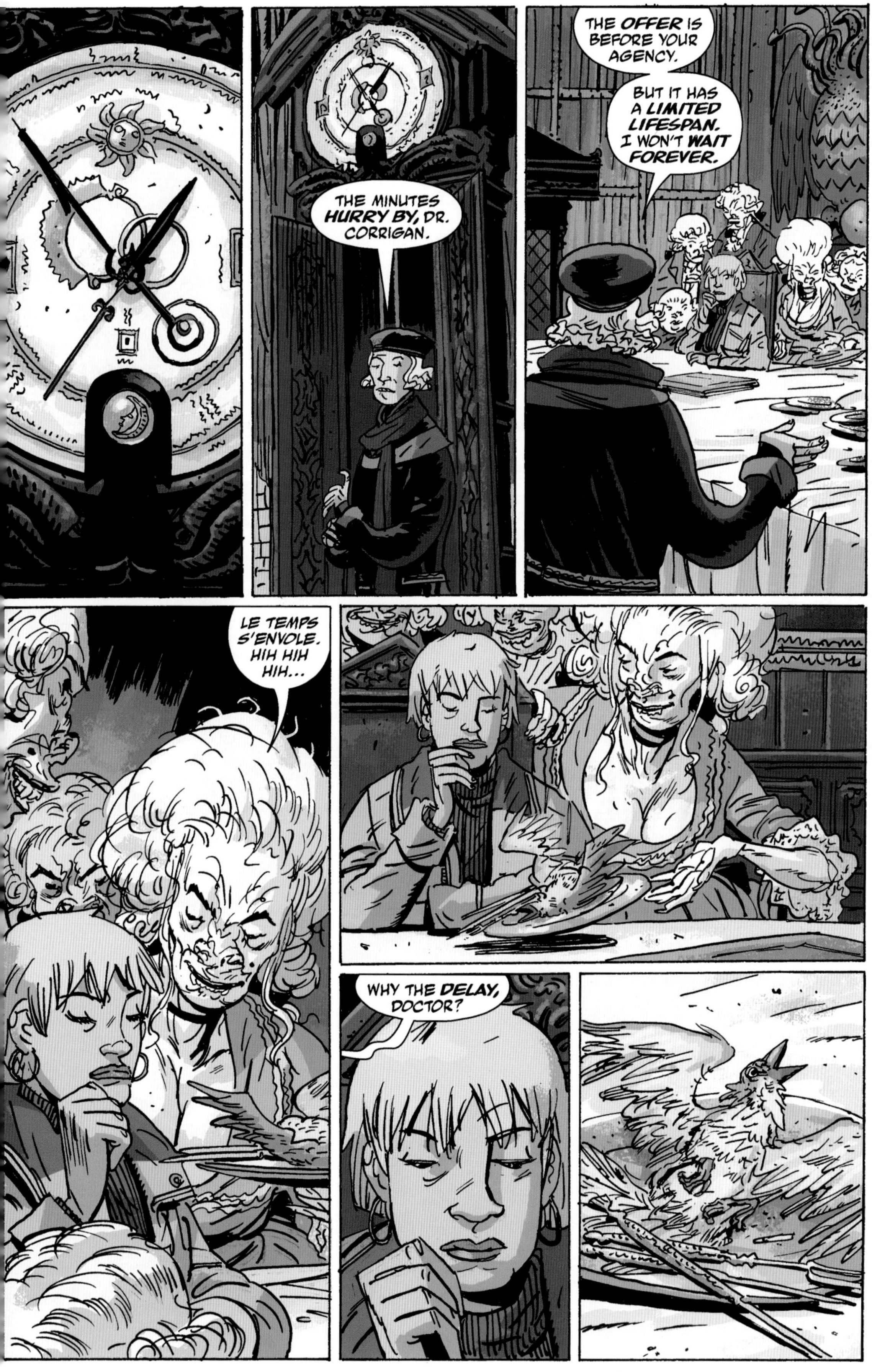
THE MINUTES HURRY BY, DR. CORRIGAN.
THE OFFER IS BEFORE YOUR AGENCY.
BUT IT HAS A LIMITED LIFESPAN. I WON'T WAIT FOREVER.
LE TEMPS S'ENVOLE. HIH HIH HIH...
WHY THE DELAY, DOCTOR?

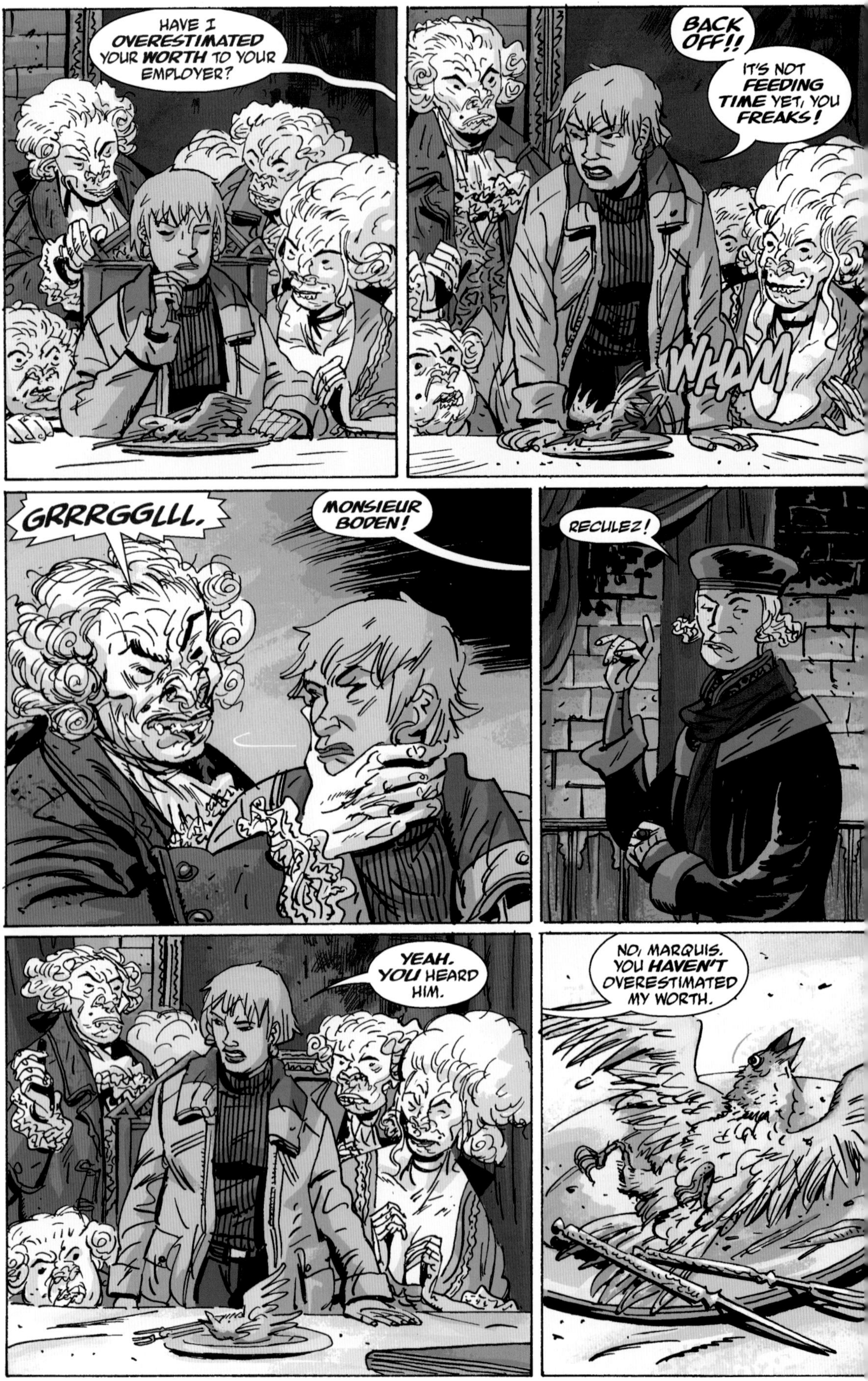
HAVE I OVERESTIMATED YOUR WORTH TO YOUR EMPLOYER?
BACK OFF!!
IT'S NOT FEEDING TIME YET, YOU FREAKS!
WHAM
GRRRGGLLL.
MONSIEUR BODEN!
RECULEZ!
YEAH. YOU HEARD HIM.
NO, MARQUIS. YOU HAVEN'T OVERESTIMATED MY WORTH.

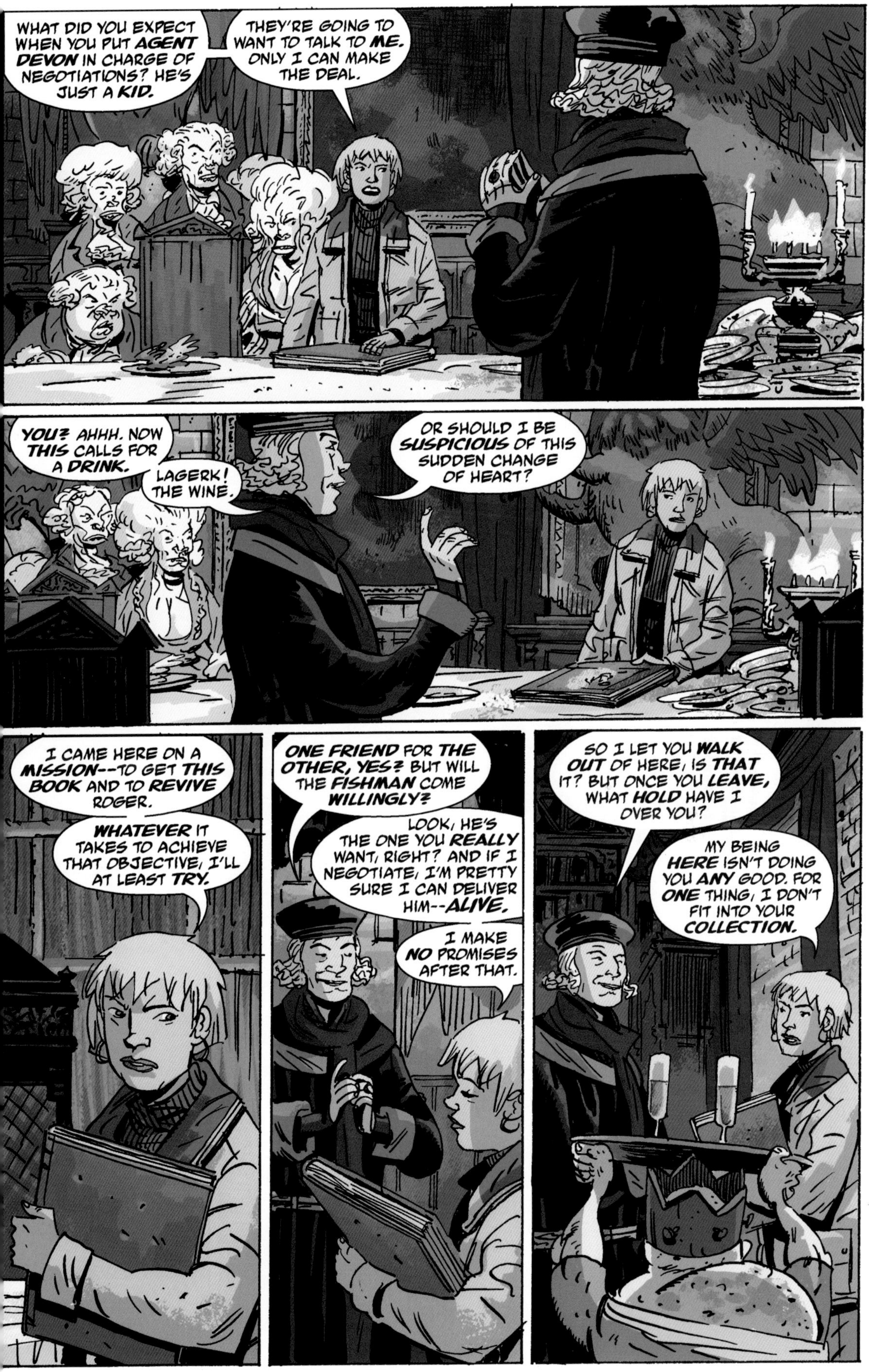

WHAT DID YOU EXPECT WHEN YOU PUT AGENT DEVON IN CHARGE OF NEGOTIATIONS? HE'S JUST A KID.
THEY'RE GOING TO WANT TO TALK TO ME. ONLY I CAN MAKE THE DEAL.
YOU? AHHH. NOW THIS CALLS FOR A DRINK.
LAGERK! THE WINE.
OR SHOULD I BE SUSPICIOUS OF THIS SUDDEN CHANGE OF HEART?
I CAME HERE ON A MISSION--TO GET THIS BOOK AND TO REVIVE ROGER.
WHATEVER IT TAKES TO ACHIEVE THAT OBJECTIVE, I'LL AT LEAST TRY.
ONE FRIEND FOR THE OTHER, YES? BUT WILL THE FISHMAN COME WILLINGLY?
LOOK, HE'S THE ONE YOU REALLY WANT, RIGHT? AND IF I NEGOTIATE, I'M PRETTY SURE I CAN DELIVER HIM--ALIVE.
I MAKE NO PROMISES AFTER THAT.
SO I LET YOU WALK OUT OF HERE, IS THAT IT? BUT ONCE YOU LEAVE, WHAT HOLD HAVE I OVER YOU?
MY BEING HERE ISN'T DOING YOU ANY GOOD. FOR ONE THING, I DON'T FIT INTO YOUR COLLECTION.

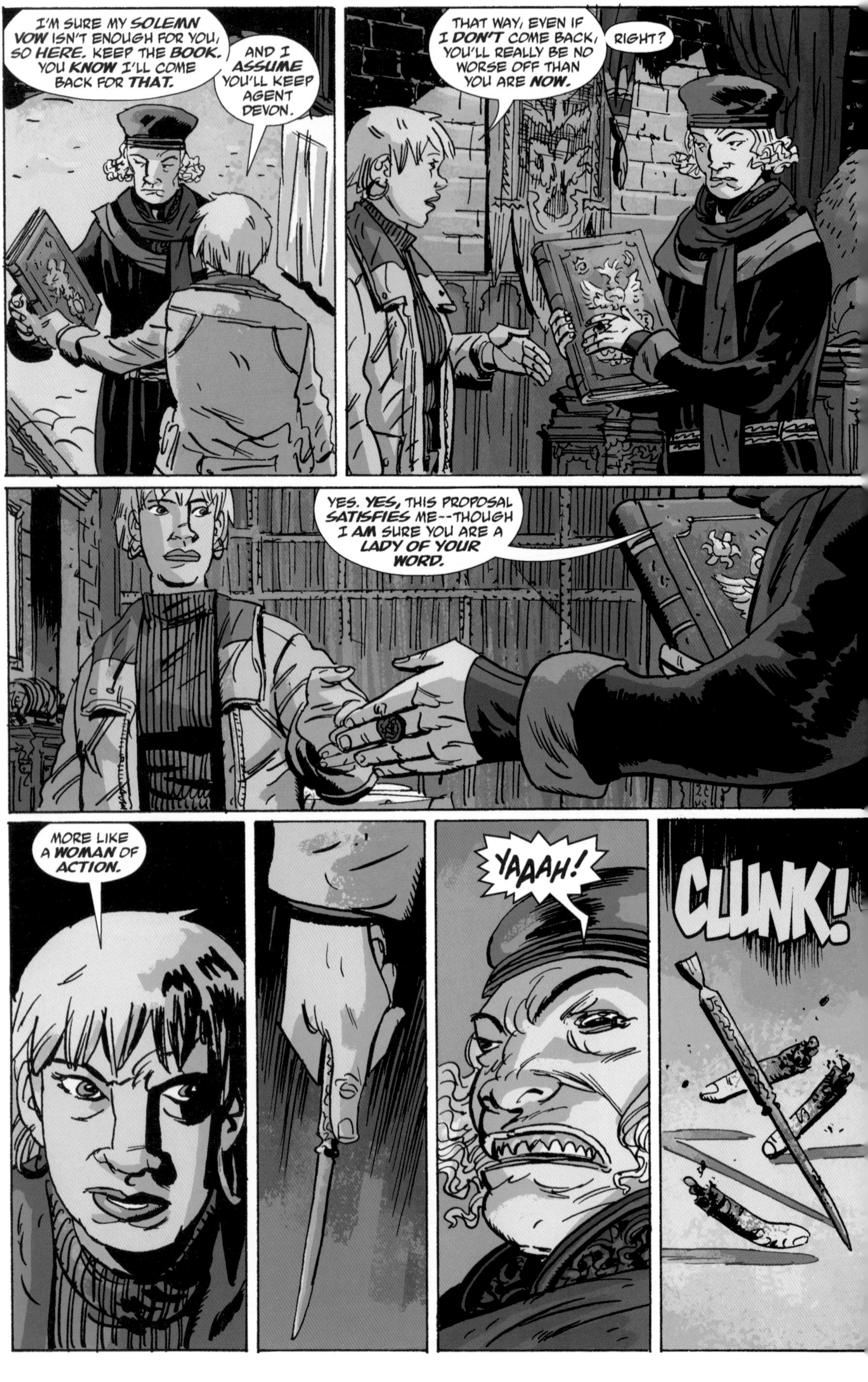
I'M SURE MY SOLEMN VOW ISN'T ENOUGH FOR YOU, SO HERE. KEEP THE BOOK. YOU KNOW I'LL COME BACK FOR THAT.
AND I ASSUME YOU'LL KEEP AGENT DEVON.
THAT WAY, EVEN IF I DON'T COME BACK, YOU'LL REALLY BE NO WORSE OFF THAN YOU ARE NOW.
RIGHT?
YES. YES, THIS PROPOSAL SATISFIES ME--THOUGH I AM SURE YOU ARE A LADY OF YOUR WORD.
MORE LIKE A WOMAN OF ACTION.
YAAAH!
CLUNK!

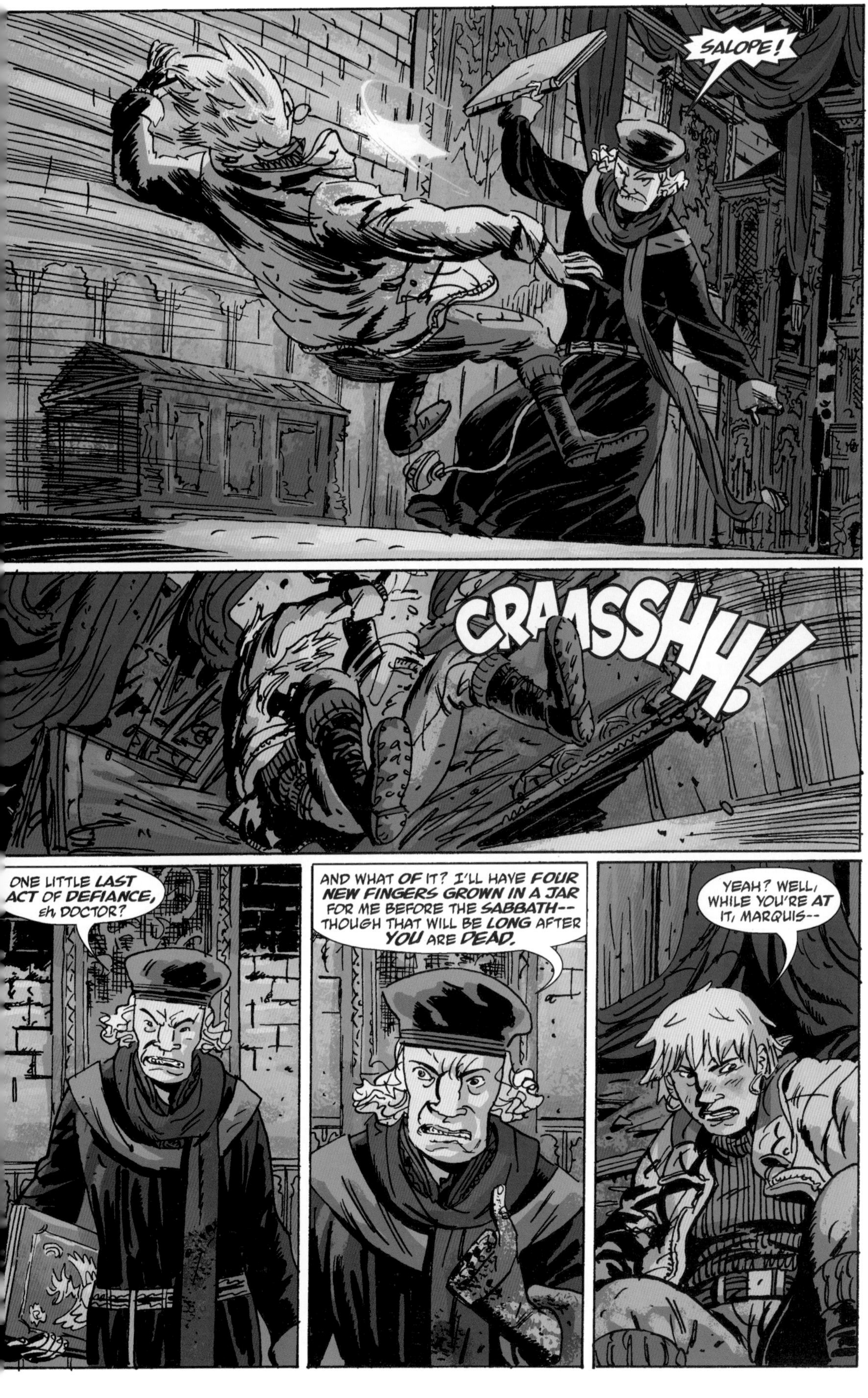
SALOPE!
CRAASSHH!
ONE LITTLE LAST ACT OF DEFIANCE, eh, DOCTOR?
AND WHAT OF IT? I'LL HAVE FOUR NEW FINGERS GROWN IN A JAR FOR ME BEFORE THE SABBATH-- THOUGH THAT WILL BE LONG AFTER YOU ARE DEAD.
YEAH? WELL, WHILE YOU'RE AT IT, MARQUIS--

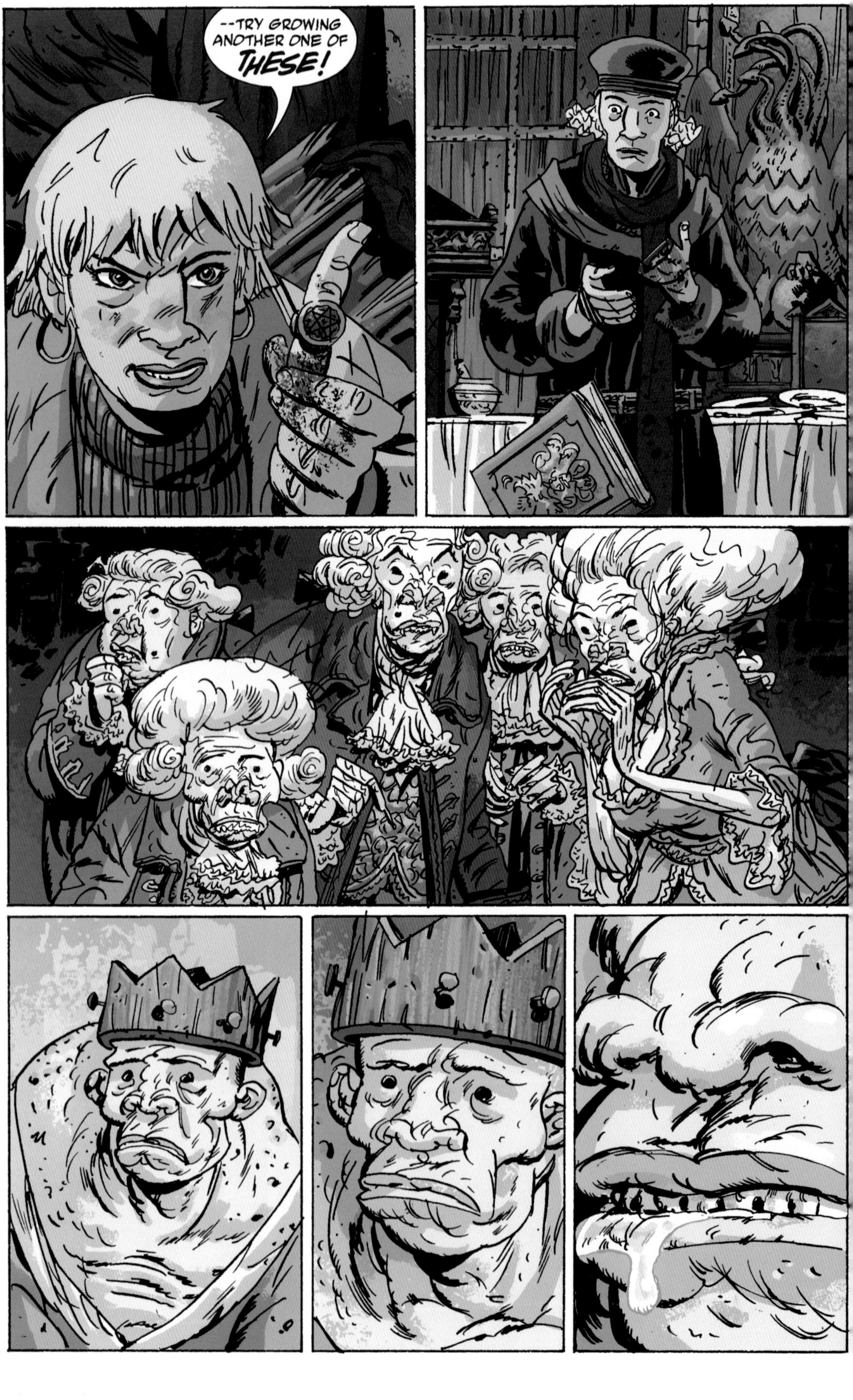
--TRY GROWING ANOTHER ONE OF THESE!

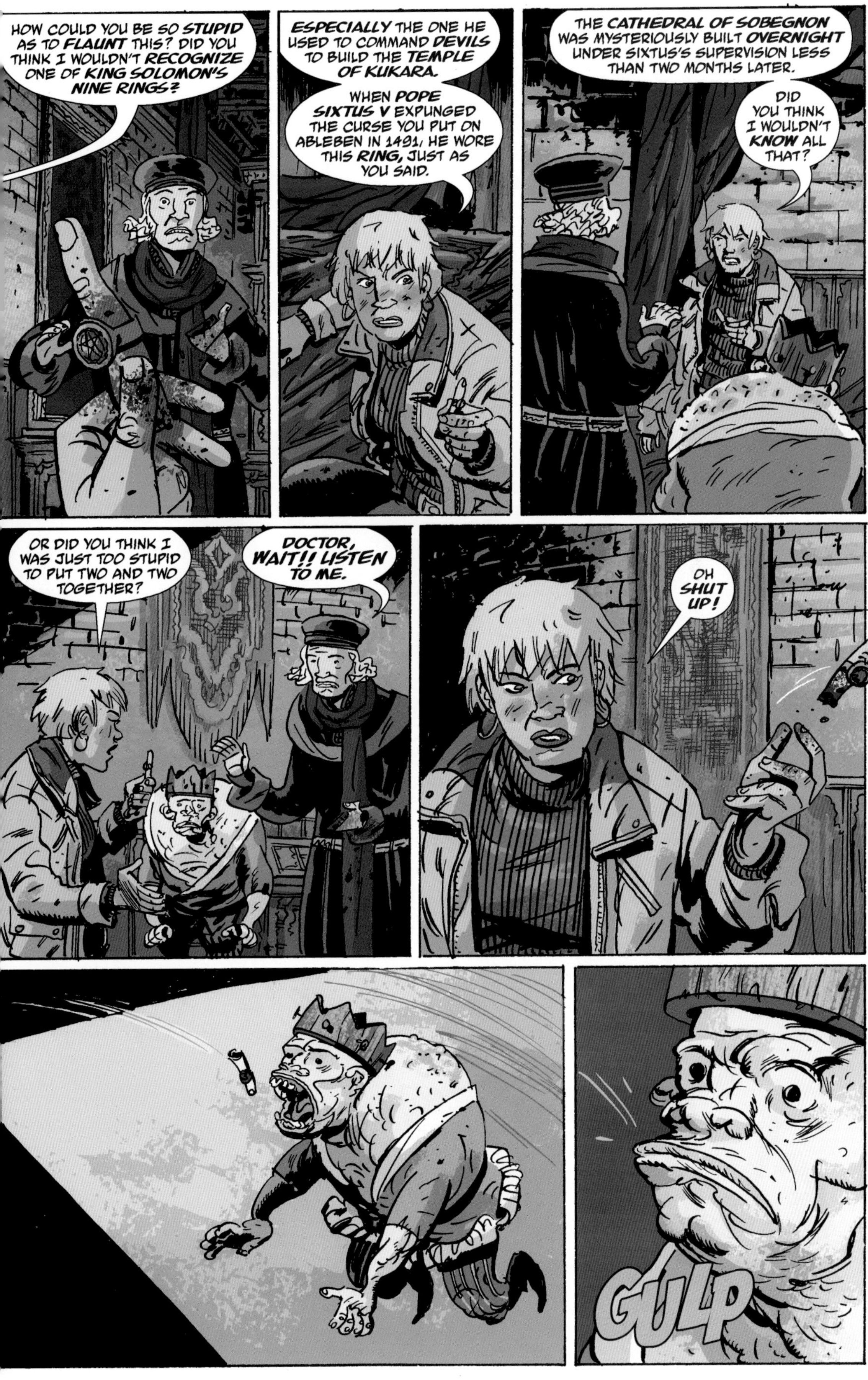
HOW COULD YOU BE SO STUPID AS TO FLAUNT THIS? DID YOU THINK I WOULDN'T RECOGNIZE ONE OF KING SOLOMON'S NINE RINGS?
ESPECIALLY THE ONE HE USED TO COMMAND DEVILS TO BUILD THE TEMPLE OF KUKARA.
WHEN POPE SIXTUS V EXPUNGED THE CURSE YOU PUT ON ABLEBEN IN 1491, HE WORE THIS RING, JUST AS YOU SAID.
THE CATHEDRAL OF SOBEGNON WAS MYSTERIOUSLY BUILT OVERNIGHT UNDER SIXTUS'S SUPERVISION LESS THAN TWO MONTHS LATER.
DID YOU THINK I WOULDN'T KNOW ALL THAT?
OR DID YOU THINK I WAS JUST TOO STUPID TO PUT TWO AND TWO TOGETHER?
DOCTOR, WAIT!! LISTEN TO ME.
OH SHUT UP!
GULP

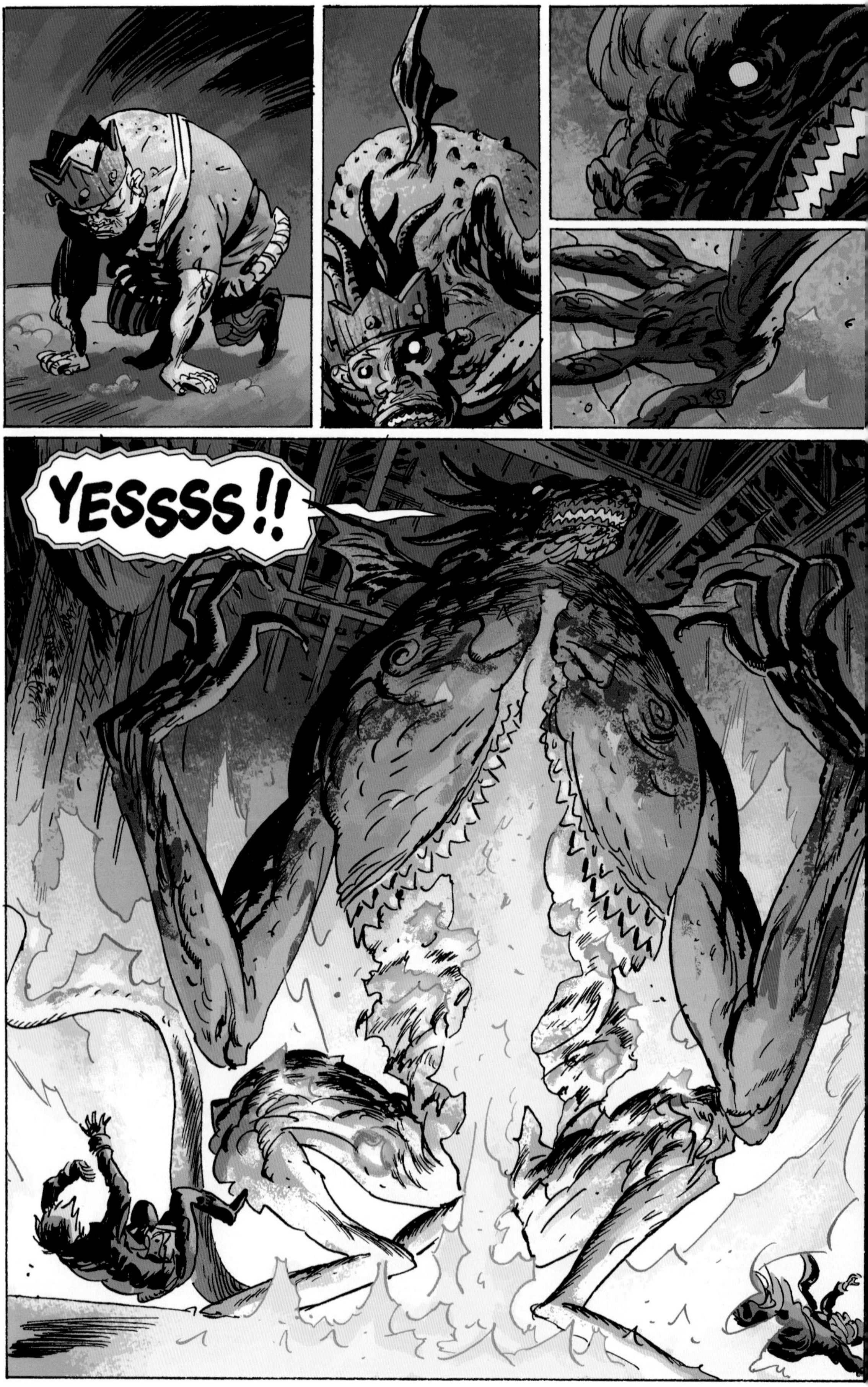
YESSSS!!

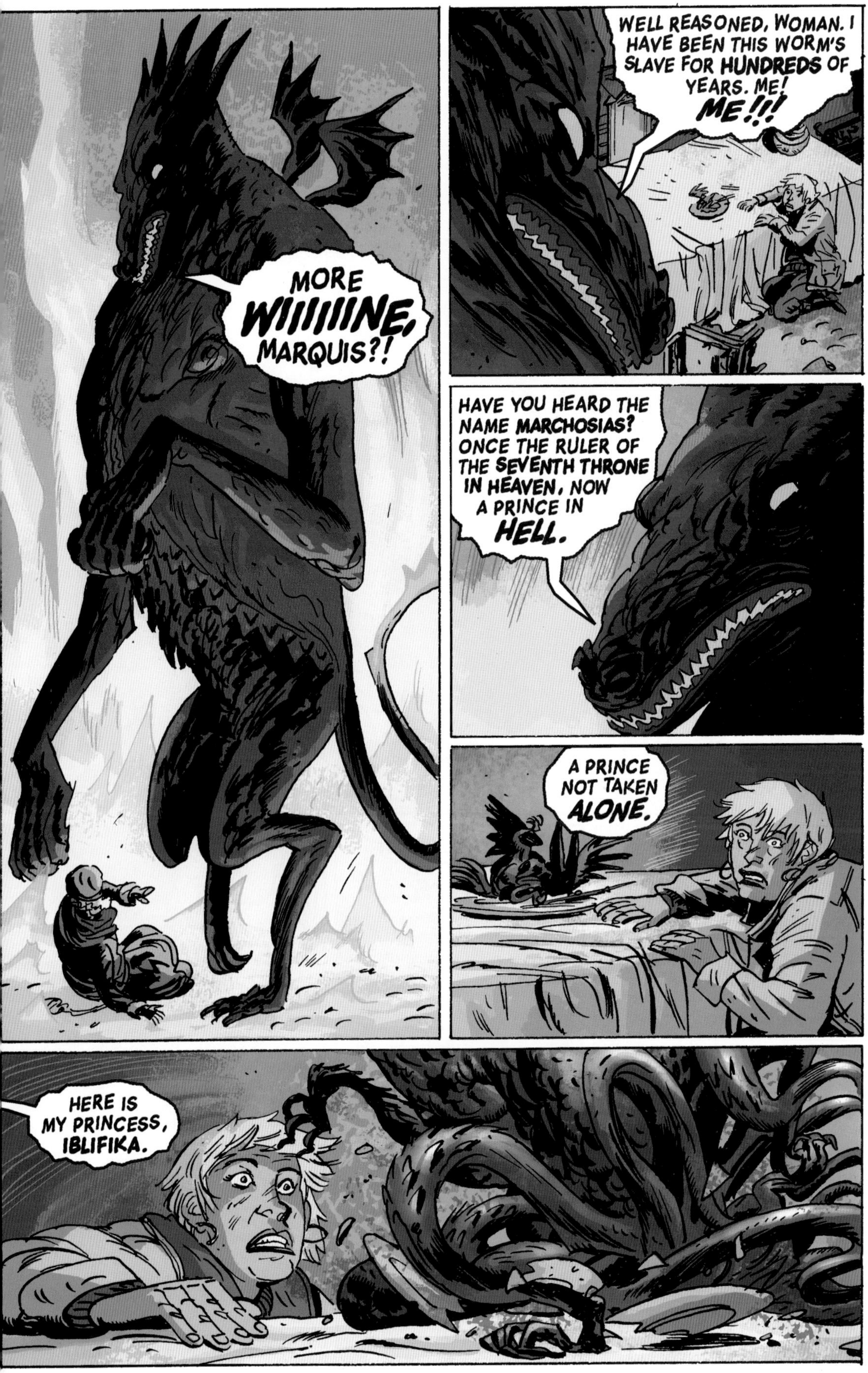
MORE WIIIIIINE, MARQUIS?!
WELL REASONED, WOMAN. I HAVE BEEN THIS WORM'S SLAVE FOR HUNDREDS OF YEARS. ME! ME!!!
HAVE YOU HEARD THE NAME MARCHOSIAS? ONCE THE RULER OF THE SEVENTH THRONE IN HEAVEN, NOW A PRINCE IN HELL.
A PRINCE NOT TAKEN ALONE.
HERE IS MY PRINCESS, IBLIFIKA.

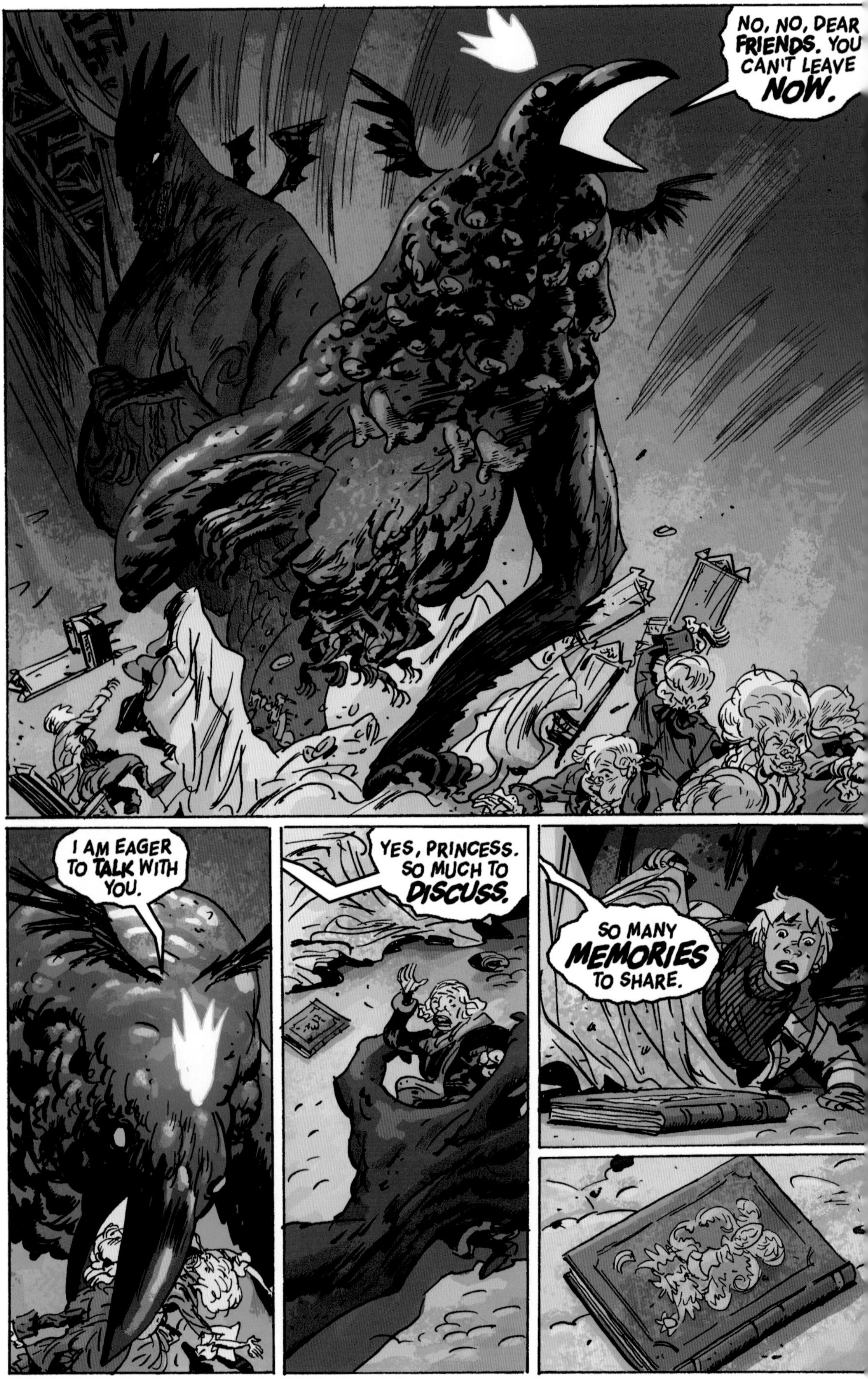
NO, NO, DEAR FRIENDS. YOU CAN'T LEAVE NOW.
I AM EAGER TO TALK WITH YOU.
YES, PRINCESS. SO MUCH TO DISCUSS.
SO MANY MEMORIES TO SHARE.

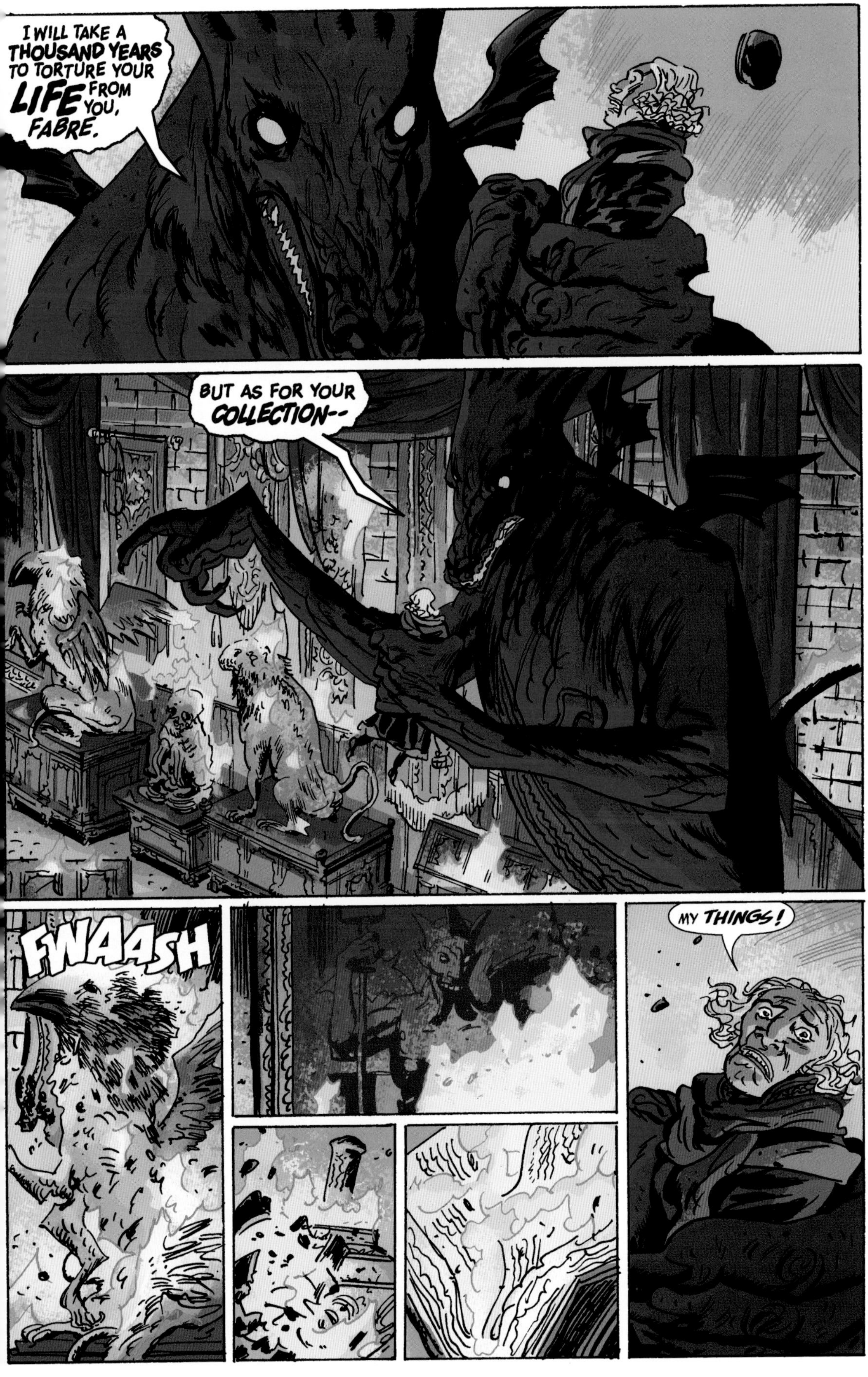
I WILL TAKE A THOUSAND YEARS TO TORTURE YOUR LIFE FROM YOU, FABRE.
BUT AS FOR YOUR COLLECTION--
FWAASH
MY THINGS!

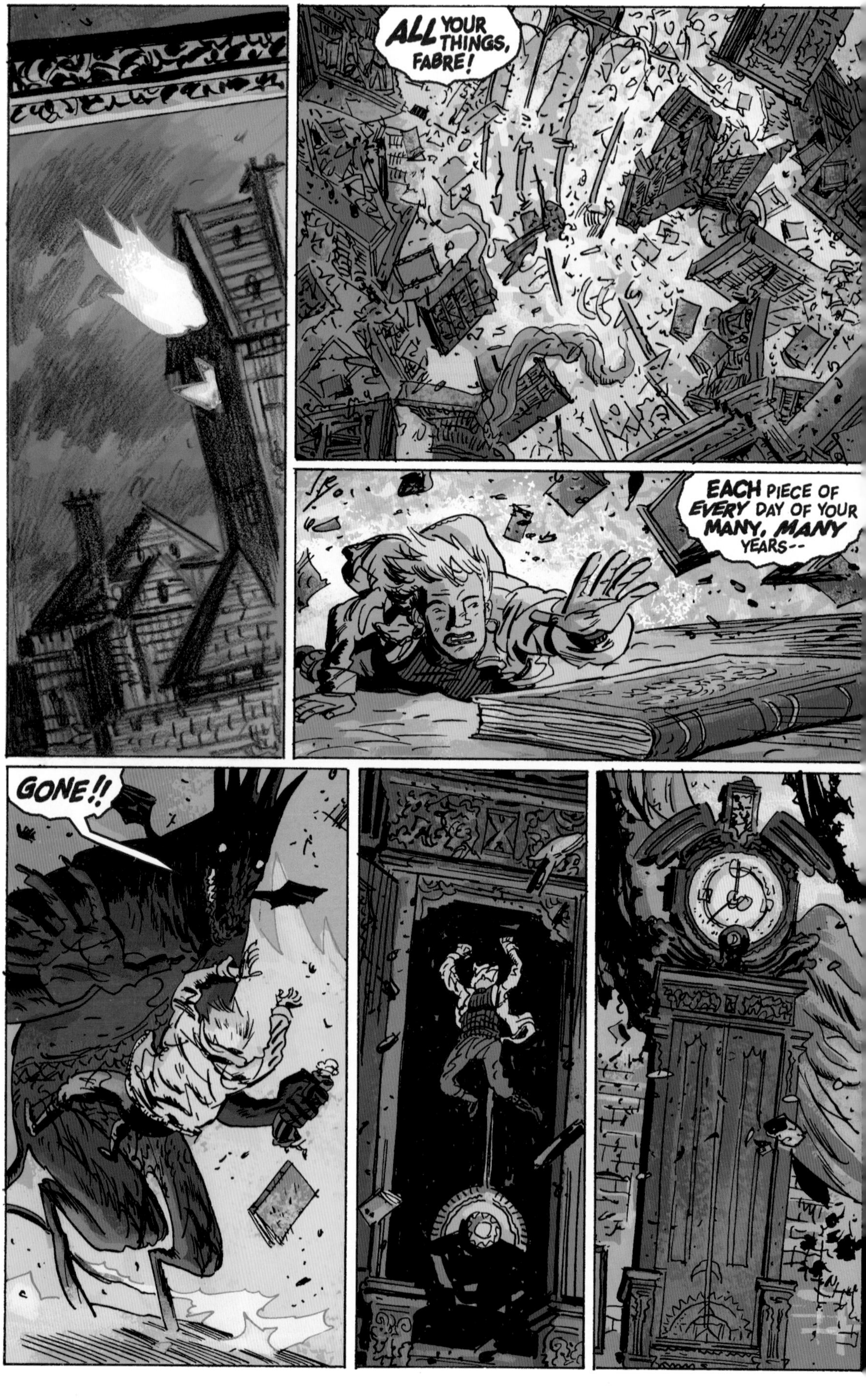
ALL YOUR THINGS, FABRE!
EACH PIECE OF EVERY DAY OF YOUR MANY, MANY YEARS--
GONE!!

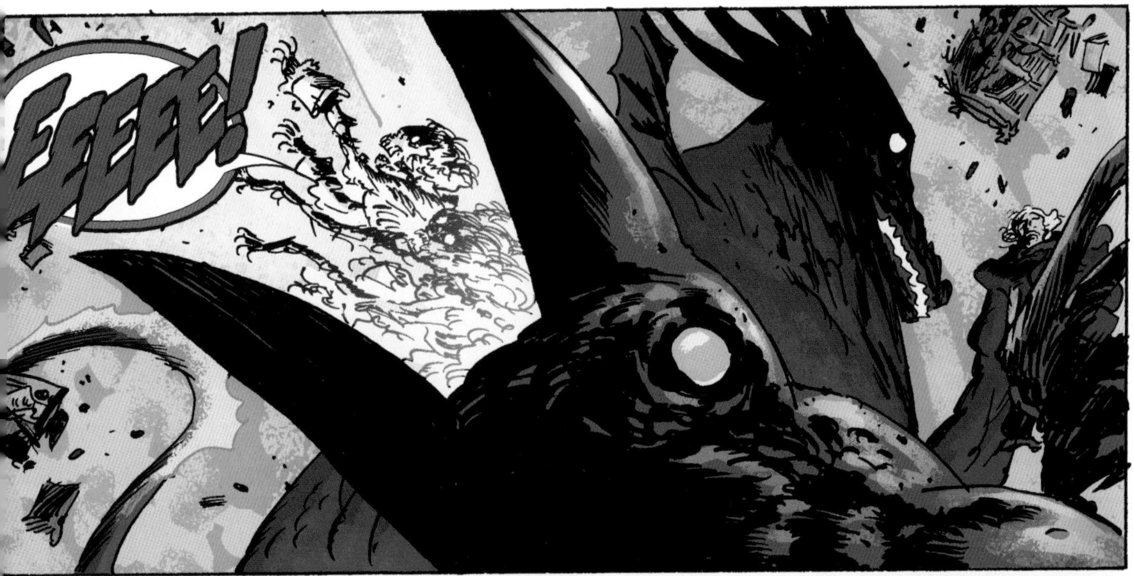
EEEEE!

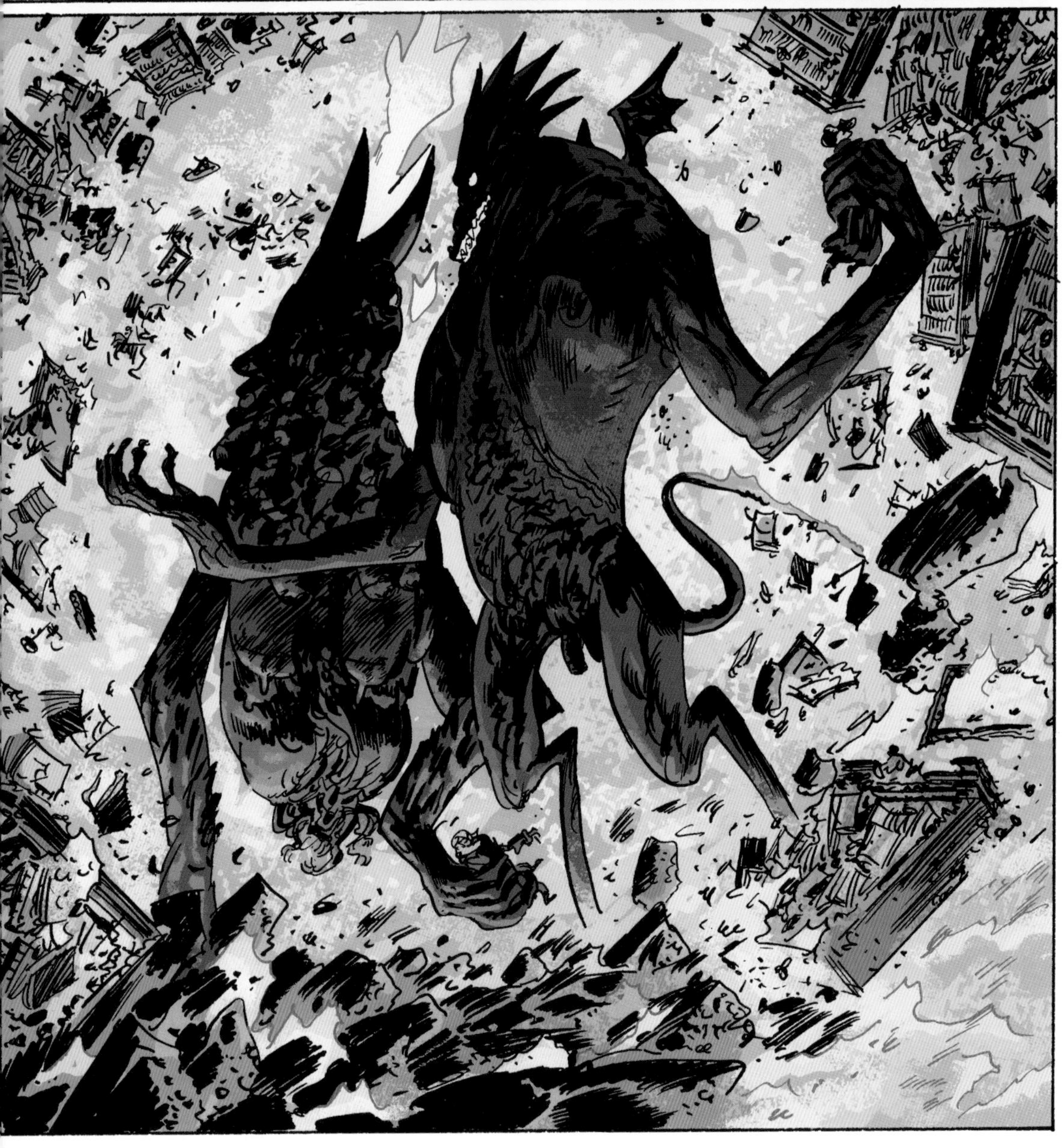

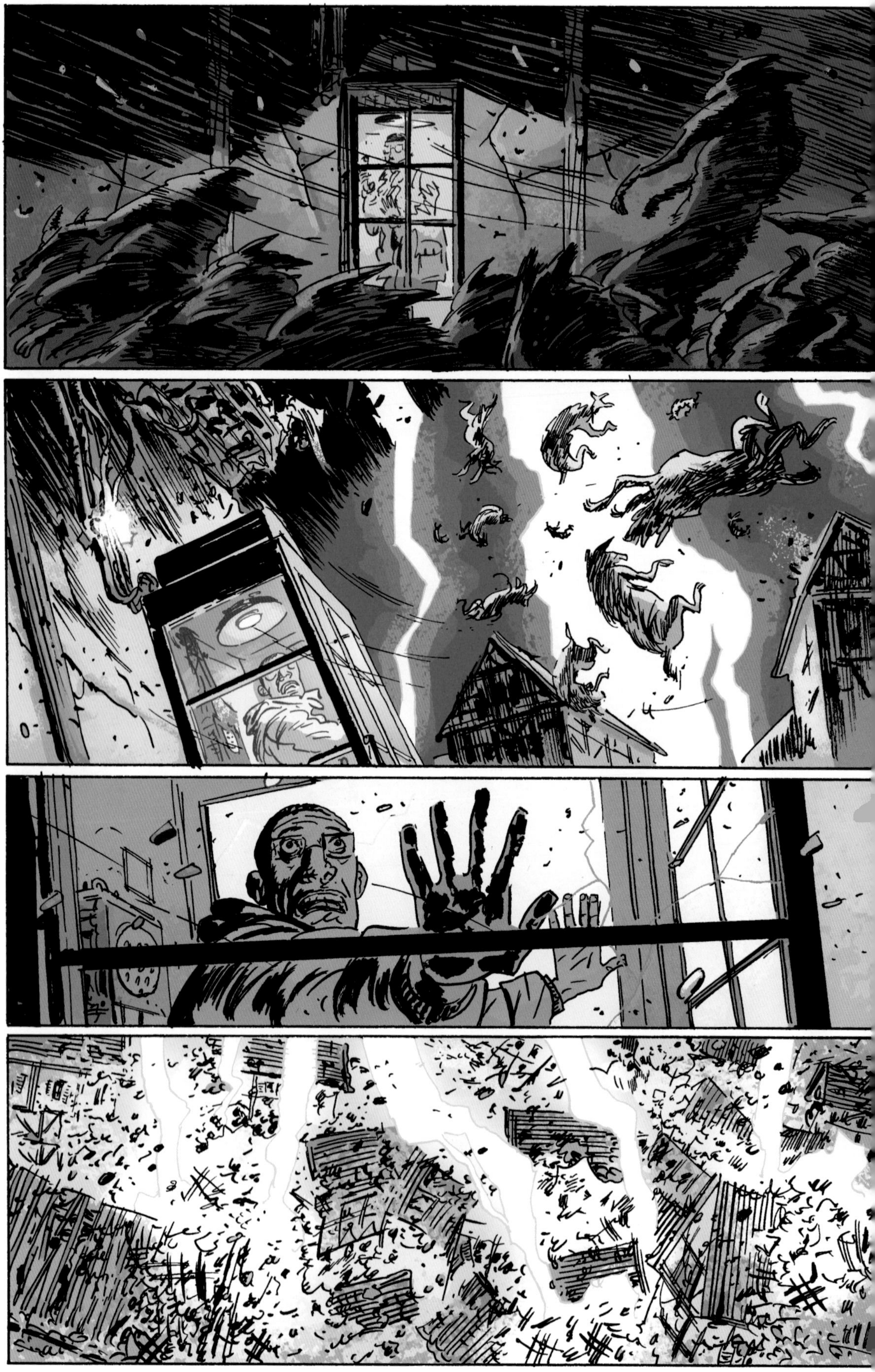

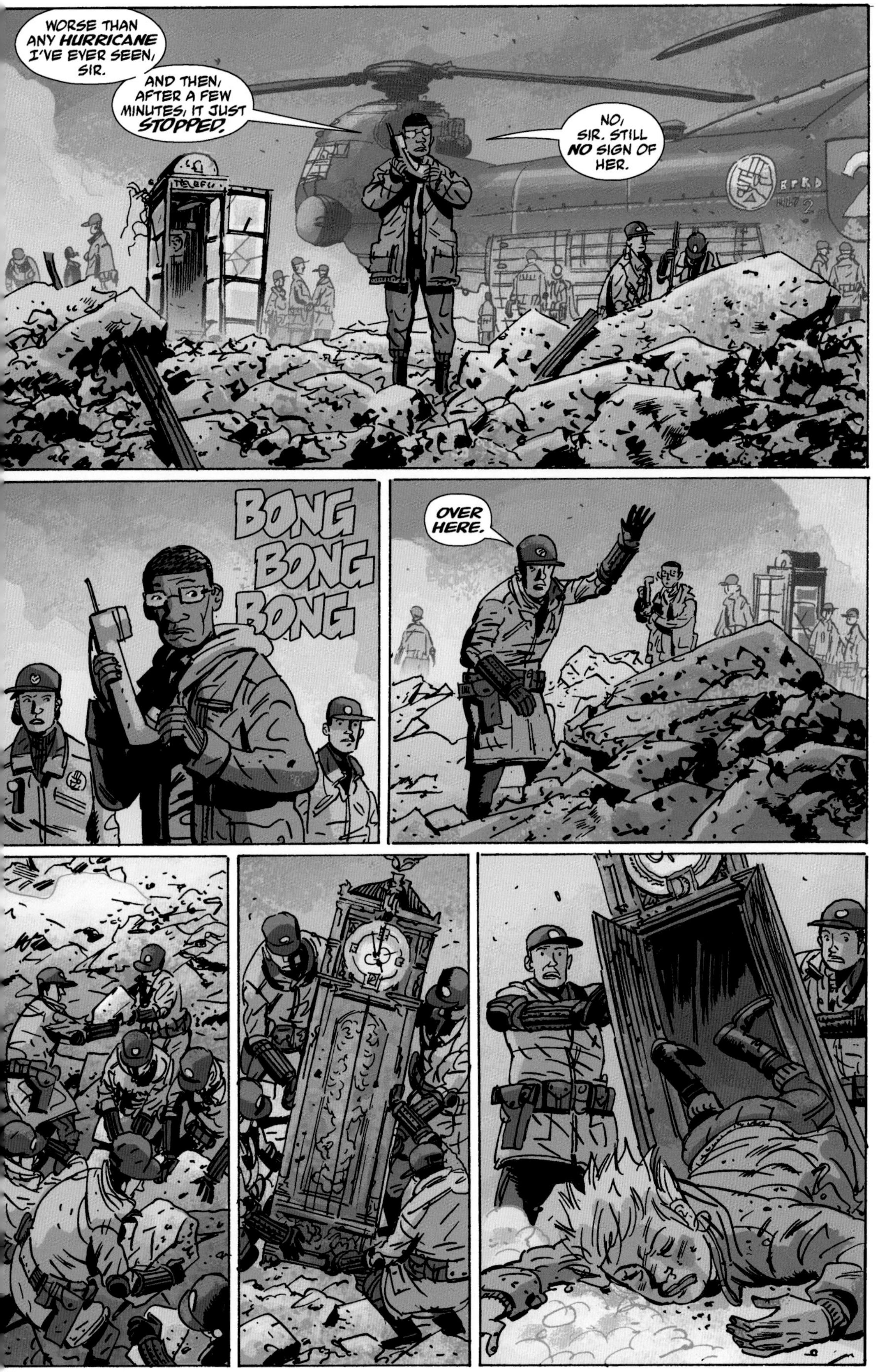

WORSE THAN ANY HURRICANE I'VE EVER SEEN, SIR.
AND THEN, AFTER A FEW MINUTES, IT JUST STOPPED.
NO, SIR. STILL NO SIGN OF HER.
B.P.R.D.
BONG BONG BONG
OVER HERE.

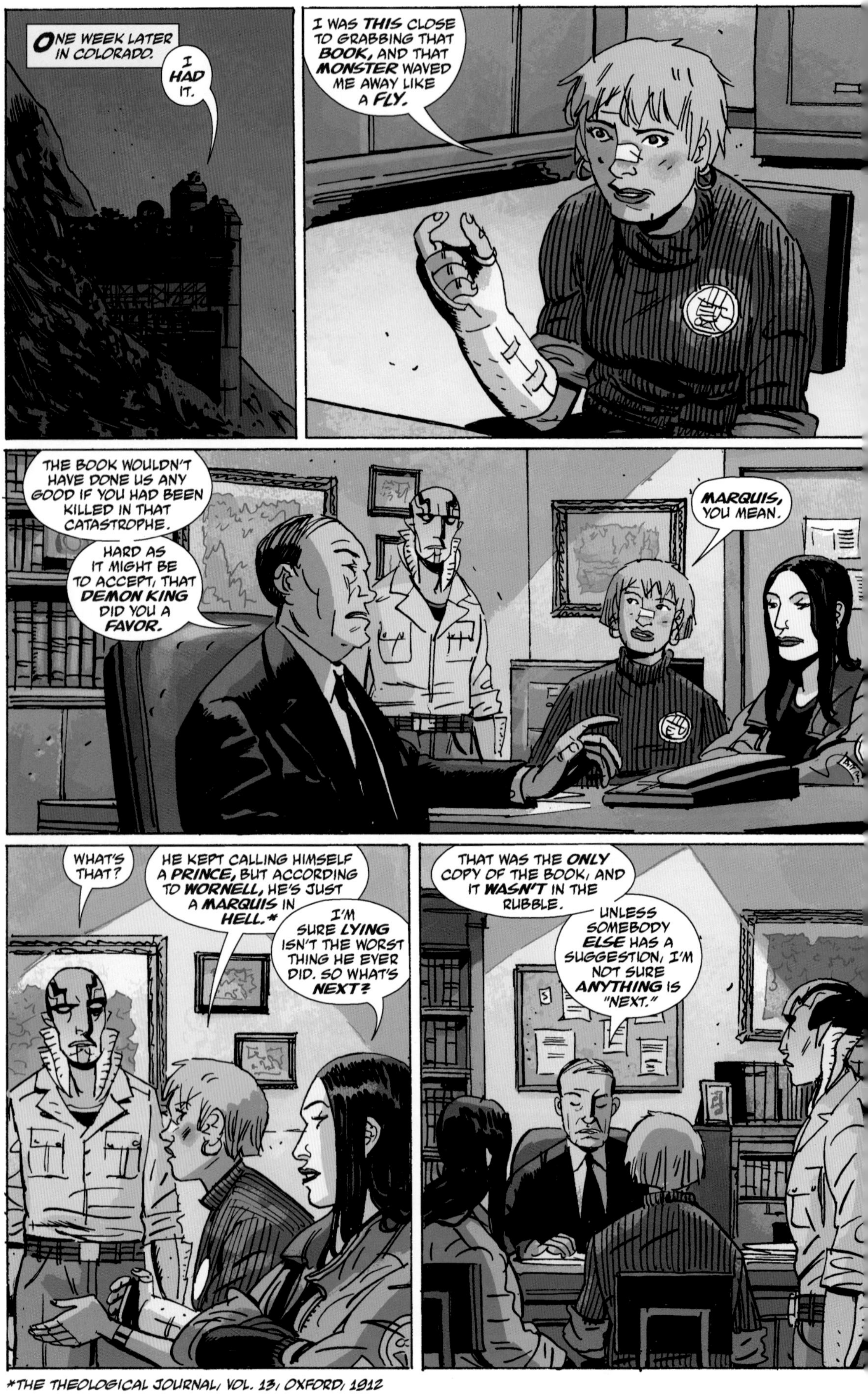
ONE WEEK LATER IN COLORADO.
I HAD IT.
I WAS THIS CLOSE TO GRABBING THAT BOOK, AND THAT MONSTER WAVED ME AWAY LIKE A FLY.
THE BOOK WOULDN'T HAVE DONE US ANY GOOD IF YOU HAD BEEN KILLED IN THAT CATASTROPHE.
HARD AS IT MIGHT BE TO ACCEPT, THAT DEMON KING DID YOU A FAVOR.
MARQUIS, YOU MEAN.
WHAT'S THAT?
HE KEPT CALLING HIMSELF A PRINCE, BUT ACCORDING TO WORNELL, HE'S JUST A MARQUIS IN HELL.*
I'M SURE LYING ISN'T THE WORST THING HE EVER DID. SO WHAT'S NEXT?
THAT WAS THE ONLY COPY OF THE BOOK, AND IT WASN'T IN THE RUBBLE.
UNLESS SOMEBODY ELSE HAS A SUGGESTION, I'M NOT SURE ANYTHING IS "NEXT."

*THE THEOLOGICAL JOURNAL, VOL. 13, OXFORD, 1912

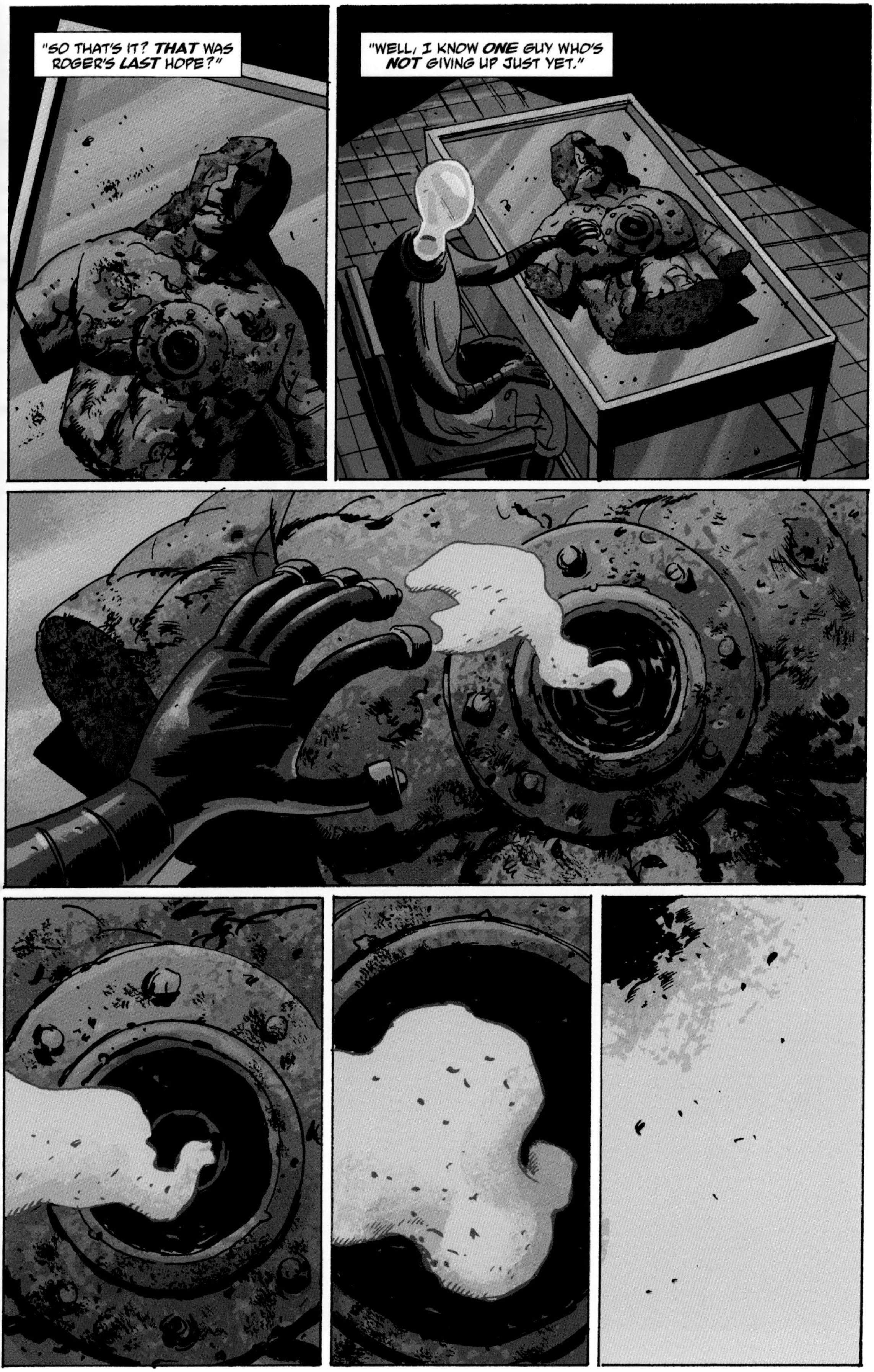
"SO THAT'S IT? THAT WAS ROGER'S LAST HOPE?"
"WELL, I KNOW ONE GUY WHO'S NOT GIVING UP JUST YET."

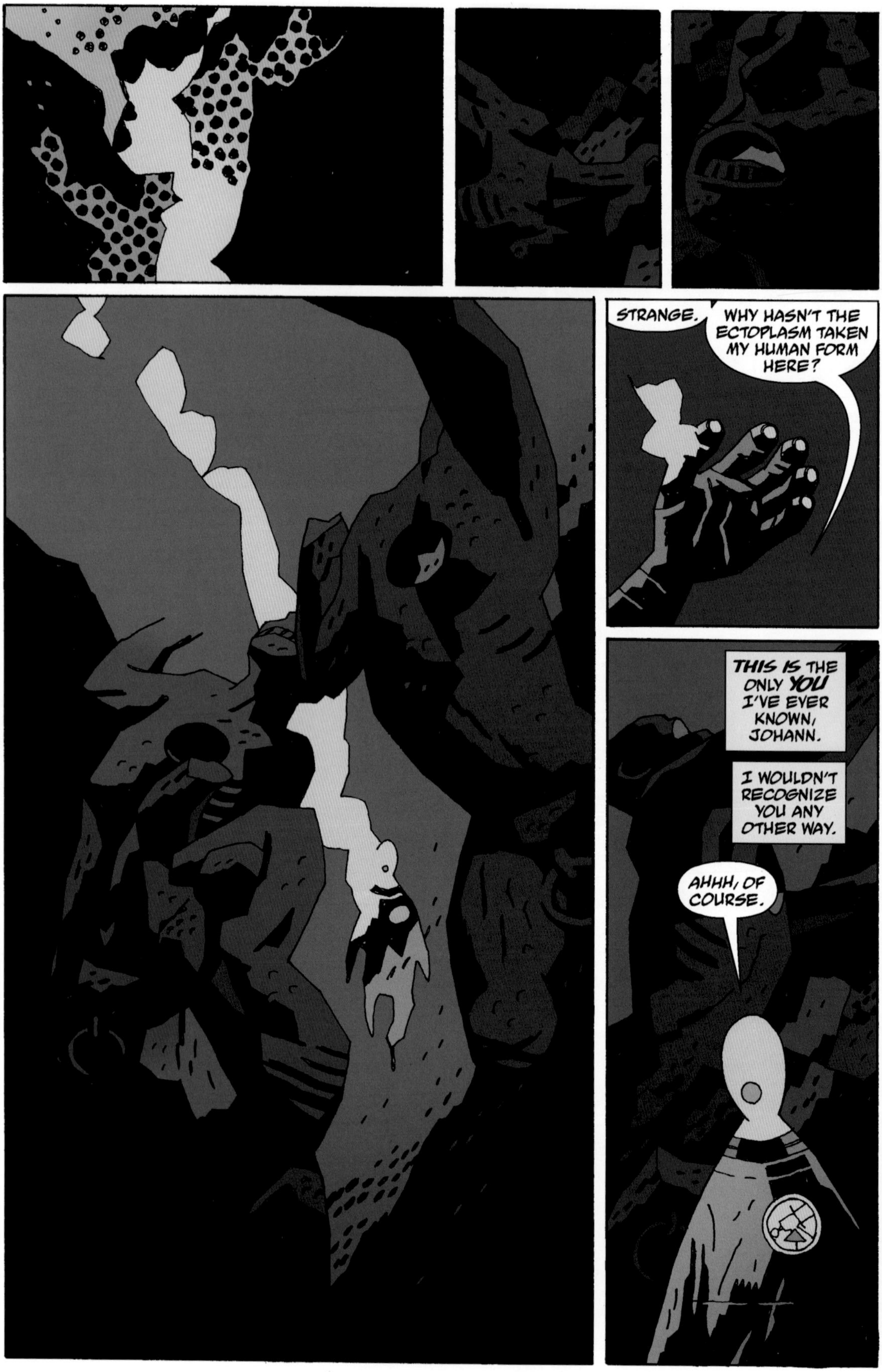
STRANGE.
WHY HASN'T THE ECTOPLASM TAKEN MY HUMAN FORM HERE?
THIS IS THE ONLY YOU I'VE EVER KNOWN, JOHANN.
I WOULDN'T RECOGNIZE YOU ANY OTHER WAY.
AHHH, OF COURSE.

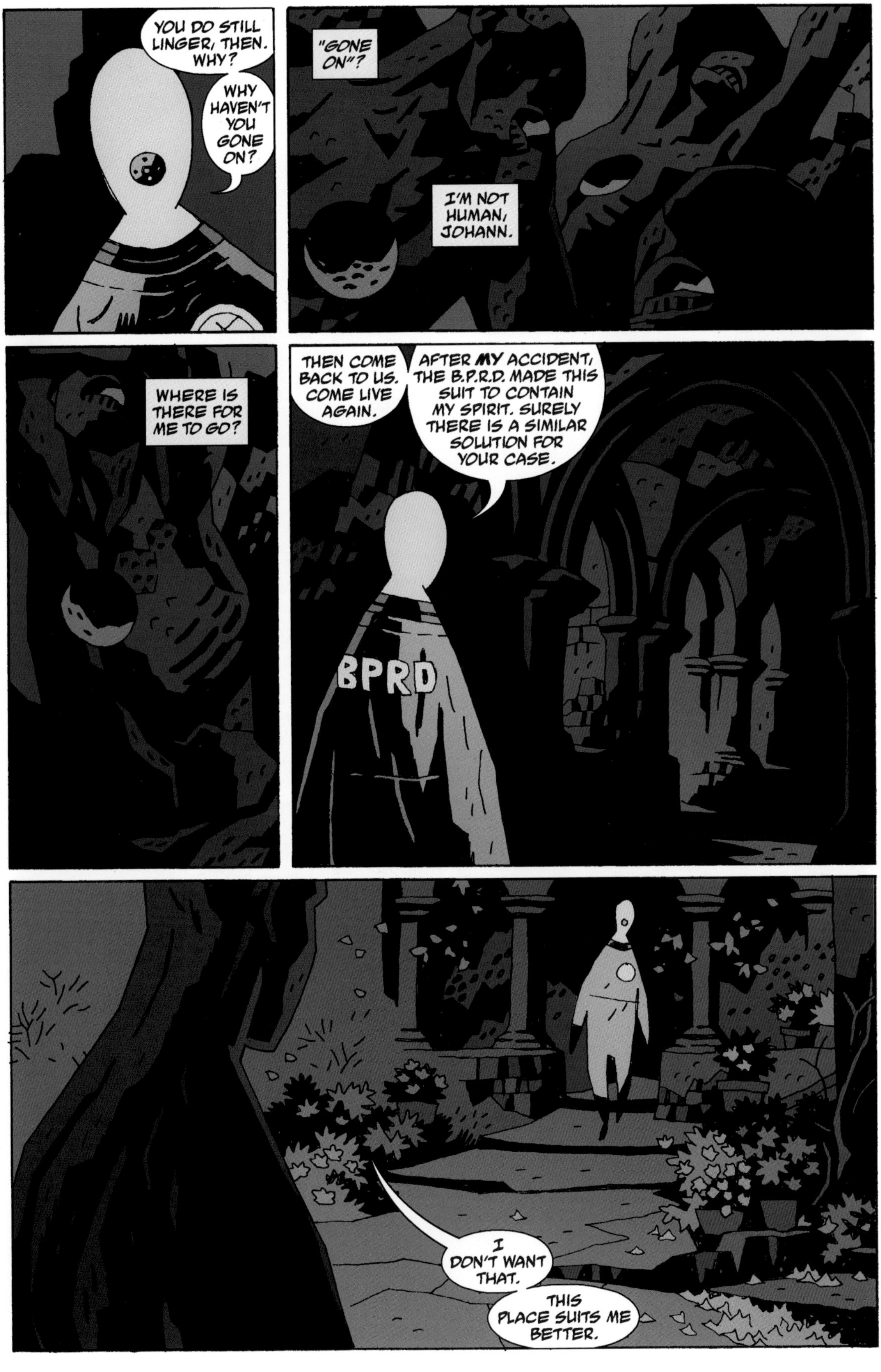

YOU DO STILL LINGER, THEN. WHY?
WHY HAVEN'T YOU GONE ON?
"GONE ON"?
I'M NOT HUMAN, JOHANN.
WHERE IS THERE FOR ME TO GO?
THEN COME BACK TO US. COME LIVE AGAIN.
AFTER MY ACCIDENT, THE B.P.R.D. MADE THIS SUIT TO CONTAIN MY SPIRIT. SURELY THERE IS A SIMILAR SOLUTION FOR YOUR CASE.
BPRD
I DON'T WANT THAT.
THIS PLACE SUITS ME BETTER.

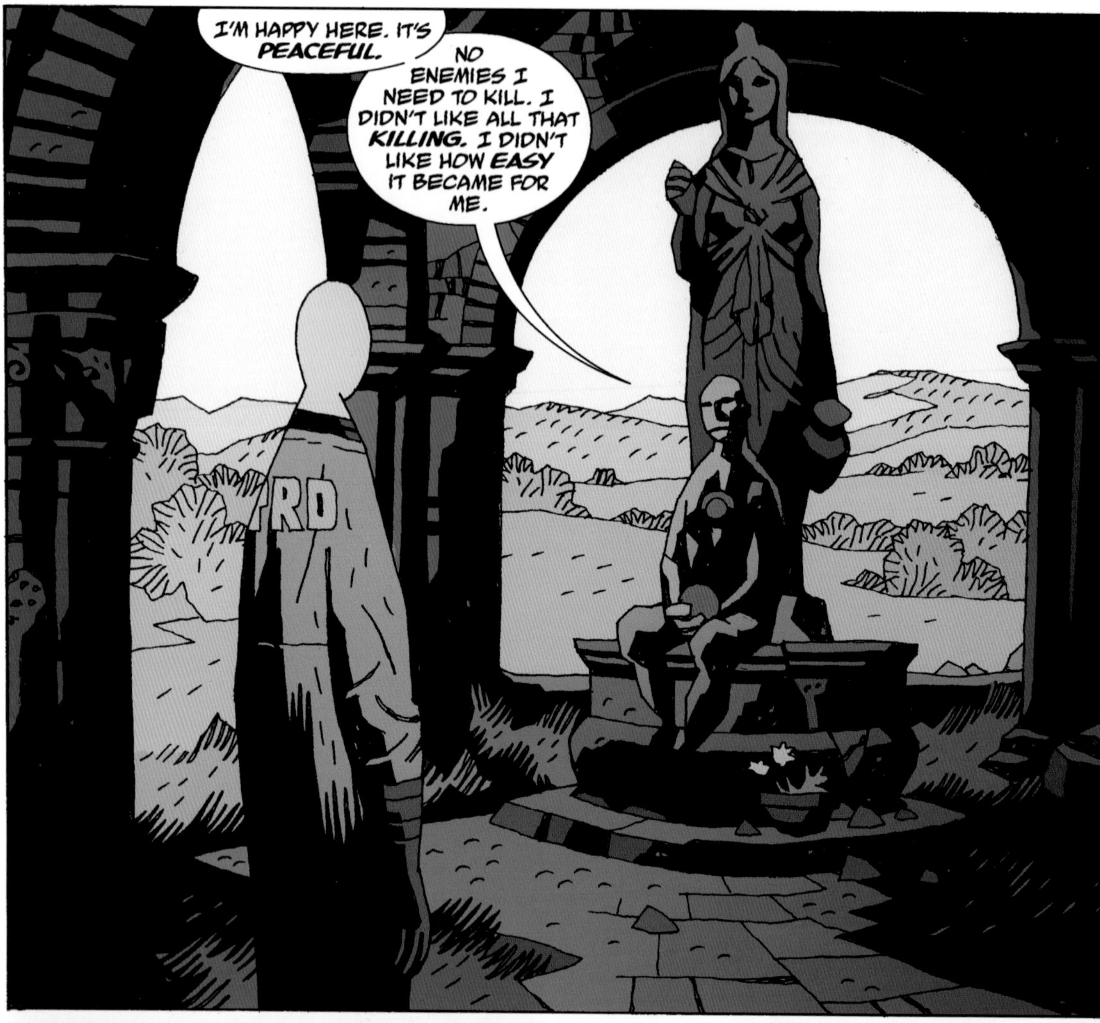
I'M HAPPY HERE. IT'S PEACEFUL.
NO ENEMIES I NEED TO KILL. I DIDN'T LIKE ALL THAT KILLING. I DIDN'T LIKE HOW EASY IT BECAME FOR ME.
BPRD

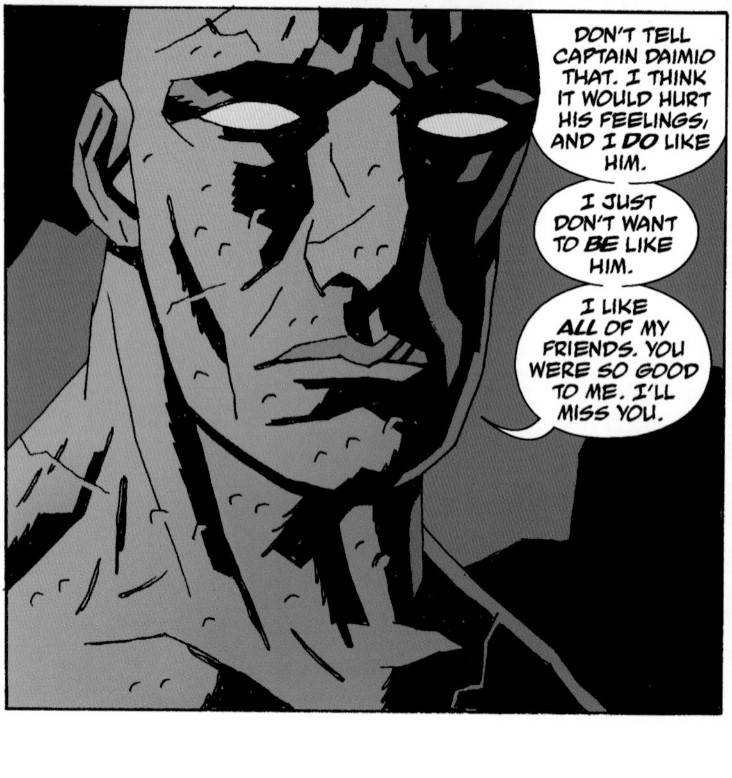
DON'T TELL CAPTAIN DAIMIO THAT. I THINK IT WOULD HURT HIS FEELINGS, AND I DO LIKE HIM.
I JUST DON'T WANT TO BE LIKE HIM.
I LIKE ALL OF MY FRIENDS. YOU WERE SO GOOD TO ME. I'LL MISS YOU.

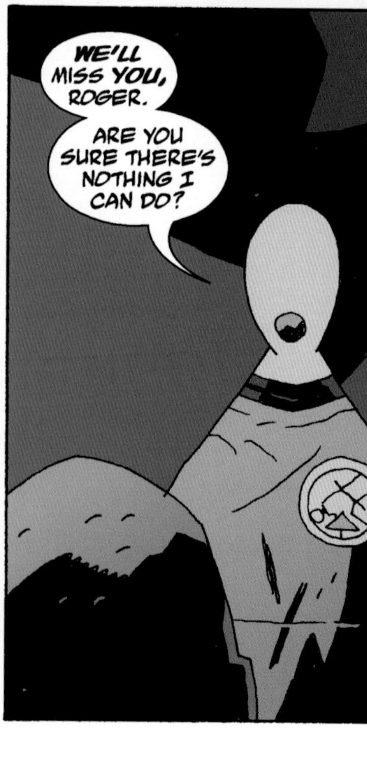
WE'LL MISS YOU, ROGER.
ARE YOU SURE THERE'S NOTHING I CAN DO?

I...I KNOW I'M *NOT A MAN.*

DO YOU THINK IT'S POSSIBLE THAT YOU COULD BURY WHAT'S LEFT OF ME IN THE EARTH--*LIKE A MAN?*

YES. YES. IT WILL BE DONE. YOU HAVE MY WORD.

GOOD BYE.

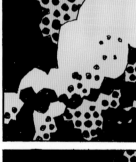

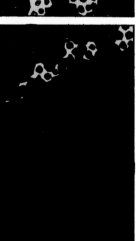

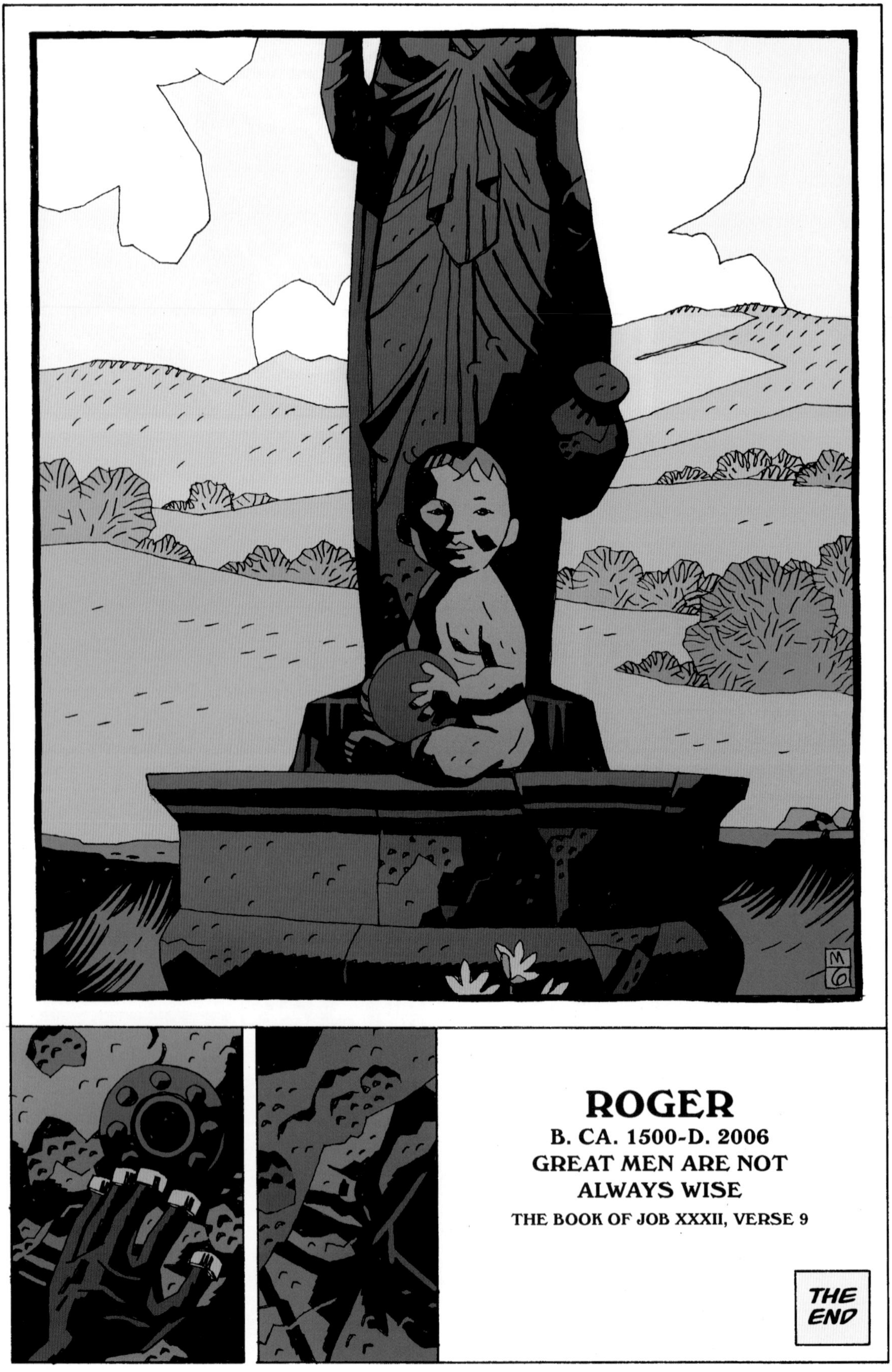
ROGER
B. CA. 1500-D. 2006
GREAT MEN ARE NOT
ALWAYS WISE
THE BOOK OF JOB XXXII, VERSE 9
THE END

AFTERWORD

This one started out years ago as a Hellboy story. Originally, Hellboy would have been the first one into the antique store, and Kate would have been the one to go in a minute later to find the place empty. There was the guy with the ring, the cut-off finger, the hunchback/demon, and the escape in the grandfather clock. I loved all the pieces and the ending, but I just didn't have a good reason for Hellboy to walk into that store. So I filed it away in my head—the Island of Misfit (broken or unfinished) Stories—and went on with other things.

A few years later, I created a Victorian occult detective character. I plotted a story, and part of it involved the phantom antique store. It worked much better now. There was a reason for the detective to go into that store (I'm not telling, but it wasn't to find a book). I added the vampires, the pathetic bird/demon tortured by forks, and the town full of werewolves. I liked it, but just never got around to doing it. The Island of Misfit (and almost forgotten) Stories is very crowded.

A few years after that, we started doing the B.P.R.D. book, and I knew I'd find a place for that antique store. As soon as we killed off Roger, I realized I had a reason for Kate to walk through that door, finally. Just about everything else in this book, including the flashback stories of Johann, Daimio, Liz, and Abe, are the work of the great John Arcudi. I wish I

could take credit for the mandrill-werewolf or the human clock, but I can't.

The Wendigo is, of course, a creature from Native American folklore. To the best of my knowledge, however, there is no monster prison in Canada.

The book, *The Secret Fire,* is our invention, but we didn't make up that stuff about the emerald falling out of Lucifer's forehead.

The picture in the antique store of Fabre's castle was probably inspired by M. R. James's short story "The Mezzotint," and the look of Fabre's vampires is definitely a nod to my favorite vampire story, Roman Polanski's *The Fearless Vampire Killers.* It was Guy's idea to give them bat noses, proving once again why he's the perfect artist for this kind of thing.

My thanks go to John and Guy for taking my little (slightly dusty) idea and turning it into something great, and thanks to Scott Allie for putting up with the bunch of us.

Until next time.

B.P.R.D.™

SKETCHBOOK

After legions of frog monsters, a Lovecraftian behemoth, and a Nazi villain in a mechanical suit, *The Universal Machine* would be a different type of adventure for the B.P.R.D. With Kate prisoner in a painting, and each chapter focusing on a different event in the team's life, a slew of new designs had to be created, and what better place to start than with an old castle on a mountainside?

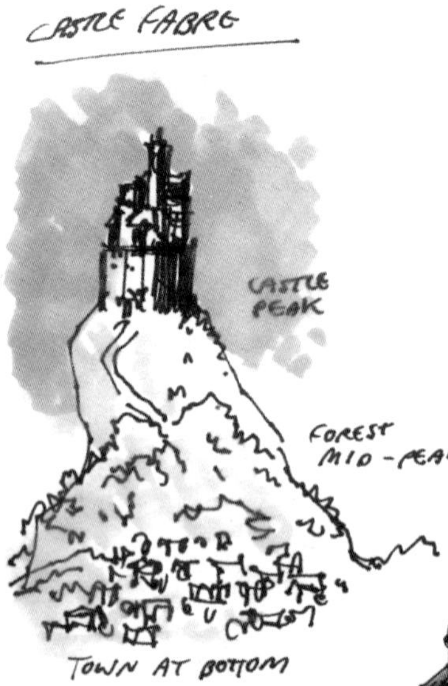

CASTLE FABRE
CASTLE PEAK
FOREST MID-PEAK
TOWN AT BOTTOM

Mike drew the first-issue cover before I started work on any designs for this storyline, so the first sketches of Castle Fabre incorporated his tower image into the architecture.

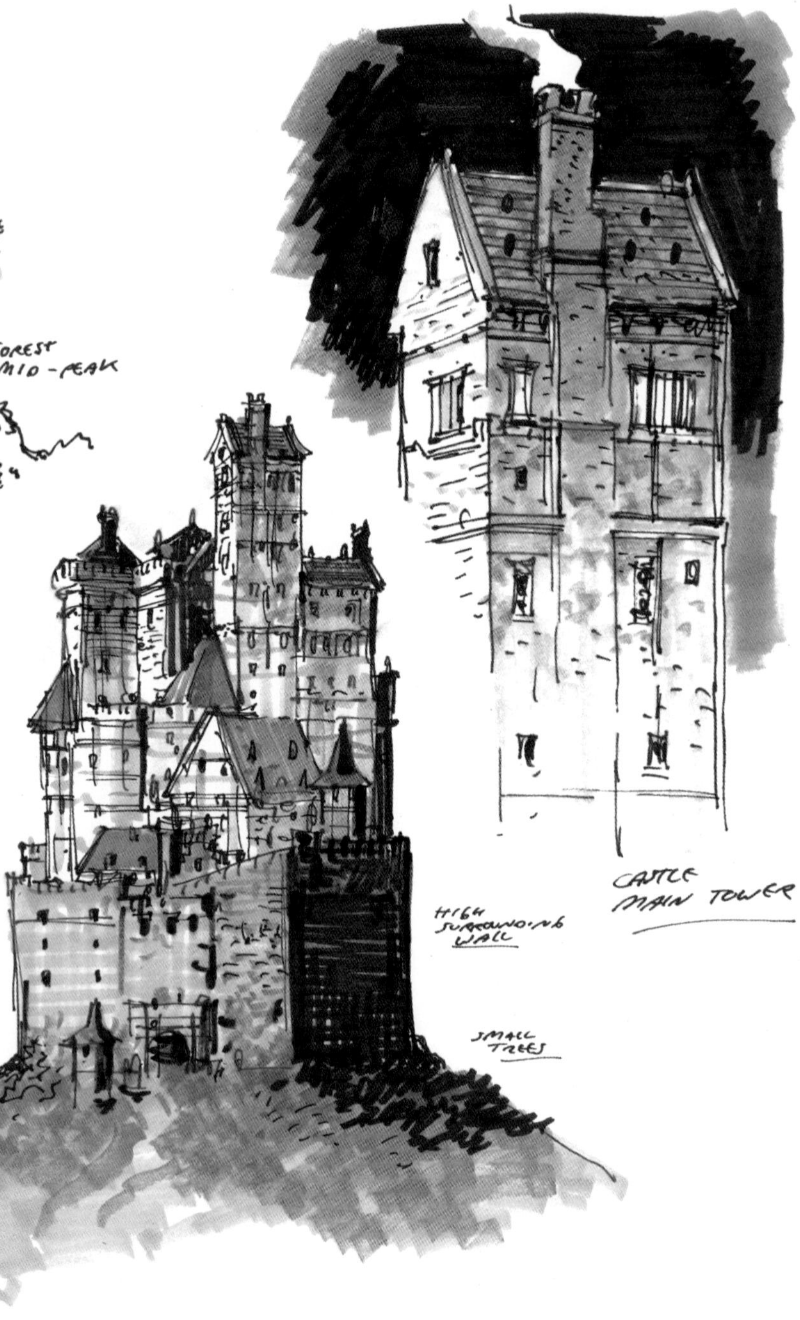

CASTLE MAIN TOWER
HIGH SURROUNDING WALL
SMALL TREES

After the initial designs, Mike sent notes on details to flesh out the castle and make it more imposing, like setting it into the actual side of the mountain so that the castle's remains would be clearer in the present-day scenes with Kate and Devon.

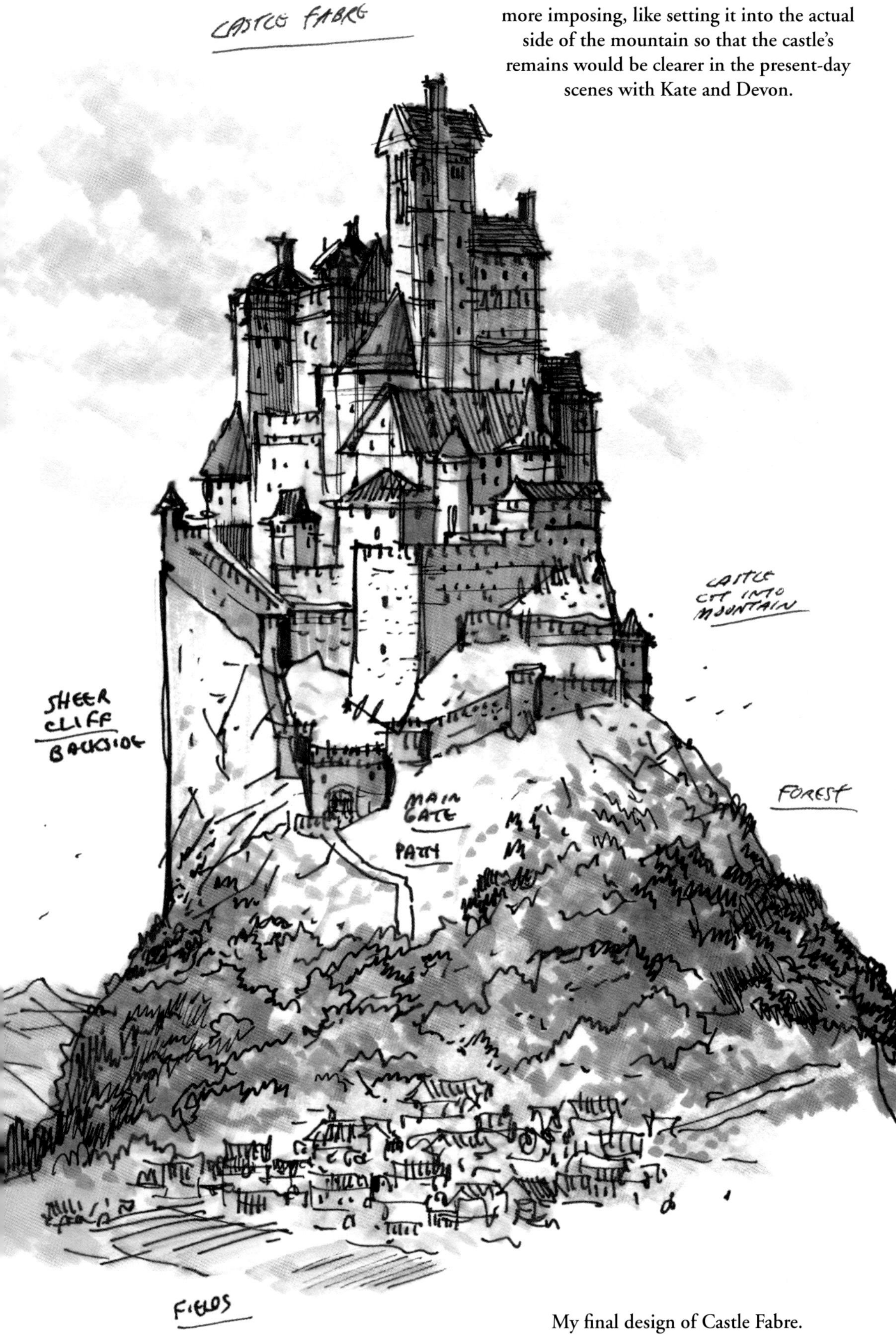
CASTLE FABRE
CASTLE CUT INTO MOUNTAIN
SHEER CLIFF BACKSIDE
FOREST
MAIN GATE
PATH
FIELDS

My final design of Castle Fabre.

Right: The jaguar-skull nun.
Below: The first designs for the "jaguar god" that came off a bit too grotesque and bizarre for a spiritual deity.

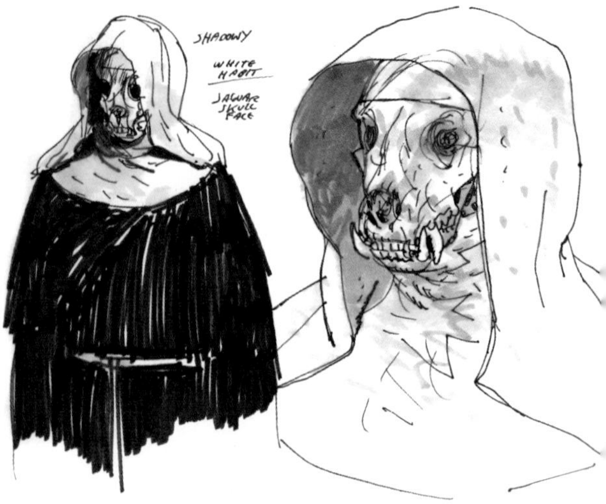
SHADOWY
WHITE HABIT
JAGUAR SKULL FACE

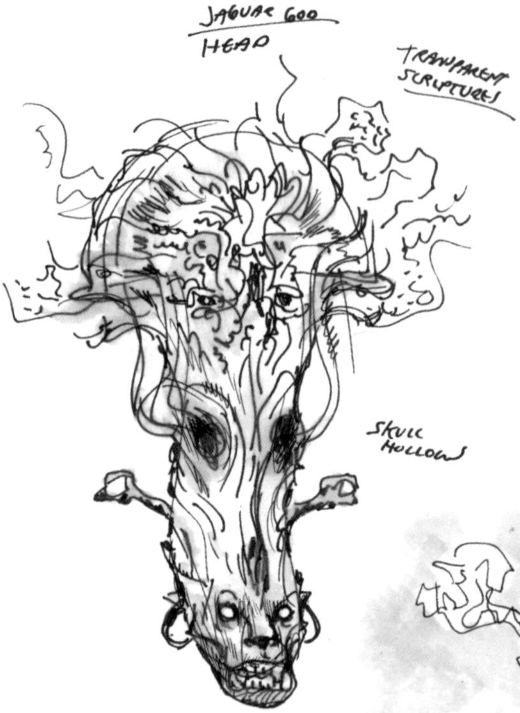
JAGUAR GOD HEAD
TRANSPARENT SCRIPTURES
SKULL HOLLOW

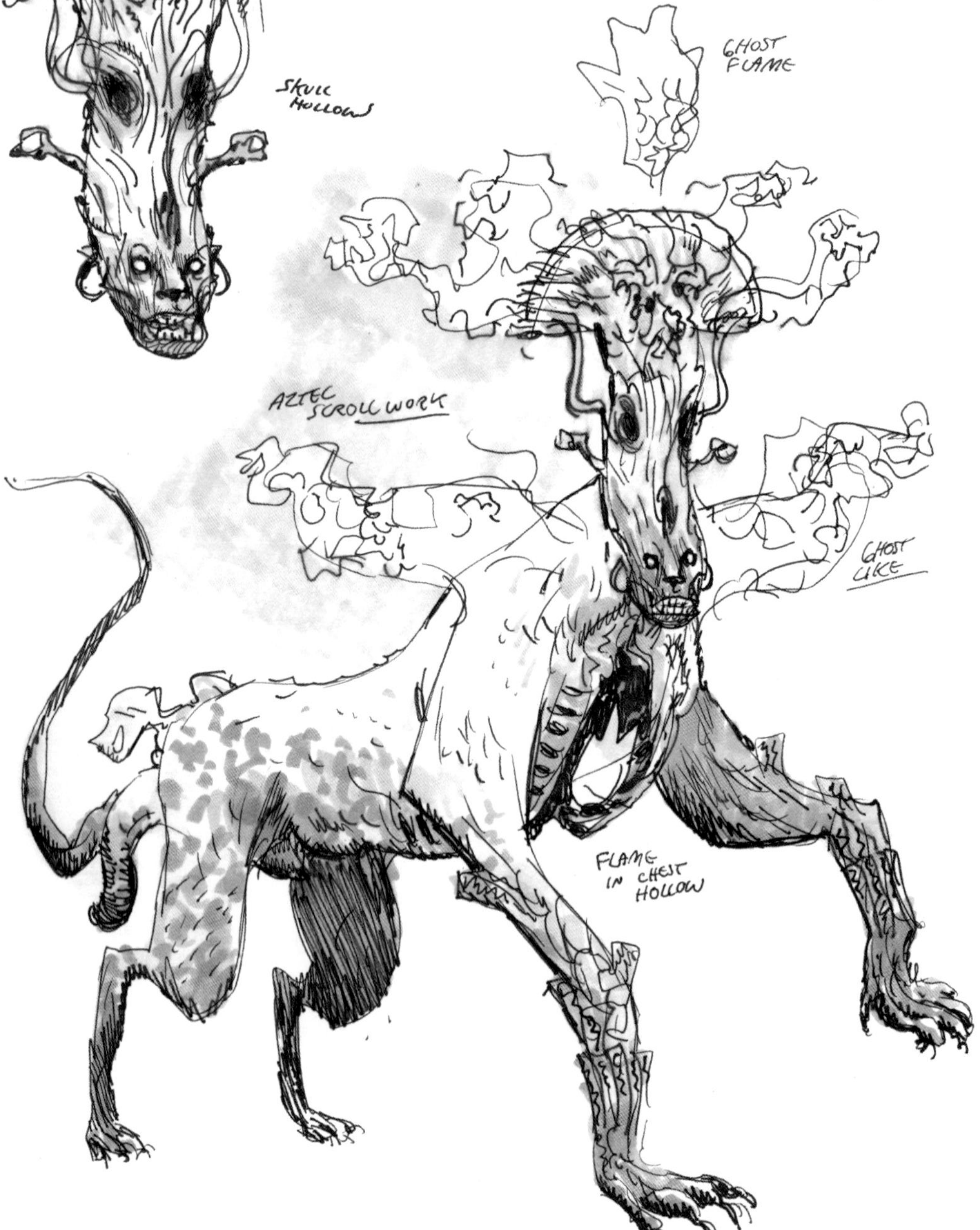
GHOST FLAME
AZTEC SCROLL WORK
GHOST LIKE
FLAME IN CHEST HOLLOW

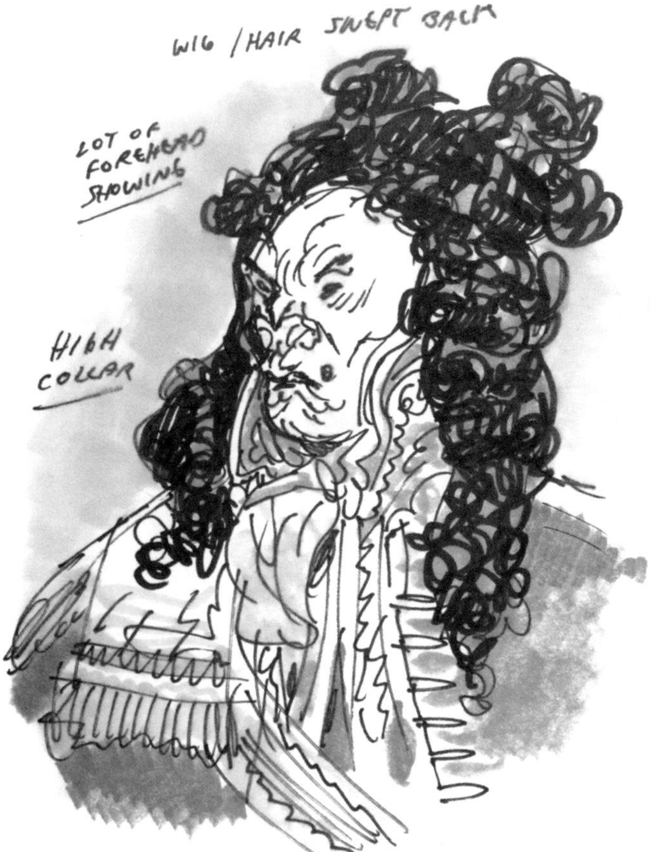
WIG / HAIR SWEPT BACK
LOT OF FOREHEAD SHOWING
HIGH COLLAR

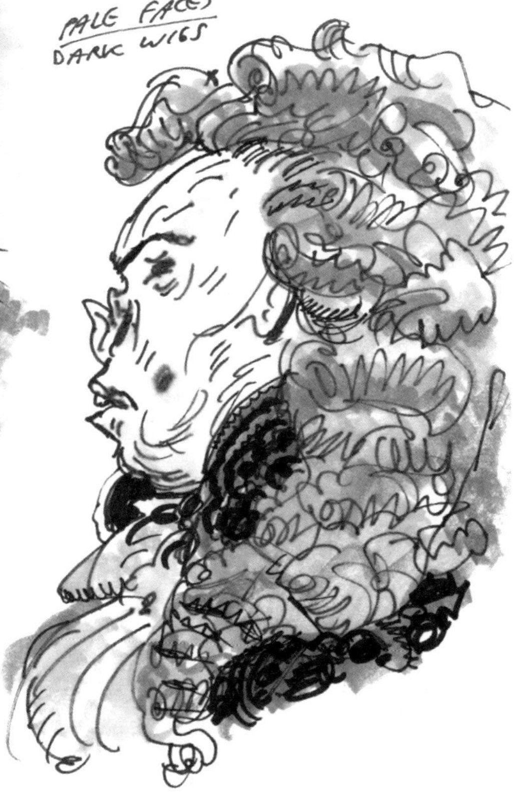
PALE FACES
DARK WIGS

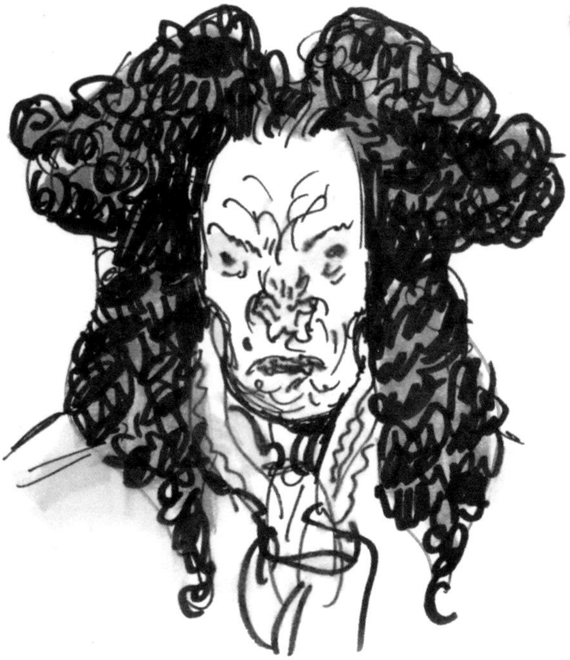

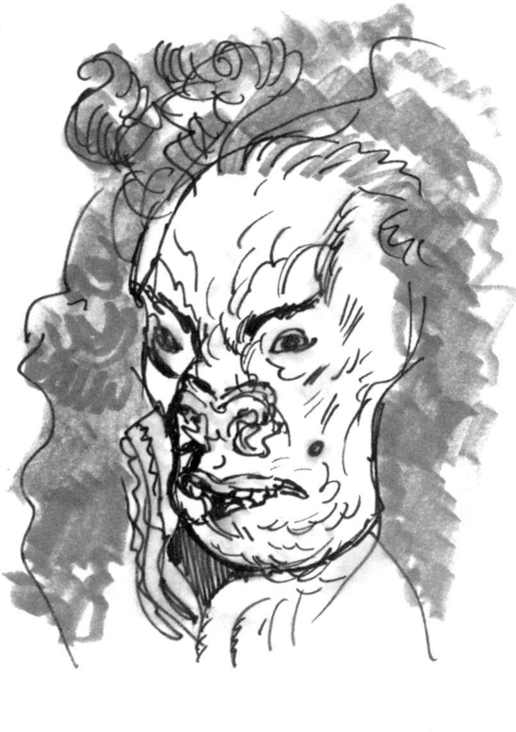

Initially I sketched out the *Court of Vampires* in 17th-century fashions. Mike asked to change it to 18th-century design as an homage to one of his favorite films, Roman Polanski's *The Fearless Vampire Killers.* In the end some of the characters' hair styles and attire would mimic that film as well.

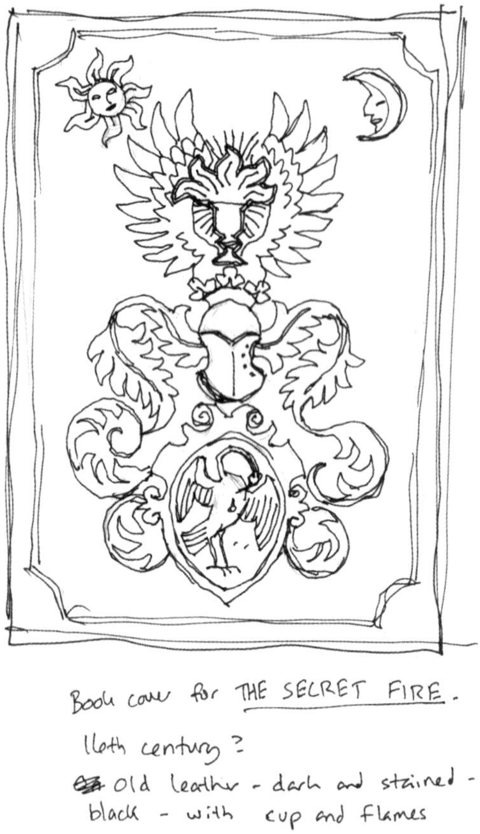
Book cover for THE SECRET FIRE.
16th century?
Old leather - dark and stained - black - with cup and flames

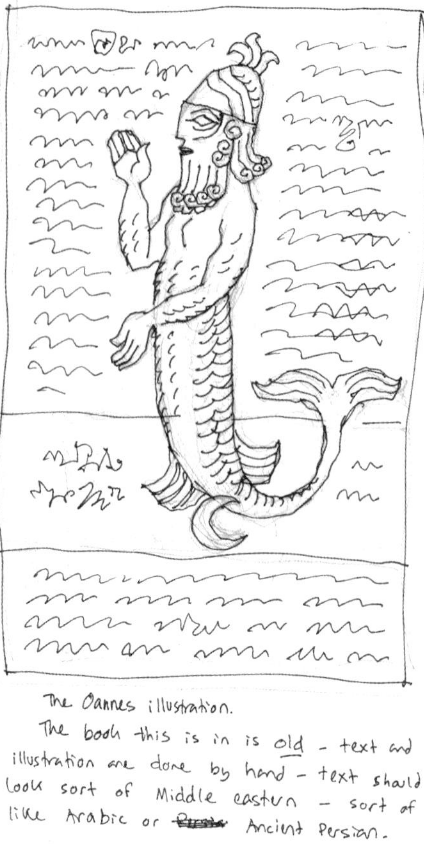
The Oannes illustration.
The book this is in is old - text and illustration are done by hand - text should look sort of Middle eastern - sort of like Arabic or Ancient Persian.

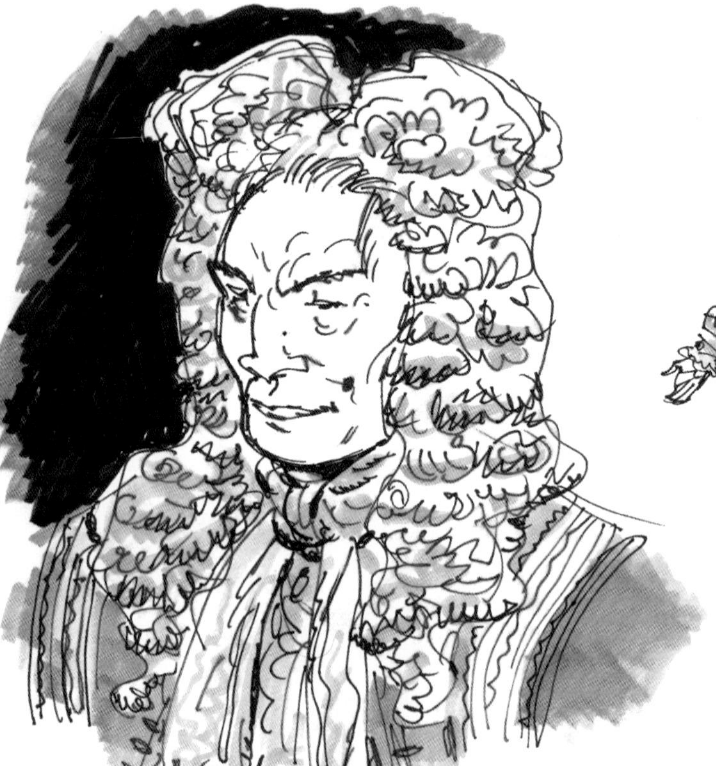

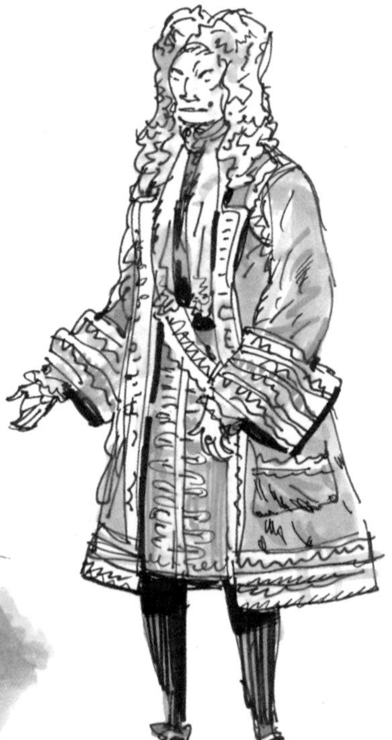

Mike's detailed sketches for *The Secret Fire* and the Oannes illustration. Above: The Marquis de Fabre gets the 17th-century fashion at first, too, as I originally thought he was part of the vampire court.

Like the Black Flame, Daryl the Wendigo was one of those characters whose design worked out from the first series of sketches.

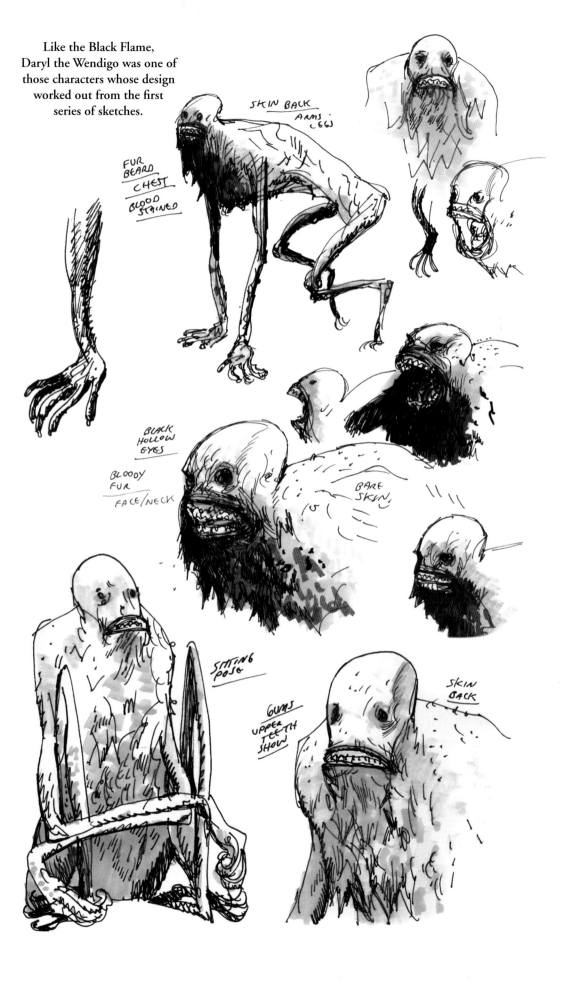

SKIN BACK
ARMS LEG

FUR
BEARD
CHEST
BLOOD
STAINED

BLACK
HOLLOW
EYES

BLOODY
FUR
FACE/NECK

BARE
SKIN

SITTING
POSE

GUMS
UPPER
TEETH
SHOW

SKIN
BACK

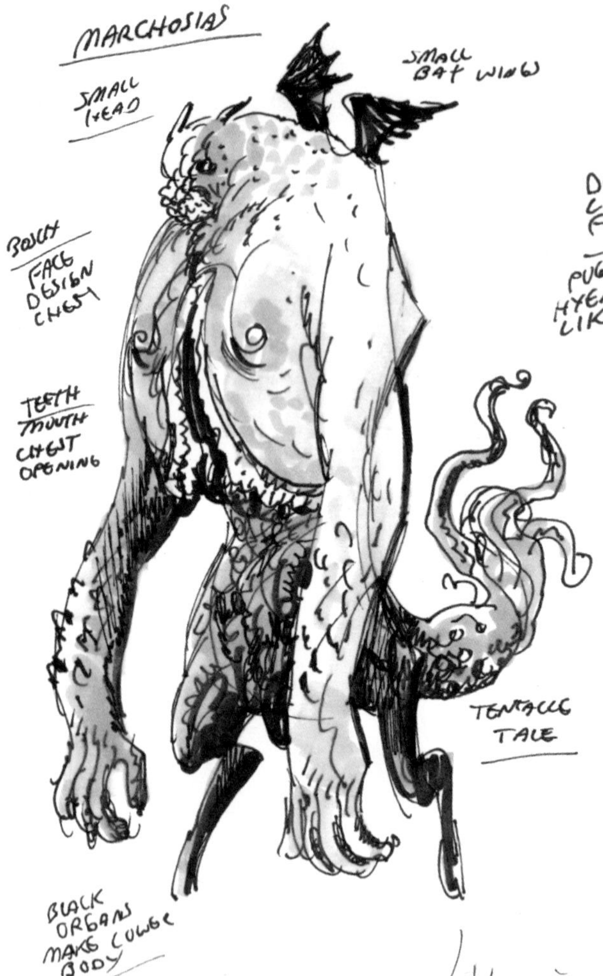
MARCHOSIAS
SMALL HEAD
SMALL BAT WING
BOTH FACE DESIGN CHEST
TEETH MOUTH CHEST OPENING
TENTACLE TALE
BLACK ORGANS MAKE COLOR BODY

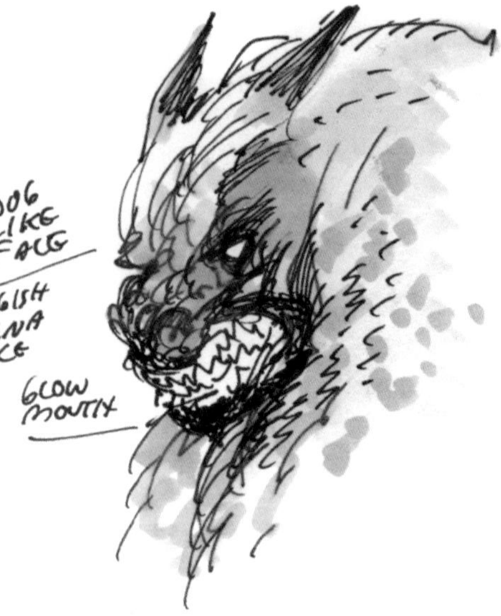
DOG LIKE FACE
PUGISH HYENA LIKE
GLOW MOUTH

The original design of Marchosias (above) was reworked to fit in with the devils of the Hellboy world, combining both animal and human shapes, but losing the tentacles and Lovecraftian bits.

—Guy Davis
Crab Pointe, MI

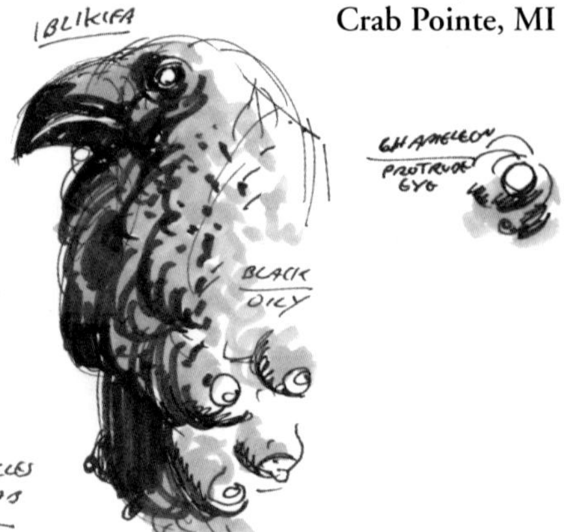
IBLIKIFA
BLACK OILY

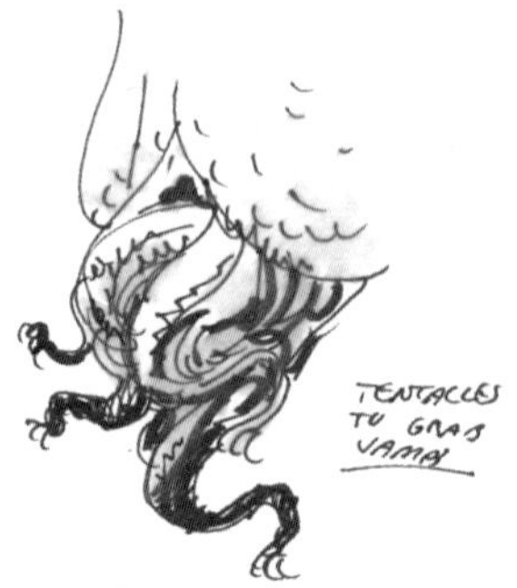
TENTACLES TO GRAB VAMPI

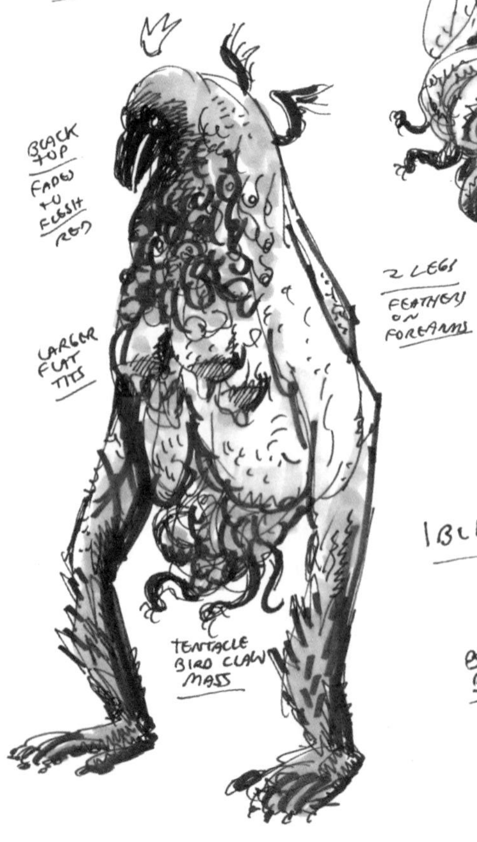
BLACK TOP FADED TO FLESH RED
LARGER FLAT TITS
2 LEGS FEATHERS ON FOREARMS
TENTACLE BIRD CLAW MASS

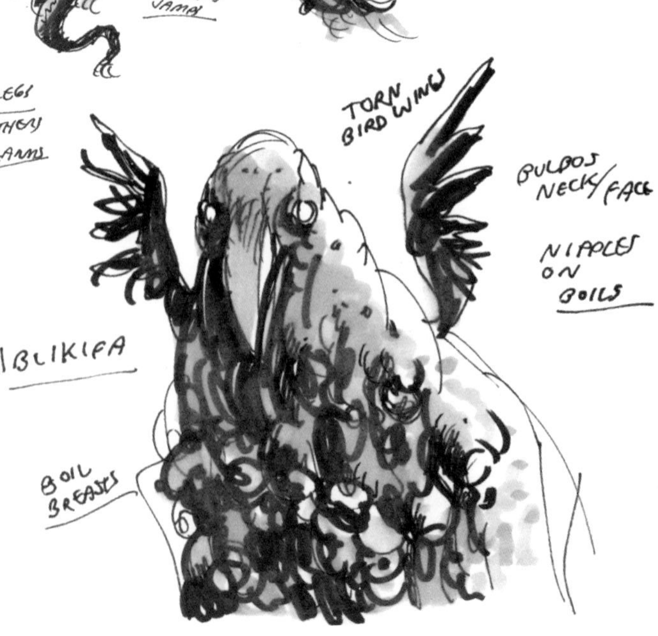
TORN BIRD WINGS
NIPPLES ON BOILS
IBLIKIFA
BOIL BREASTS

ALSO FROM DARK HORSE BOOKS

BOB FINGERMAN'S
RECESS PIECES

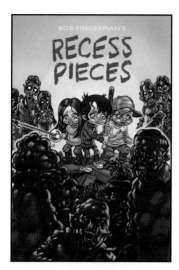

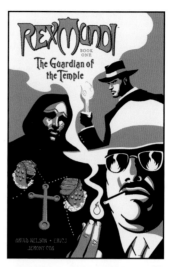

RECESS PIECES
Bob Fingerman

Bad things are brewing in the halls of The Ben Turpin School. When a science project goes wrong, only the prepubescent children are spared the fate of zombification . . . but can they escape being eaten alive? George Romero covered night, dawn, and day, but how about recess?

ISBN-10: 1-59307-450-6 / ISBN-13: 978-1-59307-450-0

$14.95

REX MUNDI
BOOK ONE
The Guardian of the Temple
ARVID NELSON • ERIC J
JEROMY COX

REX MUNDI VOLUME 1: THE GUARDIAN OF THE TEMPLE
Arvid Nelson, Eric J, Juan Ferreyra, and Jeromy Cox

A quest for the Holy Grail unlike any you've ever seen begins here—in a world where the American Civil War ended in a stalemate, the Catholic Church controls Europe, and sorcery determines political power!

ISBN-10: 1-59307-652-5 / ISBN-13: 978-1-59307-652-8

$16.95

Mike Mignola
Jill Thompson
Evan Dorkin
Kelley Jones
Eric Powell
Gary Gianni
and others
The Dark Horse
BOOK OF THE DEAD

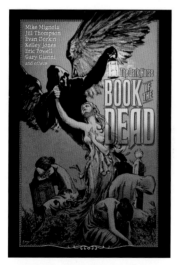

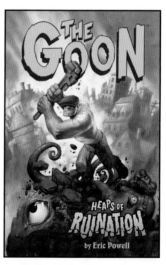

THE DARK HORSE BOOK OF THE DEAD
Guy Davis, Mike Mignola, Kelley Jones, Jill Thompson, Eric Powell, Gary Gianni, and others

Mike Mignola presents a Hellboy yarn combining Shakespeare and grave-robbing, Gary Gianni illustrates a rare story by Conan creator Robert E. Howard, and Jamie S. Rich and Guy Davis present a tale of horror and heartbreak set in feudal Japan. And that's just a taste of the tales inside this hardcover horror anthology featuring the finest talents in comics.

ISBN-10: 1-59307-281-3 / ISBN-13: 978-1-59307-281-0

$14.95

THE GOON
HEAPS OF RUINATION
by Eric Powell

THE GOON VOLUME 3: HEAPS OF RUINATION
Eric Powell

The Goon takes the fight to Lonely Street to save a mysterious gunslinger from the grips of the Zombie Priest, Modern Science triumphs over a marauding inter-dimensional lizard, and Franky and the Goon get a visit from a certain red-skinned paranormal investigator in the third volume of Eric Powell's Eisner Award-winning series.

ISBN-10: 1-59307-292-9 / ISBN-13: 978-1-59307-292-6

$12.95

AVAILABLE AT YOUR LOCAL COMICS SHOP OR BOOKSTORE! • To find a comics shop in your area, call 1-888-266-4226.

For more information or to order direct visit darkhorse.com or call 1-800-862-0052 Mon.-Fri. 9 A.M. to 5 P.M. Pacific Time. Prices and availability subject to change without notice.

DARK HORSE COMICS® *drawing on your nightmares*
darkhorse.com

HELLBOY

by MIKE MIGNOLA

SEED OF DESTRUCTION
with John Byrne
ISBN-10: 1-59307-094-2
ISBN-13: 978-1-59307-094-6
$17.95

WAKE THE DEVIL
ISBN-10: 1-59307-095-0
ISBN-13: 978-1-59307-095-3
$17.95

THE CHAINED COFFIN
AND OTHERS
ISBN-10: 1-59307-091-8
ISBN-13: 978-1-59307-091-5
$17.95

THE RIGHT HAND OF DOOM
ISBN-10: 1-59307-093-4
ISBN-13: 978-1-59307-093-9
$17.95

CONQUEROR WORM
ISBN-10: 1-59307-092-6
ISBN-13: 978-1-59307-092-2
$17.95

STRANGE PLACES
ISBN-10: 1-59307-475-1
ISBN-13: 978-1-59307-475-3
$17.95

THE ART OF HELLBOY
ISBN-10: 1-59307-089-6
ISBN-13: 978-1-59307-089-2
$29.95

HELLBOY WEIRD TALES
Volume 1
ISBN-10: 1-56971-622-6
ISBN-13: 978-1-56971-622-9
$17.95

Volume 2
ISBN-10: 1-56971-953-5
ISBN-13: 978-1-56971-953-4
$17.95

ODD JOBS
Short stories by Mignola,
Poppy Z. Brite, Chris Golden and others
Illustrations by Mignola
ISBN-10: 1-56971-440-1
ISBN-13: 978-1-56971-440-9
$14.95

ODDER JOBS
Short stories by Frank Darabont,
Guillermo del Toro and others
Illustrations by Mignola
ISBN-10: 1-59307-226-0
ISBN-13: 978-1-59307-226-1
$14.95

B.P.R.D.: HOLLOW EARTH
By Mignola, Chris Golden,
Ryan Sook and others
ISBN-10: 1-56971-862-8
ISBN-13: 978-1-56971-862-9
$17.95

B.P.R.D.: THE SOUL OF VENICE
By Mignola, Mike Oeming, Guy Davis,
Scott Kolins, Geoff Johns and others
ISBN-10: 1-59307-132-9
ISBN-13: 978-1-59307-132-5
$17.95

B.P.R.D.: PLAGUE OF FROGS
By Mignola and Guy Davis
ISBN-10: 1-59307-288-0
ISBN-13: 978-1-59307-288-9
$17.95

B.P.R.D.: THE DEAD
By Mignola, John Arcudi and Guy Davis
ISBN-10: 1-59307-380-1
ISBN-13: 978-1-59307-380-0
$17.95

B.P.R.D.: THE BLACK FLAME
By Mignola, Arcudi and Davis
ISBN-10: 1-59307-550-2
ISBN-13: 978-1-59307-550-7
$17.95

HELLBOY ZIPPO LIGHTER
#17-101 $29.95

HELLBOY TALKING BOARD
#10-248 $24.99

HELLBOY DELUXE TALKING BOARD
#10-380 $99.99

HELLBOY COASTER SET
#13-252 $9.99

HELLBOY QEE FIGURE: HELLBOY
#13-821 $7.99

HELLBOY QEE FIGURE: ABE SAPIEN
#13-822 $7.99

To find a comics shop in your area,
call 1-888-266-4226
For more information or to order direct:
• On the web: darkhorse.com
• E-mail: mailorder@darkhorse.com
• Phone: 1-800-862-0052
Mon.-Fri. 9 A.M. to 5 P.M. Pacific Time

Hellboy™ and © 2006 Mike Mignola. All rights reserved.
Dark Horse Comics® and the Dark Horse logo are
trademarks of Dark Horse Comics, Inc., registered in
various categories and countries. All rights reserved.
(BL6036)

DARK HORSE COMICS™ *drawing on your nightmares*

darkhorse.com